CODA

A TALE OF
TCHAIKOVSKY'S SECRET LOVE

ARTHUR J.
LEVY

Coda. In music notation,
a prearranged point where the performer escapes
to a new section that commences the finale.

An escape

The sign is crosshairs in a disc.

There are more things in heaven and earth, Horatio,
Than are dreamt of in your philosophy.

Hamlet, Act 1, Shakespeare

AUTHOR'S NOTE

Coda is a story stirred by personal experience, anchored to historical events. Some time ago, I inherited a stack of piano music from an old man. I turned the yellowing pages, looking for interesting pieces to play, and became fascinated by one sonata that was curiously annotated with scrawling notes. The depth of the comments gave a haunting feeling that these were not ordinary teacher's comments. This was a love letter encrypted in a scattering of loosely connected impassioned phrases. Except for the crumbling pages, I had no perspective of the period of these writings nor the motivations of the author. The enigmatic warmth of the annotations projected images in my mind of a covert relationship and a possible drama, perhaps a secret gay connection that mustn't have been discovered?

Peter Ilyich Tchaikovsky was in just that predicament. He was idolized and cherished by his Russia. Nineteenth century Russia competed with France and Germany as the center of culture. They desperately needed to parade world-known and loved Tchaikovsky as their flawless, signature icon to promote commerce as well as their culture. Tchaikovsky was flaunted as unblemished; if otherwise, it would have threatened the beloved Russia and the Tsar.

But Tchaikovsky was gay in a country that tortured, exiled and executed homosexuals. I looked at the cryptic notes in my music and pictured Tchaikovsky communicating to his lover—a plan, some cryptic plan, to elude the Tsar's spies and the powerful Russian Orthodox Church.

I assumed the writings that did survive were sought after by zealots of the Fatherland and were a deadly danger to those who possessed them.

The last year of Tchaikovsky's life, culminating in his enigmatically constructed final symphony, the *Pathétique,* is shrouded in mystery. The accounts of his death are steeped in secrecy and rumors as if published in a 19th century tabloid. This story is one interpretation of those final years. Some of the characters are purely fictional.

MOSCOW

DECEMBER 5, 2012

ANNA STOOD WITH her cheek against the heavy curtain covering the icy glass door to her shop as she listened to the rapping on the door down the street, not daring to move. Well aware that her life was in danger, she broodingly ran her fingers down the ornate carvings framing the inside of her front door, a comforting habit from her childhood. The hammering stopped and silence returned to the snow-covered street as quickly as it vanished. This time the silence gave no comfort. There was the sudden percussion of breaking glass nearby, causing Anna's pulse to quicken as she flinched from the frosted glass and wrapped her face in the velvet curtain. As the drumming sounds came closer, Anna warily peeked out from behind the curtain, then moved her head closer to the glass door and looked down the street. There were shadows coming from a block away. A curious funnel of snow swept across the street. As it dissipated, her apprehension returned. They would soon be at her door.

Anna cursed the Russian Mafia that had discovered her neighborhood and its quaint shops. At first, she had dismissed them with harsh words, but when they had threatened her customers, and eventually her grandson, she had acquiesced, feeling powerless and used. Anna took a deep breath, slowly shaking her head. This fear couldn't go on. The terror of thugs regularly demanding payment to protect her ornate display windows convinced Anna to end generations of ownership and move her shop to America. Moscow was no longer safe. It was only a matter of time before tragedy would slash her life.

As she stood slightly bent in the dark, carefully holding back the heavy curtain at the door, Anna felt a hand softly touch her shoulder. She turned and smiled sweetly at the housekeeper.

"Nadia, dear, don't worry," Anna said. "They seem to now be going in the other direction."

Nadia gently rubbed Anna's shoulder, sliding her hand down to Anna's, then grasping it. As she held Anna's hand, Nadia whispered, "Anna, we should call the police. These thugs should be in jail."

"No. For all we know, these thugs might also be the police. Be quiet; it will be all right."

Nadia pressed close to Anna. "I will get back to my work. I am staying too late already." Nadia tightened her grip on Anna's hand and then let it slide out of hers as she turned away and quietly returned to her chores in the kitchen.

Anna lingered in the middle of her shop thinking that she'd made her weekly protection payment. But it didn't mean there wouldn't be trouble. There was no guarantee that the fee was her pass to safety. She took a deep and audible breath, sizing up the difficult task before her.

She strolled among the display tables as images and stories relating to the trinkets and treasures on display slipped into her mind. She remembered hiding under the tables as a child and the wonderful fragrance of her grandmother's cooking in the adjoining apartment. There had always been classical music recordings playing in the shop, and she continued the tradition with the radio set to a Moscow station that played mostly romantic classics. Customers seemed to like the gentle ambiance and lingered long enough to become attached to some trivial ornament. Her grandfather's windup gramophone with the large brass horn still sat in the shop. It had been in the family for generations, and was priced ridiculously high so it would never sell.

Anna turned on the radio, hoping that the soft music would ease her mood. After the radio station signed off for the night, she rummaged through the old heavy wax discs for her favorite, Tchaikovsky's *The Seasons*, played on the piano. Anna preferred this intimate version to the more familiar orchestral version. She selected the last movement, a sprightly waltz that depicted the Christmas season. It accompanied the swirling waves of snow dancing along the line of neighboring shops on narrow Karandash Street.

Parting the heavy green drapes that covered the front door, Anna felt the winter air stealing in under beneath it. With her foot, she snugged the top of a long sock filled with dried lima beans against the door to block the draft. The toe of the sock rolled away from the door, signaling the futility of the task. She pressed the heavy weight of the rich green curtains against her face, knowing that the surroundings that had been so comforting all her life would have to be abandoned. She pushed through similar draperies and entered the rear apartment to get some packing supplies. She had parted those curtains countless times before, but this time she started to feel them drifting out of her life like so many of her treasures would soon leave her. But then reluctance turned to determination. She felt the need to start the next chapter of her life.

There was a huge inventory and Anna felt overwhelmed. Here was the chronicle of her family, item after item marked up like a memoir for sale but priced too high for the trade. The junk antiques were displayed prominently on tables just inside the door. She did not care if the weather drifted in and tarnished them. They were the possessions of strangers, bought for quick disposal. It was the family treasures that contained the thread of mystery.

Although it was weeks before the scheduled move, Anna felt the need to prepare one special possession right away. Hoping for solitude to compose her thoughts, she was a bit annoyed that Nadia stayed late, cleaning the stove in the rear apartment to needless perfection.

Anna ignored her and went to a small storage closet. She returned with an old bedsheet that had yellowed with age and began to tear it into long, narrow strips. Anna continued tearing the sheet until she had made a large pile of ribbons. She collected them in a wicker basket and brought them to a table in the farthest corner of the narrow shop. Anna then took a small pile of documents from a cabinet and straightened out the edges until they looked neatly stacked. She carefully folded brown paper around the stack, holding down a stubbornly folded corner with her pinky. Then Anna gently lifted the stack onto the ribbons and carefully tied them into a parcel. She pondered the importance that her grandfather placed on these papers. Into the parcel, she slipped a note written in stylishly drawn Cyrillic letters that translated as *The Music*. Anna walked back to her kitchen table and carefully set the package down.

Anna's grandfather had told her about the grave significance of this stack of sheet music, so Anna never let customers see it. She carefully took another package of similar size from a cabinet and, returning to the kitchen, placed it on top of the wrapped sheet music to keep it pressed flat. Anna carefully aligned the corners in order to keep the two packages stacked neatly. So that she, or her grandson, would not ignore what was underneath, Anna wrote *The Music* boldly on the top of the stack.

Nadia eagerly worked to complete her tasks in the kitchen and get out of the way. Anna sensed Nadia observing her obsessive precision with the packages and noticed her staying clear of the kitchen table, most likely out of fear that a careless splash would result in a reprimand. Anna lingered over the packages for a moment, straightened them once again, and then took them to the shop.

Anna thought about the new shop that she would open near her brother's house in America. He had written and assured her that she would be happy in the Brighton Beach section of Brooklyn. In his letters, he told of his new neighbors who had moved there from her district in Moscow and that she would quickly make new friends and feel at home.

Anna walked to the door once more to peek out on the street, feeling apprehensive about the sound of heavy knocking on the door a few shops away. As Anna lowered the lights in the shop to get a better look at the disturbance, her grandson, Alex, came into the shop from the rear apartment.

"You heard it, too?" Anna said.

"Yes, it's very late and I felt it was unwise to leave you alone in the shop," Alex said. He squeezed through the heavy curtain and pressed against the front door with Anna. The two studied three men banging on the shop window across the street. Anna was unsettled with the thought that these could be new thugs who would demand more protection money. One of the men was strikingly handsome and in his mid-twenties, which was around Alex's age.

As Anna and Alex watched the disturbance from her front door, a chill slipped past them from the back door and wrapped around their ankles. Anna elbowed Alex to reproach him for leaving the rear door ajar. Alex shrugged.

As Anna walked back to close the door, she saw rapidly moving shadows and heard footfalls fleeing from the kitchen. Alex noticed the movement as well and both cautiously approached the rear door as a frost-laden chill swept through the kitchen. No one appeared to be in the apartment. It was unusual for Nadia to leave without requesting payment. Anna signaled Alex to cautiously look around the kitchen. As she looked across the kitchen, Anna uttered a quiet, but mournful, sigh. She rushed to the table where the packages of music had been placed. The top package was gone. Nothing else was touched. Anna rested her hands on the remaining packet containing *The Music* and felt the heavy thumping of her heartbeat. Alex stood unmoving at the rear of the kitchen.

From around a corner leading to the hallway, a trickle of blood crept into the light. Alex cautiously followed the stream, turned the corner and stopped. With a trembling voice, he uttered, *"Boje moi!"* (My God!)

Nadia lay face down in a pool of blood.

OVERTURE TO A TANGLED JOURNEY

ST. PETERSBURG, RUSSIA, MARCH 18, 1865

IN THE ELEGANT Salon of the Michael Palace in St. Petersburg, a young man rose with slight hesitation to conduct the elite St. Petersburg Conservatory student orchestra. He bowed first to the aristocrats in the center of the audience and then, with grace, to the rest of the patrons. In measured syllables, the young conductor announced the name of the work they were about to hear and bowed gently once again. He then turned to the orchestra and, with a slight spasm of his eyebrows, lifted his borrowed baton and waited for the musicians to snap to attention. The young conductor studied the faces of the excited musicians while trying to look confident and severe, knowing that it was their debut as well as his. A slight smile escaped the tight corners of his mouth. Lowering his baton, Peter Ilyich Tchaikovsky felt a rush of excitement as the opening notes of his *Overture* tore through the stillness and filled the large marble hall.

The slender, handsome twenty-five-year old Tchaikovsky tried his best to display poise as countless critical eyes watched him conduct his debut work before the most influential members of St. Petersburg society. But as he led the orchestra through the development of the piece, his mind raced with thoughts of how the opening phrases might have been snappier, how his introduction to the audience might have been smarter, how a certain transition between melodies might have been somewhat tighter and how his shoes might have been a bit looser. Nevertheless, he maintained his appearance of serenity and studied the musicians as they glanced up now and then to their conductor. Peter breathed deeply as he savored the euphoria of the moment, and the appreciation that he knew would follow. Scanning the array of performers as he conducted, Tchaikovsky's attention was repeatedly drawn to one violinist at the rear of the orchestra. The violinist rarely looked down at his music, rather transfixed on the conductor.

As Tchaikovsky conducted the exposition of his main thematic melody, another distraction nagged at his attention. It was a subtle sound, a tinny rattling that had no place in his composition. He searched for its source, studying the orchestra members while his arms stylishly moved and guided the performance. He thought to himself, *A squeaky chair? An unbalanced music stand? Focus, Peter Ilyich, surely no one else hears the blemish.* He had a rush of anger as he sensed it coming from the right, in the cello section. He swiftly spotted the cause, a young woman—the only woman in the ensemble—wearing a charm bracelet on her right arm that jingled the metallic bauble as she played the staccato passages with her bow. Tchaikovsky felt frustrated and helpless. He tried to look away and ignore the annoying sound, trying to convince himself that the audience could not hear it. He glared with disapproval at the cellist, but ceased when he recognized her as the niece of the evening's eminent host. Once again, Peter Ilyich Tchaikovsky was humbled by his lowly social status.

As Tchaikovsky turned to the violin section, returning his concentration to the performance, he was again drawn to a violinist playing at the rear of the section. This student stood out from the others, focusing on the conductor, rarely glancing at the pages of music. Tchaikovsky caught his eye and the young man smiled and then lowered his eyes to his music with a conspicuous blush. As gravity draws a pendulum to its center, Tchaikovsky's glance kept returning to the young violinist. While the romantic melodies tugged at the emotions of the audience, it worked in subtle ways on the performers.

When the overture ended, Tchaikovsky beamed with satisfaction and felt a broad grin involuntarily appear. The violinist he had been observing smiled coyly, and with an uncontrolled reflex, Tchaikovsky winked. Tchaikovsky slowly turned to the audience, ready to receive an outpouring of appreciation. Instead of polite applause there was an ear-jarring silence. Tchaikovsky felt a teardrop beading in his eye and bowed majestically with thoughts of failure echoing in his mind. After a brief moment, starting with a lone violinist in the rear section, members of the orchestra applauded and rattled their violin bows in an unprecedented act of appreciation. Members of the stunned audience looked to others as if to see if the façade of Russian refinement permitted applause by musicians. As one diplomat stood to applaud, the audience followed politely at first and then erupted into a raucous act of apparent appreciation. Tchaikovsky held back his tears as best he could, but succumbed to emotion and let loose with a broad smile. The distinguished host stood, followed by many of those in the audience. He stepped down from the platform and briefly mingled with the audience before leaving the palace.

Two weeks later, Tchaikovsky presented his first complete string quartet to the headmaster of the St. Petersburg Conservatory, offering it for the next recital. In an offhand manner, he asked about the violinist who played in the last chair of the first violin section of the student orchestra. Interested in the way the student stared, Tchaikovsky made a vague compliment about his playing and said that he wanted to discuss technique with him. After a quick review of the student roster, the headmaster hung his head and explained in a low and cautious voice, "That student has been deported to a detention station in the far north. It says that he violated social mores regarding sexual behavior. It gives no further details. There is no time frame, which, I expect, means," and with a lengthy pause and a despondent voice, he said, "he will never return."

Tchaikovsky extended his arm in a futile expression of empathy, but upon realizing his gesture, he brushed the request aside quickly, as if he was no longer interested. As he pictured the handsome violinist, his toes curled until the muscles in his legs ached in racking pain. He casually changed the subject to his composition. "Do you think that it is too difficult?" Tchaikovsky said, as a chill coursed through his veins that would become part of his soul for the rest of his life.

Walking home from the conservatory, Tchaikovsky tried to avoid eye contact with men on the street, but often gave way to inborn curiosity. A glance here, a fleeting look there, he wondered what secrets these men concealed that if exposed would banish them to an unknown hell. He wondered if these same people might be observing him, suspicious of his secrets. As he approached an older man on the street, the stranger tipped his hat with a subtle gesture of civility and nodded to him. Tchaikovsky responded with a faint and insincere smile. He lowered his head and reflected if this would be the mask on the façade of his persona for years to come.

THE SILENCING
MAJORITY

MOSCOW, JANUARY 3, 2013

ALTHOUGH MARGO STEPPED into the hall from the wintery cold, she kept her Mouton hat on tight and the lapel of her fur coat over her mouth. She scanned the room, taking on the various men she'd seen at similar meetings before. There was Vadim Marinov, executive of the Soviet Bank, and other high-ranking dignitaries of Russian commerce as well as shadowy figures that Margo had met before.

From the determined look on their faces, she could tell that they were aware that something would be resolved here on this snowy evening. Margo watched her contact enter, and made no sign of recognition as he took his seat. The members of the secret Fatherland Society arrived in the desolate neighborhood, entered the assembly and silently sat in flimsy metal folding chairs, never making eye contact with each other. The only sound was the scraping on a rubber mat at the entrance as each person wiped the sleet from their boots. A few brushed against Margo and hung their coats on a rack made of iron pipe. The rest avoided interacting with the dismal setting as much as possible and hugged their fur as if it was their only friend in the bleak room. Their fashionable clothing made it evident that this was the upper edge of Moscow society. Dripping snow from lamb fur coats intensified the musty, clammy odor of the room. A single radiator on a far wall futilely fought the damp cold with a venomous hiss.

Standing quietly at the rear, Margo studied the crowd. One man with a full white beard, wearing a long black cloth coat with the collar turned up around his neck, chose a seat near the radiator, but after seeing a pile of dead flies rotting on the sill, changed his seat to the other side of the room. His new neighbor silently acknowledged the dingy surroundings with a telling glance. The fluorescent lights dangling from the ceiling gave the participants a pale pastiness, accentuating the somber but strange mood. This group appeared unaccustomed to being dragged out to a location such as this on a moody, gray day. No one outwardly appeared to mind; the purpose outweighed any inconvenience. Margo knew that this was no ordinary meeting. It was a showdown of grimly opposing views.

Margo took a seat at the rear and sat, motionless. Other than her, there were no women in this cabal. With her hat pulled tightly down to her eyes and her coat collar pulled high, she looked much the same as all the others. The main distinction was that she was one of the few people without a cigar or cigarette. With smoldering tobacco creating an increasingly dense smog, Margo slipped a cotton cloth from her pocket and pressed it against her face in an ineffective attempt to filter the air. She placed her free hand in her jacket pocket and checked for her Glock pistol. It was there, safe and ready for when she needed it. She folded the cloth admiring the bold Cyrillic initials, М.Д.—Margo Davidova. On her lap, she held a fist full of papers that she restlessly flicked with her fingers. There she sat like the others, waiting for the meeting to commence.

Upon seeing that everyone was seated and members were no longer arriving, a man rose from the front row and walked to the podium holding a stack of documents. From the bulk, Margo felt this would be a long oration. He began the meeting, speaking slowly in precisely enunciated Russian. "Defenders of the culture of my Fatherland, your Fatherland and that of our children, welcome to our monthly meeting. This is a special meeting. I have with me rewritten bylaws of our society that meet the requirements of a modern world. I trust that you have received your copies."

There was no reaction from the audience. Margo sat still.

"We are a steadfast society that is dedicated to the protection of the Fatherland from destructive rumors about our heroes and our ideals. We have applied inexhaustible resources dedicated to obliterate defamatory material aimed directly to destroy the reputation of beloved Russian luminaries."

There was an uneasy quietness in the room as most sat still.

The speaker continued. "Like all organisms, our league must adapt to a changing world or itself be extinguished. We have passionately defended eminences such as Mussorgsky, Tolstoy and Tchaikovsky from disgusting rumors and deceitful evidence of sexual deviance. And yet, as we do this important work, it has lost its purpose in an increasingly accepting world. That is why I have contacted our generous sponsors and had them agree to eliminate homosexuality from the list of things for which to seek and destroy evidence, however real the evidence might seem."

Margo looked around the room at the blank, emotionless faces staring at the speaker and wondered if anyone was really listening.

"After our vote this evening, we will have a simpler, more focused charter."

Margo remained inconspicuous in the last row, contented that the crowd would remain peaceful.

The speaker continued. "I have spoken to many of you and understand your disagreement with me, but I have the full support of some kind sponsors. Many of you might have believed that I have changed my opinion, but I stick to my carefully drawn position. The decision has been made as a privilege of my post. Your vote is a procedural formality. Are there any comments?"

Margo looked slowly to her left and received a sluggish nod from a portly man gnawing on a cigar. She moved the pistol from her pocket and slipped it onto her lap. She held the cold silencer in her hand as if it was a fond companion, checked that it was firmly attached to her Glock pistol, and assembled her cluster of papers as a cover. Margo stood up and walked slowly, subduing her awkward limp. She paced solidly to the podium and presented the papers to the speaker, who looked down at them. He made no visible gesture as he stared at a large cobalt blue silencer on the pistol. She pulled the trigger, which made a muffled sound, like a book being slammed shut. The speaker fell to the stool and then collapsed to the floor. Margo carefully wrapped the weapon, moved to the back of the room and once again blended in. *Well, that's done,* she thought while the audience sat as if a routine business transaction had been completed.

After a subtle nod here and there, the attendees stood and, with their heads high, marched unhurriedly to the rear and exited the building, funneling out as a homogenous group as they passed Margo, who looked back to admire her work.

Margo nonchalantly began buttoning her coat, then nodded to two men standing in a corner near the coat rack and signaled for them to move forward with a carpet, wrap the corpse and drag it out the rear exit and to a waiting truck. She calmly scanned the room before slowly walking toward the door. The room was once again empty as the radiator against the far wall hissed like a satiated demon and winter flies bounced futilely against the frost-covered window.

SHOPPING FOR ADVENTURE

MANHATTAN, APRIL 13, 2013

STARTLED BY THE ringing of his phone, Fred rolled onto his back, stretched and glared at the bedside clock. It was nine o'clock. He wiggled under the covers to grab the handset before the answering machine picked up, while thinking that this was not the way he had planned to start his Saturday. He was ready to snarl at the unwelcome disturbance until he heard the familiar and rousing voice that greeted him.

"Hi, sweetie, it's Susie. The sun is shining—you remember the sun? How about a little bit of adventure to celebrate the end of two weeks of depressing rain? Thursday morning, I swore that if it didn't stop raining that my head was going to become a sponge and swell until it exploded. Honestly, it felt as if the apartment was shrinking and in a day or two, I wouldn't fit. I'm turning into Susan in Wonderland trapped in a high-rent rabbit hole. I need sunshine."

Fred rolled over and covered his eyes. If she hadn't been such a longtime friend and confidant, he would have hung up on her. Instead, he said, "Why don't you come over and have a quick breakfast here before we go out and, as you say, celebrate the sunshine."

"I'll be right there!"

"I'll see you in a few minutes," Fred said, wishing she didn't live across the street.

After slipping into a pair of shorts, Fred padded into the kitchen to begin breakfast. Just as he pulled out a carton of eggs, the doorbell rang. He buzzed Susan in without interacting with her via the intercom, to stave off the joyous rapture a few minutes more, then crossed his arms and waited for the inevitable staccato knock before the door was flung open and Susan twirled in. She closed the door, then threw her arms in the air and melodiously said, "Good morning, sweetie."

Fred looked into the living room, raised his eyebrows slightly and continued making breakfast.

Susan twirled into the kitchen from stage left while looking up at the ceiling as if a camera recorded the event, then placed a light kiss on Fred's cheek. She plunked down on one of the two bar stools at the counter separating the kitchen from the living room.

"Smells delicious, Chef Fred."

Fred pulled a bowl of cut fruit from the refrigerator and set two bowls on the counter.

"Ahhh, what a healthful way to start the day," Susan said, then shoveled some fruit into the bowls and started flipping blueberries into her mouth while Fred put a pan on the stove and dropped some bread into the toaster.

"Fred, you're going to have to watch those eggs again. They keep rolling toward the edge of their world on the counter there. I think they're suicidal."

As Fred steadied the eggs, Susan advanced to other fruit pieces. She wiggled her tongue in her mouth as if it was an oral *Cirque de Soleil.*

"Dammit, you didn't take the little label off the peach and now it's stuck between my teeth. I hate those labels. Don't they know a peach when they see it? Do they think the checkout might've thought it was a blueberry?" Susan said.

Fred poked his fingers in the bowl and ate a peach, making *mmm* sounds, which annoyed Susan even more. She stood, grabbed her bag and started to rummage through it. "I have dental floss in here somewhere. We should start a petition at Shoprite to put an end to labels on fresh fruit."

Fred cracked four eggs into a skillet.

"We're going to explore the Russian section of Brooklyn today," Susan said as she stood up, wandered into the kitchen and peered over Fred's shoulder. "Keep an eye on the eggs, you don't want the edges to burn."

"Over easy?"

"Of course! Anyway, I'm hoping to find something nice for my sister's birthday. Maybe we could find something for your apartment. I hear that it's just like touring a Russian village."

Fred slid two plates onto the counter, walked around to the other side, sat down on a bar stool at the counter and signaled Susan to join him. As Fred ate with a hearty appetite, Susan poked at her food.

After Susan crunched the last crumb of toast, Fred got up and said, "Okay, it's time to play in the sunshine. Give me a few minutes."

"That's okay, I have to zoom over to my apartment to, ahem, freshen up. How about meeting me downstairs in front of my building in a half hour," Susan said as she spun around on the stool, ambled to the door and skipped out.

Fred cleaned up and got ready to go. He opened the door to his apartment and stared out into the hall at the row of identical doors. The hall was lifeless except for an occasional shriek from the little girl in apartment 2B.

"Well, I see that there is life—of sorts—in whine-central," Fred muttered as he swung the door closed. He caught a glimpse of an ugly vase on the shelf just as the door was closing. He didn't know why Susan had given him that thing. She'd probably wanted to lighten the load of tchotchkes in her apartment, or perhaps she actually thought he needed to have it. And now they were going shopping for more junk. He didn't know how she roped him into these things.

Fred thundered down the stairs and burst outside. He looked up at the sun and made the predictable sun-sneeze as he sprinted across the street. He paced on the sidewalk for a few minutes and then sat patiently on the cheek-wall of the entrance to the brownstone Susan's apartment was and enjoyed the sunny day while waiting for her to emerge. A short time later, another tenant, Steve, flung the front door open and squinted in the sunlight. Fred was greeted with an elevator glance from head to toe by the very handsome young man. As usual, Steve was dressed impeccably in a fitted shirt and tailored pants. With his head held high, he looked over at Fred and grinned. Humbly lowering his eyes, Fred sucked in his stomach.

Susan popped out of the door minutes later, singing "Sun, sun, sun . . . da da wah." She turned briefly to make sure that the lock clicked shut.

"Okay, so where are we going to find this Russian culture?" Fred asked.

Susan energetically replied, "Brighton Beach. We're going shopping and exploring. A whole new Russian community has grown there since I lived in Brooklyn. There are restaurants, bookstores, antique shops and a whole universe that we can discover. I feel excitement in my bones. This is going to be a thrilling day! I just know it!"

Turning back to Steve, who still lingered nearby, Susan said, "Hey, Steve honey, would you take a pic of Fred and me?" As Steve sauntered toward Susan, she rummaged in her purse, made a little whoop and exclaimed, "Dammit, I left my iPhone on the table in my apartment. I have to fly back to get it. I'm always leaving something, somewhere." She spun around and headed back to the front door. "Never mind, Steve, we'll do a selfie."

Susan ran up to her third floor apartment while Fred waited outside. Steve raised his eyebrows, smirked at Fred, then flicked his wrist in a short wave, paused a moment and ambled away. Fred threw his shoulders back, instinctively fixed his hair and then rolled his eyes. When Susan came flying out the door, they quickly walked down Charles Street, weaving down West 4th Street toward Sixth Avenue.

Fred and Susan walked to the subway entrance and descended energetically into the tiled cavern. They got on the first B train that came along and changed for the Q train in Brooklyn. They got off about an hour later near the Brighton Beach neighborhood and walked out of the train and into the bright sunlight. Susan opened her arms like a butterfly and danced around while she flapped her arms. In her sidewalk dance, she embellished her butterfly ballet as if she were budding from a cocoon. People walked past her, paying little attention.

They meandered along wide and narrow streets until they found a row of stores that looked authentically Russian, with Cyrillic writing above the English on the storefronts and flyers in Cyrillic stuck in the front windows. This was truly Little Russia, and the zest of far-off culture delightfully surrounded them. They rambled past numerous shops, studying some displays and briefly entering a few stores.

"My stomach is giving me the culinary wake-up call. It's close to lunchtime and I'm getting hungry." Susan said.

"Look," Fred said, "Ресторан, a restaurant." They lingered in front of the small restaurant nestled between the antique shops and studied the menu.

"Ah, borsht with potatoes. This is where we're going to eat," Fred said with delight.

Susan twirled around and followed Fred's lead into the little restaurant. Susan linked arms with Fred to be escorted inside.

They walked into the small restaurant that reeked with charm and delicious fragrances and sat down. The restaurant was dimly lit and heavy with the rich scent of soups and stews. "Ah, a Rachmaninoff piano concerto," Fred said as he looked at the tiny speaker near the ceiling and knew that he had chosen right. He stopped to listen, then turned to Susan and said, "Russian music, those icons on the wall. How could you be more authentic?"

Susan walked over to the display of Russian religious portraits with silver halos. "They look dreamlike," she said, then turned to one of the restaurant staff nearby. "How old are these?"

The man smiled and said nothing.

Susan returned to her seat.

"I think that they're old, probably real icons," Fred said. "That person may believe them to be the embodiment of the saints. We've stepped into another world."

As they perused the menu, Fred said, "Ahh, they have bliny, I love those pancakes. And the *pelmini*, little dumplings, I bet they're good here. I'm tempted by the *pirozhki,* sort of like Russian empanada. We can share."

"Nah, I'm eating light," Susan said. "Look around. What in this restaurant would give away that we're not in Russia? Not much. We are in Russia."

When the waitress came to take their order, Susan greeted her with the one special word she knew in Russian, "*Zdrasti*" (Hi).

The waitress responded in icy New Yorkeeze, "Yeah, hi, what would'ya like?"

As the waitress walked away, Susan whispered, "Well, that whipped me back to Brooklyn."

Over lunch, Fred said, "After we eat, we'll get back to the stores, but you're the one who buys. You have to keep a database of tchotchkes so you don't re-gift to the party that gifted you in the first place. You need a life simplification plan."

Both ordered the borsht and sandwich-of-the-day, a curious combination of roast beef and turkey. When the sandwiches arrived, Susan said, "Fred, your sandwich is loaded with lettuce and mine has none." She signaled the waitress and asked, "Can I have lettuce on my sandwich as well?" The waitress looked puzzled, but took her plate.

After the waitress returned with only a flimsy leaf on her sandwich, Susan asked sarcastically, "Can I have a leaf for the other half of my sandwich?"

The waitress appeared blasé, but Fred could sense Susan's teeth grinding in annoyance.

A bit later, the waitress rolled around and refilled Fred's iced tea, but passed Susan's. Susan looked up with incredulity. Fred raised his hand to cover his face knowing that Susan would wave to signal the waitress. Without saying a word, Susan pointed at Fred's full glass and then to her empty one.

The waitress looked a bit mystified, paused, and then topped Fred's glass. Susan was visibly irritated and lifted her glass with a demanding gesture. With a reluctant air, the waitress poured some iced tea into Susan's glass and blithely strolled away. Susan loudly growled and with a cynical tone said, "If he wasn't dead, I would write Lenin a letter about the service here."

Fred rolled his eyes. She had every reason to get angry, but what impressed him most was her ability to make things right. She had a talent for that.

The two sat quietly eating their lunch and after a while, Susan paused and with a relaxed and reminiscent voice said, "How long have we known each other? It seems like forever."

Not knowing where this was going, Fred mumbled, "It's been a long time."

Susan took a bite of her sandwich and gazed past Fred. "Under different circumstances, I wonder how things between us would have worked out."

Not wanting to be cornered, Fred lightly remarked, "Circumstances are circumstances, that's what it is." He reached across the table, put his hand on Susan's and smiled so very slightly.

The waitress brought the check and put it down on the table. Susan immediately dropped her hand on the check, looked up at the waitress and said, "Do you think you could sell me two potatoes? I'm cooking tonight and won't have time to get to the market. Of course I'll pay."

The waitress's jaw dropped as she backed away from the table.

Susan said, "And if you have one of those little salt shakers that you could include, I'll pay for that, too."

Fred looked over at Susan, smirked and slowly shook his head while the waitress disappeared back into the kitchen. She came back to the table in less than a minute to say, "No, I'm sorry, we don't have any uncooked potatoes." She looked up at the ceiling, then walked away.

Susan returned a half-smile and Fred picked up the check. Susan whispered to Fred, "If *you* had asked, I bet they would have said yes. Let's go somewhere else for dessert. I saw a bakery a couple of doors away."

They left the restaurant and walked toward the bakery. They passed a large display window of carved miniature musical instruments arranged as a symphony orchestra, which drew Fred's attention.

"Wait a minute," Fred said. "Look at this window loaded with interesting stuff. This is the place, it's like a folk museum with price tags." He focused on a set of Russian dolls decorated as a group of women wearing aprons, holding different foods. "Susan, look. The workmanship is amazing." As he pressed against the window and looked deep into the shop, he saw an old woman dusting a shelf, and as she looked up, his eyes locked onto hers. Before he could look away, she smiled and nodded sweetly.

A short distance away, Susan said, "C'mon, let's get a seat in the bakery, it's almost full. We can come back to the store later."

"Yeah, okay." Fred stayed glued to the spot and watched the old woman move about, occasionally looking back at him. His grandmother Baba had the same humble stance and aura of kindness as this old woman. He felt Susan tug at his elbow and he moved away reluctantly as the woman smiled again and lowered her head. He looked up at the name above the doorway, *Anna's Antiques*, and then nodded to the old woman.

SHADOWS

ANNA HAD SET up her antiques shop in the Brighton Beach section of Brooklyn in a similar fashion to her old shop on Karandash Street in Moscow. She positioned the items near the entrance and displayed colorful posters of similar Russian handicraft, which acted as lures placed just before the hook. The treasures she'd featured in her Moscow shop were also on display, placed against the wall in the middle of the shop, but now under modern spotlights. In places, the store looked like a museum of Eastern European artifacts, and in a way, it was.

It was early spring when Anna noticed many of the other shop owners putting chairs outside, so she had decided to do the same. She'd thought she might have time to sit outside, enjoy the warmth and perhaps chat with some of her neighbors but had soon discovered that the chair was irresistible to those waiting for their friend or partner to finish shopping in her store. *No matter,* she thought. The chair would allow those inside to store to linger longer as their companions rested. *Better for business.* She had blended comfortably into her new homeland, free of the anxiety of crime-ridden Moscow.

In the early afternoon, after rearranging a set of *matryoshka*[1] dolls and tidying up, Anna decided that was enough for a while and plopped into her comfy chair with a contented sigh. She let her mind drift while she watched the world amble by on the street. It was a sunny day and the stores across the street were brilliantly lit.

Anna was grateful for the shady exposure of her storefront. Anna felt that it was time for a glass of tea, as there was nothing else happening. She went to the back of the store and poured some highly concentrated brew into a glass, diluted it with hot water from a kettle on the stove, then delicately dropped in a few cubes of sugar and returned to her spot in the store.

When she returned, a pudgy and somewhat short silhouette hovered in the open doorway, initially motionless, and perhaps inanimate, but then moved to the side with a limp. At first Anna couldn't be sure if the person was facing inward or away. Not wanting to scare away a potential customer, Anna silently returned to her roost in the armchair. Compared to the intense sunlight, the shop was dark. Anna looked out at the silhouette, which was now nerve-wrackingly motionless. This person looked suspicious and she felt guarded and uneasy. A quick glance to the feet convinced Anna that this person *was* looking into the shop. Not wanting to move and fearing that a creak in the floor would provoke something unwanted, Anna tightened her toes and remained still. The person just stared into the store and, after a few minutes later, swung around and limped away with a robust swagger. Anna sipped her tea with a feeling of dread.

An hour later, two women, one a bit stubby and the other with a long neck, walked into the shop and lingered while chatting about a knickknack they'd picked off a table. Anna watched serenely as they advanced deeper into the shop and hovered over an assortment of quintessential Russian trinkets. She approached the women with a calculated casualness and said, "These statues are at Peter the Great's summer palace in St. Petersburg, such a grand place."

The stubby woman picked up a piece as Anna said, "Peter the Great had a desire to outdo the ornamentation at Versailles—"

---

1 Russian nesting, or stacking dolls. A Russian folk-art tradition. The word, матрёшка, is derived from the Russian female name Matryona. Many shops like Anna's would have such a display.

Anna instinctively glanced toward the store as her customer talked. There, in the window, outside the store, was the shadow again. The silhouette in the window shifted slightly, giving the outline of short, straight hair moving slightly away from her neck.

"That statue is at the center of a spectacular display of fountains," Anna said to the customers, glancing back at the window to find nobody there. The stubby woman carefully set the piece back on the table, linked arms with the other woman and, with a courteous thank you, gently hurried out of the shop.

Anna returned to her soft chair and sat staring at the front of the shop. After a while, she got up, walked around briefly and sat down. Again, she shifted her position in the chair, got up and walked around. At three o'clock, Anna felt the events of the day bear down on her and she prepared to close the shop, moving some displays to the center of the entrance aisle. As she walked over to the front door to lock up, standing no more than two feet away in the doorway was the same short, plump woman. Adrenaline rushed through her veins and an immediate cold sweat came over her. Her hands felt clammy against the edge of the door. Once again, the shadow stood motionless, but this time light reflecting from the window partially illuminated the face and her steady glare, cold and bitter, drilled into Anna's eyes.

Anna closed the door and locked it, then turned the OPEN sign around to CLOSED. For the first time, she pulled down the shade over the window on the front door, careful to keep her eyes on the woman's feet, noting that they had not moved during this whole encounter. Anna turned out the lights and retreated to the kitchen beyond the rear curtain of the shop. She was shaken and nervous. The cold sweat was now accompanied by a creeping sensation. Anna warmed some soup and had a troubled late lunch. She waited for Alex to return. And when he did, she told him nothing about the day's events.

Later in the afternoon, Alex said, "Anna, this is the busiest shopping time. Why do you have the shop closed?"

Anna thought for a moment, took a deep breath, threw her shoulders back and raised her head. She walked toward the front door as she said, "You are right, Alexei. Lunchtime is finished. This is beautiful and perfect day to welcome customers. We should be open."

MOSCOW PUB

MOSCOW, AUGUST 28TH, 1880

PETER ILYICH TCHAIKOVSKY stood by the window of the van Meck mansion at twilight and watched an eerie ruddiness settle over Moscow. Gaslights prolonged the dusk, which smoldered late into the night to illuminate more remote areas. It was in this far-flung setting that the social outcasts of society congregated. Peter was well aware that this was not the sole façade of outcasts, but rather people who dared not be revealed in daylight. The shadowy illumination of the persistent twilight afforded some protection from being identified, but a fraternity of secrecy was as much a part of Russian society as companionship. Agents of the police were considered to be everywhere and everyone. Only darkness provided a cloak.

In the late summer of 1880, Peter was mindful that he was recognizable in all social strata of Moscow. His picture appeared regularly in the newspapers and was posted on kiosks advertising performances of his symphonies and operas. His wealthy admirer, Nadezhda von Meck, supported him and invited him—no, urged him—to stay at her opulent mansion in Moscow when she was away. As much as she demonstrated her generous patronage, von Meck never met Tchaikovsky, although she socialized with other artists whom she endowed. In August, it was common for such affluent Muscovites like von Meck to vacate the city for a summer cottage in the countryside. She repeatedly offered her city home to Tchaikovsky and in the waning days of summer in 1880, he took her up on her offer.

The von Meck mansion was populated with servants and housekeepers who meticulously catered to those artists fortunate enough to be invited. They were observant of the needs of their visitors even before those guests were conscious of those needs. These invitees usually stayed to themselves and ignored others, if in fact there were any. This particular August, the guests included two musicians. At the same time that Peter stayed at the mansion, a young pianist from Paris resided there for the season as well. He had been hired to teach music to Nadezhda's children and to play duets with the wealthy philanthropist. The pianist was happy to escape the summer heat of Paris and to obtain lucrative employment at the same time. He was in no hurry to return to Paris until the summer had ended. His name was Claude Debussy and he had just turned nineteen, more than twenty years Tchaikovsky's junior. They had many conversations about new trends in music over a glass of schnapps on the terrace overlooking the gardens. Even though Claude was less than hesitant to press the value of new ideas, he felt privileged to begin a friendship with the internationally acclaimed master. They talked about the new impressionism in French art and how it was being echoed in music in strange and mysterious ways. Tchaikovsky loved Claude's spirit and honest enthusiasm, and as they walked the grounds of the von Meck mansion, they developed a closeness that belied their generation gap.

On one occasion, the two musicians played a game that only the most highly skilled could. One would play a short melody on the piano and the other would extemporaneously play variations on that theme. Claude Debussy would offer an intricate melody and then laugh as Tchaikovsky would ornament it with emblematic Russian variations. "Oh, Maestro, you have brought my Paris theme to Moscow beautifully." Their friendship grew swiftly and unusually strong as they playfully exhibited their uncommonly fine skills.

Peter went to his bedroom late on a Saturday evening, fetched his coat and scarf and quietly slipped out of the mansion and onto the chilly streets of Moscow. Most of the staff had gone to bed and several servants had the night off. Ordinarily, a footman would have rushed to meet the departing guest and offer a carriage.

Peter walked alone in the cool night air, deep in thought of the revisions he was making to his second symphony. He had written to Nadezhda about this and felt an obligation to make it ready for performance upon her return to Moscow. Lost in thought, Tchaikovsky followed the trail of gaslights until it ended and, isolated by a tunnel of contemplation about his loneliness, he kept walking into the deepening sunset. The smell of cooking meat wafted from the affluent homes. As he walked, these fragrances changed to roasted potatoes.

Nearing eleven o'clock, on a street illuminated only by the rays of oil lamps leaking through distorted windows, Peter stopped inside a small pub to be amongst the warmth of anonymous conversation. This is where he felt best. Peter sat in a shadowy corner and patiently waited for service while he became absorbed in a pair of musicians playing poignant music on folk instruments. Some patrons sat at other tables quietly chatting while others stood silently holding hands in the shadows. Tchaikovsky looked through the smoke-filled pub and into the distance with an empty stare until a man in uniform moved toward his table and slowly sat. This was no stranger, and as Peter searched his mind for the man's identity, the man put his hand on the table as a gesture of friendly introduction. At that moment Peter shrunk back in his seat and recognized the footman from Nadezhda's carriage house.

Tchaikovsky's face dropped as he remembered the incident at the salon years ago where an affectionate young violinist was sent to a northern detention camp for his illegal affections. With the chilling realization that he had surely been recognized, Peter stood, hurried to the door and, pulling his collar up high around his neck, paced quickly back toward the mansion in Moscow. The clicking of his heels on the narrow cobblestone street echoed from the surrounding high walls. Peter wasn't sure whether it was his footsteps alone that be heard, so he quickened his cadence, listening to the ambient sounds, never quite convinced that he was unaccompanied. He pulled his collar a tad higher and walked a bit faster, anxious for the sanctuary of the von Meck mansion. He hoped that his only companion was his loneliness. But everyone watched and everyone was watched.

EXPLORING BRIGHTON BEACH

BROOKLYN, APRIL 13, 2013

IT WAS APPROXIMATELY two-thirty when Fred and Susan stepped out of the bakery, with Susan still complaining about the service she'd received. Fred was still intrigued by the imaginative display of colorful nesting dolls in the window of Anna's Antique Shop.

"I can't believe they wouldn't tell me what spices were in those cookies. It's not like I'm going to mass-produce them," she said.

Fred rolled his eyes.

"I just wanted to learn something. They should have felt the compliment," Susan said.

"I know," Fred said with a distant tone, picturing the vibrant Russian folk art he had seen.

"And she always gave you the bigger cookie."

"It's because you're a woman."

"I know." Susan huffed, scanning the street and wiggling her finger to the left. "Let's go in that direction. We haven't been over there."

Fred looked back at Anna's Antique Shop, crinkled his nose in disappointment and thought that he would get back to that shop one way or another.

Fred and Susan ambled along the street and aimlessly peeked into one window after another. Fred glanced back at the shop once more, thinking of the old woman he saw through the window. He also recalled seeing a stocky woman take a few steps backward from the shop, then turn and limp away with heavy footfalls.

The street ahead was thick with people weaving around Fred and Susan. When they reached the corner, Fred looked back once again, paused and then turned left and a while later pressed to another left turn. Fred looked at his watch and saw that it was getting late. "Sus, let's circle around. It's going on four o'clock and I wanted to see that antiques shop."

"Sure, let's do it."

When they returned to Anna's Antique shop, Fred saw the shade being pulled up and the old woman turn the CLOSED sign around. As he moved from one of the display windows to the other, he said, "Susan, looks like we timed it just right." He shielded his eyes from the glare and pressed his face against the display window, trying to see deeper inside. In the deep shadows in the rear of the store, he saw a handsome young man pick up some boxes and disappear through curtains. Fred heard the door unlock and then open.

The old woman swung the door open wide and placed a bulky iron statue against it as a doorstop. She stepped outside, looked at Fred and Susan, nodded, and pointed into the shop. Fred politely nodded and slowly stepped toward the door. He saw the old woman lean out and look the other way down the street. She folded her arms across her chest, took a deep breath and softly said, "Please." She pointed inside the shop.

Susan said, "You were closed for a while, I noticed when—"

"We just had lunch a few doors away," Fred said.

The old woman gave them a questioning frown, then opened her mouth and displayed a cheerful welcoming look one gives a relative returning from a lengthy absence. "At the bakery, so good. Yes, so good." The old woman stepped back as if to draw Fred and Susan deeper into the shop. "Welcome to my shop. My name is Anna."

"My name's Fred, and this is my friend Susan. We were admiring your display."

"Yes, I saw you. It is beautiful day. Everything in shop is from places in Russia, some old, some new." She led the way and turned on some lights. As she spoke, she periodically turned to look back at the front door, then looked back and smiled gently.

Stepping inside the shop, the dim lighting and soft music gave Fred the feeling that he'd crossed a great divide from the outside world. Anna turned back, glanced once again the door and said, "Come, look around."

Fred looked over at Susan, who raised her eyebrows in approval. It was a relief to get off the busy street. Here, it was calm and peaceful, with the rows of nesting dolls and carved puppets giving it the playfulness of a sophisticated toyshop. The mixture of exotic rose-like scents and musty smells evoked another culture. There were fragrances unlike any they sensed in other shops. It stirred a vague feeling of hunger, but for what was not clear. Still, the shop felt as if it contained something special that Fred or Susan lacked. Paradoxically, soft classical music coming from the darkness in the rear of the store made it feel ghostly quiet.

The shop was narrow, with the left side far deeper than the front area. Susan walked toward the dimness of the narrow section in the back while Fred examined some old cups. He kept an eye on Susan and Anna and could hear conversation.

Anna followed Susan to the rear of the store and said, "You are liking Russian antiques? You would be interested in something, perhaps?"

"This shop has very nice feeling," Susan said, dropping the *a*. Fred hoped that Susan wouldn't continue the dramatized Russian accent.

Anna quickly said, "And your husband?"

Susan tilted her head and softly said, "Oh, my *friend* . . . Fred."

"Fred?" Anna queried.

Susan fondled a small vase. "Fred Novik."

"Ah, Fred Novak," Anna said.

"No, Novik. It's an Americanized name," Susan said, then called across the store. "Fred, could you come back here for a minute."

Fred sauntered over, pausing at the brightly colored tapestries along the way. "What was your family name originally?" Susan asked.

"It was Tochinovich, but my grandparents changed it to Novik to make it seem more American when they came here from Russia. People think it should be Novak, but it is No*vik*."

In the dimly lit room, Fred noticed Anna's brows lift and her forehead wrinkle as she said, "Torchinovich is normal Russian name. You meant To*r*chinovich, yes?" Anna rolled a sustained 'r' to accentuate the difference.

Fred smiled slightly as he explained, "No, it is Tochinovich. Who knows how long ago the 'r' might have been dropped, but as far back as we go in our family tree it was Tochinovich."

A bit flummoxed by the name, Anna turned to Susan and said, "Enjoy your search." She turned, but did not move for a long time before ambling away slowly. "Tochinovich, Fyodor[2] Tochinovich," Anna repeated in a whisper.

As Fred wandered the shop, he hummed along with the music while his fingers involuntarily moved with the sound of the piano.

Susan started whistling with the music, which Fred found grating and put his finger up to his lips to stifle the irritation. Susan stopped with a look of contrition. They both wandered around the tables looking for nothing in particular.

"It's Tchaikovsky," Anna said from across the room with a thick Russian accent.

Fred smiled at her. "The Seasons, Tchaikovsky's own piano arrangement."

The woman smiled. "You know it."

"Actually, he wrote it originally for piano. My grandmother used to call it *Ochen kracevyeshe*," Fred said

Her eyes lit up. "Very beautiful."

"Yes."

Susan meandered toward a heavy green curtain at the rear of the shop. Fred turned away from her to look at a small sculpture, then heard her gasp. Fred turned quickly to see what had happened and found a young man—probably in his late twenties—appearing from nowhere and standing in front of Susan.

---

2 Fyodor is a common Russian nickname for Fredrick.

While Fred and Susan wandered the shop, Anna kept an eye on the front door for any activity from the street. She was still uneasy about the theft of the bundle marked *Music* in her Moscow store and what it could possibly mean for herself and her family. But it was Fred and his unusual name that made her think.

This Fred knows Russian music, Anna thought as she wandered to the back of the shop. Everything seemed to be happening again, as if the problems in Moscow had followed her to America. The unbearable was relentless. The package of music in the hands of a Russian was a perilous target. Perhaps an American should keep it safe.

Her grandson was unpacking some boxes at the far end of the shop. She'd brought him here to keep him safe. Alexei was standing beside Susan and talking to the couple. Anna was fearful for her grandson and always suspicious of strangers speaking with him. She watched the boy interact with the American couple. All seemed friendly. She relaxed.

A short while later, Susan meandered toward Anna and said, "How do you like living in New York?"

Anna shook her head and looked up to find Susan looking at her, eyes wide and smiling. "We have been with this store three months almost," Anna said. "Many things from Russia, very nice. You are looking for something in particular?"

Susan's face grew cold, almost as if she was ready to negotiate the price of an object. "A musical instrument for a friend, a very talented friend. Perhaps a piccolo or a flute."

"Ahhh, I see," Anna said, amused by Susan's fake accent. "Perhaps you have a Russian background?" she said with a smirk. "Maybe family still in Russia?" Anna said with businesslike enthusiasm. She thought for a moment, opened her mouth wide and said, "*Pikkolo fleyta* (flute), let me see."

"Ah," she pleasantly exhaled. "Da . . . da . . . one moment, please." And she hurriedly shuffled to the curtained off area. Less than a few minutes had passed and the drapery parted.

"Come, *poojzhalsta*" (please), Anna said, then peeked over to Fred, who held up a vase and flicked it with his finger to listen to the chime. She tapped him on the shoulder and said, "There are no cracks in that vase." She signaled Fred to follow her into the back area.

"Come, please." Anna gestured the group to gather around a wooden table with a shiny green and tan enameled metal top, then pushed a plate of cookies toward Susan. "Here, made today. Enjoy."

"No, thank you," Susan said while Fred slipped one into his mouth.

"Just like my grandmother made," Fred said.

Anna edged the plate closer to Fred. "Here, have more."

Throughout all of the hospitality, Anna studied her customers. The name *Tochinovich* kept echoing in her head. *Could it be? Could it be possible? Tochinovich*, she thought.

Anna watched as Fred chewed his cookie and said, "You like?"

"Very much," Fred said, then took another bite.

"Well then, perhaps I have something else you may like," she said, glancing over at Susan, who seemed curious about what she was getting at.

"Hopefully not more cookies," Susan said with a grin.

"No, no more cookies," Anna said, then stood up. "*Izvinite menya*" (Excuse me).

As Anna walked out of the room, she caught Susan glance over at Fred as he mouthed *Excuse me* to her. *The silly girl*, Anna thought.

Anna grabbed the velvet-lined piccolo box, then paused and thought about the music. She could give this man and his friend the music and save herself and Alex from further danger. Nobody would think this man had such a thing, plus he would probably keep it in good condition. His family name, *his name*.

She removed her hands from the box, then thought about the ominous figure she'd seen in the shop entrance. *What if it all happened again? What if they found her and came back for more evidence and found it? What would happen to Alex?* She turned toward the doorway, then back to the package of music. She grabbed the box containing the piccolo and walked back out to them.

Anna brought the small case to the table and opened it to reveal purple velvet lining cradling a black wooden piccolo from the 1920s with silver mechanism and keys. She watched Fred's eyes widen and his mouth open slightly as he leaned forward. Fred put his hand on the box and Susan picked up the instrument. It smelled musty, so there was no expectation that she would bring it to her lips, no less play it.

Anna enthusiastically said, "Go ahead, you try it."

Susan quickly put the instrument back in its case, showing that she had no ability to play it.

Anna quickly said, "Yes, a bit dusty. You like music?"

Fred tilted his head down, looked away and quietly said, "Music is my life."

"I see," Anna said, wondering why he would be so shy about such a thing. She reached over the table and placed her right hand over Fred's folded hands and looked him in the eyes. "You have good friend in this girl."

"Friendship goes both ways," Fred said.

"Yes, yes, I believe it does." Anna looked over at Susan, whose cheeks had a crimson glow.

As they studied the craftsmanship, Anna said softly and with obvious affection, "Sixty dollars. You pay cash, no tax."

Fred reflexively grinned, raised his eyebrows and said, "That's a fraction of its value."

Anna nodded and said, "Good, I will wrap it for you."

Fred took three twenties out of his wallet and put them on the table. Susan and Fred looked at each other as if they had just robbed the kindly old woman blind. Fred started to draw additional money from his wallet, but Anna put her hands on his and said, "That is fine. You will love instrument. I will be happy knowing it is in the right hands."

Anna held the money and broadened her closed lips just enough to reveal a slight smile. She watched Fred and Susan get up and slowly walk toward the door.

"Please, do not go yet," Anna said. "The instrument needs cleaning. The instrument is old. It will need some work before it can be played. My grandson has friend who will do it—not cost too much. Alexei, *poojzhalsta*." Anna waved Alexei over. "I see you have already met my grandson, Alexei."

"We spoke with him briefly," Fred said.

"Please, let me formally introduce Alexei."

"Alex," the young man blurted out while giving Anna a pointed glare.

"Alex," Anna said. "These young people wish to forget their heritage. It break my heart."

Alex smiled pleasantly at Susan, then turned toward Fred and let his eye rest on him a bit longer than necessary.

Fred awkwardly said, "Nice to formally meet you, Alex. Your grandmother has an amazing shop here." Alex reached out, shook hands and smiled.

Anna said quietly to Alex, "это хорошие люди, держать их близко."[3]

Alex fumbled with a piece of paper, then wrote down the name of the instrument restorer, paused a moment and then added his own name and phone number.

Fred took a card from his wallet and slid it across the table to Alex.

Anna watched as Fred gazed at Alex. His gaze was more than just any look one man would give to another. It was a look she'd seen before, one of longing and desire. Yes, she thought, this man will work. He will do what I need because of his desire for Alexei and his love for all things Russian. Anna had set the hook. "Frederick Tochinovich. Can it be? I see a way," Anna slowly said as she envisioned Fred having the music. No one would suspect him of having the music, and because of his interest, he would take good care of it.

Alex was in bed and unable to sleep. He couldn't stop thinking about Fred and his friend, Susan. He rolled over and hoped to fall asleep. After a while, Alex raised his head and looked around his small bedroom above the shop and listened to Anna sleeping in an adjacent bedroom. Shadows from the dim nightlight in the bathroom accentuated the darkness, making the space feel unbounded. The only sounds were of slumbered breathing with the occasional snort. Through the slightly opened windows, he could hear the occasional snore of nearby neighbors punctuating the deadly stillness.

---

3   "These are good people. Keep them close."

But somehow the stillness of the building was different. He listened carefully to the empty shop downstairs. *Was that a door handle?* He listened again. Nothing. Was he hearing things? Then there was a dull thump, barely recognizable, then silence again. He had to be imagining it. Perhaps it was the remains of a dream. He closed his eyes, but couldn't help but continue to listen for strange sounds. There was something unusual that gave him a creepy, chilling sensation. Then he heard glass breaking downstairs. He got out of bed with a slight tremor and then tiptoed out of his bedroom to check on Anna. Her door was closed. He cracked it ever so slightly and peeked inside. Anna's wheezing assured him that she was secure and unmoving. Then he heard movement downstairs and a creak of the floorboards. He slowly tiptoed from his room to the top of the stairs and paused to listen.

Alex descended one stair at a time to sneak a peek at the intruder. Although his hands trembled on the handrail, he stood motionless, looking down to the kitchen below. Seeing nothing, he descended further, bit by bit, feeling his toes on the edge of the stairs. Feeling a rush of outside air at his feet, he was now sure that the intruder had entered through the front door, broke the glass and unlocked it from the inside.

In the darkness of the kitchen, he slid his hand against the wall until he hit the knife rack. He then silently took a large carving knife from the rack. Although he trembled, he felt surprisingly firm in his bearing. With little time for planning, he decided to surprise the intruder and chase him from the shop. He swept the air around him with the knife as a sort of batting practice in the event that it might be used.

Through a crack in the curtains separating the shop from the kitchen, Alex saw the narrow beam of a flashlight sweeping across the shelves. He heard the sound of papers and magazines being torn from the shelves and thrown to the floor. There was a flash of bright light, then he caught sight of the intruder, who looked short and pudgy. Alex rushed from the curtains, waving his knife and shouting as loud as possible, "Get the hell out my shop!"

With his head thrown forward, Alex saw a bright flash accompanied by a loud thud as he was thrown to the floor.

Anna woke to the sounds of a scuffle in the shop below. She jolted up in bed, but kept quiet. She was suddenly transported back to Moscow and the trouble she'd had there. *No,* she thought, *this cannot be happening.* She strained to listen and heard someone gasp. She grabbed her robe and scurried down the stairs.

In the dim light Anna saw Alexei on the floor, a pool of blood beneath his legs. She rushed to him and cradled his head in her arms. "Alexei, my baby, Alexei what has happened?"

As Alex slowly regained consciousness, he looked down to the bloody floor and then up to Anna. "I guess I dropped the knife on my thigh and cut myself. I thought there was only one of them."

"Oh, my Alexei," Anna said as she combed through his hair with her fingertips and felt her cheeks dampen with tears. Seeing him move with an occasional groan and deciding that he was all right, she began to sob loudly.

"I thought we left all of this behind in Moscow. When will it end?" Anna cried. "Will it ever end?" She hugged Alex and kissed his forehead as Alex twisted to sit up. With a determined voice, Anna said, "Tomorrow we will fix this."

They cautiously went to the open front door, then closed and locked it. Alex taped some cardboard over the hole in the glass, climbed back up the stairs, then they went back to bed.

Neither slept.

Anna sat at the kitchen table sipping tea with Alexei as she thought about the danger from the previous night. No matter how much she tried to forget them, thoughts of Moscow came to mind. Alexei, her grandson, her treasure, had almost died. He'd been injured, stabbed. And for what? For music. No, *the* music.

"We can't keep that music here any longer," Alex said. "The music must be moved to someone we can trust so that it will be preserved. And who that is, I don't know. We can't put it into a safe-deposit box. These thugs will still believe that we have it. Why don't we just conspicuously give it away? Whatever it is about that stuff, it isn't worth what we're going through. I do not understand why valuable antiques are pushed aside while our lives are torn apart just for some sheet music."

Anna quickly looked away, then stood up from the table and softly asked, "Do you want some toast with your tea?"

Alex rested his head in the palm of his hand with his elbows on the table as Anna fumbled by the stove droning in a distinctly audible voice. "The time has come. Tochinovich—I can't believe it."

Alexei is right, Anna thought. *We can't keep the music here.* She wouldn't be able to live with herself if Alexei was seriously injured, or worse. If she could find a new home for the music, then she and Alexei could remove themselves from the shop for a few days, enough time for the thieves to ransack the shop and find nothing.

"And I think you should get a dog," Alex said. "You're alone a lot of the time and it would keep you company."

"I agree. I'll name it Sassy. Go upstairs, get Fred's phone number. I want to talk to him."

Fred wasn't home, so she left him a message.

Fred returned the call later that day. "Hello, Anna? You called?"

"Yes, Fred. Come back to our shop to see something that I believe you would be very interested in seeing. It will be something that goes with the instrument, something important."

"Something important?" Fred said.

"Something you should have." The conversation went on for a short while and then Anna hung up.

Two hours later, Anna heard the doorknob rattle followed by knocking on the plywood panel that covered the door. Anna walked into the shop and saw Susan's face pressed against the window with her hand above her eyes. A few minutes passed until Anna unlocked the door and graciously welcomed Fred and Susan inside and led them to the back of the shop and into the kitchen. She offered them a seat at the kitchen table, and then some refreshments.

"What happened here?" Fred said, looking back at the door. Anna did not answer as they walked toward the kitchen.

Thundering footsteps came from stairwell and Anna raised her chin and rolled her eyes. "My grandson," she said. "Alexei."

"Alex," Alexei said sternly as he bounded into the room.

"Alex. I'm sorry. My grandson, Alex."

Fred and Susan stood and warmly greeted Alex. As Alex sat down at the table, Anna stood up and went to the rear of the shop area. She returned in a few minutes with a package, cradling it tight to her bosom as if she was protecting a foundling.

At the table, Anna caressed the package and rotated it as if she was taking a final look before sending it off for adoption. The package was tied with ribbons made from torn white sheets, yellowed with age. Anna rested her hands on the package and signaled everyone to sit. Her fingers nervously repositioned the package very slightly as she looked up at Fred and Susan. Alex showed no visible reaction.

In the dimly lit room, Anna looked directly at Fred while her aged hands gently caressed the top of it like a lover. With a sadness in her eyes, she said, "I know that I am making you curious. Please, forgive me. There is so much music and history and love in this package. This is a treasure, something that cannot be lost. This is my gift to you. Keep it in safe place. It is extremely precious, and could possibly be a part of your heritage."

Anna watched Fred glance at Susan, who seemed about to jump out of her seat and grab the package. Anna's fingers closed around the package and then tentatively opened it. With a visible spasm of hesitation, she slid the old bundle toward Fred and gently took her hands away. With the same graceful movement, Fred put his hands on the parcel and ushered its journey toward him.

Fred quizzically smiled at Anna and mouthed "Thank you."

Anna softly smiled back.

Anna put one hand on his and the other to her lips. She interrupted him, speaking in a barely audible voice not intended for Susan nor Alex to hear, "You will see. Look for the name Tochinovich in the music." Anna brought a plastic bag to the table and slid the package inside, then said even more softly, "Yes, Tochinovich."

Fred and Susan exchanged good-byes with Anna, who gave a light hug to Susan, then one to Fred; Alex boldly grabbed Fred's arm as their eyes met. There was a slight hesitation as Susan and Fred faced the door, then they all slowly paced toward the street. Anna watched as Alex placed his hand on Fred's shoulder with the hushed promise that they would soon meet again.

Susan and Fred took their newly found treasure and stepped out into final rays of daylight. They glanced back in through the window and squinted at the reflections of the street, then joined hands and turned away.

Anna crossed her arms as she watched Fred and Susan walk down the street in the last hours of sunlight. She grinned slightly, then turned toward Alexei and said, "It is done."

MUSIC AND ANNOTATIONS

MANHATTAN, APRIL 16

ALONE IN HIS apartment, Fred was drawn to the package from Anna's shop. Susan was away for the day and Fred couldn't wait for her to come home to see what Anna had given him. Fred set the package of music down on the table, then slowly opened it. A musty scent rose from inside the package, tingling the surrounding air like a haze of incense in a gypsy tent. There were well over a dozen folios of sheet music inside, which Fred gracefully slid from the container and placed on the table.

Fred stared at the first piece of music in awe. Before he tried to translate the Russian notes scribbled on it, he studied the piano score, a Tchaikovsky waltz, one that he had played in a piano recital as a child. The paper was old, with notes in Cyrillic scrawled in random directions. It was dated 1892, and after a short dash to his computer in the living room and a quick check on Wikipedia, he mumbled, "My God, a first edition."

He carefully thumbed through each page, all of which was piano solo. Some of the pieces had the name *Pyotr*[4] hand-written

---

4 The Russian name for Peter.

in Russian characters; others had just the Cyrillic initial P [П]. Fred sifted through the pages looking for a date embedded in the Cyrillic handwriting and found several, mostly in the 1870s. He sat at the table looking at the folios and wondering what could have made this batch of music so important that Anna had given it to him for safekeeping.

Looking through the sheet music, he thought he needed to share this amazing experience with someone. He thought about his brother John, then sauntered to the living room and sat down at his desk, placed his hands on the keyboard and stared at the ceiling for a moment.

Dear John,

I got an amazing package of ancient sheet music today from an old Russian woman. When I opened it, the scent reminded me of when we used to hide in a closet in Baba's house. It was a mind-blowing feeling of being one with antiquity.

I carefully slid pieces off the stack trying to decipher the titles with my meager knowledge of the Russian language. Sprinkled in with the Russian titles were some German titles. These were immediately recognizable, but were less interesting. One rarely sees music titles in Russian and I was intrigued. I selected one title on a worn piece of music that I thought translated as The Seasons, *by Tchaikovsky. It had a translation of the Russian at the bottom of the title page in French, which I can handle pretty well, as you know. I put it on the piano easel and started to play it. This piece is usually heard played by an orchestra, but Tchaikovsky wrote it originally for piano. I know that because it was played in a concert I went to some years ago and I was a bit amazed to see that mentioned in the program notes.*

I opened to my favorite part, June. *It has such a soulful melody that I was humming it before I got to the page. As soon as I started playing, I was sure that my translation was correct and got some confidence in recognizing Russian words. But what was most* interesting is that the music was littered with comments in Russian, likely from a teacher. My piano teacher frequently jotted comments in my music, usually disparaging ones. I assumed that these were similarly caustic and derogatory. Although I've seen it on occasion, compliments are rarely marked in music. I played, noting the comments, but the fact that they were in a stylistic Russian script meant, as you can imagine, that I understood virtually nothing.

And then I singled out a word, written in a bold hand in the Cyrillic letters, which I understood as passionate and then a few words later, heart. I don't know why these words translated so easily. But I remember grandma Baba using them.

Passion of the heart? That's a bit unusual to see in the music, I thought to myself, and I played on. As I played, I thought of my student days and my piano teacher, Mrs. Gordon. I remembered when I played a Brahms piece, she said, "This is the first time that you have made music." She took her dull red pencil and leaned over the music. I watched with affection as she drew a small heart over the passage that I had just played. I felt a bond, a fondness for my teacher as she acknowledged her pleasure. I wondered how much of that rapport was expressed in the Cyrillic printing on what I was playing. There was certainly a large amount of writing.

There was one more thing that drew my attention. The writing was all at the same slant. Annotations in my music were done in random directions, depending on where my teacher was hovering. Someone standing over a student and scribbling on a vertical page did not do this. This was done at a desk.

One more thing drew my attention, the writing was done most at its simplest technical parts, where the music least filled the space on the page. And this particular piece is technically facile. Usually, in my experience, the teacher had the most to write where the music was the most demanding. There was clearly a strange pattern.

I became more and more curious to know what went

on between the teacher and the student. Surely these were more than instructional comments. Although I played past these scribblings, the pattern of the writing kept flashing in my mind. I must confess that the whole thing gives me a creepy feeling. And then I thought back to the shop where I got this package and the old woman who gave it to me. I have been gradually getting the feeling that there was more to this gift than I thought. It's all kind of weird.

Say hi to Andy,
Love, Fred

Fred scanned the letter, clicked the "Send" button, and sat back in his chair. He couldn't wait to tell Susan what he had found. He carefully packed up the music and slid it in the piano bench. It was suddenly a prized possession with a value that he could not imagine. He started to understand why Anna grasped it so hauntingly and lovingly on the table in her shop. What he could not understand is why she gave it to him.

Fred reached in his pocket for his iPhone, but it wasn't there. He stood up with a dazed feeling and saw it lying on the kitchen table. He went to it and called Susan.

"Susie, you know that package that we got at the antique store in Brighton beach? Well, it's amazing in a million ways. I think that it might be really important, but I'm not sure. I want to go back to that store and find out more. I want to know why it was given to me. Y'wanna join me? I would love to get some of the Russian writing translated. It would be a kick."

"Oh, sweetie, I can't do it today. I have a meeting with the Fabulous Film Forum group. How about we go back on Saturday?" The disappointment in Susan's voice turned to suspicion after a pause. "You know, I don't get it. What was that old woman doing giving stuff away? Yeah, I want to go back and get a better sniff of this fish."

BACK TO ANNA'S SHOP

BROOKLYN, APRIL 21

THE RAIN CAME down hard, making it dismally dark as it slid down Fred's raincoat and soaked into his jeans. If he wasn't so full of questions about the music Anna had given him, he wouldn't have bothered going outside on this Saturday afternoon.

"Fred," Susan called out in the distance.

Fred turned to see her lagging a good six feet behind him, then looked at the open mouth of the subway station across the street. He pulled on the hood of his raincoat as he waited for traffic to clear before jumping over the puddle and crossing the street.

At the top of the stairs, Fred looked around at a bleak streetscape as drops fell off his hood and down his cheeks. He waited for Susan to catch up, then swiftly stepped down to the dank station. He was relieved to be in a dry place. Fred and Susan ambled to the center of the platform where, without saying a word, they waited for their train. A sudden cold wind roared from the tunnel followed by a screeching train.

Fred gazed around the car but saw only images of the music sheets flash before him. He wanted to know more, but didn't know exactly what he would say to Anna. The two took the subway exit and walked to Anna's shop. The street seemed more distant now. Last time they were on this street, the crowds and noise made it seem friendly; now, the absence of others gave it a cold feeling. He didn't know if the emptiness of the street was due to the heavy drizzle or if it might be some religious holiday he didn't know about.

When they found the shop, it was closed. Plywood covered the glass door, so the two of them tried to see through the tinted glass side windows, but without lights on inside, it was impossible to discern anything except dozens of cheap trinkets roughly piled on a table near the window. Fred stepped back, looked at Susan, who seemed disappointed, then looked down the street. All the shops on the street seemed to be closed, except for the restaurant where they had eaten on their last visit. "C'mon," Fred said as he pointed to the restaurant.

They wandered around the restaurant looking for a sympathetic person. Fred said, "Susan, that woman over there, she looks like who we want."

Susan walked up to the woman and asked, "Do you know Anna from the antique store down the block?"

Fred said, "We need to see Anna. It's important."

The woman stared silently at them.

Susan quickly said, "We've enjoyed eating here before. And I must say that my life went through a sort of transformation when I had the borsht."

Fred hoped that Susan would slow down on the hollow accolades, fearing that it might backfire and ruin any chance of getting help.

The woman looked at Susan and gave a slight smile. "Anna? You know Anna?" the woman said to someone behind a partition.

"Ah, Anya . . . *Da*, Anya!" The woman nodded spiritedly and stepped out from behind the partition. "Let me make telephone. I ring her for you."

The woman went to a telephone on the wall and dialed carefully. "Anya?" The next thousand words were totally unintelligible, but sounded encouraging. She put the phone back in its cradle with gentle precision and walked back to Fred and Susan. "Go to shop. Anya will open door for you."

"Let's do it," Fred said to Susan as they left the restaurant and hurried down the street to Anna's shop.

Approaching the shop, Susan said, "There's Anna outside, by her front door. She is too sweet."

"Welcome, welcome," Anna said as she swept her hands toward the entrance. "I somehow expected your return." Anna clasped her hands together and raised them to her bosom. She walked well ahead of Susan and Fred and toward the back of the store.

"Fred, look at this," Susan said. She pointed to the fragments of glass inside the door frame. "Something has happened here, and it doesn't feel so good."

They paused for a moment, looked at each other and then hurried to catch up to Anna.

Anna ushered them to the small kitchen in the back and put a pot of tea and four mismatched cups on the table. "You have looked at the package of music?" Anna said. "You have questions—I am not surprised. Please, sit down." A dog squeezed under the table and licked Fred's hand. "Oh, Sassy likes you, a good sign," Anna said.

Fred grinned, then pet the dog's head. When Sassy went to the corner of the kitchen to lie down, Fred smiled at Anna and said, "There's a lot of notation in the sheet music."

Anna nodded, "Yes, notes. Many notes."

"My Russian just isn't—"

"It's passable," Susan quickly added.

"And I would like to read the notes."

"Which are amazing, I'm sure," Susan said.

Anna nodded, "Yes, notes. Many notes."

"There are a lot of questions. The writing in the music, it's unlike any teacher's notes I've ever seen. I'm curious as to what it might mean," Fred said.

Anna softly smiled and nodded. She held up her hands and said, "Please, just one at a time."

Someone bounded down the stairs. Fred turned to see Alex emerge from the stairwell.

"Alexei," Anna said, giving him a stern eye. "Barbarians walk in such a way."

Alex shrugged, then pulled up the empty chair to Fred's left and dropped himself into it.

Alex slid one of the cups to him, poured a cup and sat quietly listening to Fred and Susan.

"The handwriting is hard to read. I can get some of the Russian but the words that I do get make no sense where they're put," Fred said.

Anna slowly nodded.

"The words that I do get are very unusual for a piano teacher."

"Yes."

"I would like to understand it, the writing."

Anna reached and out and held Fred's hand. She smiled up at him and said, "How much do you understand?"

Susan blurted out, "Enough to come here."

Anna glared at Susan, then turned her attention back to Fred. "How much do you understand?"

"Not very much."

"But enough to know that it's very curious," Susan said.

"There is much for us to discuss," Anna said.

"What happened to the front door?" Fred said.

Alex cleared his throat, then looked up at Fred and said softly, "A few days ago, someone broke into the shop. Nothing was taken, but there was some damage. Apparently they did not get what they were looking for."

"The shop?" Fred asked, a bit perplexed.

"The broken window in the door," Susan said.

"Yes," Alex said, his soft brown eyes holding Fred captive. "Nobody was harmed, thankfully."

Fred looked down at the table. "Thankfully." He felt a hand on his left arm, then looked up to see Alex gently lick his lips.

"I can help you translate the notes," Alex said.

"Can you tell us why people want the music?" Susan asked.

"It is historical document," Anna said. "It is part of our history."

"But—"

Anna stood up and tapped Susan on the shoulder. "Come, let me show you something."

"But—"

"Come, let the boys talk." Anna clasped her hands together and took in a deep breath. "I have something amazing to show you."

Susan looked back at Alex as Anna started to lead her to the front of the shop. Anna hesitated for a moment, then turned around and looked directly into Fred's eyes. "The package that I gave to you is now yours." She paused and as if choosing her words carefully. "But it is not only yours. It belongs to the world. It is important. It is—I believe the word that is used is *heritage*—perhaps your heritage. You must be careful with it. When you decide to tell someone that you have it, choose *very* carefully." And then she leaned toward Fred, placed her hand on Fred's shoulder said, "Take care, as we say, *Tisha, tisha, Misha na krisha.*"[5] She gave a slight pause, "*DoSvedonya.*" Anna topped off the gesture with a comforting smile, lowered her head and then left the room.

Alex got up and fetched a piece of paper for Fred to write down his address and telephone number. "Here, you write it. If I do it, I will screw it up."

After Fred handed the paper back, Alex looked at it and with a broad smile, said, "*Do Skorovo Svedonya.* I'll see you soon."

"Yes, *skorovo,* soon," Fred said, while he got lost in Alex's brown eyes.

Fred walked briskly along the sidewalk while Susan dragged behind. Fred swung around to allow her to catch up. "Well, Alex was interested in you," Susan said with a sigh, then raised her eyebrows as she gave Fred a sideways stare.

"That doesn't mean anything," Fred said.

"Don't patronize me. I've lived in New York long enough to know better."

Fred turned around as Susan stood up and said, "I still think that something is fishy about all of this."

Silence.

They continued walking, and after a while, Susan said, "Do you think it's some sort of sting operation?"

Fred was still thinking about Alex.

---

5   Quiet, quiet, Misha [listens] on the roof," a simile for "the walls have ears".

A HISTORY

WHEN FRED ARRIVED back at his apartment, he sat down at his desk and wrote another email to his brother.

Hi, John,

When I got home from the old Russian woman's antique shop, I played the piano pieces again carefully, keeping my eye on the densely patterned handwritten notes. I am certain that there is something unusual. I took some of my old music and put it on the piano to examine my teacher's notes, only to find that my intuition was correct. My music has the teacher's comments scrawled at odd angles depending where she stood. The jotted notes in the old music are not scribbles at all. They were all carefully written at the same angle. And the neatness led me to believe that they were written, not on the piano, but on a desk, carefully crafted all at once. The days pass slowly as I await Alex's visit and the translation. I can only imagine what secrets are embedded in the blocks of writing. I keep remembering the old woman obsessing about our

old Russian family name, Tochinovich. We know
that there are no other families with that name.
What's the big deal?

Alex arrived at one o'clock on Thursday wearing a pair of khakis, Puma sneakers and light pink oxford shirt and seemed eager to get to work.

"I think that we're about to have an adventure," Alex said.

"It was good of you to come here." Fred put his hand out expecting a polite handshake, but Alex passed his hand and gave Fred a gentle but sweet hug. Feeling the warmth of Alex's body brought a smile to Fred's lips and stirred a desire he hadn't felt in years.

"An adventure, huh?" Fred said with a slight grin.

Fred put a pot of tea on the table to make Alex feel at home while he set out on the translation.

Alex smiled broadly and asked, "How about a Diet Coke?"

"You got it," Fred said. *He's escaped from the glass-of-tea culture,* Fred thought as he rummaged in the refrigerator for a diet anything.

Fred brought the can of soda over to the kitchen table and set it on a napkin as Alex brought the package of music to the table, where he spread out the sheets. Alex slid the can to the far edge of the table away from the music and then moved the copy of *The Seasons* to the top of the pile and reverently put his hands on the pages. As he looked at the title page, he slowly moved his fingers around the edges, pressing the pages flat onto the table as he sat back for a moment and then did it again.

Fred brought out a pile of pages that he had printed from the scanned originals. "Here, I scanned the music into my computer last night. You can write the translations on the copies next to the Russian script."

Alex gazed into Fred's eyes and smiled before looking down at the pages.

Alex set to work writing on the copied pages. Fred was amazed how enthralled Alex was by this project, writing continuously.

"You do understand that this music is from one of Tchaikovsky's students, don't you? His name was Ivan. I haven't seen his last name yet, but *Ivan* is written on the cover in many places." Alex raised his eyebrows. "And you do understand that these comments were written by his teacher."

"Yes, yes, I understand that," Fred said impatiently. "My music is also littered with my teacher's scribbles."

Alex smirked. "But here the instruction is signed as *Pyotr* in many places and in some places *P.I.T.* That would be Peter Ilyich Tchaikovsky. You have here original copies of the teachings of Tchaikovsky. In fact, it appears that the music was once owned by Tchaikovsky himself."

"Please continue the translation," Fred said. "We're in a new and exciting place now, we need to make the most of it."

As Alex worked, Fred paced around the apartment, first replenishing drinks and then putting out a small bowl of pretzels. Fred didn't want to hover, but couldn't resist watching Alex work, following the movement of his pen. He went over to the sofa and lied down. His eyes closed as he heard melodies from *The Seasons* in his head.

Alex worked for more than an hour and suddenly, with a reflexive jerk, stiffened his hunched body upright and stared spellbound at the sheets of music. He piled the music into a neat stack, then went over to the sofa and sat down where Fred's feet were curled up.

He looked at Fred fast asleep and felt bad that Anna had used him to keep the music safe. If only Fred knew how dangerous it was to have this music in his possession. He took hold of Fred's left foot, feeling his toes inside the thick cotton sock. How beautiful this American was, how sweet and inviting. He wanted to lie next to him, curl up and feel the heat of his body. But they were working on a project together and the last thing they needed was to be distracted by romance.

He held Fred's foot and watched him snooze.

MODIA'S DISCOVERY

MOSCOW, OCTOBER 20, 1890

IT WAS UNUSUALLY sunny in Moscow. Although it was late October, when the melancholy of winter starts to steal in bit by bit, 1890 continued to be a stellar year for fine weather. Making the most of a stream of sunlight brightening his workspace, Peter sat at the piano in his small Moscow apartment with his hands hovering over the keyboard, reviewing the piano version of his beloved ballet, *Sleeping Beauty*. He understood well that it was customary for his publisher to demand the highly marketable transition from the sumptuous score of the orchestra to the solo piano. He had just finished playing a small section and felt quite content with the arrangement. Tchaikovsky contemplated the revenue that he would be getting from his publisher as music enthusiasts in St. Petersburg and Moscow would rush to buy a copy to display on their parlor pianos. Until his score was published, Peter depended on the small cadre of students to supplement his salary at the Conservatory. He could always fall back on the generosity of his benevolent admirer, Nadezhda von Meck. Nevertheless, he enjoyed meeting fresh students in the hope that he would experience the thrill of discovering a new genius. On this day, Peter Ilyich would do just that.

His brother, Modeste, had recommended a new student for Peter's consideration and facilitated an audition. Modia, as he called his brother, had frequently selected wealthy students often related to the upper crust of Moscow. Sadly, they were usually untalented and unmusical, with an air of indifference to Tchaikovsky's prominence and skills. In his letters, Modia referred to these snobbish students as *neekulturni*, an insulting designation for the enduringly uncultured. Tchaikovsky, reluctant to waste his time on the *neekulturni*, was resigned to catering to their demands in order to supplement his income. Modeste dutifully recommended those that were of nobility and could pay large sums for lessons and then coolly boast that they studied with the great Peter Ilyich Tchaikovsky.

In spite of Peter's fame and good looks, he felt isolated and extremely lonely. He was close to his family, but they were scattered in various cities that were more than a day's voyage away from Moscow. Travel was very tedious in all but the summer months. Tchaikovsky learned to covet his time alone to work, but it did not ease his lonesomeness. Solitude eventually became his sanctuary, filled with musical imagery. Tchaikovsky suffered the tremendous social pressures on a famous single man in 19th century Russia. Society had forced him into a marriage that he despised and ultimately, painfully, dissolved. He turned exclusively to his greatest passion, music. Although his main interest was composition, students, even the *neekulturni*, were a necessary part of his schedule.

There was another aspect to Modia's scouting that added a bit of spice to his discoveries; Modia had an eye for good-looking young men who had a place in his own fantasies. On those infrequent occasions when he got together with Peter over a glass of vodka, the salacious imageries were a lurid part of Modia's inflated tales.

Modeste had attended a concert of young pianists at the St. Petersburg Music Conservatory in late September. These concerts were quite common since they served as a way for students to experience an audience, and for local music lovers to hear free concerts. Out of the array of performers at this recital, one in particular captured Modia's attention. Modeste noted his name on the program, Ivan Tochinovich. Ivan was both visually and musically stunning. Modeste was so fixated on Ivan's exceptional presence that at times he barely focused on his playing. Instinctively, Modeste endeavored to initiate and maintain an acquaintance with this appealing young man. He approached Ivan after the concert at an informal reception, standing just out of range of the circle of friends and admirers, watching Ivan humbly react to the compliments of enthusiasts. Modeste observed another student approach Ivan, shake his hand, and then slowly slide his hand away from Ivan, prolonging the contact as long as possible. No one else would have noticed this moment of clandestine intimacy, but Modeste was aware. Modeste patiently waited for the moment that he could break in and introduce himself. He was so captured by the young pianist's personality and stature as well as his talent that he could hardly choose the proper words.

Ivan was shy, which made it a bit easier for the garrulous Modeste to strike up a conversation. Ivan was extremely cautious as well. Modeste piqued Ivan's interest when he boasted about his brother. Ivan had dreamed of studying with Tchaikovsky, as many musicians did, but not only was he unable to afford the tuition at the Moscow Conservatory of Music, he had no standing to warrant an interview with the maestro. Talking fluidly to sustain the momentum of the interaction, Modeste vibrantly assured Ivan that he would communicate with his brother about the possibility of a scholarship to study with the famous Tchaikovsky. Modeste repeatedly tried to navigate the conversation away from Peter to satisfy his own interests, but at this moment Ivan had no interest in anyone but the grand celebrity. Eventually, Modeste gave up trying to promote himself and gave every indication that he would recommend Ivan to his brother. Later that night, Modeste extolled the musical excellence of his newest discovery in a letter to his brother.

Peter had heard these exaltations from Modia before and smiled as he read the latest. Modia's acclaim of Ivan was different from previous recommendations. Notably, he did not underscore the wealth and social position of his discovery as he usually did. Rather, he emphasized the arresting charm and musical talent. Peter saw something distinctive in the unusual choice of words, which stirred his interest. He did not expect to see explicit romantic thoughts that may have been on Modia's mind put in writing. It was well known that government agents often scanned mail, and suggestive text could be dangerously incriminating. Peter wrote back to Modeste, giving a date and time for an appointment to meet the young pianist and perhaps begin his first lesson.

For the next several days, Ivan prepared for his audition with the great master, the icon of Mother Russia. He practiced a few notoriously difficult piano pieces until they were as good as he could get them. He played them in the blind darkness of night so that his fingers instinctively aimed for the correct keys. He chose the piece that he played in the recital that charmed Modeste, imagining that in some way his performance of that particular piece had some enchanting attraction.

At last, in mid-October, the day to travel to Moscow arrived. Ivan set out his best clothing and polished his boots. He turned in front of his small mirror a number of times in an attempt to assure himself that this audition, his only chance at a satisfactory first impression, would be successful. As he examined his posture and appearance, he shivered with the anticipation of meeting the renowned maestro. He sensed that this was to be the single most important encounter of his career. Ivan hoped Modeste had conveyed his musical achievement to Peter, making the legendary musician at least somewhat interested in receiving him. He was unaware at the time that more about him than his musical skills had been communicated.

Ivan booked a carriage to Moscow, the train being far too expensive, and prepared for the journey. He squeezed into his seat in the coach along with five bulky passengers ballooned by heavy coats. The musty odors of the interior were overwhelmingly smothered by their cloying cologne. Ivan relaxed his mind to a pleasantly hypnotic state, trying to imagine what his destination would bring. Eventually, Ivan drifted into a deep slumber, immune to the elbow that poked at his rib with each bump in the roadway and impervious to the woman facing him who commented bitterly about everything. Ivan, in his dreams, flew above all the immediate discomfort, picturing engravings of the

luminary he would soon meet. His eyes closed, Ivan soared in
the clouds with the music of the great maestro filling the space.

Although Modeste gave Ivan an intriguing recommendation,
Peter had reserved expectations. He tidied his flat somewhat, a
common drill to ready for a student audition. Peter pulled some
freshly written sheets of manuscript from the piano, dusted the
notes and the puddles of fresh ink with talc and blew the drying
dust off the page. He piled the pages away from the piano and
cleared his table of partially empty glasses of tea to prepare for
his visitor.

In Moscow, the weather turned cool, but the days still
sparkled. It was an October Monday, the start of the workweek,
and Peter was restless, having been pulled away from the
overdue project of finishing his piano transcription. He stared
at his score lying near the piano and in his mind he heard the
boldness of a full orchestra surround him. From his far left, an
unfitting bell tinkled. Annoyed by the jarring sound, he looked
up from the score and tried to dismiss it with a contemptuous
glance. He tried to regain his pleasurable mood when he realized
that the bell above the door was jingling. Peter glanced up at
the tangle of pulleys and levers connecting a wire to the outside
handle. The bell rattled again, now more assertively. As he
opened the outside door the glare of the low autumn sun burst
into the dark hallway, giving him an indistinct view of Ivan,
his new student, precisely on time—a good start. The visitor
stood at attention, his fingers nervously trying to fiddle with the
buttons on his neatly pressed jacket. Peter showed Ivan into his
parlor and escorted him to the piano. As a manner of decorum,
he scarcely looked at Ivan. Ivan stood awkwardly next to the
piano, surveying the room, awaiting further instructions.

Facing away from Ivan, Peter calmly walked toward the
tarnished samovar on the credenza. Fumbling with a cup of
sugar cubes, he said, "Would you like a glass of tea to drive the
chill away?" It was an awkward moment that Tchaikovsky found
as stimulating as the applause at one of his performances.

Peter finally glanced at Ivan, trying not to stare. But he was virtually spellbound. Ivan stood with a posture that made him look taller than his natural height. He had light-colored hair, perhaps blond, with strands of light brown. His luminous green eyes were transfixed on Peter. Perhaps he looked at Ivan's eyes a bit too long. Ivan lowered his head, displaying a shy nature while at the same time awkwardly stepping forward. As a reaction, Peter stepped back, but reconsidered and regained his position.

Tchaikovsky was tender and accommodating to a nervous student. He displayed an unanticipated humility and charm, the persona of a giant towering over Ivan and at the same time, an affectionate human being. Ivan grinned with tight corners on his lips that slowly grew into a broad smile.

Peter was captured. He knew that there was no stepping back from this moment.

Nothing was said.

A POETIC CRYPTOGRAM

FRED SAT BESIDE Alex and studied his translations. *Let your passion lead the way. Heartfelt love leads to a true finale.* Fred looked at them again before Alex moved the page and continued reading.

"Yes, these are more than teacher's notes," Alex said as he smiled at Fred. "Tchaikovsky was doing something quite unusual here."

Fred put his hands on Alex's shoulders. "It feels like a love letter of sorts," Fred said, looking down at Alex's full lips and holding himself back from kissing him.

Alex looked into Fred's eyes. "Yes, quite astonishing."

Look ahead to the coda—let romance be the guide. It was as if a cork had been removed from an old bottle of unlabeled wine and a complex perfume of poetry had emerged.

Alex and Fred reread the comments as if they were a continuous text throughout the entire suite, all the way through *The Seasons.* When they got to the *December* waltz at the end, Fred said, "My God, we're reading a cloaked message. This has every sign of a love letter from Tchaikovsky to his student."

"A love letter written in code? No, this is more than a love letter," Alex said pensively, looking directly into Fred's eyes. Fred looked at Alex sitting so close to him with words from the yellowed pages flashing randomly in his mind: *passion, love.*

"This is amazing," Alex said, turning his gaze back to the music. He flipped back a few pages, then placed one of them in front of Fred.

"Did you see this?" Alex said, pointing down to his notes.

"Tochinovich," Fred said softly.

"It's Ivan's family name." Alex met Fred's gaze, then slipped his hand over Fred's. "It's what your name was, your family name."

"My last name is Novik."

"How many immigrants shortened their last names to appease Americans unfamiliar with their language?"

"Which is what Anna thinks."

"It is what my grandmother knows," Alex said. "She's a very wise woman."

"I've never known anyone outside our family who has heard of another Tochi-*novich*," Fred said. "I suppose that there could be several family lines that have that name, but I doubt it. I know of Torchinov as a common shortening, but outside of our family. Not our name."

Alex thumbed through the pages of music and showed Fred. "Look, here it is: Точинович. So that's why Anna mentioned heritage. There is a chance that you are part of this mystery and all the dangers that it brings."

"Dangers. Really. People have been murdered to keep this sort of romance hidden from the public," Fred said softly.

"My grandmother felt that you should have this," Alex said.

"Me?" Fred was perplexed.

"Your family name."

Fred's eyes grew wide. "You think because of my last name—"

"We know it," Alex said.

"And you knew about this all along?"

"Yes." Alex turned to Fred. "I saw it in the music about an hour ago. I didn't know how to tell you. I don't want you involved in this, but I'm afraid that it's too late. We have to be careful."

Fred hung his head. They wanted him to have this because

of his name. It felt absurd, but he believed Alex. They were both weary.

"So this is a love poem," Fred said softly.

"Between not only a teacher and his student, but between two men," Alex said.

Fred swallowed, then looked down at the translated notes.

Let your passion lead the way, heartfelt love.

Alex said, "A crime punishable by death."

Fred placed his right hand over Ivan's and said, "Not much has changed."

"These pages are dangerous," Alex said. "This is why my grandmother wants you have them."

Fred looked at Alex quizzically.

"This is as dangerous today as it was when it was written," Alex said.

"Why? This is the 21st century. So Tchaikovsky was gay; not a big deal."

"We're talking about Russia," Alex said. "There's widespread belief, in a nationalistic cult of sorts, that Tchaikovsky being gay is a malicious rumor. Then, to come up with proof in his own handwriting that their national icon had a gay lover is damning. I suspect there's more than that written in these pages. They'll want to destroy it all."

"She wants me to hide it."

"To keep it safe."

"I see," Fred said, moving away from the table. He walked across the room and glanced out the window, looking down at the people milling about on the street below.

"She trusts you."

"You knew," Fred said softly, keeping his back toward Alex. "You came here to translate some notes acting as if you didn't know what they said, but you knew what they said all along."

"I only knew what my grandmother told me."

"But you knew she needed me to keep something hidden." A sudden pang of regret filled Fred's chest. He slowly shook his head. "You came here to play along, to play me."

Alex walked across the room, then back to Fred. A horn relentlessly honked outside, breaking the spell. They moved to the window and silently watched the people walking below.

Alex placed his hand on Fred's shoulder. Fred didn't move. He then stepped away, letting Alex's hand drop.

"Fred, please. You must trust me. We aren't, as you say, playing you." Alex once again put his arm on Fred's shoulder.

Fred didn't move, instead he let Alex keep it there so he could feel the warmth.

"I came here to help you understand what it is my grandmother is trusting you with," Alex said.

Fred closed his eyes. "Why didn't she tell me?"

"She was desperate and afraid you would say no."

"She would have found another sucker."

"But she had you, Fred Tochinovich," Alex said softly. "Like the music, you have a history. A connection."

"She should have told me."

Alex slid his hand off Fred's shoulder. "I'm sorry."

Fred swallowed and stared out the window. He looked down at the people below, looking so small as they milled about not knowing that something as important as a romantic poem between doomed lovers was three stories above.

"I can take it back," Alex said.

"It can't be archived?"

"It would be destroyed."

"How?"

"Russian nationalist zealots would find a way. They know the music exists. They just don't know where it is . . . now. They are hellbent on destroying it."

Fred nodded. This was too important to allow that to happen.

"My grandmother can find another way to keep it safe."

"No," Fred said softly, and he felt Alex's arm on his shoulder move ever so slowly.

Fred said, "It's been thought that Tchaikovsky was gay, but now we have proof. Not only that, we know who his lover was. Who was this Ivan? Was he a famous performer, at least known in the music circles of that time? This opens up a whole new aspect to Tchaikovsky's life and perhaps motivations for composing. But one question keeps haunting me."

"What is that?"

"The phrase that you translated, *Look ahead to the coda.* There is no coda in the work."

Alex looked at Fred. "That is mysterious. I wonder . . . "

Alex stood next to Fred and stared out the window. "There are volumes of letters that Tchaikovsky wrote. There are innuendos. Some historians believe that a few acquaintances were more than that. Isn't it strange that the only letters by Tchaikovsky that survived don't mention a lover? The fact that these love letters that we now have are coded into a teacher's comments in piano music confirms that Tchaikovsky was very cautious. Everyone in Russia was cautious in those days."

"He must have loved Ivan very much to go to such length to keep their romance alive," Alex said.

"They could have been put to death for this, but they must have been in such awe of romance, so dangerous that it had to be so very secret."

"Yes," Alex said softly, then looked up at Fred. "Everything is still the same."

Fred swallowed. "No, not only in Russia."

"Tchaikovsky must have been watched every minute, everyplace he went. What a life!" Alex said. "I knew this music was important and dangerous, that it had something to do with Tchaikovsky, but I didn't know exactly what. I'm not sure how much my grandmother knows about it."

"But she knows it's dangerous."

"There are people out there who would kill for it."

Fred's eyes grew wide as he took in a deep breath. "Would kill?"

"Have killed," Alex said.

"And she gave this to me?"

Alex turned and sat on the windowsill. "There was another package," he said. "I believe it also was music, but I do not know what was in it."

"Like this one?" Fred asked.

"Yeah. Anna kept the two packages together. That other package was stolen from our shop in Moscow. I'm sure that we will never see it again."

"I bet that Anna was really shocked when that happened," Fred said.

Alex quickly said, "Anna was devastated when it was taken. And it was taken right under our noses. We were less than five meters away. Our housekeeper and friend was murdered."

Fred put his arms around Alex's waist and pulled him into a tight hug. "That was a lesson," Alex said softly as he tightened his embrace. "We have to be very careful to protect ourselves and this music. That there is real danger is certain."

"I believe it." Fred said.

"There was a break-in at the shop here in Brooklyn recently."

"Was anyone hurt?" Fred said.

"Well, I'm here."

"Oh, Alex," Fred said, sighing deeply. "What can we do?" Extending his arms, he placed them gently on Alex's shoulders.

"This," Alex said as he put his arms around Fred and pulled him in tight.

"Alex," Fred mumbled. He kissed Alex deep and long.

SEARCHING FOR SHUMKA

BROOKLYN, APRIL 26

"HE FEELS USED," Alex said to Anna while he sat at the kitchen table in the rear of their shop drinking his morning coffee.

"I'm sorry to hear that," Anna said as she poured tea in a glass and carefully measured some sugar. "There is alternative to Frederick Tochinovich keeping the package of music."

"And what's that?"

"Shumka," Anna said.

"Shumka?"

"You need to talk to Giorgi Shumka. He would understand gravity of this situation and will gladly keep the music safe. Yes, go to Shumka. You go, better than me."

"Who's Shumka? Where does he live?" Alex got up and poured more coffee. "How do you know him?"

"He is from our neighborhood in Russia. He is distant relative, very much removed. I have lost track of where he lives, but I know he is in New York City."

"Anna, I'll do what I can, but this isn't Karandash Street. New York is a big place. And if Shumka knows you, why do I have to go?"

"You will find him. He will be very happy that you brought music to him. He would not see me. In Russia, we did not end on good terms. Alexei, be careful and make sure that Fred is careful. If Fred decides to not keep music, call me and I will get more details. I think Mussyinka might know, she knows everybody's business." Anna put a teaspoon of tea to her lips and blew on it. "Yes, Shumka, perfect solution," she said, then sipped from the spoon.

Alex arrived at Fred's apartment shortly after noon. He sat at the counter facing the kitchen while Fred cleaned the stove. "Would you like a cup of coffee?" Fred said.

"No, I'm already fired up. I have an idea."

"About the music?"

"Yeah. We have a friend of the family, well, he's actually a distant relative. Anna tells me he's connected with the Russian community in New York."

"How could he possibly help?" Fred said.

"He should see the music. Anna says that he should be happy to keep it safe. We could have him read the text. There might be something more between the lines, as you say. Maybe something more is hidden in the poetry." Alex stood silent for a moment, staring down at the carpet, and then slowly paced in a circle. "His name is Giorgi Shumka. That's all I know. We have to do some research, but we'll find him and he'll take the music off your hands. Anna seems to be sure of that."

"And I wouldn't have the music anymore?"

"That's right. You give the go-ahead and I'll get more details from Anna and we can go to Shumka—or not."

Fred hung his head, and after a moment said, "Yeah, let's do it. Call Anna."

Alex dashed across the room, picked up the phone and rapidly dialed. A short time passed during which he spoke in rapid Russian, presumably to Anna. He waved his hands at Fred, requesting a pencil and paper and then scribbled some notes. Alex hung up and said, "Anna didn't have the address. I have to call her friend, Mussyinka." He began to dial the number he had just written.

"Good luck," Fred said.

Again, Alex spoke in Russian, only this time more slowly. He wrote more notes on the pad and then stood motionless with his eyes staring at the ceiling. He made a few acknowledging grunts and hung up.

"Shumka lives somewhere near here in lower Manhattan on Bleeker Street. She gave me an address, one-sixty-one or something; she wasn't sure, but she gave me landmarks. It seems that he lives near a fish store that has *Zen* and *Mystical* in its name. Mussyinka went on and on with some gossip about another Russian guy who lives one block away that has nothing to do with our interests, but she just felt like talking. I tried to hang up sooner."

He took the phone from Alex. "Okay, let's get over there. I'll call Susan. She'll want to come along and she's very resourceful. We'll need her, I am sure of that."

"Hi, Susan, we're going over to Bleeker Street to find a Russian scholar who can tell us s'more about the music and possible hold it for safe-keeping. Would you like to come?"

"I've been thinking about this fabulous music," Susan said. "The more I think about incredibly well-preserved documents with scribbling by an incredibly famous person, the more I want to see incredible proof."

"Susan, you are the eternal skeptic. We're going, are you coming?"

Susan whined. "Paper of that age would be pickled and crumbly by now. My God, it's about a century and a half old. How come it is in such good condition? I have a feeling that you are on a fool's errand."

"We don't have enough information yet to apply logic. It's too soon to try to interpret," Fred said.

"Yeah. Of course I'll go with you. I'll be over in a few minutes."

Fred, Susan and Alex walked along Bleeker Street to Shumka's apartment looking for the landmarks that would assure them they had the right address. Fred had the package of music wrapped in a plastic bag and then stuffed in The Brown Bag pressed under his arm disguised as the spoils of a shopping day. He looked down at the bag and wrapped the carry strings tight around his fingers. He was confident that the music was safe.

They proceeded slowly along the busy street, looking for the address and the prescribed landmarks.

"C'mon, this is the street. Let's get moving. It's near a fish store and has *Zen* and *Mystical* in the name," Fred said, leading the pack and hoping that it would be an easy find.

"Half of these doors don't have an address on them. How do they get mail? Do we know what we're looking for? Everyplace here looks like it was converted from a mystical shop or is being turned into one. Don't these people have real lives?"

"Susan, come on," Fred said to keep focused.

Susan walked close to Fred and said, "You know, if this Shumka thing doesn't work out, I know this guy I used to see, Howard, an expert musicologist. Yeah, Howard Brodsky."

Fred tried to hurry Susan along. There were plenty of doors pressed between storefronts that were clearly entrances to apartments. Alex walked fast, getting far ahead of Susan and Fred.

"So what do you think, Susie," Fred whispered, "about Alex's description of this magical Russian expert?"

"Alex might have a point. Besides, I like the way he says it," Susan said.

Fred slowed down a bit. "Don't trust him just because of his sexy foreign accent. He seems to know what is going on."

Susan quickly said, "I still think about the possibility of a contrived façade."

"Be fair to the guy. Don't let everything he says be a test of his legitimacy," Fred said quietly as they fell further behind.

Alex looked back, saw the group lagging and stopped until they caught up.

Slowly, they continued their hunt for the mystifying doorway. "There's so much traffic here. I don't get a good view across the street," Susan said. "Are you sure we're on the right street?"

"Mussyinka said Bleeker Street," Alex said. "No," Alex said, "*Bleeker*. I know we're Russian, but I understand what she says. Bleeker. Okay?"

Fred stopped walking and was looking across the street, at a restaurant with the word *fish* in the name. "I think this is it, there's a store that sells souvenir-type junk nearby."

Susan and Alex followed Fred as he crossed the street.

Fred held the package tight to his chest and looked at the sign above the storefront window. *The Art of Zen.* Could this be the place, he thought, then glanced at the dirt-encrusted door to the left of the shop entrance. "Hey, guys," he called out, "I think this is the place. Look at the sign." He pointed up at the store name. "The number on the door is rubbed off, but this must be it. Let's do it."

Fred directed their attention to the four doorbells with empty name clips below each. He tried to peer into the window, but the dust and grime made it nearly opaque. He rubbed his hand across the window, leaving a broad trail of smeared glass behind. Now he could see through, but the only illumination was a bold streak of light that matched the curvature of his smear.

Fred mumbled, "This is hopeless." He tried to see inside, then cautiously tried the doorknob. It was locked, but the door yielded to a gentle push. They quickly stepped inside. Fred unconsciously rubbed his hand against his pants, then said in disgust, "From the window to my pants. What a souvenir." He peered ahead. "How deep does this narrow hallway go? I can't see a thing and I'm afraid to touch anything."

Fred stepped into the dirt-encrusted vestibule and looked around. The announcements taped to the wall were from months past and the mailboxes looked as if nobody had used them in years.

"This is disgusting," Susan said. "Do people actually live here?"

"Man, I would hate to have to squeeze furniture up to the second floor on that stairway," Alex said.

Alex spotted the name on the mailbox. "Shumka, there it is. First floor, so it appears. That is, if they're in order."

"Well, let's get going. We can't stand here and look like we are intruders," Susan said.

Susan wandered to the back of the entrance to a door nearly concealed by darkness. The light from the streak in the glass in the exterior doorway penetrated into the hallway, but not quite to the apartment door. Susan looked up at the 15-watt bare bulb hanging from a cloth-covered wire. Pointing to the light, Susan whispered across the hallway to Fred, "Hopeless as that is to do its job, it seems appropriate for the setting."

Fred instinctively put his arm out to grope in the dark. *No wonder no one cleans here,* he thought, *it's nearly pitch black.* He turned to look back at the light at the front of the lobby when he saw a profile in the window of the outside doorway. He squinted to see better, but the dust trapped by the greasy window made the shadow seem indistinct and ghostly. The stationary silhouette spellbound Fred. As he stared at the figure, he wondered if he should warn the others, but as he watched, it noticeably swayed from side to side. With a sense of alarm, Fred put his hand on Susan's shoulder and then on Alex's and turned them to see the outline.

"Don't move," he whispered.

They stood motionless, waiting for something to happen.

Slowly, the three slinked back into the lobby, trying to blend with the shadows near the staircase. The front door to the street creaked open. A figure stood in the doorway and looked around. Fred froze. The figure then stepped outside and hovered by the door and then moved away. They stood motionless against the staircase.

Alex whispered, "I know that person. She has been walking around our shop. I've seen her on several occasions. What the Hell is she doing here?"

"I'm afraid to say what I'm thinking," Fred said.

Susan said, "This is starting to creep me out."

"Let's get on with it," Alex said. "Try this door down here." He walked boldly over to the door and knocked sharply. As they waited in the quiet darkness, there was the sound of shuffling. The door cracked open enough to see the eye of a man peering out.

"Is this the home of Mr. Shumka? We were told to come here by Mussyinka," Alex said.

There was a low murmur from behind the door and then in the whiney voice of a man rasped through the crack, "Who are you?"

Alex rattled a few sentences in Russian. The only word that Fred could make out was *Mussyinka.* The door shut and after a chain rattled softly behind the door, it cautiously opened fully.

Susan mumbled under her breath, "Jackpot."

Shumka stood in the door and welcomed the group inside. He stopped for a second, looking out, and then closed the door and bolted it shut. He spoke to Alex in Russian for a bit. Then Alex gestured to the others to sit, making the letter *T* with his fingers, signaling to the others to sit down for a glass of tea. He shrugged his shoulders and Fred nodded and made the *OK* symbol with his fingers. Fred stood while the others took a seat.

FRIENDSHIP LOST, LOVE FOUND

MOSCOW, NOVEMBER 5, 1890

IVAN SETTLED INTO his tiny room in a boarding house on the outskirts of Moscow, thinking about his new teacher, teetering between apprehension and unrestrained joy. It was that kind of day, with nothing going wrong. It was the first day of his serious studies and he was anxious to perform.

The melodies he had practiced echoed in his head and his fingers pulsed in response. He quickly dressed and dashed downstairs and onto the street. On his way to a café two blocks from his room, he decided that breakfast was an unnecessary luxury on this eventful day. He entered for a cup of coffee, but fragrances lured him to a plateful of eggs mixed with chopped ham. He ate impulsively, until he was stuffed and somewhat sluggish. This was not what he'd wanted. He ordered strong coffee and drank until he was ablaze like a lightning storm. He thought about walking the streets until his mid-morning appointment, but decided it would be best to return to his room and sat with his eyes closed, trying to rest. The caffeine did not cooperate.

At nine-thirty, he walked to Tchaikovsky's flat fully prepared to reinforce the good impression that he had made on his first meeting. The arrival was cordial, but stiff. Ivan greeted Tchaikovsky with a formal "*Gospahdeen* (Sir), Maestro."

Tchaikovsky responded with a polite gesture and invited him to take off his coat and become comfortable. He sat far across the room as if he was in a recital hall. Ivan breathed into his closed hands to warm them up as quickly as possible and then sat at the piano waiting for the master's nod to begin.

Ivan played the first movement of Mozart's sonata number 14 with grace and a delicate power. He phrased the passages so that they spoke to his audience of one in an intimate salon. When he finished, he continued to face the keyboard and waited an insufferable time for Tchaikovsky's comments, giving Ivan a prophetic feeling of displeasure.

"Why did you choose the Mozart sonata in C minor?" Tchaikovsky said.

Ivan thought a bit, then said, "Unlike any previous Mozart sonatas, it begins in a minor key, but that dark position is filled with energy and gradually is overcome, bursting with joy. It reverts to the somber position, but regains strength again and thrives. This is biographical. It attests to Mozart having developed his own voice, a sort of freedom from the tyranny of his father and expressing his own life. It is my life. It is all of us."

"Have you prepared anything else?" Tchaikovsky asked.

"I have." Ivan sat back down at the piano. He glanced at Tchaikovsky and started playing a romantic piano ballade that had never been published. Ivan played it with warmth and passion, his fingers singing the melodies with the love that was conceived with the composition.

Shortly after Ivan began the piece, Tchaikovsky stood, but did not move from his position across the room. He looked alarmed and stood motionless as Ivan played the markedly tender piece. Eventually Tchaikovsky took a handkerchief from his pocket and held it briefly in his hand and then touched his cheek to meet the tears.

"Why did you choose that composition?" Tchaikovsky asked with unease.

Ivan hastily said, "I've offended you, Maestro Tchaikovsky. Please, I am so very sorry. I should have never—"

"No, not at all," Tchaikovsky said. "He was my friend; Kolodka was my friend."

Ivan, more uncomfortable at what he had done, blurted, "Please, my apologies."

Tchaikovsky continued in a dreamlike voice. "He died so young. I played an early version of that composition on a visit to St. Petersburg four months ago. My friend, so creative, so wistful." Tchaikovsky slowly approached Ivan with his arms lifted. His face was vacant as he said, "I loved him."

"I understand," Ivan said.

Tchaikovsky, still tearful, turned his back to Ivan and quietly muttered once again, "Oh, Kolodka," then sobbed into his handkerchief.

"I knew that you were close. I visited his family in St. Petersburg and asked to see the final manuscript. His mother was pleased to show it to me. I studied it as a gift to you. It was never published and may never be."

Ivan stood, and while clasping his hands in reverence. Tchaikovsky paced forward, then grabbed Ivan. In that hug, Ivan felt the gratitude and reverence for Tchaikovsky's lost friend.

Ivan said, "*Gospahdeen* Tchaikovsky—"

"Please, call me Peter."

Their hug intensified, then Ivan felt the warmth of Peter's lips against his neck. Tchaikovsky hummed Kolodka's romantic melodies.

SHUMKA'S APARTMENT

MANHATTAN, APRIL 26

FRED STEPPED INTO the dimly lit apartment and was accosted by the scent of cooked cabbage, fried potatoes and, oddly enough, Pine-Sol. As he looked around, he found the apartment orderly except for a bookcase bursting with papers and books. There was a stack of newspapers next to the bookcase that started from white at the top and progressed to dark amber at the bottom. Fred thought the apartment seemed light enough, but the dimness gave a sensation of thrift he'd always associated with the elderly. Susan gently closed the door, making as little noise as possible. Fred looked back at Susan and noticed a beam of light from the outside entry slither under the door and rake across the floor.

With a blank stare at the door, Shumka motioned for Fred to join Susan and Alex and sit at the enameled kitchen table littered with Russian newspapers and assorted debris. Not knowing what to do next, Fred glanced at Alex, who in turn said something in Russian to Shumka, who responded in Russian before getting up to fetch a green washcloth from the sink. The group sat, watching Shumka shuffle the newspapers into a ragged pile, sit them on an empty chair and briskly wipe the enamel top of crumbs and tea stains. Alex continued to speak in Russian to Shumka, who occasionally nodded, eventually bobbing with unbroken rhythm. Susan got up and meandered around the room, browsing at the piles of Russian papers, then turned to Fred and shrugged.

Susan joined Alex and Fred at the cleared table while Shumka went into the kitchen. Alex followed him into the kitchen. Fred almost gasped as Shumka walked into the dining room with a tray of assorted glass jars filled with some sort of amber liquid. Shumka arranged the glasses delicately in front of each guest, appearing now to be quite pleased with the unexpected company. The tea was in tall and narrow goblets and reminded Fred of how his grandparents reused the glasses that held votive candles. He glanced across the table at Susan, who eyed the refreshments suspiciously, then glanced at Fred and cocked her head. Susan picked up her glass, looked at it, then looked at Fred and mouthed, *Uncle Misha.*

They all waited silently around the table under the bare bulb hooded by a round metallic shade that could have been a flying saucer prop from a 1940 science fiction movie. As Shumka leaned down, deep wrinkles around his eyes and on his neck became apparent.

Fred slipped the package of music from the brown shopping bag, set it on the table and began to unwrap it.

"This place is like a museum of Russian culture," Susan said.

Shumka gave them a dull grin and nodded, then turned toward Fred as he removed the paper and opened the package of music.

Susan pointed at something across the room and blurted out, "And those nested dolls are lovely!"

Again, Shumka turned to her with an insipid smile, then looked back at Fred.

Finally, Fred had the music folder unwrapped on the table and laid it in front of Shumka. Shumka opened the folder and slowly flipped through the sheets. He turned the folios on their back one by one to survey the entire package before delving deeper. Everyone was quiet while Shumka looked through the music. Shumka grunted and murmured a few times, then turned a few pages and grunted approvingly once more.

He studied the cover page for *The Seasons*, nodding as if he were examining photographs of an old friend. He then started turning the pages slowly. When Shumka got to the handwritten text, he stopped and in a droning voice, began to translate aloud.

"Passion, heartfelt, love. Ahh," Shumka mumbled. "This was for good student."

Fred peered at the sheet in front of Shumka, noticing that he was close to the section where Alex had pointed out emotional phrases. Shumka began to read aloud, first in Russian and then in English: *stimulate to brilliance*, and a bit later, *descend into collapsing darkness*. He bit his lips then paused.

When he finally finished perusing the pages, Shumka looked up and rubbed his forehead. His eyes grew wide and his lips trembled as if searching for words. Shumka picked up his glass of tea, then placed it back on the table without taking a sip. He kneaded his palms and rubbed his hands on his pants as if they were not clean enough. Shumka pointed to Tchaikovsky's signature and said, "Pyotr." He paused. "Pyotr Ilyich Tchaikovsky. *Boje moi!*"

Shumka took a deep breath, then said, "In this music is a letter—no, a poem—to his lover. It is so beautiful. The words are scattered over the pages. He must have been very much in love with her. What was name of her? Let me see."

Shumka turned back the pages to the beginning to see the name written in a fine point pen at the front of the music, anxious to get inside the folio. He pushed his glasses down his nose, turned the page again and looked back once more. Shumka pressed his palm against the top of the sheet music, looked from Alex to Fred and said, "You know what you have here?"

Fred said, "What do you think?"

Shumka pointed at the word *Koда*, saying aloud, "Coda."

Shumka turned to the December waltz, looked up and said with wonderment, "This was secret message. It was love letter from Tchaikovsky to his student, Ivan. This is name of student? Here is again, *Vanya.*"[6] Shumka stared ahead, looking far into the distance, beyond the apartment walls. "Pyotr Ilyich Tchaikovsky's lover was man. A student."

---

6 Vanya is a common nickname for Ivan in Russia.

"Yes, we know," Fred said softly. "Tchaikovsky had a gay romance."

"How did you find this?" Shumka said. "How do we know these are not, how do you say?"

"Counterfeit?" Susan said.

Shumka nodded. "Yes, that is what I mean."

Alex said, "These have always been in our family's possession."

"There was gossip about Tchaikovsky," Shumka quietly said.

With a subtle grunt, Shumka stood up from the table and collected the papers into a pile and bounced them on their ends until they were neatly together. In an irritated voice, he blurted in Russian, "*igra, vykhodka, otvyecheneya.*"

"He thinks this is a game," Alex said, frustrated. He said, 'None of this is real—this is counterfeit.'"

Shumka threw up his hands and stood up. "*Slukhi, nikogda ne gomoseksualist, Eto frantsuzskiy spletni.*"

"He thinks that Tchaikovsky was the victim of nasty rumors. He was never a homosexual. It is the French that make this gossip persist," Alex said.

Shumka walked away from the table and into the kitchen as if he had been dishonored. The group sat at the table speechless. A moment ago, he was certain that this was a finding of historical importance but now, he appeared offended that the icon of his Fatherland has been insulted.

Fred was silent as he watched Shumka amble over to a dimly lit corner, followed by Alex. He couldn't believe Shumka had taken such offense to this proof of Tchaikovsky's sexuality. He suddenly felt as if he had caused Shumka's anger and that he had to do something to calm him down. Fred walked up to Shumka and Alex and said, "Mr. Shumka, might I ask why you were so unhappy with what you read?"

Shumka slowly and pensively replied, "Tchaikovsky is great Russian hero. Story of his death was told by my father. Tchaikovsky, the great composer, greatest in the world, was an ailing man. His marriage unhappy and his music, so autobiographical, at the end showed this very much."

"That's very interesting," Fred said, slowly guiding Shumka back to the table where Susan quietly waited.

Alex steered Shumka back to his seat and they sat with the

music in front of them. Shumka, with idle fingers, reached out and brought the music closer to him and started looking once again. "Maybe forgery? But handwriting is old style. If this is imitation, it is old imitation."

As Shumka studied the manuscripts once again, his eyes opened wider and his brows lifted. "I believe this is Tchaikovsky handwriting, so much detail about events and place. Strange. If this was to be damaging gossip, it would be to the main point. This says nothing, and perhaps everything. Oh, what we have here."

"Whatever truth this is, it must be preserved," Fred said.

"Mr. Shumka, we want you to keep this music safe. You understand more than anyone of us what this means and how valuable it is," Alex said.

"This would be a valuable addition to your library," Fred said.

Shumka started to cough, which made him look more distraught. Susan emptied her pockets onto the table and slid a hard candy across to Shumka. He accepted the candy, and as his coughing stopped, he turned to Susan and nodded. She fidgeted with her keys and other objects on the table until Fred put his hand on hers to stop the distraction.

There was an awkward silence, a sadness in the air. "I think I understand," Fred said. "The Russian authorities couldn't arrest Tchaikovsky. He was all they had. He was their rock star."

Shumka rose to his feet, agitated. "This music, this does not belong here, with me or with you. This is history, it needs to be in a museum."

"It would be destroyed," Alex said.

"Not if it you choose the right one," Shumka said. "There is one I know of in the city."

Fred leaned back in his chair. "I'm still haunted by the idea that Tchaikovsky would go to such an extent to write in code?"

Shumka said, "I admit, homosexuality is not a secret today, but the proof, ah, the proof. It is dangerous thing to hold in one's hand. I agree with you, there is something more in this poetry, though."

"Someone collected these pieces containing encrypted love letters. Moreover, they preserved them carefully." Fred turned to Alex and said, "Did Anna ever talk about what she had in this collection?"

"I watched Anna pack this music for the move to America. She wrapped a lot of things, but this was treated differently, as if it was more precious than any other thing."

"Ivan was the lover of one of the most famous people in Russia," Susan said. "One can only wonder how he felt, the responsibility he had."

"Mr. Shumka, you said something about a Russian museum. Would you keep this package of music and make sure that it is safe?" Fred asked.

"Very dangerous material. Hoodlums will destroy papers," Shumka said.

Shumka continued to study the documents spread out on the table. He moved folios and turned pages over carefully, making notes on a yellowed pad. Suddenly, he grunted a spasmodic whoop. "There is more. I cannot believe what I see written here. Dangerous, *ochen' opasn"* (very dangerous).

Shumka looked through the pages of music while Fred sat watching him, then noticed a break in the light under the door. It was subtle, and he had to keep his eyes on the bottom of the door to make sure he actually saw it. The break in the light moved again, almost like someone standing at the door and listening. He prodded Alex and nodded toward the door.

Alex's eyes grew wide as he noticed the break in the light.

Fred tapped Alex on the shoulder and pointed to the shadow, and then put his finger to his lips. Fred then tapped Susan's hand and once again pointed to the shifting shadow. Alex quietly moved to Shumka and put his hand on his shoulder. Shumka looked up, somewhat annoyed, then saw the shadow under the door.

Shumka turned around and examined the doorway. "Maybe Mrs. Potolsky getting mail," he mumbled acting annoyed by the distraction and turned back to the sheet music spread out in front of him. "You realize what we have here?" Shumka exclaimed in a slow calculating manner. "We have evidence of a plan. It is here, in his own handwriting. A plan." He glanced back at the door and then to his notes. Shumka kept repeating and mumbling as he continued to write. "There is a secret code here. I think I see it now." He hesitated a bit. "I need to study more." Shumka looked back at the door and studied the shadow.

Fred glanced at Alex.

Shumka looked up and whispered, "Generations ago, Russian bureaucracy would have done anything to destroy this evidence, anything. I would not be surprised if same organizations persist today to destroy it. In fact, I will hide these documents." As quickly as his face turned to alarm, it turned back to that of the placid host. "Would you like more tea?" he said as he began clearing the table.

Susan tapped on Fred's shoulder and then looked over at the shadows coming from the bottom of the door. Fred then picked up a pen, slid a piece of paper over and hastily wrote, *We're being observed. Someone has been listening to us.*

Shumka stood up and examined the door. His hands rose to his mouth and he murmured, "This become serious." He waved his hands, pointing to the music. "We hide it here," Shumka whispered. "It will be safe." He grasped the wrapping and pressed it on top of the music, looked around the room, then took ten inches of newspapers from the totemic pile in the corner of the room, opened one newspaper and slid the music inside. Then he replaced the papers to the pile. Given the heft of the pile, it seemed that it would take weeks to sift through and find what had been slid within the stack. It instantly blended into the massive pile and vanished from sight. "Is good. Music is safe here. Now you must leave." Shumka vigorously waved his hands to marshal the three guests to the kitchen. He placed the brown bag on the kitchen counter and pointed to a door that led to a garden outside the kitchen. He raised his finger to his lips as the other hand frantically hurried them along, fitfully moving back and forth while barely in a whisper, he repeated, "*Teesha, teesha*" (quiet, quiet).

"No," Susan said, stopping at the door to the garden. "We can't leave it." Susan snatched the brown bag off the kitchen counter and darted back into the apartment, slipped her fingers into the stack of newspapers at about eye level and rummaged for the package of music. She found it almost immediately, stuffed it into the brown bag, clutched it to her chest and headed back toward the kitchen door. "Now, we know it's safe." As she passed Shumka, she paused briefly, leaned and gently kissed his cheek. "Thank you, Mr. Shumka."

Shumka stood by the table whispering, *"Teesha, teesha."*

Fred looked back at Shumka and gave him a slight grin and a wink before Fred slid out the door and joined Alex and Susan in the small garden. Fred waved his hand and Shumka nodded in return.

FLIGHT FROM SHUMKA'S

MANHATTAN, APRIL 26

SUSAN AND ALEX quietly slipped toward the adjoining alley. Fred held back a moment, looked through the kitchen window and once again waved goodbye to Shumka. Fred quietly closed the gate and ran down the narrow alley quickly joining Susan and Alex. They passed an occasional fenced in garden, which gave an intermittent respite to the urban blight. He followed Susan and Alex as they took a left down another alley.

Fred said, "Is this tangled path going to get us out of here?"

"These alleyways are connected," Susan said, pointing to a narrower alley that looked as if it hadn't been walked in years.

"I feel like we're walking in circles," Fred said.

"I know these types of alleys," Susan said. "We'll find an alleyway that will lead to yet another alleyway and away from this neighborhood."

Alex stopped, pried open a decaying wooden gate draped with barbed wire and said, "Let's hide in this garden for a while until this blows over."

"No, let's get the hell out of here, and do it fast," Fred whispered.

Alex grabbed Fred's arm and Fred pulled him close in a tight hug. Fred felt Alex's heart pounding and grabbed his hand. He held Alex's hand tight until Susan turned back and anxiously whispered, "C'mon."

As they turned to the left, Susan pointed to the sunny area at the end of the alley and motioned to head in that direction. They quickly walked to where it opened onto the street. Suddenly Susan halted, thrust her hands in her pockets and exploded with, "Oh shit, I left my keys at Shumka's!"

"We can come back for them tomorrow," Fred said.

"I need them," Susan said with a whine. "The keys to my apartment are there, along with a few other irreplaceable items."

Alex said, "Sue—"

"No, I have to go back. It'll be fast. I'll catch up."

Fred said, "Dammit, We'll stick together." Fred and then Alex turned around and headed back with Susan.

Fred mumbled, "These alleys don't look the same when you see them in reverse. Are we on the right track?"

"If a rat in a maze can do it, we can. C'mon," Susan said as she pulled ahead.

When they turned into the alleyway of Shumka's apartment, Fred lurched ahead to grab Susan's arm and whispered, "Wait."

There was a commotion coming from Shumka's apartment. Fred placed a finger over his lips to hush them, then spotted a garden with a small shed that looked like it would fit all of them snugly. He looked at Susan, then the shed.

Susan shook her head emphatically until Alex grabbed her arm and pulled her through the knee-high weed-covered garden, climbed over some discarded crates and paused in front of the shed.

Fred got inside and noiselessly moved a rake and shovel to the far wall, then slid to the right to make room for Susan and Alex.

"It stinks," Susan whispered, then Alex covered her mouth.

The back door to Shumka's apartment opened, banged shut, then creaked open again as two people spoke to each other in Russian. It sounded as if they were coming close to the garden.

"Oh my God," Susan whispered softly.

"Shhh," Fred said. "Now they're walking the other way, I think."

After a few minutes, all was quiet and Fred pushed the shed door open and leaned out. "Let's go," he said quietly and they emerged from the shed.

Susan brushed the filth off her blouse and said, "God, was that the worst."

The gate was open when they arrived back at Shumka's. Fred looked over at Susan and Alex and shrugged. Fred felt his chest tighten with dread, then tapped Susan on the shoulder and put a finger to his lips.

Susan stared at Fred, her eyes wide.

Alex slowly shook his head.

What? Susan mouthed.

Fred pointed to the open gate, then mouthed, *It was closed.* He then pointed to the open kitchen door.

"I'll wait here," Alex said, and stayed at the edge of the gate peering into the alley. Fred stayed close behind Susan as they hurriedly walked back into the kitchen. She softly said, "Mr. Shumka, we're back. I forgot my keys."

Fred wandered through the apartment astonished at the scattered papers, books dumped on the floor and upset furniture. The shelves were now empty and one dangled precariously. The drawer of the desk was upside down with it contents scattered nearby. Carpets were bunched like a rag bundle against the wall. Fred quickly glanced at the massive pile of newspapers in the corner that once stood upright and for a short while hid the package of music. It was now strewn across the floor as if kicked one way and then another. The disarray of the room was in stark contrast to the disquieting stillness.

Shumka sat slumped with his head on the dining room table and his back to them. Fred took in a deep breath and held it.

"Hello, Mr. Shumka," Susan said cautiously as she took a step toward Shumka. "It's Susan."

Fred placed his left hand on Susan's shoulder, gently holding her back.

Susan pulled away and took another step closer, then another. She reached out and tapped Shumka's right shoulder. "Hello, Mr. Shumka?" she said softly. "Mr. Shumka, we're back. I forgot my keys."

Susan walked around the table keeping her eyes on Shumka.

When she reached the head of the table, her eyes grew wide and her hands flew to her mouth. She took a step back.

"What is it?" Fred called out, rushing toward her. He turned to find a puddle of blood pooled in front of Shumka's head. Shumka's twisted face, smeared with blood, stared up at her with glassy, unblinking eyes. Fred tugged at Susan's arm, but she stood frozen at the end of the table. Shumka was crumpled into his chair, his head askew on the table. Blood dripped over the metal table from a slice in Shumka's throat, then onto the chair and down to the floor.

Susan pointed to Shumka's clenched fist and the fragments of paper still clasped in his fist. She said, inhaling, "He must have—"

"God, this is awful," Fred said.

Susan tried to avoid looking at him, but Shumka's head was turned toward her and his eyes stared with a hypnotic hold. Susan hastily snatched her keys off the table, then grabbed Fred's hand and dashed about the room.

Fred said, "We gotta get outta here."

Susan pulled away from Fred and said, "We can't just leave Shumka."

"Come on, Susan, we know they didn't get what they were looking for," Fred said, taking Susan's hand and pulling her toward the door. Susan held the brown bag tight to her chest and dashed out the kitchen door to the garden. Fred closed the door tight.

"We have to get as far from here as possible," Susan said. "Dear Lord, this is all much more terrifying than we could've imagined."

Alex looked terrified. "What?"

Fred pulled Alex close and whispered, "Shumka's dead. The murderer can't be too far from here. That's what we heard in the alley."

Alex stood frozen.

"Alex," Fred said, "We gotta go." He pulled Alex along until Alex kept pace on his own.

"This looks like a fast way out," Alex said as they fled into the alleyway and toward a fence adjoining a large house. They continued to scramble, each grabbing onto the other for support as they climbed over dented steel garbage cans to mount shabby fences.

As they approached MacDougal Street, Fred put his arms out, stopping Susan and Alex. He glanced left and right for a brief moment to see if anyone looked threatening or suspicious. The mass of people on the street flowed like molten lava, silently walking, offering a cover. Fred hoped that it would be easy to blend in with the crowd. The three crossed MacDougal and proceeded down Minetta Lane toward Sixth Avenue.

Susan looked around and said, "There's a lot fewer people around now. I'm not sure if this is a refuge or more exposure. I can't think."

Fred said, "Let's calm down. Walk steadily now and hope that no one looks suspicious."

They spilled onto the street, collected themselves and then started to walk amongst the crowd. Fred noticed Alex look back a few times and gave him a slight nudge with his elbow.

"I think we're being followed," Alex whispered.

"You're kidding," Susan said.

Fred fought the urge to look back. Instead he took hold of Alex's hand, then looked over at Susan and nodded to cross the street. "I've seen that man before," Alex said. "He came into Anna's shop several times."

Susan said, "You know, I believe I saw someone behind us from my home street a ways back but it couldn't have been."

The man, way behind them, started to walk briskly in their direction. He was large with an uneven lumbering stride, gaining ground with every step.

"My God, he has a knife," Susan said, and clutched the brown bag tighter.

Fred groaned. "He's gaining on us."

"Listen to me," Alex said. "I'll wait here." Alex pulled Fred toward him and gave him a hug. "Go across the street like we're parting ways." He gave Fred a brief kiss on the cheek. "I'll meet up with you later." He gave Susan a brief hug, then gently pushed her back.

"I don't want to leave you here," Fred said as he slipped away.

"What's going on?" Susan whispered as she and Fred hurried across the street.

"I don't know," Fred said.

When they got to the sidewalk, Fred looked back to see a man gaining on Alex. Susan gasped, and he grabbed her arm to keep her from going back. They had to trust that Alex knew what he was doing.

"Fred—"

Fred pulled her close and forced her to walk with him. He looked back to see Alex duck into an entrance.

"But, Fred—"

"We have to trust him," Fred whispered as he quickened his pace.

"Hurry," Fred said as he pulled Susan across the street and Alex slid into a nearby doorway.

The burly man approached Alex and slowed down. Across the street, Fred tightened his grip on the package when he noticed that the man saw what he was holding. The man tightened his grip on the knife and held it close to his chest. Traffic on Sixth Avenue alternated between combative and furious and then to an uneasy stillness as the light on Bleeker Street turned red. The traffic stopped on heavily travelled Sixth Avenue. Engines purred like restive lions, but no cars moved.

Alex was across the street, motionless in the doorway, studying the traffic on the avenue, his eyes fixed on the traffic signal as he watched it change from red to green and back to red.

A chill ran up Fred's back as he saw the assassin stand squarely in front of Alex. Susan stood on her toes, grabbed Fred's hand and squealed, "Oh, my God, his knife."

They were powerless to do anything as the monster stood over Alex as if he was about butcher an animal. Fred and Susan teetered on the edge of the curb, watching Alex intently, unable to do anything. Fred wished Anna had never given him the music.

The thug took a deep breath.

Alex remained still.

Fred cried out, "Run, Alex, Run!"

As the assailant reached back, the traffic light went to yellow. Alex jumped out from the doorway sideways, slipping past the brute and dashed onto the avenue. The man with the knife chased after him, jumping into the middle of Sixth Avenue.

The light on the cross street turned red. The man was gaining on Alex. A taxi zoomed past Alex, grazing his left shoulder, then struck the man chasing him straight on, flinging him into the air and onto another lane. The man moved his arms, twisted to his knees and then tumbled back to the street. He raised his head and stared at Fred, a drool of blood dripping from his chin. A second taxi streaked past the first taxi and ran over the man.

Susan stood with her jaw hanging on the other side of the street. As her arms fell to her sides, Fred took the brown bag and held it tightly. Alex ran through the traffic, joined Susan and Fred and they ran away from Sixth Avenue. After a short time, they paused for a sustained group hug, then, still trembling, the trio walked briskly back toward Fred's apartment.

Susan asked, "What gave you such confidence that that brute would stay with you and not come for us?"

"Thugs like that guy will pick one out of the herd, one that he perceives as the weakest, and attack, ignoring the others. But he would have come for you next," Alex said.

"We've got to call 911," Susan said. "It's a matter of safety to involve the police."

Alex argued, "We have to distance ourselves from the incident in every way, at least for the time being. Lay low, that's what we have to do."

"What'll happen when they find Shumka?" Susan said.

"They'll find that thug lying in the middle of the street with a knife that has Shumka's blood on it. That's all they'll need to close the case," Alex said.

They slowly approached the busy corner of Seventh Avenue, walking each abreast on the sidewalk, numbed from the day's events. Suddenly, a young man rushed into Susan, tripping her into a planter alongside the road. She grabbed Fred to try to regain her balance and in the awkward acrobatics, Fred dropped the package containing the music into the street. Alex dove to recover the music as the runner dashed ahead without looking back. He handed the brown bag back to Fred.

They walked down Barrow Street for a ways and stopped in front of the Barrow Street Music School. There was piano playing part of a Tchaikovsky concerto. It sounded perfect. It was repeated, sounding perfect once again.

Susan pointed to some steps in front of a brownstone just across the street and gestured to Fred and Alex to sit down. Fred climbed up a couple of steps and sat down behind Susan. He put his hands on her shoulders and moved them gently down her arms. Alex sat down next to Fred and put a hand on Fred's lap.

Susan said, "What are we doing? People want this package at any cost. Shumka is dead. We should turn the music over to a museum or something and not get involved any further."

After taking a deep breath, Fred said, "I've been upset since we learned what we had here."

Susan said, "This is affecting my life and I want this affair to change directions right now. Let's get this music back to Anna."

Alex appeared disturbed and a quiet eruption of emotion brought moisture to his eyes. "We have inherited a responsibility. I can't let this extraordinary evidence of an important gay romance be destroyed. I've experienced this type of hate in Russia, it flows from the Russian Orthodox Church like opium to budding addicts."

Fred nodded.

Alex said, "Thugs who'll stop at nothing to destroy this evidence about Tchaikovsky to protect an archaic philosophy of state-endorsed homophobia are falling from trees. Shumka was killed to keep it a secret. We have the key to that secret, whatever the hell it is."

They sat on the steps and listened to the nineteenth century Russian music played again and again. Fred looked down at his fist tightly strapped with the handles of the brown bag that held not just the music, but a truth about one of the greatest Russian composers of all time. Susan let out a soft sigh while Alex leaned against Fred, who in turn wrapped his arm around him, then kissed the top of his head. Fred closed his eyes and let the moment take him.

It was eleven o'clock when Fred climbed into bed thinking about Alex and Anna and how he couldn't believe a package of music could cause such a mess. Bloody images kept flashing before him. As much as he wished Alex could be cuddled by his side tonight, he understood Alex's need to be with his grandmother. He grabbed the remote from the nightstand and flipped on the news.

The opening credits rolled, then the local news anchor came on.

"A man was found dead in his apartment tonight."

Fred's eyes grew wide as a photograph of Shumka came up in the upper right corner of the TV screen. He grabbed his cell phone and dialed Susan, who answered on the first ring.

"I just saw it," she said.

PROTECTION

FRED WOKE THE following day feeling groggy and thinking about Shumka and the people who were after the music. He slid to the edge of the bed and sat with his bare feet on the cold wood floor. He needed to make sense of this, but how? Then he thought about Alex. Alex would know. He sat at the edge of his bed and looked back at the rumpled sheets, then reached for his phone and dialed.

"Alex, it's Fred."

"Hey, what's up? You okay?" Alex said.

Fred took a deep breath and wished he'd figured out what to say prior to calling. "I keep thinking about yesterday. My head's spinning. I don't get it. I don't know what to do or how to go about dealing with this."

"So you need answers."

"I need something."

"Just a minute," Alex said, then there was a muffled conversation in what could have been Russian, Fred couldn't tell. Then Alex came back to the phone. "Come by for breakfast. My grandmother is going to make us blini."[7]

"Can I bring Susan?"

---

7   Russian pancakes similar to crêpes.

"I'll ask," and this time, Fred clearly heard in the background, "*Da, ochen' khorosho,*"[8] and then Alex, "Of course. Seeya in less than an hour."

Fred straightened his bed as he dialed Susan.

"G'morning, Sus. You okay?"

"I didn't sleep, kept waking up with images. You don't want to know."

"I spoke to Alex. We're going over to Anna's shop for breakfast with Alex."

"Good, I'd like to get Anna's view on things. I think she knows more than she lets on."

"I'll meet you downstairs in fifteen minutes. I have to jump in the shower," Fred said.

"I'll be there."

Still in a daze, he watched the water cascade down the shower wall and imagined blood dripping down the package of music. He stood still as the image of a lifeless Shumka hunched over and staring up came to mind. He let the shower run on his face as if that would erase things. If he carried it with him to Anna's shop, he would have a chance to safeguard it. It would be risky, but at least he would be in control. He didn't want to carry the package, but he also couldn't abandon all responsibility for safeguarding it.

As they walked to the subway station, Fred said, "Susan you're dragging. C'mon."

"I can't get Shumka out of my head."

"I know."

Susan heaved a sigh and said, "If it weren't for us, he'd still be happily sitting at his table sipping tea from his glass."

"We can't think like that. Let's go."

"I guess I know what's in the package," Susan said.

Fred said, "I can't keep this package tied to me wherever we go and I can't leave it in the apartment." He carried the Big Brown Bag tightly under his arm with the handles twisted painfully tight around his fingers. "If someone wants to snatch this bag from me, they will have to rip off my hand."

"God, what a freaky thought," Susan said.

Fred squinted over his shoulder and pressed the whole

---

8 Yes, very good.

package under his elbow. He stared over his left shoulder and then looked up at the fire escape as they passed. The shadow of someone approaching from behind seized Fred's attention and he took Susan's elbow and pulled her to the side. After the stranger passed, they continued to walk toward the subway entrance.

They arrived at Anna's shop, finding Alex at the front door looking out the window next to the closed sign. Without a greeting, Alex opened the door, let them in, locked the door behind them and led the way to the rear of the shop and upstairs to the apartment. As they entered the kitchen, Anna turned from the stove and approached Fred and Susan with a restrained smile and emotionlessly said, "Have a seat. Your blini will be ready in a moment." She poured coffee into four cups on the table and returned to the stove.

They poked at their pancakes, eating very little, and without saying a word. Anna sat down at the table, postured stiffly for a moment, then relaxed in a slump.

Anna placed her left hand on Fred's back while pouring him another cup of coffee. "Such horrible thing," she said. "Shumka, such good man." She paused a moment, then made a sweeping cross over her chest. "And you, Fred, I am so sorry. I thought, I thought it would be simple."

"You should have told me."

Anna walked back to the stove. "I was afraid you wouldn't take it. I also thought you would never figure it out, that it would be safe with you and you would never see it as anything more than music. Who would suspect you?"

"But that's no longer the case," Susan said.

"No, it is not."

"The man who did that horrible thing won't be doing that again," Susan said.

Fred said, "But remember, we heard more than one voice in the alley. I'm afraid this isn't over."

"I feel like everyone is watching," Alex said. "Every window, every doorway, everyone on the street. We can't keep doing this, walking around with the music on a leash. We have to hide the music in a safe place. Fred, what about your apartment?"

Anna turned to Fred softly said, "I'm sorry that I have changed your life. I can only hope that this is the end of trouble."

Susan said, "My life changed when I saw blood dripping off of Shumka's table. Alex is right. The music must be totally hidden. I never want to see—"

"We should call the police," Fred said.

Anna straightened up. "No, no police. Police can't be trusted."

"This isn't Russia, Baba,"[9] Alex said.

Anna waved him off. "Police are all the same."

"No, this isn't Russia," Susan said. "I think we can trust them."

Anna turned from the stove and glared at Susan. "For music? You Americans have no respect for such things. They will not understand the Russian people. They think Russians are like in the movies and cartoons. They will see music and think we're crazy."

Fred looked at Susan and raised his eyebrows. She had a point, even if he didn't fully agree with her about how Americans saw Russians.

Anna took her cup from the table and ambled away. Staring at the wall, she said, "Those people, those terrible people will still believe that the music is here."

Alex shook his head, then said, "No, we will fix that." He took a few bites of his pancakes, then stood up and said, "We should go. We have a lot to do." He went to Anna and gave her a prolonged hug, turned away, then went back and hugged her again. "Baba . . . It will be all right," he said softly.

Susan reached out to hold Anna's hand for a moment "We'll be back for a visit soon. The blini were wonderful, thank you."

Fred said, "Thank you."

Anna squeezed his hand.

Alex led Fred and Susan downstairs and to the door and outside, where they stood and waited for Anna, locked the door behind them. Fred turned back to see Anna smile through the window as they walked toward the subway.

They approached Fred's building, opened the door and climbed the stairs. As they entered the apartment, Susan took a

---

9 Russians often call their grandmother *Baba* although, strictly speaking, it should be *Babushka*.

deep breath. "Am I the only one who's nervous about what to tell the police when they question us about Shumka?"

"How will they know we were there?" Fred asked.

"They'll know I was there. They have my fingerprints from my visa when I entered the country," Alex said. "Then, they'll go for Anna and eventually you two."

"But surely they found the killer dead on the street," Susan said. "Wouldn't they stop there?"

"Only if they can make the connection," Fred said.

Alex slowly nodded.

Fred sat down on the sofa and looked over at Alex, who plunked himself down in an overstuffed chair next to the sofa and stared at the floor. "I wonder if that thug was swept up by some accomplice and vanished. Remember those other voices in the alley. Maybe we really should hand this over to the police?" Fred said.

"The police will do nothing," Alex said, his voice sullen. "They won't understand what this is. Anna said the same thing."

"But we need protection," Susan said.

Alex's eyes were rimmed with dark circles. He shook his head, looked up and said, "If we go to the police, then these thugs will know where we are."

"Shit! And now we're all at risk," Susan said. "Great!"

Alex stormed out of the living room, then the bathroom door closed with a thud.

"Perhaps I should go," Susan said softly, then gathered her purse and bent down to give Fred a kiss on the cheek.

"Everything is going to be fine," Fred said.

Susan forced a smile. "I know."

Fred walked Susan to the door, then walked over the bathroom and took a deep breath before walking inside. Alex's palms were pressed against the sink and his head hung low as he looked down at the basin. Fred reached out and gently placed his right hand on Alex's shoulder.

"I'm sorry," Fred said, his voice soft and calm.

Alex turned and clutched Fred tight as he let out thundering sobs. "He's dead because of me."

Fred held Alex tightly as they walked back to the living room and sat together on the sofa. After a while, Alex said, "They saw us at Shumka's, so they know that either you or Susan has the music. Our shop has been ripped already. They wouldn't come back there." He put his hands over his face and said, "You or Susan, we have to assume that they'll come after the music."

"So what do we do, sit here with a gun pointed to the door? And what about Susan?"

"One at a time. You have the music. We should hide it somewhere in the apartment," Alex said as he looked around the room.

"That's crazy. Do you want to find me hanging over the kitchen table like Shumka?"

Alex started to wander the around the apartment. "Picture Shumka's apartment all torn up. Where didn't they look? They ripped up the rugs, tore everything off shelves, refrigerator, oven, broke up cabinets,"

"It's hopeless," Fred said as Alex walked into the bedroom.

"No, no," Alex mumbled as he looked around. He walked into the bathroom, then into the living room. "Fred, come in here. If we take out that new recessed medicine cabinet, there's bound to be enough space in the wall either above or below it. It's screwed from the sides, not the top. They'll open it up, but they'd never think to rip it out."

"Yeah, it'll be a mess to do that, but it's good." He turned to Alex, hugged him, then looked again at the cabinet.

"But what about Susan?" Fred said. "If they ransack her place, we've got to send the message that they were expected, but there's nothing there."

"Okay, we should plant an inviting distraction in Susan's apartment. If these murderers find a package, it would be the decoy, giving us warning to do something."

"Let's do it tonight," Fred said as he slid the package of music behind his dresser, then he and Alex left the apartment and went downstairs.

Susan was outside of her building talking to a neighbor. They waited until Susan was alone, walked up to her and told her the plan.

Susan said, "The plan is fine, although I'm not enchanted with the idea of luring grimy goons to my apartment." She looked up at her window and reached out for Fred's hand. "I guess there's no choice. Let's do it."

"We've got to appear as casual and unaware of what's out there as possible," Alex said.

Although Fred didn't want to come out and say it, he was amazed at how Alex had put himself into lethal danger to help them. He turned to Susan and said, "Dammit, I can't get the image of Shumka's eyes out of my mind."

"I know."

Standing outside of Susan's apartment, Fred couldn't help but take a good look at Alex, sweet, attractive, smart, brave Alex. He reached out and held onto Alex's hand, giving it a squeeze, then hugged him tightly.

Alex looked up at Fred and squeezed tighter until tears started to trickle down. When Fred felt Alex's tears on his cheek, the pent up emotions of the past two days escaped and his tears began to flow. They stood there with their cheeks pressed together until Susan put her arm over Fred's shoulder. She joined the hug and the three stayed tightly together for a few moments. As they separated, Fred held on for a moment and then let Alex's hand slip slowly away.

Alex leaned in to Fred and Susan and said, "Let's go upstairs and set up the packages now."

"It's getting late and I am totally spent. How about doing it first thing in the morning?" Fred said. "We'll do a much better job of it if we're not exhausted."

Alex and Susan agreed.

STRATEGY

MANHATTAN, APRIL 28

STILL DREAMY AND not quite awake, Fred buried his face in his pillow, terrified by the grotesque images of his apartment torn up like Shumka's. He rolled to his left side, opened his eyes and peeked at the glowing numbers of the bedside clock.

"Two-fifteen," he mumbled, then turned on the lamp next to his bed and looked at Alex sleeping sweetly and wondered what he was dreaming about. Reluctant to disturb the angelic image, he leaned over and planted a soft kiss on Alex's cheek.

Squinting into the light, Alex said, "What's the matter?"

"Sorry, but I can't sleep knowing that the music is sitting out there. We've got work to do. Go splash some water on your face and let's get the bathroom project done."

Alex rolled over and moaned, "What? Can't it wait 'til morning?"

"I'm hyped," he said, kissing Alex once again. "Sorry to wake you, but I really need your help. We've got to get Tchaikovsky's vault ready."

Still in his pajamas, Fred went to the dresser and fished out the package of music, held it at arm's length and stared at it.

"You're going into hiding, my little Russian bear," he said as he put it down on the chair. He noticed that his hand still had red lines from where he'd gripped the string handles of the shopping bag. He mumbled, "This is like a Shakespearean curse."

"Let's take the medicine cabinet out of the wall before we do anything else and see what we've got," Alex said. "I have a hard time seeing enough space in there for that package."

"Okay, I'll get a screwdriver; we'll see. But we've got to be careful that we don't make it look like it's been mucked with. Don't scratch the walls."

They took everything out of the cabinet and piled it into the sink, carefully removed the recessed medicine cabinet from the wall and placed it in the bathtub. "What a mess," Fred said. He shone a flashlight into the opening, looked above it and probed around with his hand. "There definitely will be enough room just above the cabinet cutout if we take out some plaster chips."

Fred got a plastic bag, wrapped the package and slid it up into the medicine cabinet cutout. He wrestled with some loose lath boards, made a shelf inside the wall with duct tape and a piece of lath and jiggled it until the package stayed securely. "There, that looks good. Now, let's get the cabinet back in place and clean everything up. I think we're good."

After everything was placed back in the medicine cabinet and the wall wiped clean, Alex said, "Well, we're done for the night."

"Not so fast. Let's get the decoy all prepared so we can bring it over to Sus's apartment tomorrow morning."

"Is this a dream?" Alex said. "I could drop back to sleep right now. It's three-thirty."

"Dream? This is a nightmare. And if I don't get everything ready, this dreadful dream will join me for the rest of the night. I'll get some tape."

Fred went into the kitchen, piled a stack of magazines on the counter, stood back with his head tilted and said, "This looks pretty much like the heft of the music package, don't you think?"

Silence.

Fred turned around and saw Alex sleeping on the couch. He smiled, went to kitchen and pulled out a bag and some tape. He wrapped the package of magazines and stood back to admire his work. He went over to Alex and softly said, "Let's go to sleep. I think I can deal with my nightmares for now."

Fred awoke a few hours later, washed, then called Susan.

"Good morning, Sus. We got a lot done last night, so we'll be over in about an hour and set up your part?"

An hour later, Fred walked out his front door holding the package of magazines in his left hand and Alex's hand in his other. They paused to hear the door click closed and then confidently walked over to Susan's building.

"Fred, do you think you could be a bit more casual with the package?"

Fred and Alex walked up the front steps to Susan's house and rang her bell. The door buzzed and they walked in while Fred took one last look back at the street.

Susan was waiting with the door. Fred held up the package. "Here's the decoy. Pretty good, huh?"

"Pretty convincing," Susan said, leading them into the foyer. "I have to say, ever since we were at Bleeker Street, I haven't been able to sleep. I can't shake the feeling that eyes are on me wherever I go."

"I know, we're planning for a break-in here, but we have no choice at this point. Where should we hide it so it won't be too hard to find?" Fred said as he wandered around the entrance and into the living room. He looked in the bedroom and said, "How about at the bottom of your hamper with some laundry piled on top?"

"Oh, be real," Susan said from the foyer. "Come out here."

As Fred stepped into the foyer, she said, "That old dumbwaiter is crying out to be the obvious hiding place." She went over to the dumbwaiter, opened it and bounced back as a musty draft wafted in her face. "Whew, that was waiting a long time to escape."

Fred reached in and explored the side to locate the wooden railings that once guided the floating shelf. He poked his head inside, looked up and down and said, "This brownstone must've been a grand building."

Susan put her finger to her lips and pointed down the shaft

as she mouthed, *They can hear you.*

Fred leaned in and placed the package of magazines against the railing. He turned to Susan and mouthed, *Lots more tape.*

After the package was secured inside, Fred closed the door.

Alex whispered, "Well, we did it, and I think we did it well."

"And now we wait for a Russian jihadist," Susan said, trembling.

Fred held Susan's hand and gave her a tight hug. "Oh, Susan, we'll figure out a way to see this to the end."

Back in his apartment, Fred looked at his hands and was pleased that the lines from the handles of the shopping bag were receding. He let out a deep sigh, went into the bedroom and luxuriated in a state of collapse on his bed. Alex kicked off his Pumas, then tenderly fell next to Fred and partially over him. Fred placed his head under Alex's chin and they fell asleep.

There were no nightmares.

LOVE, LESSONS
AND LANDLADIES

MOSCOW, NOVEMBER 1892

THE DARKNESS OF winter prowled up to the doorstep of Moscow, mocking Peter Ilyich Tchaikovsky's euphoric mood. He assumed that Ivan had exhaustively studied the pieces assigned to him when he returned to Peter's flat on Wednesday, November 9, more than two weeks after his previous visit. The maestro had expectations that Ivan would not flag in his efforts to reinforce the impression he had made and was certain that Ivan was well prepared.

After Ivan folded his heavy coat and removed his outer boots, he was offered a seat in Peter's studio and they had the usual small talk and a glass of sweet tea. As garrulous as Peter was, Ivan was reserved and hushed. Tchaikovsky wished for a repeat of the emotion-filled interaction of the previous visit, but did not want to appear persuasive. Ivan followed Peter's lead, sat down at the piano in the parlor and played the first piece. More than before, Tchaikovsky was to be captured by the poise and physical charm as much as by the performance. He stood transfixed as Ivan sat at the piano waiting for his next command, perhaps a critique.

Peter walked over to the piano and said, "Let us hear the etude played once again." He sensed Ivan's thrill to play an encore and assumed that he had worked hard to perfect the piece. One performance from this charming and talented young man was far too fleeting.

Peter concentrated on the performance, slowly pacing as Ivan began to play. He stopped behind Ivan, closely watching this new student perform. Tchaikovsky's senses raced ahead of his ability to react. He was riveted by Ivan's light, slightly ruffled hair, the faintest fragrance of cologne and the sound of fine music. Tchaikovsky watched Ivan's hands move over the keyboard with grace and precision, and where he ordinarily would be critical, he was enthralled. Peter felt nuances in the music, perhaps nuances that he fabricated in his own mind, but nonetheless he sensed them. The aura of Ivan before him, playing with grace and passion, captivated all his senses and made Tchaikovsky dreamy.

Peter returned to his role as teacher, and as a further test of Ivan's proficiency, Peter set some new music on the piano easel. Tchaikovsky instructed, "Please, play up to tempo," a common test of technique. Ivan accepted the challenge with self-confidence. As Peter reached his arm over Ivan's shoulder to turn the page, Ivan tilted his head ever so slightly to allow it to brush along his cheek. The touch, so ephemeral, yet so electric, made Tchaikovsky back away, hiding his blush. They both understood the chemistry that was manifest. Without saying a word, Tchaikovsky brought some Mozart music for four hands and sat on the piano bench next to Ivan. The two entwined their musical passion and rocked gently, turning occasionally and smiling because of their mutual achievement. There was the intermittent tutorial about the interpretation, but for the most part, it was sheer fun.

The lessons repeated every Wednesday. Soon they were twice a week and then three times a week. Peter moved all the students who had appointments on Wednesday to alternate days of the week. Soon his other students were packed into appointments on just a few days of the week, when he did not meet with Ivan. Peter was happy and hopeful of the future for the first time in recent memory. He dined with Ivan often and was seen with his new student by his many friends. He wrote to his brother, Modia, but his letters never mentioned Ivan by name. He described his happiness in coded phrases that his brother all too well understood.[10] Peter was absorbed by the companionship of his new student and they spent many evenings together discussing music, friendship and life in the harsh world of Russia.

Late one evening, while Peter and Ivan were having a quiet time in each other's arms, there was a knock at the door. Peter put a finger to Ivan's lips to let him know to be quiet. He did not want her to think he was there.

"*Gospahdeen* Tchaikovsky," his landlady called out in a hushed voice.

Peter looked at Ivan, his eyes wide.

She screeched in the smallest possible whisper as if something might be wrong, "*Gospahdeen* Tchaikovsky."

Then, from a poke of the landlady's toe, the door slowly swung open, causing Peter to freeze as he saw his landlady holding a tray of poppy-seed strudel, her eyes wide with fright. The doorway framed an image that Peter feared would cause unwelcome consequences.

The landlady stood gaping at Ivan and Peter, who were standing together, not fully dressed, and without saying a word, she gently placed the tray on the floor and turned around. She stood for a moment with her back to the doorway, looking up to the heavens. As she trotted toward the stairs mumbling and crossed herself repeatedly in broad sweeps. Peter Ilyich and Ivan stood frozen in a failed tableau displayed to a cruel and critical audience.

Peter looked at Ivan's terrified face, and for a brief moment felt the gravity of the encounter. But his soberness vanished quickly and a stifled chuckle cascaded into a giggle and broke into a drunken laugh. Ivan's face glowed and his rosy cheeks nearly eclipsed his sapphire eyes. This was a happy time to be coveted, but their carelessness would have a price.

Ivan asked in a cautious voice, "Is this how it will be, evading every suspecting eye? Will people ever see past the crushing influences of Russian inhumanity?"

Peter walked to the other side of the room with his head

---

10   In letters to Modia that exist today, Tchaikovsky referred to his sexual attractions using vague Russian words with no English equivalent.

down, and after a short time turned to Ivan. "In one edition of the Beethoven piano sonatas there is a misprint. A C-sharp is printed as a C-natural. The printing is so blatantly wrong that any sane pianist would make the correction with little thought. If the correction is not made, the sound is a terrible assault on the ears and the intellect. Nevertheless, one occasionally hears that sonata performed with that wrong note. The pianist would rather have his ears abused with what he must know is wrong than oppose the presumed authority of Ludwig van Beethoven, the great master. The offensive error is repeated in concert again and again by trusting musicians with the fear that disobeying master Beethoven is beyond their domain of influence. Authority, whether real or perceived, is hard for some to challenge no matter how it affronts them. This is the Orthodox Church."

Two weeks after the incident involving his landlady, Tchaikovsky sought out a new home. He bought a house in the village of Maidanovo near the village of Klin, which was convenient to both Moscow and St. Petersburg. These were the halcyon days for Peter. He spent time with Ivan walking through the autumn countryside, playing piano duets and working on his compositions with a newfound contentment. Their love strengthened each day. Tchaikovsky recommended Ivan for performances in both Moscow and St. Petersburg. He attended many concerts in which Ivan performed, being as obscure as possible to avoid drawing undesirable notice to himself. Because of the inevitable attention he would attract when they went to concerts together, Pete always arranged the seating so that Ivan was placed in the row in front of him. The mores were onerous and Peter did not want his public to see him with a partner. Even though life could not be better, there was a nagging memory of the encounter with his former landlady and he dreaded the thought that the price for that incident might have to be paid someday.

Filled with the sanguine outlook of love, Peter sketched out sections of his new ballet, *The Nutcracker*, and filled it with grandeur and playful optimism. It was quickly drafted to the point where a piano version of some of the major parts could be played for colleagues in a private soirée. It was a grand recital filled with friends anxious to hear the newest fantasy work. Although the attendees were critics and music composition professionals,

Peter arranged an invitation for Ivan. Ivan sat in the front row and was mesmerized by the splendor of his lover playing the piano, debuting his new music. After the musical, they attended a reception but stayed a safe distance apart to avoid planting seeds for malicious blather. At the end of the reception, they slipped out of different doorways and left St. Petersburg together in a waiting carriage. Both Peter and Ivan had grown wary of idle and cruel gossip and were mistrustful of observers.

But Peter was stealthily observed regardless as he moved about in his daily activities. His reputation throughout Europe made him an immutable treasure of Russia. Friends, rivals and enemies alike paid close attention to the activities of the celebrity. The Tsar had him followed and observed during his trips to Paris, Prague and other major cities. Peter, believing that his private life was disregarded when he was far from home, allowed his passions to guide his actions. As Ivan frequently accompanied him and shared his living quarters, a slanderous reputation started to form in the inner circles of some dangerous organizations. There was growing concern that Peter Ilyich Tchaikovsky could soon become more of a liability than a treasure to the Fatherland and the institutions that boasted of him. All of Europe was watching the icon of Russia, waiting for something new that they could use to celebrate Russian culture or perhaps defame.

THE BROWNSTONE

MANHATTAN, APRIL

ENJOYING THE SPRING sunshine, Fred strolled down to the corner store to get some bagels for breakfast while Alex showered. Once on the street, he paused to notice a short stocky woman moving into the basement apartment in Susan's building

When he got back to his apartment, he said, "Looks like Susan's got a new neighbor."

"Why don't you call Susan over for breakfast and find out—what do you call it—the dirt?"

Fred nodded and dialed. "Hi, Sus, how about coming over for brunch? Got some fresh everything-bagels from Sol's, just what you like, what could be better?"

A short while later, Susan buzzed and Fred let her in. "We've got a new neighbor. The name on the doorbell says Margo."

"That's it? Margo. No last name, just Margo? Is this like *Cher* or *Madonna*?" Alex said, laughing.

"Have you talked to her yet?" Fred said.

"Not yet, she took the apartment a few days ago," Susan said. "She's already got Verizon over, which is an amazing feat. I'll catch her when she's settled in."

Later that day, while walking down the street, Fred and Alex saw a mover's truck and a woman come out of the basement apartment stomping with a limp and shouting at the movers. "Couch in the front room, desk in back. C'mon, Kong, don't doddle."

Fred turned to Alex. "Pretty assertive, huh?"

"Assertive. I call that obnoxious."

The woman screeched at the two workmen, her voice echoing between the buildings, "And one of you is tracking mud into the house!"

"The street's turned into a fun-house," Fred said.

Alex laughed, "Isn't that what you call the New York voice?"

Fred said, "No, she's way beyond what you think of as the New York voice. This is high-test acid."

"That voice has an edge like a knife dangling across your throat," Alex said. "She really is a piece of work."

When they got to Fred's building, Fred and Alex continued watching the woman's tirade. She was stopping traffic, yelling at the movers and onlookers and even blocking traffic.

A taxicab blared his horn and yelled, "Hey asshole, move that fuckin' truck."

The woman left her post at the side of the moving van and swaggered like a limping longshoreman from the front of the brownstone to the taxicab. The cab driver salivated as he escalated his profane screaming to welcome her arrival. "Here comes the dumb-ass bitch that's screwing things up?"

Thumping her limping leg on the sidewalk, the woman marched solidly, where they shouted at each other and their hands flew up and down. Seconds later, the yelling and honking stopped abruptly.

The woman walked casually back to her post directing the movers. She then directed the van to park a bit farther up the street and mostly on the sidewalk. As the traffic slowly rolled by, the drivers gawked at the furniture on the sidewalk that had disrupted their travel. The cab driver, with his head hung low, looked the other way as he passed the brownstone.

About half an hour later, Fred's doorbell rang with Susan's moniker short-short-long signal. Alex buzzed her in.

"What gives with this Margo woman? Did you see the scene on the street?"

Susan said, "Yeah, Cut her some slack. After all, she is new to the neighborhood. Let her look around. Her life's just been upgraded to the best house on the best street in the best city. Let her wallow in it." Susan sat down at the kitchen counter. "Okay, so she's not in the best apartment. Her life has room to grow. And you have to feel just a little bit sorry for a pudgy woman with a leaping limp."

"I don't know," Alex said, "She's like a Disney character." He laughed. "Maybe Cruella. You've got t'love her."

"Moving is nerve-wracking. I feel for her," Susan said, walking to the window and looking out. "I noticed that the moving van was from Sid's Furniture Rentals. This must be that poor woman's first apartment."

"For her first apartment, she seems like she knows what she's doing," Alex said.

A few days later, when Fred and Alex were visiting Susan, as Fred walked up the front steps of the brownstone, the woman poked her head out of the basement entrance and with a drippy saccharine tone, yelled, "Hello-ou!"

Fred shyly looked at her, not knowing if this was the right moment to welcome her to the neighborhood.

"Hi. I'm Margo. I've seen you coming and going over the past couple of days. Do you live here?"

Fred blankly stared at her.

"Visiting a friend?"

Silence.

"I thought it would be nice if you were a neighbor. Guess you sort of are," Margo said with a tight smile while raising her eyes in an almost alluring flirt. With the corners of her mouth in a twisted smile, she said, "So who are you visiting?"

So sweet, but too sweet, Fred thought. "Uh, we're, uh, going up to Susan's apartment," Fred said as he turned away.

"I like to get to know my new neighbors," Margo said. "I think I'm going to love this street."

Fred returned a vague smile and stared at her pale, doll-like face with black bangs, blushed cheeks and severe eyeliner. Her eyes drilled at his as if she was a hypnotist. "A pleasure to meet you," Fred said, then rushed past her and up the stairs to the entrance of the brownstone.

"Likewise, I'm sure," Margo said. "Can you recommend a nice place to go for dinner?"

"Luigi's. Best Italian in the area."

"Thanks."

As Susan buzzed them in, Alex turned to Fred and whispered, "She's certainly not shy. That was pretty intimate," Alex quietly said. "She practically ignored me."

Fred looked back down to the basements steps to find that Margo was eyeing him, her seductively corrosive smile sending a chill down his spine. Fred marched into the front door trying to pretend that the icy smile was gone.

Fred and Alex entered Susan's apartment and made their way into the kitchen.

"I just ran into your new neighbor," Fred said.

"I met Margo today, too," Susan said. "She seemed comfortable talking to me."

Fred said, "What did you tell her?"

"Not much," Susan said.

"Just a sec," Fred said as he went to the dumbwaiter, quietly opened it and peeked in and then soundlessly closed it. When he got several feet away from the dumbwaiter door, he said, "I just want to make sure that our handiwork is as we left it. All good."

Susan rummaged in a kitchen cabinet and put a plate of cookies on the table. "Margo does have the gift of gab. We've talked several times the past few days. She wanted to know where to get stuff, y'know, like dry cleaning."

"What does Margo do?" Fred said.

"I don't know. She's around the apartment a lot. She must work from home, whatever she does."

Fred raised his eyebrows and reached for a cookie.

Susan said, "She's new to New York and is probably eager to make friends. So far, her only fault is that she's a bit chatty."

"And you certainly can hold your own," Fred said, leaning back in his chair.

"*Tête-à-tête* tabloid, is that what you think?" Susan said.

"No, what I'm getting," Fred said, teetering in his chair, "is that this building thrives on gossip."

Susan thought for a moment. "Yeah, I guess that's it. Fun, huh?"

Alex said, "How about we go out for a light lunch? I'm going to have dinner with Anna tonight."

"How is Anna doing?" Susan said.

"I don't want to leave her alone too much, especially with what's been going on. She's constantly mentioning Shumka, and, well—"

"You're right, Alex, Anna needs your support," Fred said. "She shouldn't be by herself, especially now."

"She mentions that she's uneasy. I can see it," Alex said.

"So for lunch, let's go to that new place near the corner," Susan said.

When they got outside, Fred, Alex and Susan strolled toward the restaurant. Fred said, "Have you ever been in the second floor apartment?"

Susan changed her tone. "Oh, yes, the flagship apartment."

They looked back at the curved bay window that extended across the front of the building.

"The entire apartment is sheer luxury," Susan said. "It has the highest rent on the street."

Fred said, "I've met the two guys who live there, both are good-looking men. They're nice, but for the most part, they keep to themselves."

Susan said, "I've met Allen, but only seen Steve."

Fred said, "Yeah, Steve is referred to as a pretty boy. He's one of those impeccably dressed Bloomingdale salesmen. I would guess that every gay man who wanders into the men's department where he works is struck by Steve's looks."

"So they hang around long enough to buy something," Susan said.

"I would guess that this Steve guy knows how to use his looks as a blunt sales instrument," Alex said.

Susan said, "I wonder how many moths he has to lure into his web to afford that wonderful apartment. It is expensive."

"Don't forget, Allen lives there, too," Fred said.

They turned the corner and paused. "What a great day," Susan said. "My apartment may not be nearly as opulent as Steve and Allen's, but it has its own type of luxury."

"It's the furnishings," Fred said. "You've filled it with the entire spectrum of *tchotchkes* from artful to kooky and beyond tasteless, but it works. I can't explain why."

"Tasteless?" Susan said, taking a few more steps. "The best part of the apartment is that I can see far down the street in both directions,"

"And you also have an outdoor cocktail lounge on your fire escape landing just big enough for Alex and me to join you," Fred said. "I like the three tiny chairs that you stuck there."

Susan said, "With that large window wide open, my cocktail lounge extends the guest room. I love it."

They reached the restaurant and were seated for lunch.

The next day, Susan visited Fred and Alex for dinner in Fred's apartment. "Thanks for having me over," Susan said. "I needed to get out of my apartment for a bit."

"Oh, apartment building politics is the same all over the world," Alex said.

"Nah, I just needed a change."

"But I would guess that if you wanted to hear what's going on, you could pony up to the dumbwaiter and crack it open a bit," Alex said.

"A couple of weeks ago, when Allen was out of town, I heard moaning from two guys," Susan said. "Nice relationship they have."

"Inspiring," Fred said. "Sound checks in, reverberates, and doesn't leave, sort of like an audio roach motel. I suppose it could escape to some other apartment if they had their dumbwaiter door open."

"The dumbwaiter, ahh, where privacy goes to die," Alex said.

Food was served and the conversation ended for the time being. A short while later, Susan said, "So if I have a date over, I have to stay away from the dumbwaiter or else the word will get out to anyone hanging around the shaft. The problem, really, is that all the quality guys I date turn out to be gay. I rarely have repeat dates."

"Oh, you'll find someone. You're a catch," Fred said.

"That's a small consolation. I really need some male companionship to share the best apartment on the best street, in the best city in the world." She paused a bit, put her arms on Fred and Alex's shoulders, and said, "With my best friends."

Susan's cell phone rang a grating melody, causing Fred to turn to Alex and gently shake his head and roll his eyes. She looked at her iPhone to see who it was and, looking at Fred, raised a finger and said, "Just 'sec . . . Hello."

Silence.

"Sounds interesting. One second."

Susan turned to Fred and Alex and said, "Are you free tomorrow night? Steve and Allen are having a small cocktail party and we're all invited."

Fred turned to Alex, who nodded, then said, "Sure, we'll come."

After Susan put her phone away, Fred said, "What's the occasion?"

"Apparently, Allen's been away—y'know he's a flight attendant for Delta Airlines. I understand he's being transferred to Boston. Steve is staying. Allen brought home wine from France and they're having some friends over."

"Oh, so they're inviting us so you won't complain about the noise. Got it," Fred said.

At six o'clock the next evening, Susan, Fred and Alex went to Steve and Allen's apartment. The door was open and conversation from a dozen men rattled through the hallway. Allen greeted them at the door.

"Would you like a glass of wine?" he said, then turned toward Susan. "We have cranberry juice for you, Susan. I'll put it in a wine glass, like the grownups."

"Thank you," Fred said as he took a glass and sniffed it.

Turning to Alex, Allen said, "You two are in an apartment across the street, aren't you?"

Alex blushed and said, "We're in the process of—"

"We are," Fred said smiling at Alex.

Susan, Fred and Alex stayed together as they wandered around the apartment, talking briefly to guests as they passed.

"Stunning apartment," Fred said to one of the guests.

"What a bay window," the guest said as he led Fred and Alex to the bay window that spanned the width of the living room. "The view is delicious." He looked down at the street and nodded to a couple approaching the front steps.

Susan stepped back into the foyer and signaled Fred and Alex to follow. "Look, they've covered their dumbwaiter with that huge painting of a male nude with an unrealistically muscular body diving into a pool."

"I think the bare dumbwaiter door had more art value," Alex said, laughing. He quickly stifled the laughter as Steve approached.

"Hey, guys, there's some people on the terrace who want to meet you," Steve said. "I think you'll like them."

"Terrace, my ass," Susan whispered to Fred as she tailed behind. "It's a fire escape." Once they entered the bedroom and approached the window, Susan said, "Okay, the way they have it decorated, I'll give it balcony status, but terrace, no way."

Fred climbed up the risers against the large window and stepped out. The fire escape was uncomfortably crowded; some guests were sitting on the steps going up to Susan's apartment. One couple had climbed up to Susan's floor and was sitting on the chairs that Susan had set out.

Allen went on the fire escape landing and signaled Susan to come out. "I hope you're okay with this," he said waving a bottle of wine toward the string of men on the fire escape. "Here, try the Chateau Margaux. Delta's been good to me."

Susan smiled and nodded. "It was nice of you to invite us. Did you invite the whole building?"

"I thought about asking that new woman that just moved in, but she's distant and in your face at the same time. I don't need that."

INTERMEZZO

MANHATTAN, APRIL 29

IT WAS FUNNY, but Fred watched Alex straighten the magazines strewn on the coffee table before taking a seat next to him on the sofa without thinking twice about it. Fred liked that Alex was becoming a part of his life.

"Y'know, Anna likes you a lot," Alex said, then gave Fred's left thigh a pat.

Fred cocked his head, then asked, "Why do you say that?"

"She doesn't make a fuss about me spending so much time with you. Anna treats you like you're a long-lost relative. That's a treatment that I don't get to see very often," Alex said as he leaned over and planted a soft kiss on Fred's cheek.

Fred smiled and said, "I'm getting very fond of her. Anna's cooking brings back memories of my grandmother. It's nice to sit in her kitchen and see how happy she is preparing dinner. I'm getting hungry just thinking about it."

The telephone rang and Fred closed his eyes hoping that it wasn't Susan. He really wanted some alone time with Alex. "Hi, it's Sus. Remember Rob, my flying instructor, the pilot? I told you all about him last week. Well, Rob and I are going out for Chinese, The Winking Wok. Please join us."

"Slow down a second. You've had two lessons and you're dating your instructor? The last I heard, it was a just a cappuccino in the flight simulator."

"Yeah, well, I'm not sure I like this flying thing, but the instructor is sweet. You'll love to meet him."

"Things are moving fast with you and, what's his name, Rob."

"He's really good-looking and he's been nice to me—kinda flirty. We've had one date."

"So it's bail out of the lessons, but keep the instructor. Way to go, Susan."

"I'll probably take a couple of lessons more before I drop out. Rob makes the whole thing seem attractive. So, dinner?"

Fred shouted into the next room to Alex, "We're going out for dinner with Susan and her boyfriend *du jour*. Okay with you?" And before there was an answer, Fred said, "Yes."

"I can't believe Susan is involved with a new man so fast," Alex said as he and Fred walked down the street, heading toward the Winking Wok. "Think it'll last?"

"She says he's a looker," Fred said, then pulled Alex close to him, "so don't go stealing him away from her."

"Stealing," Alex laughed and hissed his *S*, which made Fred smirk. Alex grinned as his eyes grew wide before letting out a sexy roar. Fred couldn't help but keep smiling.

When they arrived at the Winking Wok, Alex held the door open for Fred, who blew him a kiss as he walked inside. They scanned the dimly lit restaurant and found Susan sitting with a dark-haired man with chiseled features and a scruffy face. In a row of two-person tables, a pair of tables had been pulled together to accommodate the foursome. It was early and the restaurant was sparsely populated.

"He looks dreamy," Alex said.

Fred turned to Alex and whispered, "Not bad. I'm glad Susan snagged a good-looking guy." Then, staring at Alex, he said, "You don't have to gape at Rob like a tourist in Times Square. Behave yourself." He approached Rob and said, "Hi, I'm Fred, this is Alex."

Rob stood up, extended his hand and said, "Hi, pleased to meet you."

"Susan tells me that you're a flight instructor," Fred said, shaking hands and trying to avoid looking anywhere but Rob's eyes.

"I'm a pilot," Rob said. "I fly a corporate plane and instruct on the side."

As the standard conversation starters became stagnant, they all sat down and Susan said, "Ain't this nice." She reached both hands across the table and touched hands with Fred and Alex. Rob placed a hand on Susan's and there was a brief period of smiles until the waiter arrived, distracting the group as menus were passed around and studied.

Customers arrived at an increasing rate and were seated randomly in the restaurant. A bit later, the waiter brought a new customer to the far end of the row of tables near Susan, Rob, Fred and Alex. The patron stood for a moment looking across the room before sitting down.

Alex turned to Fred and said, "I think I know that woman. I think she lives in my neighborhood." He looked toward the woman and smiled. "I've seen her around our shop."

She cocked her head, smiled in return, then slowly walked up to their table.

"Hi, I'm Sophie."

Alex stood up. "Hi, Alex."

"I think we have relatives in the same neighborhood in Brooklyn," she said.

Alex smiled politely and nodded.

"Well, I just wanted to say hello. Perhaps I will see you around. It was a pleasure to meet you," Sophie said, then walked to her table, sat down and smiled at Alex once again before burying her face in the menu.

Fred turned to Alex and said, "Who is that woman?"

"I'm not sure," Alex said. "In the Brighten Beach enclave, most people are from the same area of Russia, probably from Moscow. Who knows if we're somehow connected?"

Susan leaned over and whispered to Fred, "Sophie smells like an entire magnolia tree. You think she might have overdone it a bit?"

Fred leaned back in his chair, then forward and with his mouth nearly against Susan's ear, "Be kind, although I tend to agree with your nose."

"What is it about the aroma of Chinese food that makes everybody salivate?" Susan said. "Let's order and get this party going." She opened the oversized menu and said, "What's good here?"

"I think I've seen Sophie around the shop," Alex whispered to Fred.

"Well," Susan said, "what's good here?"

At a table across the room, a cell phone rang with an excerpt from a reggae band. A woman grabbed her bag, rummaged for the phone and snapped it open. As the woman spoke, Susan exclaimed, "My God. Could she talk any louder? She talks on her phone like she had a tin can on a string. Don't you absolutely hate it when people use their cell phones in a restaurant?"

Alex's cell phone rang. He looked at Susan and Fred, then down at the screen. His eyes grew wide, then he put the phone to his ear. "Hello. *Da?* . . . *Nyet! Boje moi!* We'll be there as soon as possible."

Alex was pale he hung up and placed the phone on the table.

"What's wrong?" Fred asked.

Alex softly said, "That was Katyusha." He stood up and took a quick breath. "Anna is missing."

Susan gasped as Fred turned to look at Sophie, who quickly looked into her bowl of soup.

WHERE IS ANNA?

NEW YORK CITY, APRIL 29

FRED PLACED HIS right arm around Alex's shoulder as they walked onto the street. "I'm sure it's not what it looks like," he said softly, although he didn't really believe it himself.

Alex slowly shook his head.

"Maybe she went to the store," Fred said, putting his hand under Alex's chin and lifting his pale face. Fred's heart sank as he looked into Alex's lifeless eyes. "Let's get to the subway. I bet she'll be home by the time we get there."

"She never goes out at this hour—it's nearly nine-thirty. And Katyusha never calls. Her voice, the sound of it . . . I'm scared."

Fred held Alex and softly said. "We'll figure this out. Try to keep it together."

Alex put his left arm around Fred's waist and held him tight as red and yellow light lit the sidewalk from the pulsing *Cholula* sign overhead. Fred looked back to see Susan give Rob and hug and a kiss in the doorway to the Winking Wok before sending him on his way.

"I've never heard you mention Katyusha. Is she a relative?"

"No," Alex said as looked up at the throbbing *Cholula* sign. "She's the next door neighbor, a close friend of Anna's."

When Susan met up with them, Fred said, "We should call the police."

Susan shook her head. "They won't do anything until she's missing for twenty-four hours."

"No police," Alex said.

"But we have to," Fred said.

"No!" Alex said. "Anna said no police, so no police."

Fred looked at Susan, who shrugged.

"Let's get to Anna's," Fred said. "The subway is down the street."

It was ten-thirty when they reached Anna's shop.

"Why don't you keep an eye out on the street and call us if you see anything strange," Fred said to Susan when they reached Anna's shop.

"Good luck," Susan said as she took a step back and looked around

Alex trembled as Fred opened the door. They stepped inside, then Fred closed and locked the door.

Alex walked ahead and turned on some lights, then softly called out, "*Anna. Anna.*"

They slowly walked through the store, keeping quiet and listening. They paused when they reached the kitchen. Fred looked at Alex, whose eyes were wide as he slowly nodded. They stepped inside the kitchen, then heard barking from upstairs.

"Sassy," Alex said, then quickly ran upstairs. He came to the top of the stairs and quickly opened it. Sassy bound out, jumping on him with large paws and flopping ears while Alex gave her a hug. Sassy put her paws back on the floor, then turned toward Fred and barked.

"No, that's Fred. You remember Fred," Alex said as he put his arm on Fred's shoulder. "He's fine."

Sassy ran down the stairs, got to the bottom and sniffed before turning to look back at Alex and Fred. She let out a whimper.

Alex called out for Anna, but there was no response.

There was the scent of food, as if somebody had recently finished cooking. He stepped into the kitchen and looked around.

He took another sniff. Pot roast? There was a large pot on the stove that was warm to the touch. He lifted the cover and was overwhelmed by the fragrance of pot roast. "This pot roast must be only a few hours old. It's still warm."

Alex walked up to him and stared into the pot. "We have to go next door and talk to Katyusha."

Fred nodded, then they walked outside. There was a light on upstairs in Katyusha's apartment above the shop next door, so Alex rang the bell. He stepped back to check the light upstairs while Fred waited at the door. There was a short buzz, then Alex leapt at the door and pulled it open. They rushed inside, then upstairs, where Alex swiftly knocked on the door.

There was shuffling inside, then a soft voice said, *"Shto?"* (What?)

"Katyusha, it's me, Alexei."

The door opened a crack and an old woman stared out, her eyes set in wrinkles. She nodded, then she closed the door and chains rattled before the door opened fully and she stood there, looking older than Fred had expected, her dark hair streaked with gray.

"Alexei," Katyusha said with a frail and shaky voice. "What is it you want?"

"I need to talk to you about Anya."

She pointed a crooked finger at Fred. "And who this is?"

"Fred, Katyusha. He's fine."

She stood back and motioned them to enter and she closed the door behind them.

"I heard Anya," Katyusha said as she walked into the living room. "There was lot of noise, but not loud. Just a lot of sounds coming through the walls, footsteps and the voices of men. Sometimes I heard Anya. She sounded afraid."

"Did you call the police?" Fred asked.

Katyusha let out a huff, then pursed her lips and shook her head. She glared at Fred. "Police no good."

Fred said, "But—"

"No good," Katyusha said as she put up her hand.

"Tell us what happened," Alex said softly.

"I ran down the stairs to go to Anya's apartment. When I got to front door and opened it, I saw large car. Two men were holding Anya. I wanted to scream, but could not make sound. They lifted Anya off the ground. I see her legs running in the air as she is pulled into car. I think there was also tape across her mouth." Katyusha paused. She took a deep breath, then her lower lip trembled slightly and she closed her eyes.

"Is that when you called me?" Alex said.

Katyusha nodded. "I did not know who else to call."

Alex said, "Did you go to Anna's apartment?"

"*Da.*"

Fred said, "And?"

"Her door was open and furniture messed up. I straighten things up for Anya. And then, on the kitchen table, I found letter. I looked at letter for a while and wanted to hold it for you. I am sorry, I opened it. I do not understand it anyway."

She handed the letter to Alex, who read it aloud.

> *Your grandmother will soon be in Moscow. If you want to see her again, send package of music. Deliver music to 46 Karandash Street, Moscow on May 24 at 23:00 hours. If no one there to meet you, leave on doorstep. Then you will see your grandmother.*
>
> *If package not authentic, your grandmother will die. No police.*

Alex softly said, "That's the address to Anna's old shop in Moscow, where we lived."

"Alex, isn't it time we call the police?" Fred said.

"They'll kill her."

"You do what they say," Katyusha said. "You will get Anya back."

Fred's eyes grew wide. "But you can't—"

"There is no choice," Katyusha said. "I will take good care of Sassy."

"Thank you, Katyusha," Alex said.

AFFIRMATION

MANHATTAN, APRIL 29

ALEX LAY IN Fred's arms on the sofa as Fred wondered what was going through Alex's mind.

"You seem kind of distant, like you're in another world," Fred said as he stroked Alex's hair.

"I'm worried about Anna."

"Do you think we should go to the police?"

Alex snuggled in closer to Fred and rested his head on his chest. "No, no police. She wouldn't want that."

"Then what are we going to do?"

"What the note said."

"We ought to fly to Moscow right away," Fred said as he sat up in the sofa. "They're saying that it's going to be more than three weeks until we can get to Anna. Are we just going to hang around here until then?"

"They're taking her by boat, probably on a merchant ship. That could take a couple of weeks. The thought of Anna held on a boat for all that time makes me sick," Alex said.

"Why so long?" Fred said.

"A merchant ship is only way they could get someone out of the country and into Russia so they can slip through immigration.

These ships make some stops. It takes a while. Yeah, my dear Anna is cramped into some rusty shitcan."

Alex paced for a minute, then said, "In a few days I'll phone some of the old neighbors in Moscow and ask if they've seen anything. It's funny that everybody watches everybody, but nobody wants to talk. I'll wait a few days, then I'll call every few days."

"Do you think that you'll learn anything?" Fred said

"Who knows? We can't just sit here."

Fred let out a sigh as he held Alex tighter. "Do you have any friends in Russia that you could contact?"

Alex said. "I did have one, but it's been years since we've talked."

"We're going to find Anna," Fred said as he pulled Alex closer to himself.

Alex said softly. "She's been watching over me all these years, and—"

Fred kissed the top of Alex's head wishing he would see reason and change his mind about going to the police. "We'll go to Moscow and get her."

"Thank you," Alex said, then let out a long sigh. "I've tried to convince myself that things were worse in Russia than they are here. But they are the same. *Dyerma sluchayetsya*, or as you say, shit happens."

"Your friend in Moscow, could he help us with this?"

"Boris. I don't know where he is," Alex said softly. "Poor Boris."

"What does that mean?"

"Tough life. He was terribly bullied."

"We all were hounded by bullies at one point or another," Fred said.

"No, not like Boris. He tried to make friends but he made bad choices—they were the most malicious. Boris was a target to tease. He was the fat kid in the neighborhood. The children in the neighborhood repeated slurs mocking Boris and his family," Alex said.

"Mocking?"

"Cruel rhymes."

"Wow," Fred said.

"I was his only friend. He was short, stocky, with a round face and a vanishing neck. He was poor and never stuck up for himself, which made him an easy mark."

"Kids can be cruel."

"It's not easy to be poor in Russia."

"It's not easy to be poor anywhere. He must have been glad to have a friend like you."

"In some ways, we had each other," Alex said softly. "And then we grew up. It's funny how people drift away."

"You don't know what happened to him?"

"He worked in his family bakery for a while, then got involved with the wrong sort. He did all kinds of favors for Anna. She was fond of him."

Alex's eyes had moistened some, so Fred pulled him in close.

Fred's phone rang. It was Susan. Alex let out a sigh when Fred put the phone to his ear and said hello.

The doorbell sounded with a short-short-long buzz. Fred and Alex popped up from the sofa.

"Come for breakfast at my place," Susan said, then hung up.

TEMPEST IN THE BROWNSTONE

MANHATTAN, APRIL 29

"WHY DON'T WE see a movie to take our minds off things," Susan said as she sat next to Fred on the sofa.

Alex held himself back from rolling his eyes. Dropping his hands in his pants pockets, he leaned against the wall, then heard someone talking through the dumbwaiter. He listened closer. Russian, it was clearly Russian.

"*Skoro . . . Ya znayu, gde muzyka,*" a woman said. It sounded like Margo.

"Alex," Fred said.

Alex put a finger to his lips as he glared at Fred.

"*Yest' slishkom mnogo lyubopytnykh sosedey.*"

There was silence.

"*Dover'tes' mne. Tam budet neschastnyy sluchay. Musor ne budet.*" It was Margo.

Alex's eyes opened wide and he pressed his ear against the dumbwaiter door.

"*Oni govoryat Moskvu; oni nikogda ne budut tuda dobrat'sya.*"

Go, Alex mouthed, then pointed to the front door. He stood and listened, then shook his head as he heard more of the conversation.

Susan and Fred stood up.

"I've been dying to see that new French movie downtown," Susan said loudly.

"*L'Air du Temp,*" Fred said. "It's been getting great reviews."

Alex rolled his eyes as he followed them into the hall.

Susan locked up, then they rushed out of the building and onto the sidewalk.

They followed Alex down the street, then stopped in front of the subway entrance. "We have to get our tickets to Moscow tonight," Alex said.

"We have to shop for a decent price," Susan said.

"They want to kill us," Alex said. "We've got to be careful."

Fred said, "What?"

"Margo knows that we're going to Moscow," Alex said. "They have no intention of letting us leave."

"Margo. I knew it," Fred said.

"I don't get it," Susan said. "We're being directed to go to Moscow to exchange the music for Anna's life and yet Margo is—"

"There's more," Alex said. "She says she knows where the music is. Holy shit! The devil is here and she's living below you, Susan."

"Oh my God," Susan said. "I'm still single."

In the early evening, as she was leaving, Susan stood at her door with the key in the lock when she heard some movement below and then a voice. She began to lock the door to her apartment, then stopped and listened.

"Hey, Steve, I've been thinking."

She paused at the sound of Margo's voice from below.

"Y'know, Steve, now that Allen's gone—your apartment is so large, you should have someone share the rent with you."

Margo's voice was sweet, cloyingly syrupy.

"I'm fine, but thanks for thinking of me."

Susan slowly twisted the key and turned toward the stairs, but stopped as the floorboard under her foot creaked. She listened.

"I'm not talking move in, just share the rent. I would make my office your spare bedroom. I wouldn't be any nuisance. You deserve it."

"No, you're very kind, Margo, but thank you—no."

Susan quietly opened her door, walked inside and called Fred. "How about getting together tonight. We have lots to talk about. I'll bring dinner."

Susan arrived at Fred's apartment a few hours later. She stacked frozen veggie burgers on the counter, and holding up a container, said, "Here, I brought something new for dessert, couscous and blueberries. You'll love it."

As Susan worked on the final touches of dinner, Fred and Alex sat quietly at the counter blankly looking at scratches on the surface. With a wedge of cheese on a wooden board in her hand, Susan walked to the counter, heaved a slow, heavy sigh, and said to Fred and Alex, "I feel like I'm living in a nightmare." She looked into the distance as she thought about how simple things were not too long ago, then placed the cheeseboard on the counter and sat down.

"We're in this nightmare together. My imagination couldn't do worse," Fred said, looking across the room and then at Alex.

Susan went to the kitchen drawer, got a knife and placed it next to the wedge of cheese on the board. "I can't live in my apartment without thinking about Margo. I should stay here, with you."

Alex said, "Every time I think about Anna stuffed in a room somewhere, I get a chill."

"There is no room for you in this little apartment," Fred said. "Sorry, I know what you're going through."

"I live in that cozy brownstone above that subterranean demon while Anna is being dragged over the high seas." Susan said as she poured the tea. "Do we even have a plan to get her back?" She set the dinner plates on the table.

Alex picked up the knife and sliced a wedge of cheese, then lifted the knife and stabbed it into the cutting board. He stood up and said, "They could be putting a knife to Anna's throat and we're just sitting here having high tea. We're doing nothing!"

"We're *going* to Moscow," Fred said.

"Of course we're going to Moscow," Susan said.

"Let's get the tickets tonight. We can go right away," Fred said.

Susan cocked her head. "Now? Moscow? They gave us a date that's three weeks away."

"We don't have a choice, we have to find Anna," Fred said. "We can't sit here doing nothing."

"You heard Margo, they're not going to let us leave. We're hunted here and we'll be hunted in Moscow," Alex said. "Except here you know how to deal with it. In Moscow, well, you have me, but that's not enough. I have a feeling that rushing off to Moscow so soon is a bad idea."

"What about the police?"

"We'll deal with that later."

"What about going to the American embassy in Russia?" Susan said.

"More bureaucracy? Nah. Let's get our tickets now," Alex said as he opened Fred's laptop computer. He worked on the computer while Susan set the table for dinner.

"Something interesting," Susan said. "I went over to the managing agent for the building to ask about a new fridge and while I was there I paid my rent. I saw some checks on his desk, and one was for apartment two." Susan put dinner on the table and sat down. "It appears that Steve's rent is coming from someone named Harry Peterson. Steve lives alone, but doesn't pay the rent, at least, not all of it."

"None of these flights make good connections." Alex said.

"Try Travelocity. Then compare results with Orbitz. There are others that are pretty good," Susan said in a matter-of-fact tone. "You can do that later. Don't let your dinner get cold."

Fred joined Susan and Alex at the table and silently ate.

Susan looked up at the ceiling and mumbled, "Think about it. Steve isn't paying all of the rent, but Margo is offering to pay half. She's up to something."

"I'm thinking that we shouldn't go to Moscow too soon. How can we be sure that Anna has really left the country? I mean, what can we believe in that ransom note?" Alex said. "You think these thugs get an award for honesty?" He typed, paused, and typed again. "Every night, in the dark, I look up and see Anna's face and I think about that note. It would be hell in Moscow, waiting and not being sure. We'll travel days before the date on the ransom note, not weeks. I want to feel sure that she's there before I get on a plane."

Fred walked over to Alex and put his hands on Alex's shoulders, then leaned over and kissed the top of his head. Fred rubbed Alex's shoulders and heaved a heavy sigh.

"So," Fred said, turning to Susan, "in the midst of all our problems we find that Steve has a sugar daddy. How sweet, a wealthy admirer investing money in his toys. That's how he affords the rent. I'm not surprised, Steve *is* really cute."

"Cute, but not my type," Fred quickly added. "And that snake in the basement wants to get into his second-floor apartment . . . closer to you."

Susan brought dessert to the table and said, "I got this recipe for blueberries in couscous on the Internet. What do you think?"

Fred took a spoonful, scrunched his nose, then said, "I think we should feed the rest to Margo. Thank you for dinner, Susan."

Alex shook his head. "Margo on the second floor. That's really scary. She has her eye on you, Susan." Alex collected the dishes, brought them to the kitchen and began to wash. "She must have seen us bring The Big Brown Bag up to your apartment."

"Thanks for dinner, Susan. It was great," Fred said. "Alex, as soon as you're finished, let's work on flight reservations."

"Sorry about the dessert," Susan said, then wiped the table, stood for a moment with her arms wrapped around her chest. "And now back to my perch above the den of the beast." Fred hugged Susan, then planted a light kiss on her cheek.

Alex put away the clean dishes, went to the laptop computer, then typed and clicked. "Delta has nonstop flights. We might pick one of those." He leaned back and with a light kiss on Susan's cheek. "Yeah, thanks for dinner; it was delicious."

Two days later, Susan sat at her front window looking down at the street below and watched an elegant black BMW convertible slowly drive by. It was nice to see a classy tourist in her neighborhood.

An older man got out of the BMW and walked quickly toward her building. As he turned to the front steps, she thought that he must be Harry Peterson.

Susan pressed her face to the window so she could see closer to the building. As the man climbed the first couple of steps, she saw Margo pop up from the basement stairs. There was an interchange and the man hurried up the stairs. She heard the front door slam shut and the sound of quick footfalls on the stairs. She peeked down as Margo slowly walked back to her apartment with a contented swagger.

Susan walked to her kitchen thinking about what she saw. She mindlessly opened her refrigerator, slammed it shut, then thought that she needed to get out of there.

CINCO DE MAYO

MANHATTAN, MAY 5

ALONE IN HER apartment, Susan put down her cup of tea, then ambled over to the dumbwaiter. She looked at the door, crossed her arms and thought about opening it to see if the decoy was still there. Thinking it was better not to jinx the setup, she turned away and started to walk back to the kitchen. A whining creak came from the dumbwaiter, so she went back as quietly as possible, then gently opened the dumbwaiter and looked inside. Her eyes were drawn to the light coming from below. Susan peeked down through decades of cobwebs and saw the light at the very bottom. *Who else had their door open?* For a few moments she stared down the dusty shaft, then gently closed the door, leaving it open a crack.

Later that morning, while she was reading, there was a soft ringing echoing from the dumbwaiter. She gently placed the book on the floor and walked to the dumbwaiter. Margo answered in Russian, so she backed away and threw her hands up to her face, then quietly slipped her iPhone from her pocket and started recording. The tone of Margo's speech varied from calm to creepy, with long periods of silence followed by an occasional *da* (yes) and sometimes *nyet* (no). The conversation went on for several minutes until she heard Margo say *do zavtra* ('til tomorrow) and then the conversation stopped. Susan slowly closed the dumbwaiter door, stopped recording, then slipped her phone into a pocket, dashed out her door, down the stairs, and fast-walked a short way down the street, her fingers twitching as she dialed Fred.

"Hi, Fred. Yeah, crappy Cinco de Mayo to you, too. Something is going on here. Margo has her dumbwaiter propped open, probably a venting event. It was so weird, I had to leave the apartment. Is Alex there? There was more Russian conversation. Alex needs to hear this."

"Did you get anything?"

"Why bother? It's all in Russian f'crissakes!"

"Alex is here. Come on up."

Susan rang the doorbell and was instantly buzzed in. She bolted in and dashed up the stairs, finding the apartment door open and Fred waiting with Alex.

"Let's hear it," Alex said.

Susan sat on the sofa with Fred and Alex on either side and played the recording. Partway through the recording, Alex stood up and put his hand to his mouth.

When it was finished, Alex said, "Margo is promising to get something at any cost—I assume it's the music. And then she promises to take out the trash. *Vynesti musor* means take out the trash. It's a gangster idiom in Russia. It means, well, get rid of people, like murder."

"You sure of that?" Susan said.

"Russian *is* my native language," Alex said, then dropped back down onto the sofa. "I just hope that *we* aren't the trash."

"But we are," Fred said. "Did you get anything else?"

"She said in a couple of different ways that she would take her time and do it right."

Fred got up from the sofa, went to the kitchen and returned with three cans of soda. He sat across from Susan and Alex and said, "Don't erase that recording. It's freaky in itself, but considering what's been going on, it's terrifying. You've got to record anything that you can, Susan. It might come in handy later on to have a record of this." He sat down and popped the tab on his soda, then put it down on the table.

"Do you think there's a connection with Margo and Anna?" Alex said.

"Holy shit," Fred said, then picked up his soda and took a gulp. "Is it possible that Margo kidnapped Anna, or is at least part of the plan?"

"Never mentioned. In all the conversations that we've heard, she never heard her say anything about Anna," Alex said. "I've listened for any reference to kidnapping. All we know for sure is that she's involved with the music."

"And she thinks that I've got it," Susan said, then reached for her can of soda. "Why else would she be farting around with Steve?"

Alex said, "I don't think she really knows anything, for sure. As long as Margo doesn't get her hands on the music, we're safe. If she does, we're dead."

Susan leaned back and said, "That's something. And on a different note, I got an invite slipped under the door this morning for a party in Steve's apartment tonight. I'm sure everyone in the building has been invited. I think we should go."

"Wait a second," Alex said. "If everyone in the building is there, that must include Margo. We could slip down and look through her apartment. Who knows what we'd find, maybe something about Anna."

"Are you out of your mind? Breaking and entering? Do we need something else on our plates at this point?" Fred said.

"Hold on," Susan said, then stood up and walked around the room. "I like it. But how would you get into Margo's apartment?"

Alex said, "That's less of a problem than you think. I have a friend, Dmitri, who can enter a locked door like it was wide open. I've seen him do it."

"Alex!" Fred said.

"Okay, but I wasn't involved. He brags about it all the time," Alex said. "I think it's worth the risk, even though the risk is, well, deadly."

Susan went back upstairs, stood in front of the dumbwaiter door and stared at it. She rolled up a magazine, and used it to prop the door open a crack. She pulled the club chair closer to the door so that she could hear what was going on while she read on her iPad in the dark.

She couldn't see the decoy, but the magazine sticking out of the dumbwaiter reminded her that they were the hunted. She got up from her chair, listened closely with her ear against the open crack and heard nothing. A musty draft drove her away and she plopped back into the chair, listening and thinking about the craft of the shaft.

An hour later, Susan dozed off, curled in her comfy chair.

A short while later, a voice resonated up the shaft that sounded like Margo speaking Russian. She picked up her iPhone and started recording. Street noises, squeaks of tinny trumpets and the beat of shallow drums through her kitchen window annoyed Susan, so she marched to the kitchen and slammed the window shut. Worried that the loud bang could echo to the open dumbwaiter, she walked back to her chair, squirmed a bit and, convinced that the tone had not changed, went back to the kitchen window and sat on the sill. Feeling alone with strange voices beaming into her apartment, Susan went to her bedroom, closed the door and waited. When the conversation coming from the dumbwaiter shaft ended, she picked up her phone, stopped recording, then called Fred.

She whispered, "I'm going crazy here. I'm getting foreign languages through the dumbwaiter and all kinds of annoying sounds coming from outside, as if a piñata of trumpeters opened up and littered the neighborhood. And on top of that, odd things from downstairs are happening. Something is going on here. You should be over here with me to get it."

Susan went to the window and opened it once again to let some fresh air in as someone in a faraway crowd whooped out, "*Olé!*"

A while later, Susan buzzed the front door and waited with her door open to welcome both Fred and Alex. Happy to have someone else in her apartment, she softly said, "Margo is freaking me out. It's better if Alex hears it directly."

They listened at the dumbwaiter door for a minute, then Susan pulled the magazine tube out and let it close. "Wouldn't you know it, she's gone now. I guess you came over for nothing."

"Do you think that she's eavesdropping on *us*? Maybe she wants to see what we're up to?" Fred said.

"The next time her dumbwaiter door is open, let's announce plans to be away and see what she does," Susan said. "Have a cup of tea. She'll be open for business soon."

"Are you crazy? If we corner her like that, she could gun us down," Alex said.

"But she doesn't have the music. That's our safeguard," Fred said.

About a half hour later, Susan heard creaking coming from the dumbwaiter, lifted her head and said, "Here she is."

They walked over to the dumbwaiter, opened the door and looked down to see the light in the shaft, then stepped back.

"How about going out to the movies this afternoon?" Fred asked. "There's an afternoon showing of an early Woody Allen movie at the library."

"Great, let's do it. We'll have to rush over now to make it."

Then quietly closed the dumbwaiter door. They walked out and into the hallway, then went down the stairs chatting loudly as they walked out the front door, then tiptoed back up as stealthily as possible and reentered Susan's apartment. She slowly closed the door, locked it and they sat down on the sofa together.

They waited silently.

After half an hour, Fred leaned forward and quietly said, "This is stupid, nothing's gonna happen."

Susan pushed Fred back. He closed his eyes and slumped in his seat.

About forty-five minutes later, a scratching sound came from the apartment door. Susan grabbed Fred's arm and pointed to the door. Fred was about to speak, but Susan put her finger to her lips and Fred nodded. She got up, quietly walked to the door and stood still as the scratching continued. Fred and Alex got up and waited behind her. As the doorknob slowly turned, Susan grabbed it and yanked it open. Margo stood there with a stunned look and her mouth open.

"Oh. Ahhh, glad to see you're home. I thought I smelled smoke and thought I should see if there was any danger. I guess all's okay." Margo shrugged, nodded awkwardly and then dashed down the stairs.

Susan shut the door and locked it. "I guess we won't be seeing her up here again."

"She's a scary piece of work. Now it's our turn," Alex said. "Let's figure out what we're gonna do tonight. I can get Dmitri over here in short order."

"Here's the plan," Susan said. "I'll slip down with Alex. Fred, you stay with the party. If you see Margo getting ready to leave, text message me on your iPhone. We'll get out in plenty of time."

"I think that you should stay with Margo," Fred said. "You can stall her better if there's a problem. I'll have a text ready to go and signal back that I got your tip-off."

"But Susan, you'll have to stay close to Margo while we're downstairs," Alex said. "You can't let her out of your sight."

"Don't forget to take pictures," Susan said.

Alex slipped out his phone and running his fingers over the screen, said, "I'm getting Dmitri to come over."

After Fred and Alex left, Susan stood in front of the dumbwaiter door fighting the urge to open it and listen. Then she heard a ringing telephone echo from the dumbwaiter.

Later that evening, Susan waited outside the brownstone for Fred and Alex so she could accompany them to Steve's apartment for the Cinco de Mayo party. She watched people start to trickle in, some of them glancing at her and nodding.

It was nearly eight o'clock when Susan saw Fred and Alex ambling toward her building with a young man with dark hair and a square jaw she assumed was Dmitri. Susan waved excitedly and walked toward them to greet them for the party.

"Judging from the crowd that already arrived, I can see that this is going to be interesting," Susan said.

When they entered the building, she said, "Wait 'til you see it. Margo's greeting the guests at the door to the apartment, oozing her brand of hospitality like a cake-decorating bag exudes buttercream laced with venom. Scary, huh?"

Trailing on Fred's heels, Alex said, "I hope that our plan tonight works out. I can't wait to get some info on Anna, although I'm kind of afraid of what we might find."

Fred turned to Alex and softly said, "Now I feel like we're doing something."

Once inside Steve's apartment, Susan, Fred and Alex stood in the archway between the living room and the kitchen and observed everything.

"I'm not in the mood for any of this, but I don't want to retreat into the woodwork either," Susan said. "Look at the loads of food everyone's brought."

Susan studied the first-floor tenants, Jane and David, as they unloaded a few bottles of tequila onto the kitchen counter. Susan overheard Jane say to David, "Do you think anyone will know if I just dumped my homemade caponata from a jar?"

Margo walked to the kitchen and walked past Fred and toward Dave as she said, "Hi, good to see you again. It's been a long time."

Jane frowned as she turned to Dave and said, "You know that troll?"

Dave said, "Are you kidding?"

Fred nudged his elbow into Susan's ribs as he pointed to a pair of men wearing sequined bolero jackets who had entered with a flare. "Look at that pair."

"They're a scream," Susan said, followed with a loud, "Hah."

The two danced their way over to Susan and said, "Hi, I'm Michael, he's Russ; we're friends of Steve. Olé. And you?"

"I'm Susan and this is—"

"Here's where the party is." Margo appeared out of nowhere and grabbed Michael and Russ's arms and pulled them away. She joined their hands, spun them onto the dance floor and vanished as quickly as she appeared.

As Michael and Russ pranced around the floor, Susan said to Fred, "What was that? And look, Harry seems to have noticed Margo's behavior and looks more annoyed than I am."

Susan poked Fred and nodded toward Margo, who exuberantly greeted each guest as they entered.

"Is she playing the hostess?" Susan whispered as Harry extended his hand to an arriving guest and Margo silently slipped in between with a welcoming smile. "It's his party. I should get over to her and pretend to be a collaborator so we can join at the hip while you . . . y'know what."

"Geez," Fred said, "now's the time to tie yourself to Margo."

Harry turned back and forth with short, deep breaths.

His cheeks were getting red. Susan pinched Fred's elbow and whispered, "He's not taking this well, is he? Okay, wish me luck. It's Margo and me against the world."

"Alex, Susan's just attached herself to Margo," Fred said. "We should start moving."

"Just a sec, I'm taking some pics of Margo in action. I think we should have some documentation," Alex said as he lowered his iPhone to his waist, looked down and tapped the screen. He slipped it into his pocket and said, "Let's do it."

Fred caught Susan's eye as Susan subtly nodded. She started talking to Margo, turning her away from the door.

Fred and Alex scooted down the stairs and out the front door, where Dmitri was waiting. Dmitri reached into his pocket and pulled out an array of odd-looking rods. They went down the basement with Dmitri and watched him insert one rod, then another into the keyhole. In less than twenty seconds, he pushed the door open a crack, looked back at Fred and Alex with a subtle grin, then pushed the door fully open.

"I wait across street to lock," Dmitri whispered.

Alex and Fred entered the dark apartment and locked the door behind them. "Use your iPhone flashlight?" Fred said.

Alex paused with his light shining on the dumbwaiter door. It was held ajar by a rolled up newspaper. Fred whispered, "C'mon, there's nothing we can do about that now. C'mon."

They walked to a large bedroom in the back of the apartment that had a desk and two file cabinets along the left wall with a single bed at the far wall. On one side of the bed was a nightstand squeezed between the bed and a closet door, on the other a dresser. Except for a computer screen and keyboard, the desk was covered with stacks of paper with some stacks neatly piled on the floor nearby. A printer was on the floor next to the desk.

"What a mess," Fred said. "We have to look fast."

Fred carefully sifted through stacks of papers on the floor. "Here's some in Russian. Alex, come over here."

Alex carefully thumbed through a pile of papers on the desk. "Holy shit! These are invoices, in Russian. Most are for one

Moscow address."

"What do you mean by *most?*" Fred said.

Alex picked up a notebook and flipped through the pages. "She has a few years of notes here about different jobs she's worked. It's like a diary for the Russian Mafia." He took several pictures with his iPhone. "Here are some recent entries for April. She has notes about, 'the target located in the brownstone,' as she puts it." Alex turned to Fred holding up the notebook, "She's targeting Susan for the music."

Fred started looking through drawers in the nightstand. The top drawer was filled with neatly arranged red and green boxes. He carefully lifted one of the boxes labeled *Lillier & Bellot .45 Auto* and had pictures of bullets on the side. He whispered, "Hey Alex, holy shit, here's a drawer full of ammo. My god, 45-caliber, this is serious stuff. Now I understand what 'taking out the trash' means."

He laid the box on its side, photographed it, then carefully put it back and photographed the open drawer. There was one worn box labeled *TulAmmo, Made in Russia.* Fred picked the box up and showed it to Alex.

Alex came over and looked at the open drawer, photographed it as well, then closed the drawer. "We should get outta here."

"Not yet." Fred went to the computer on the desk and touched a key. The screen lit. He tried a few simple passwords. The login screen never changed.

"Fred, we gotta go."

As Harry came from the kitchen smiling with a tray of hors d'oeuvres, Margo lifted the tray from his hands and passed it to Jane, who served the guests. Harry took a deep breath and tightened his fists, then went back into the kitchen.

Susan said, "Margo, this is a really good party, but Harry seems to be having a not-so-good time."

Harry looked out at the crowd from the empty kitchen.

"He's fine," Margo said and walked away from Susan.

Susan kept a grip on her iPhone.

Steve started some Mariachi music, then someone yelled,

"Conga line!"

Susan grinned as one guest put a large, outlandishly decorated sombrero on Harry's head, and for the first time she saw Harry beam with a broad smile. The conga line merrily progressed around the apartment with Margo breaking into the line with her ungainly limp, pushing Harry behind her while Susan sat and watched the clock on the wall. A quarter of an hour passed and they weren't back.

Margo coughed a few times, moved toward the apartment door, looked back, then opened the door.

Susan grabbed for her iPhone and texted Fred.

NOW

She waited for a response.

Nothing.

She sent a text message again.

No return message.

Susan looked up as Margo left the apartment and headed for the stairs. She ran over to Margo and said, "Margo, wait, I wanted to talk to you about . . . about, oh, rent increases."

"Later," Margo said as she headed down the stairs.

"No, we have to talk now, because tomorrow—"

"Not now," Margo said, looking Susan straight in the eye, then turning and continuing down the stairs with her uneven step.

Susan stayed close behind Margo, trying to keep a credible distance. She fumbled with her iPhone and hit the message button again and texted, *xxx!!!*

At the landing, Margo turned and stared at Susan.

Susan said, "I really need a breath of fresh air."

She followed Margo out the front door and paced on the sidewalk as Margo followed the basement steps.

Margo's phone rang. "What now?" she said, then answered, speaking fast and indistinctly.

Susan texted again.

"Alex, the door," Fred said. He looked at his iPhone, which showed that there was no service. "Shit, there's no cell service in the basement."

Alex and Fred turned off their lights and moved toward the back of the bedroom. The front door creaked open as Fred quickly pointed to the closet. They pressed into a closet as deep as they could while Margo said, "Gotta go now, I'll lose reception in a second. Yeah, yeah, yeah. *Do zavtra.*"

The apartment door slammed shut, then there were Margo's limping steps on the floor followed by a brief sound of water running.

Fred peeked out the closet door and noticed the computer screen. It was brightly lit. He tightened his lips. Then it timed out and went dark.

Lights were turned on in the bedroom, shining under the closet door and making the floor in the tight space glow. Fred held Alex tight and tried not to breathe. It was hot and there was an oppressive stink of mothballs.

Margo shuffled around the apartment, slammed some drawers, then there was silence. Just outside the closet door, the bed springs creaked, then there was the sound of papers being shuffled.

Fred closed his eyes and pictured Margo sitting just a few feet away.

There was more movement away from the closet, then there was knocking and Susan called out, "Margo, Harry wants to talk to you."

"Yeah, I'll be right up," Margo said, "Tell him to hold his horses."

Fred held Alex tight in the closet and barely breathed. The noxious smell of mothballs triggered the urge to cough, but Fred bit his lip, pressed his eyes shut tighter and tried to hold his breath.

"Okay," Susan yelled.

The light under the closet went black, then there was Margo's distinct footsteps heading away from them, then the door to the apartment opened and slammed shut.

"Let's get out of here," Alex said, pushing open the closet door.

They turned on their flashlight apps and headed for the door.

"Wait," Fred said, "She left her cell phone on the dresser, and it's still unlocked."

He grabbed the phone, then went to her call log. All her phone calls were in the US. He moved to her photos and saw pictures of buildings, then noticed a few pictures of Anna's shop. He showed the pictures to Alex, whose eyes grew wide, then he wiped the screen and carefully placed it back where he'd found it.

They ran out of the apartment and into the street, where Dmitri was waiting.

"I can lock door now?'

In Steve's apartment, Alex walked up to Susan and said, "Would you like a drink?"

"Thank God," Susan said, grabbing Alex by the shoulders and hugging him.

"You did good," Alex said.

"Let's go," Susan said.

They said goodbye to Steve, thanking him for the invite, and walked upstairs to Susan's apartment.

Once inside, Susan said, "Well, what did you get?"

"From the ammo stashed in her drawer, we can say that she's got a serious gun somewhere. Outside of that, we found nothing about Anna," Fred said.

Alex dropped on the couch and lied down. He closed his eyes and yawned.

"Wait here with me. This evening ain't over yet," Susan said. She wedged a book into the door of the apartment so that it was slightly open. "Not enough to be obvious, but we can hear."

"Susan, it's after midnight. I'm getting ready to call it a night," Fred said, pointing to Alex, who was spread out on the sofa.

"Wait a bit. The only ones left in the apartment are Margo, Steve and Harry," Susan said. "A toxic brew. Just wait."

A door slammed, reverberating through the stairwell. There were shuffling.

"What was that," Fred asked.

"Someone's hanging out in the hallway," Susan said.

"You ugly little bitch," Harry called out. "You think that smile is teasing me? I'm gonna—"

"It sounds like he's going to explode," Susan whispered, then leaned toward the door.

Margo screamed, "Harry, you dampened the spirit of the party by being there!"

Harry yelled, "It's you, you fuckin' bitch you, you—"

"Well then, fuck you," Margo snarled.

Harry stomped down the stairs and slammed the front door to the building, reverberating longer than Fred thought possible.

Then, in muffled voice, Margo said, "Drop dead. I can't wait."

Alex lifted his head from the arm of the sofa. "What's going on? Have we heard anything more about Anna?"

CRYPTIC HANDWRITING

MANHATTAN, MAY 6

WITH HIS HEAD in his palm and both elbows on the kitchen counter, Fred scanned the articles as he flipped through the morning newspaper. Then he noticed the headline, *Man Killed on Taconic Parkway*. His heart skipped a beat when he saw the name *Harry Peterson*. He couldn't believe it. He stared at the page and imagined the ghostly glow of Harry holding a tray of hors d'oeuvres. He took a deep breath.

Alex walked out of the bedroom and looked over at Fred. "Is everything okay?"

Fred spread the newspaper out on the counter. "Alex, look at this. My God, Harry Peterson was killed on the Taconic Parkway last night. He crashed into an abutment."

Alex walked closer and looked over Fred's shoulder. "The guy from the party last night? Holy shit."

Fred's phone rang.

Fred picked up the phone and said, "Sue, listen to this, Harry's dead, a car accident. The paper says there was one witness."

Susan shouted, "What?"

Fred leaned over the newspaper and read, "A witness said that he swerved to avoid hitting a car crossing in front of him. The witness said he was driving erratically."

"I was just dancing with him. What the hell is going on? Should I come over? This is giving me the creeps."

"Come on over. We should talk about this," Fred said.

"Give me a few minutes."

Fred hung up the phone and turned to Alex. "Susan's coming over. She shouldn't be alone right now."

"Good, you can talk about Harry with her. I've got to go over to Anna's shop to see that everything's all right there. I'll be back in a few hours."

"Probably not a bad idea. Don't stay too long," Fred said then walked over to Alex and gave him a hug. "We'll go out for dinner."

"I'll grab a light lunch in Brooklyn, I need some time alone," Alex said. "Do you think Harry was part of Margo's trash to be taken out?"

Fred blew a kiss across the room. Alex smiled and returned the kiss, then waved and quietly closed the door.

Fred stood poised by the door, buzzed Susan as soon as the doorbell rang, and left the apartment door slightly ajar.

Out of breath, Susan flung the door open and said, "I just had the strangest interaction with Margo."

"Really?"

"Yeah, she was standing outside my building as if she was waiting for someone. I just gave her a polite hello, trying to maintain my momentum."

"Momentum, very important," Fred said.

"She couldn't believe that poor Harry, as she put it, was driving so fast after drinking so much."

"Our world is getting strange," Fred said.

Susan said, "I thought he didn't drink, at least that's what he said when I offered to get him one at the party."

"She creeps me out," Susan said. "Where did Alex go?"

"He goes out to Brooklyn every other day to check on Anna's place to make sure it doesn't look abandoned. This is killing him, but he's been acting pretty brave about the whole thing. Let's go out to get some lunch. I need some air."

The next evening, Susan slid her comfy chair next to the dumbwaiter, propped the door open and sat back with a copy of *Trouble in Flatbush*. After a while, she was on the verge of falling asleep when she heard some noise emanating from the dumbwaiter. Susan leaned forward and slowly got up from the chair.

Margo's voice rattled up the shaft. "Yeah, Monday—I have full access now. No, I'm not giving up my apartment."

Really, Susan thought, *access to the main part of the building.*

After a pause, Margo said. "*Vy poluchite paket v svoye vremya.* Yes, of course, you'll get the package in due time. I'll pay his whole rent if I have to."

Susan put her hand on her forehead. *Fred isn't going to believe this phone conversation.*

Margo's voice rattled up the dumbwaiter shaft a bit muffled, but understandable. "It'll work. I'm paying half the rent; he has no other choice now. *Eto proizoydet v blizhaysheye vremya.* Soon." There was a lengthy pause, then she said, "*Do zavtra*" ('til tomorrow).

Silence.

Susan shook her head as she sat back down and wondered how Steve could give her the keys to his apartment, then she got a chill from the back of her neck to her toes.

She phoned Fred. "Fred, I can't stand being so close to that troll, but I'm afraid to let her out of my sight. And, by the way, all is well with the you-know-what."

Susan glanced at some books on the shelf, grabbed them and set out for the library. She saw Margo on the street talking to Alex and slowed her walk to hear as best she could. Alex looked agitated, trying to break away.

"Y'know, Alex," Margo said, holding on to Alex's shirt at the elbow and raising her voice. "Steve has an interest in Fred, and from what I've seen, the feeling is mutual."

Alex shrugged and tried to politely pull away from her grasp.

"I thought you and Fred were a couple. Maybe not for long."

"What?" Alex said. "Look, I've got better things to do than—"

"If I were to say more, I might be interfering, but I'm not the kind of person to gossip."

Alex looked stunned. He jerked his sleeve and without saying another word, pulled away from Margo and marched briskly away.

Margo turned and walked toward Susan. Susan slipped around the corner, but looked back and saw Margo grin as she walked away. Susan mouthed, *That bitch.*

Susan pulled out her phone, and tapped her thumb on the screen. "Hey, Fred. Yeah, me again. You wouldn't believe what I just overheard. That limping gnome is at it again."

Alex urgently unlocked the front door, dashed across the hallway and swung around the bannister railing and up the stairs to Fred's apartment. He flung open the door to the apartment and walked over to Fred, who was sitting on the sofa.

"I can't decide if everything is going to shit, or I just don't know what," he said, then dropped into the soft chair next to Fred.

"What?" Fred said.

"This letter was waiting with the mail at the shop. I can't fuckin' believe it. Here, read it," Alex said as he threw the envelope at Fred.

Fred slid the paper out of the envelope and studied the writing.

Do what they want and everything will be as good as Putin.
Anna.

Under that sentence, in a different jagged penmanship, it said, *This is not game. Do not play with Anna's life.*

"What is this?" Fred said as he looked over the envelope. "It's postmarked Newfoundland. *Newfoundland?* Wait, let me look at a map."

"Better yet, let me use your laptop," Alex said. "They've got to be traveling by boat." He opened the laptop and started typing. In a few moments, he said, "I found a web site called *Shipfinder* that shows all merchant ships and stuff about them. I think I have several ships that Anna might be on. They're off the coast of Newfoundland and headed for the Gulf of Finland. I bet one is heading to some small port in Russia. It makes sense, they don't have to go through St. Petersburg customs to get to Moscow."

"Wow," Fred said, "that explains a lot. Now we know why they're giving us such a long time to get to Russia."

Alex slumped deeper into his chair. "First of all, it means that they're heading to Moscow on the standard route by way of the Gulf of Finland and they stopped in Newfoundland. So they're about a third of the way there. I bet they go through that tiny port town, *Sestroretsk.*"

"Okay, we figured that they would go by boat," Fred said, giving the letter back to Alex.

Alex closed the laptop, stood up and went to the kitchen window. "Second, that is definitely Anna's scrawl, but she doesn't write that kind of stuff. This shit about 'as good as Putin' is not the sort of thing she would say. All the way back, I thought about that."

"I know," Fred said, pacing to the kitchen then back to the living room. "She's mentioned Putin a few times. She doesn't like him."

"Like? Like? She hates him, blames him for what made us move here in the first place. There's something there."

"So what does she mean?" Fred said.

"I don't know," Alex said, holding the letter up to the light as if there might be more to see.

"Just a sec," Fred said, opening the laptop and typing quickly. "What was that website that tracks merchant ships? We'll find which ones left New York recently."

"Shipfinder.com," Alex said. "It should still be there, in the browser."

"Yeah, here it is, the entire fleet of merchant ships and we can track where they are and where they're going. Pretty impressive."

"Find a ship headed toward Russia from New York that recently passed Newfoundland," Alex said, breathing down Fred's neck.

"There are too many ships to be sure which one. I'm afraid we won't know anything more by doing this. Most of them make lots of stops. All it explains is why it takes weeks to get to Moscow.

Anyway, what would we do if we did identify the ship?"

Alex backed away. "We could call the Coast Guard and tell them about a kidnapping."

"And what if the kidnappers thought it was better to dump Anna off the ship rather than be arrested? How much better off would we be then?" Fred said. "Maybe they'll do that anyway." Fred breathed deeply, then leaned forward and closed his eyes. "How horrible."

"My world is going to shit and that's what you have to say?" Alex said as his eyes filled with tears. "Is that what you want?" He picked up the note from Anna, looked at it tenderly and then walked to the door.

"No, Alex, you're upset for no reason. You don't understand—"

"Maybe I do," Alex said. "Maybe you should talk to Steve about it. I'm going back to Brooklyn."

Alex slammed the door shut behind him.

Fred ran to the door and yelled, "No!"

The outside door slammed, so he grabbed his phone and dialed Alex. When voicemail picked up, he hung up.

Two hours passed and Fred could not stay in his apartment replaying the look on Alex's face as he stormed out, so he dragged himself downstairs and meandered about the neighborhood with his hands in his pockets and hoped Alex would call. He desperately wanted to explain the misunderstanding to Alex, but was also afraid that repeated attempts would make things worse. But what else could he do? As it was, he had no idea why Alex would behave in such a way.

Two days passed and Fred still hadn't heard from Alex. He wanted to know more about Anna's note and was pained over his last interaction with Alex. When the phone rang, Fred ran to the phone, ready to say *Hi, Alex,* but one glance at caller ID and he calmed down. It was Susan. He picked up.

"I haven't talked to you in a couple of days. The drama over here continues. Margo and Steve are not the happy couple. Not surprising, Steve doesn't need Margo."

"That's not my problem. I can't get ahold of Alex."

"What does that mean?"

"Oh, I haven't heard from him since he marched out. I don't know what to do. I'm lonely, worried about Anna and feel lost. Is your part of the world any better?"

"That *is* my world. Do we have anything more to go on about Anna?"

"Not much."

"This is torture," Susan said. "I feel drained. Do you mind if I come over just to hang out and read? I won't be a bother."

"Of course. It would lighten my spirits. Seeya in a bit."

Susan arrived a short time later with a book, dropped in the club chair and said, "You can ignore me if you want. I'm quite used to that."

Fred said, "Let me make some tea. I got some really great cookies at Ferraro's in Little Italy yesterday."

They sat at the kitchen table, sipping tea and sampling cookies. Fred said, "Worrying about Anna is even more trying with Alex not around."

"I know. And what's the story with Steve?"

Alex walked up the street toward Fred's apartment with his hand in his pocket, his fingers wrapped tightly around the key to Fred's apartment. He opened the street door and walked lethargically up the stairs. He paused at the door and heard Fred speaking.

"Steve is putting the make on me. He calls on occasion for no particular reason. The conversation is something like, 'Hey, It's Steve. I wanted to ask you some things. Can I come over?' and then it's up to me."

"That's a bit awkward," Susan said.

Alex leaned toward the door to hear a bit better.

"I'd rather not have him near me. The whole thing is unsettling."

Susan said, "Maybe Steve just needs a friend. If he wasn't gay, I'd step in to be that friend."

"I feel like my life is in a downward spiral and the worst part is that I feel the same for Alex. I would love to convince Alex that this Steve thing is nothing, but I don't think he would believe me."

Alex leaned against the doorjamb and pressed his ear against the door.

Fred said, "Yesterday, Steve called. He reminded me who he was, like I needed that. His sink wasn't working, so he said, and he couldn't reach the landlord. 'Could you come over to take a look at it?' he said."

"Did you go over?" Susan said.

"He whined about how I know how to deal with that kind of thing."

"So?"

"He was begging. He said he was desperate and kept pleading. I felt sorry for him."

"I'm afraid to ask what happened."

"I went over and started to look at the fittings, then Steve put the make on me."

Alex's eyes widened.

"He made his move, so I pulled away and left before he went further."

Susan said, "Did anything happen?"

"Not exactly."

Alex jammed his key in to the lock and flung open the door.

"Alex, where have you been? I'm so happy that you're here. I was worried sick about you," Fred said.

"No, where have *you* been?" Alex said as he entered.

Fred said, "Just helping a tenant in Susan's house fix some plumbing."

"You mean Steve?" Alex shot back.

"Yeah, he called, I went and fixed it and that was that," Fred said, uneasily. "Why do you ask?"

Susan backed away and sat on a bar stool at the kitchen counter.

"I saw Steve on the street a couple of days ago. He waved and said, 'How's Fred', and then grinned like something was going on between you two. It was like a slap in the face," Alex said as he turned away from Fred.

"Alex," Fred said, spreading his arms toward Alex.

Alex backed off and turned. "I could read Steve's arrogant face like a book."

"No, Alex. It's not like that."

Alex said, "With all that is going on with Anna, this is what you do to me? Now is when I need you . . . I need you the most and now is when . . . oh, fuck off. I need some space. I can do this myself." He walked toward the door.

Susan shouted, "Wait."

Fred said, "Alex, no. I didn't do anything wrong." Fred approached Alex, but Alex turned his head away, then dropped it and stared at the floor.

Susan said, "Stop it! Can't you see what's happening? Margo is using Steve to split us up. If she can wedge in using Steve, she can deal with us one at a time. Sneaky, huh?"

"You're right. Alex, listen to Susan."

Alex mumbled, "Fred and Steve. You want to put that on Margo?"

"Don't you think that she's bought Steve by paying his rent, or at least part of it?" Susan said,

"I don't know, but I don't trust her. She's lethal and we have to stick together." Fred said.

Alex lifted his head, then got up and walked out the door.

Susan gave Fred a hug, then said, "Give him a little time. He feels helpless now. It'll all be okay."

At dinnertime, Fred opened the refrigerator to find something to eat. He stood staring at the shelves for a moment, then he closed the refrigerator and went back to his chair. He held his phone and selected Alex from his contact list but never called. He didn't know what to say.

The next day, the phone on the kitchen wall rang and Fred ran to answer it hoping it was Alex. He enthusiastically answered the phone, "Hello? Al—"

"It's me, Steve."

Fred pulled the phone away from his face, wanting to slam it down. He looked at the phone and heard Steve faintly babbling. He put the phone back to his ear and started to speak, but then quietly hung up the phone. He thought, this business is toxic. He didn't want to be part of it.

Walking to dinner that evening with Susan, he said, "It wasn't that long ago that I thought I would never find a soul mate."

"I know. Every time I meet a nice guy that word, soul mate, pops into my mind. Then it trickles away into nothing."

"But I've found my soul mate," Fred said. They turned the corner. "Now, with everything happening, it's falling apart. I want to strangle Margo and Steve."

"A soul mate . . . precious, don't let yours fade away."

They walked to the next street and stopped for a traffic signal. Susan said, "And I've got Margo, Steve and Harry's ghost—I don't like it that Margo can be in the apartment right below me whenever she wants."

"All I want is to be sitting at a table having tea with Anna, Alex and you. Will things ever be right? I'm not sure I know how to laugh anymore," Fred said.

They entered the restaurant, sat down and Susan reached across the table and put her hand on Fred's. They had dinner, then Fred walked Susan back to her building and he returned to his apartment.

Later that evening, alone in his apartment, Fred stood in the bathroom looking at the medicine cabinet that concealed the package of music and had the dispiriting thought that if there was anything good about the whole mess, meeting Anna, discovering Alex, it had vanished. He looked at his reflection and thought about how tired he looked. *Could it be possible to lose Alex over a silly misunderstanding?* He lowered his head to the sink and let warm water flow over his hair and over his face.

Fred meandered into the bedroom. The apartment felt small and stale. He grabbed his phone, his keys and dashed out of the apartment. Without thinking of a direction, he just walked. Although the street was crowded, it felt empty and purposeless.

Alex sat in the rear of the antique shop in Brooklyn with his head in his hands and his elbows in the kitchen table. If Margo could be responsible for Harry's death, what else could she do? Alex stood up, took a deep breath and pulled out his iPhone. He texted Fred:

Sorry for the rant the other day. I will never let anyone come between us. Fuck Steve, fuck Margo. I love you.

Alex closed up the shop and was lumbering toward the subway when he got a text from Fred:

I love you more than you know. I need a hug.

Alex quickened his pace.

Coming out of the subway in Manhattan, Alex took a deep breath and looked up at the sky, which seemed more deeply blue than ever. As he walked from the subway, he saw Steve and greeted him with a wide grin. Steve looked him in the eye and said nothing. It was a beautiful day. He spread his arms and zigzagged on the sidewalk to end of the block. For the first time in a while he felt like things were back on track and that they were going to find Anna.

The May afternoon was warm and Susan felt that the apartment was dreadfully stuffy. As she got ready for the evening out, she walked around the apartment fanning herself with an old *Life* magazine. She opened all the windows a bit, not too much in case of rain. It was cooling off outside with late afternoon breezes starting. Susan glanced at her watch and realized that she had lost track of the time and needed to dash to get ready for her film forum. She rushed to get dressed, thinking about how she did this every Tuesday.

Susan ran down the stairs, out the front door of the building and found Margo sitting on the front steps between her and the sidewalk. Margo smiled. Susan paused for a moment, thinking that Margo surely wouldn't kill her here on the sidewalk, but perhaps might follow her and maybe push her on to the tracks of an approaching subway train. She mumbled, "Excuse me," and walked briskly down the street. She watched the shadows around her wondering if Margo's shadow might appear behind her.

Margo began to vigilantly stalk her prey. She understood Susan's timing from previous Tuesday nights and knew when she would return. Margo watched Susan speed down the street and turn the corner. She reached into her pocket and rattled the keys, then took out the key to the front door and walked inside and up to Steve's apartment. She knocked, even though she knew Steve was at work, then slowly put the key in the lock and entered.

Margo felt the flash of adrenaline peaking and quickly slipped open the window and stepped out onto the fire escape.

SOMETHING NOT RIGHT

MANHATTAN, MAY 14

THERE WAS AN unfamiliar odor at the door of the apartment when Susan arrived home from her film club. She opened the door and warily walked in a couple of steps into the dark apartment. She stepped back to the door, ran her hand along the wall until it landed on the wall switch and hesitated, listening for any sounds. She was about to turn on the lights, but stopped and listened. Nothing. Susan quietly closed the apartment door, then went into the living room and sniffed. The air smelled faintly musky, almost like cologne.

Susan peered into the apartment as far as possible, but with only the glow from a streetlight below, she could see very little. Standing still, she listened for anything unusual, but all she heard were the typical sounds, a creak in the floor, a drip from a faucet. Yet the elusive feeling that her space had been violated persisted.

She kicked off her shoes, then stepped quietly toward the lamp next to sofa, paused, and then turned it on and quickly looked around. Nothing appeared out of place, yet something about the apartment felt wrong. She took off her sweater and threw it on the sofa, then went into the kitchen to make a cup of tea.

She wandered to the bedroom. The room seemed fine, and then she noticed the pillows on the bed. The plum pillows were always lined up against the navy pillows with a pair of tiny, faintly striped pillows against these. She liked to arrange the small pillows with the stripes vertical, but now the stripes were horizontal. Then she noticed that the drawer on the nightstand was slightly open. An eerie feeling came over her.

The teakettle whistled. Susan poured herself a cup and headed toward the dumbwaiter. The door was closed. *That's odd. Thought I left it open.* Sticking her arm inside, she reached up and felt for the package Fred had left. It was gone. Her heart sank. She held her sticky fingers under the light and saw that they were smeared with blood. The burglar must have scratched a finger on a sharp edge and kept on probing.

Oh God, she thought as she rushed into her bathroom, ran some water over her hands. She then grabbed a scarf from her bedroom dresser, wrapped it around her neck, and quickly left her apartment and went to Fred's place.

The doorbell to Fred's apartment chimed rapidly. Before Fred could get to the door buzzer, the phone rang. "It's Susan. I'm downstairs. Buzz me in."

Fred pressed the button to unlock the front door, then said, "Alex, Something's wrong. I hear it in her voice."

Susan bound up the stairs, then grabbed Fred in the hallway and gave him a long, tight hug. They went into the apartment and closed the door. "It happened. The package is gone."

"Holy shit," Alex said, "When?"

"Just now," Susan said as she showed Fred and Alex her wrist, which still had blood on it, then went to the kitchen sink and scrubbed her hands. "It had to have been Margo who broke into my apartment. I can't stay in that building."

"Sit down, Susan," Fred said, giving her another hug. "You poor thing. Try to relax, there's nothing we can do now."

"Now that whoever ransacked my apartment knows that I never had the music, what's the plan? Where is the music anyway?" Susan glanced at Fred and then slowly looked over at Alex. "They'll think that we're playing games, lethal games."

"The real package is in a secure place," Fred said as he went over to the kitchen table and wiped it over and over. "It's fine until we exhume it for the trip."

Alex said, "We've gotta get out of here and get to Moscow."

"A snack would be nice," Susan said.

Alex got to work on Fred's laptop computer.

Fred got right to work at the stove. The aromas of the grilled cheese sandwiches with slices of tomato filled the apartment while Susan and Alex frantically searched for air flights to Moscow.

"We're dashing off to Moscow, assuming Anna was really taken there. How do we know that for sure, taking directions from sickos?" Alex mumbled as he typed. "You think I know what I'm doing? I've never done this before. What's the best website?"

From the kitchen, Fred said, "Try Travelocity, Hotwire and Orbitz."

"I got this, don't worry," Alex said.

Fred shook his head while sprinkling some oregano flakes on the tomatoes, then grabbed the spatula and flipped the grilled cheese. "Just get a direct flight."

"Fred, you certainly know how to cater a crisis," Susan said watching Fred work in the kitchen. She went to refrigerator and brought a Diet Coke to Alex working on the computer. "Here. How's it going?" He took it from her without looking up, opened it and took a straw from Susan, then continued to click the mouse.

Alex continued to suck on the straw long after the soda can was empty. He finally looked up and said, "There're a few choices, but not many nonstop. Aeroflot is cheap, but we might wind up in the ocean."

Fred walked over to Alex with a small bowl of M&Ms, leaned over Alex's shoulder and said, "What choices do we have?"

Susan watched over Alex's shoulder.

"I think we should shoot for May 20th. That would give us a few days to get acclimated before the ransom date," Fred said. "And don't worry about the price, let's just go. I don't want to drag it out on a stopover."

Alex scrolled the flight lists, then said, "We have to get round trip tickets so that we can be sure we have a means to come home no matter what happens."

"Make sure the tickets can be changed if we have to change the date," Susan said. "Who knows when we'll be coming home?"

"Nonstop is more than I expected, about two thousand dollars each, not much better if we use Aeroflot. I don't have that kind of money," Alex said.

"Alex, we're certainly not going to let money be a factor." Fred rubbed Alex's back affectionately while he hovered, and then bent over and placed a light kiss on the back of Alex's neck. "This one's on me."

After about ten minutes of working, Alex announced that the best he could do was to get a pair of tickets for nineteen hundred dollars each, leaving in time to be in Moscow a few days before they were supposed to meet the abductors.

"Book them. I'll get my charge card so that you can get two tickets now."

Susan handed Alex her charge card and said, "Make that three tickets. I'm in this up to my ears. And besides, I'm not staying here alone waiting for my throat to be slit." She sat back down and said. "Split the cost fifty-fifty."

"Wait a minute. There's another problem that we haven't talked about," Alex said. "What do you think happened when the police found Shumka lying in a pool of blood? If they dusted for fingerprints, they would have found that we were there; and as far as fingerprints go, mine are on record. They fingerprinted me when I entered the country, so they have my prints on file."

Fred looked quizzically at Susan, then back at Alex.

"They're going to find my fingerprints at Shumka's," Alex said. "If they haven't already."

"There's a new kink," Susan said.

"This is more than a kink. How am I going to leave the country? And If I do manage to slip out, how can I get back in? I don't have the same passport as you guys. I'll be noticed and snagged immediately."

Alex sat down on the sofa next to Susan and took her hand. "I was checked by customs and immigration when I came here. There's no getting around that fact that I'm in the database."

Susan got up, paced a bit, then moved behind Alex and put her hands on his back. "Everyone's in some database."

Alex slumped on the sofa with a soft moan as his head hung down.

"If the police are looking for you, you'll get red-flagged at the ticket counter," Susan said as she paced with her hand on her chin. "I used to date a guy named John who works for US Trans Airlines. He'll do anything I ask, if I ask properly." Susan walked confidently to her bag, rummaged for a bit, then pulled out a composition book with a black speckled cover. She fumbled through the notebook. "I'll call him and see if he'll book the tickets for us. He owes me big." She mumbled, "Offhand, I can't remember why, but I am sure he remembers. Ahh, here it is, John, I'm sure he'll help us out."

Susan picked up a phone and dialed. She twiddled a pen in her fingers ready to outline a plan. Alex sat down across the room and watched attentively.

"Hi, John? This is Susan . . . Susan Bacon . . . Fabulous. How've you been? Been a while, hasn't it?"

Susan listened for a bit, nodding and rolling the palm of her hand in a circle as if to hurry the conversation along.

"John, you're still working for the airline, aren't you? Good. I need your expert advice."

Fred sat back in his chair and relaxed for the first time that day as he watched Susan's theatrics, interposing reminisces about past dates with the task at hand. She omitted interactions with the police and the detail of reentering the country, but that was for a later time. For now, John was her big hope and Susan seemed to be in total control. After a while, Alex got up, walked up to Susan and waved to roll ahead with the script.

" . . . So we'll see you on May 20 at 7:30 in the evening," Susan said, then hung up, grinned, and raised her hands in the air while doing a happy-dance.

"What's the plan?" Alex asked.

"We meet John at the Hertz car rental counter. He'll be in uniform with our IDs and boarding passes and escort us through security as associates of some form or other. We'll never have to show passports or anything. I think he's bringing some sort of badges that we can flash. The only catch is that we cannot check baggage, we can only bring carry-ons. I knew John would come through. He hates all the official stuff."

"Susan, why don't you sleep here tonight? I wouldn't want you alone in that building after all this."

"Thank you," Susan said. "Maybe I'll be able to sleep."

DEATH SENTENCE

MOSCOW, FEBRUARY 15, 1893

PETER ILYICH TCHAIKOVSKY was greeted at the portico of the imposing residence by a servant with a vague, plastic smile on his pallid face. Peter Ilyich stood tall but felt fragile with the massive stone pillars surrounding the entrance looming over him. As the butler parted the dark mahogany doors and ushered Peter into the cold vestibule, a wisp of air escaped from the passage and into the bitter night. The massive hall was decorated with gilded carvings and evergreen boughs were draped on the marble walls in an incomplete dismantling of ornamentations from the holiday season. But the fanciful decorations were incapable of lifting his mood above the feeling of dread that Peter had that night.

He entered slowly, with the impression that he was the alone in the mansion. It seemed to be more a deserted museum than a home, perhaps a lifeless mausoleum. There were three dark doors in this great reception room, the one in the center, oversized and two on either side that appeared to barely clear one's head. The butler pointed to a huge chair and quietly disappeared behind one of low, heavily carved doors, leaving Peter alone. As Peter awaited his host, he lowered his head and gazed at the pattern on the polished marble floor, which sparkled from a mixture of flickering candles and gaslights. Even with his heavy coat still hanging on his shoulders, Peter felt the coldness of the house steal through the layers of clothing. He stood motionless as he waited to learn the purpose of the invitation. As he waited, a chill made its way deep into his soul, giving him unsettling thoughts of what was to happen.

After several long minutes, the butler returned and signaled Tchaikovsky to follow him through the low doorway on the left side of the reception room and into a dim room. Peter complied, and given the unexpected warmth of the room, surrendered his coat and hat. The room was heavy with draperies but otherwise sparsely furnished, except for a long table in its center, two tables in the corners at the far end with large ornate candelabras and a narrow, long sideboard against one wall. The long banquet table was covered with an ivory damask cloth boldly stitched with flowers. The air hung heavy with a blanket of vapor from a conflicting diversity of scented candles, some of which flickered alone in a pool of liquid wax; others bent away from their cluster as if frozen in an attempt to escape. Alone, Peter sluggishly paced the room as if he were a caged animal in a private zoo. As he paced, his eye fixed on a single candle on the sideboard. The steady light captured his eyes and as he stared at the radiance, and he imagined the first time he saw his beloved Ivan standing in the doorway of his home, glowing in the morning sun. It was a glimpse of heaven, the furthest sensation from his current surroundings.

Peter sat at the head of the table and stared at the ensemble of high-back chairs evenly spaced side by side. For a moment they seemed animated, as if trying to squirm free from captivity. He tried to convince himself that it was the flickering shadows from the candles and the gas-lit sconces. Nothing could be animated in this foreboding setting. Tchaikovsky's eyes began to droop, dulled by the lengthy wait in the shadowy room.

After a while, a line of elderly men paced slowly into the room from behind a heavy tapestry at the opposite end. Peter stood in recognition of their authority. The men took their places, standing behind the chairs at the table and waited silently. A few moments later, a man in a thick, dark robe entered and stood behind the chair at the opposite end. A butler slipped into the room with a ghostly silence and pulled the chair back for the man in the dark robe. It was Anatolyi Krakorentsky, a prominent elder advisor to Tsar Nicholas and trustee of the law school that Peter had attended as a young man.

As Peter choked on the fumes from the burning wax, he felt the dull sting of an impending twist in his destiny. He studied the faces of the assembly as he tried to find one, if any, who might be a friend. A few hung their heads in circumspect silence while others stared ahead like trained animals fearing the consequences of straying from the pack.

One man with a somewhat small stature had an angry expression on his pudgy moon face. He was restless and shifted in his seat in an increasingly agitated manner. He broke the silence with a snarling voice as he said, "Let's get this going. We have some serious work to do tonight in the name of God, the Tsar, and our Fatherland."

Peter turned his head and studied the face of this angry participant; he had seen him before, but struggled to remember where. No matter where it was, this member was provocatively familiar. He diverted his glances to the table and then across to the tapestries on the wall. Nevertheless, as if by a lodestone, his eyes were drawn back to the man, then recalled who he was and looked away so he would not display any recognition. This man, this irate participant had been at Sergevich's country home.

Peter, knowing the severity of their crime, believed Sergevich had been extremely careful with the guest list. He was confused when he looked back at the moon-faced man sitting before him. This man is also known in the circles of the Russian Orthodox Church as an important, pious follower. *Yes,* Peter thought, *it was he who spoke out publicly when two men were honored in a small church for being together for four decades, a sort of same-sex spiritual union. It was he who condemned the ceremony and proclaimed that it had permanently soiled the church so that God would never again enter the edifice.* Peter started to grind his teeth. *It was he who instructed the building to be burned to the ground to sanctify the spot. It is he who drove the congregation to an angry frenzy. And he is drawn to other men as much as I.* Peter began to tremble at the concept that a man covertly guilty of the same crimes to which he was to be accused was now taking control of the assembly.

The leader, Anatolyi Krakorentsky, began in a whisper, "Pyotr Ilyich, you have become a national treasure for our Fatherland. More correctly, your name is a national treasure to our Fatherland. All through Europe and America, the name Pyotr Ilyich Tchaikovsky brings pride to our great nation. This has an important effect on our commerce, our trade and our national identity. Ultimately, this pride and commerce brings power and security in a troubled world. Amongst other things, Russia depends on your name in order to prosper.

"Europe, and the world for that matter, look to Russia for greatness and honor. There is nothing that can be allowed to tarnish that. No one, no matter how great, can be allowed to blemish the name of Russia. Neither you, nor any little significance that you think you have, will soil that name and dishonor Russia and our beloved Tsar throughout the world."

Peter's head grew heavy. Unexpectedly, Peter was comforted by a new melody in his head as Anatolyi Krakorentsky droned on and on. At first the melody was an amorphous, distant and sweet sound, but it slowly and persistently came closer until it dominated all the other sounds in the room. The orchestra in his mind played a mournful theme and transported Peter to the Grand Philharmonic Hall in St. Petersburg. He was no longer alone in the chamber, but surrounded by the spirits of friends who loved him and treasured his work.

Anatolyi Krakorentsky kept rambling and admonishing. "You created this national treasure and brought it to the rest of the world. But a dark stain has soiled the tapestry that we proudly display. Only you can prevent this cultural wealth from being destroyed. If you do not, forces that you are unable to stop will destroy it from within. The forces of decency will tug at you until you must fully expose the sins and the shame. You must take action to prevent the eyes of Russia and all of Europe from watching our dignity and honor crumble.

"It must happen within the next three weeks," Anatolyi Krakorentsky demanded as his voice rose in a chanting tone. "You must take the necessary action to end your deceitful, illegal, and dishonorable life. We demand bereavement so that the vital reputation of Pyotr Ilyich Tchaikovsky may live."

As Peter listened to Anatolyi Krakorentsky's mantra, the melodies of a new work continued to drift through the hall as if an ensemble played in the deep shadows.

"A flask has been prepared for you. I am told that it is not an unpleasant drink and it will provoke a dreamlike effect. It will be your final dream and you will depart this earth with honor."

The sadness was swamped by the haunting and beautiful melody that echoed through his sentience in the dankness of the room. In Peter's mind an orchestra played his symphonic fate and despair with a beauty that overpowered the dark solemnity of the council. The rank fumes of the candles turned into incense that set the stage for an interplay of lingering melodies.

Peter sat in stillness as he once again stared down at the designs in the tablecloth. There in the damask he saw Ivan dancing among the swans, beautiful Ivan. Peter Ilyich's breathing was so shallow that he might have stopped breathing right there. Yet he raised his head and surveyed the table surrounded by his judges. The velvety sounds that swirled in his head were no longer a ballet from his past, but a new symphony. The work had begun coming to life.

Resigned to his fate, Peter asked, "I have but one request. I must have sufficient time to finish my symphony. Then I will do as you ask." Peter looked deep into the eyes of his judges and watched for their reaction. As they slowly nodded, the melodies of his passion unfolded in his mind. It would be his final and fullest communication to Ivan, it would express his heartfelt love.

Anatolyi Krakorentsky put both hands on the wooden box next to him and pushed it toward Peter. He cocked his head to one side sympathetically, much like a puppy sensing his master's distress shares the pain. One would have expected an audible whimper as he took his hands off the box and gave it up. The box passed down the table from hand to hand. As it passed to the hands of the closeted council member, it was given a conspicuously forceful thrust down the table. Peter Ilyich took the box and remained seated as all the others at the table stood up and solemnly walked out of the room. The sounds of his nascent symphony were almost too loud to bear as Peter sat and watched the candles flicker and one by one burn out. Peter Ilyich sat at the end of the now empty table as the servants entered the room to return the chairs to their unfilled precision. As he looked at the box before him, he felt the marble walls of the smoke filled room crush down on him as his head collapsed forward.

His carriage waiting, Peter took the box and returned to his house. He put the box on the table in the foyer and tightened his coat around his neck. The building was like a coffin to Tchaikovsky and he needed to walk in the cold night air. His companion now was the resonance of melody, simultaneously passionate and wistful. It haunted him and at the same time, propelled him. He felt a driving force to express his emotion. There was a compelling need to broadcast his feelings to the world and to express the secret manner in which he led his life.

When Peter returned from his walk he immediately started writing his most passionate love poem to Ivan.

A defiant thought coursed through Peter Ilyich's mind, becoming more and more credible until it became a strategy that could not be disregarded. He developed a plan to communicate to Ivan. The communication was to be encrypted so that it could not be understood by anyone but Ivan. If any hint of a plan fell into the wrong hands, it would be fatal for Ivan. Yet the coded arrangement had to be clear so no errors could be introduced by misinterpretation. The key to the plan had to be lucid to Ivan, but yet invisible to all others.

Peter Ilyich set to work with renewed enthusiasm. He had been planning a new symphony for a while, his sixth, and had sketches and some orchestration completed. That work was a contrived expression of grandeur that no longer suited his spirit. It was to be abandoned, perhaps revisited at a future time.[11] His new harmonious expression of transcendence and hope was about to be conceived as his new sixth completed symphony. In these grave moments, when Peter Ilyich Tchaikovsky was simmering with an emotional explosion that could hardly be contained, he needed to express himself in the way he found most meaningful.

---

11 These sketches were later discovered, unfinished. Russian composer Semyon Bogatyrev reconstructed Tchaikovsky's seventh symphony from these sketches and premiered the symphony in 1957 in Moscow.

AIRPORT

MANHATTAN, MAY 20

IN THE EARLY morning, Fred took his suitcase from the hall closet and opened it on the kitchen counter. He took a piece of stiff cardboard that he'd cut and made sure it fit tight enough over the music, then covered that with a piece of nylon cloth that Susan had hemmed to fit snugly inside the suitcase, then glued it to the inside walls and bottom of the suitcase. When he was done he stood back and said, "Damn good, if I must say so."

Alex walked up behind him, looked inside the suitcase, then gave him a kiss on the cheek.

"Let's have some breakfast," Fred said.

After breakfast, Fred and Alex went to the bedroom to gather clothing to pack for the trip. Fred stacked his sweaters, a nylon jacket and an ample supply of underwear and socks next to the suitcase to get an idea of the bulk. Alex heaped a few things on the bed, then put some of the things back on the dresser. "I don't need all this stuff. I can buy what I need in Moscow," he said.

At noon, Fred sat on the edge of his bed next to his open suitcase and watched Alex, who was perched on the windowsill, hypnotically staring out at the cars below as they slogged through the steady drizzle. He walked over and slowly massaged Alex's shoulders.

"This gloomy rain doesn't help matters one bit," Alex said. "I can't believe the day to go to Moscow has arrived. It feels like we've been waiting forever and, boom, it's here. Spring is damp over here, but it's colder in Moscow." He opened the closet door, looked inside and said, "I'll take a heavier sweatshirt." He pressed the sweatshirt into his suitcase. "I hope Anna's warm."

Fred looked at his open suitcase sitting next to Alex's and shook his head. "What if they decide to search my luggage?"

Alex gave Fred a hug. "It's going to be fine, don't worry. To the x-ray it'll just look like a bunch of papers."

"I'm starting to freak out a little," Fred said as his cell phone rang. He answered. "Hi, Susan, how are things going? All packed?"

"She's driving me crazy," Susan said. "It's like she knows something is going on."

"Who?" Fred said.

"Margo. I bumped into her on the street and she said to have a nice trip. How did she know we were travelling? And her voice was strange," Susan said.

"Oh, don't worry. C'mon over when you're all packed. I'll make something to eat and then we'll be on our way," Fred said. "Good, seeya in a bit."

Fred started to pile his clothes into the suitcase, then looked over at Alex's pile and said, "Are you sure you're taking enough clothes?"

"I'll do a little shopping in Moscow. Stuff is cheaper there and I know all the stores. There, I'm done packing. Wait a sec, I want to take a sweater for Anna that I brought from her cedar chest. She'll like having it when we find her." He put his handkerchief to his face, then wiped tearing eyes. "If we find her." Fred pulled him close and hugged.

They both zipped their suitcases and wheeled them to the living room near the apartment door.

The doorbell rang and Fred buzzed Susan in. He opened the door, heard her suitcase clanking on the stairs below, then leaned over the railing and shouted, "Wait, I'll be there in a sec." He went downstairs, took the heavy suitcase from Susan and dropped it. "My God, Susan, what do you have in here? I hope the plane can lift off with this on board."

"I'm prepared for all kinds of weather," Susan said as Fred got a better grip on the handle and heaved it up. "Plus, I had to cram in all the electrical conversion plugs and maps that a tourist might need."

Susan nervously went to the kitchen window, looked out and shouted, "It's here! Let's do it."

With a soft grunt, Fred took Susan's luggage downstairs first, then ran back up for his. Fred and Alex rolled their luggage down to the front lobby. First Susan, then Alex and Fred darted from the front door to the taxi though the drizzle. Fred looked up at Susan's building and noticed some curtains on the second floor moving as if somebody had just stepped away from the window. Fred put his arm on Alex's shoulders and said, "We'll be having tea with Anna before you know it."

They squeezed into the back seat of the taxi, then the taxi pulled onto the street. They arrived at the terminal at ten minutes to six. Fred paid the driver and Susan added a large tip.

Once inside the terminal, Fred wheeled his luggage into the men's room, found an empty sink and splashed cold water on his face. Grabbing both sides of the porcelain sink, he stared at himself and wondered what he had gotten himself into. All of this was over notes jotted on sheet music. It seemed ridiculous, but it was happening. He looked down at the water swirling into the drain and thought about Shumka, blood and assassins.

"Fred, we have to go," Alex said as he walked up behind him. "Susan's getting more controlling, we need to get her under control."

Fred lifted his head, then dried his hands and followed Alex into the busy terminal, where Susan was shifting from one foot to the other waiting for them. She glared at them and then strode quickly along the concourse to the Hertz car rental counter. The Hertz booth looked abandoned except for an idle female attendant sitting stiffly while looking at her monitor. Next to the Hertz counter, there was a row of connected chairs against the wall and Alex sank into one of the seats and put his feet up on his suitcase. "It's good that we got here early. Hanging around a bit is cooling my hysteria," Alex said.

At seven-thirty, Susan stood on her toes and looked toward the far end of the concourse as if she was staring at the end of an infinity mirror. Fred fidgeted with the zipper on his suitcase. Alex stared into the distance hardly blinking. Several minutes passed before Susan anxiously said, "He'll be here any moment."

Alex stood up and said, "God, what if we're at the wrong terminal? Is there another Hertz?"

"Alex, keep cool, if you can't trust Susan—"

"Then what? When do we panic? Tell me. I'm ready now," Alex said.

"I'm going to phone the airlines desk," Susan said, then fumbled for her cell phone and hastily dialed. "Hello, is John Milotti available? I need to speak to him. It's urgent."

There was pause, then Susan's jaw dropped and her face became colorless. She put down her phone and turned to Fred and Alex and said, "John called in sick, he has the flu."

"You're kidding," Fred said.

"No, but he has an envelope waiting for us at the desk. I'll get it. Wish me luck; we've got to get on that plane without showing passports. I'll be back in a minute. It's just over there." Susan rushed off.

"I can't believe this is happening," Fred said as Susan scurried off to the desk and elbowed her way to the front of the line. She leaned over the desk, had an animated conversation with the clerk, then turned around and rushed back to the Hertz desk holding a manila envelope.

She walked up to Fred and Alex, opened the envelope and took out some papers. "Thank God," she said, "there are three boarding passes and some official-looking medallions."

Fred said, "Now we have to worry about getting through security."

Susan fumbled a bit and said, "Well, mine looks okay and here's yours." She handed Fred and Alex their papers.

Fred looked at his boarding pass, his eyes opened wide and his face turned pale. "Whoa, what is this name, Ronald Miller? What's the name on yours, Alex?"

Alex reached out for Fred's hand and said, "It's not my name, probably better. As long as it's a real boarding pass, it'll be all right."

Susan said, "Sorry, I never told John your names. At least we have something to board the plane. I'm sure John thought about what he was giving me."

Fred raised his arms and grunted, "What now?"

The woman behind the Hertz counter looked up and smiled, then looked back down at her screen.

They wheeled their suitcases slowly toward the line of people waiting for security screening, then stopped about forty feet away. Alex surveyed the crowd while Fred noticed a security guard walking past a line of wheelchairs near the entrance. "Alex, hold onto my suitcase," he said, then walked to the wheelchairs, grabbed an empty one and wheeled it to Susan and Alex.

"Alex," Fred said, "sit your ass down here and let's get through security and on that damn plane."

Fred wheeled Alex to the disabled line while Susan followed. While they waited in line, Fred whispered to Susan, "Follow my lead."

When they reached the head of the line, Fred took a deep breath and said to the security agent, "My patient has a severe neuromuscular disorder and needs meds in a few moments or we'll have a tragedy. This line took longer than I ever thought it would. Could we do this quickly?" He looked into the agent's eyes, "Now."

"Stand to the side and give him whatever he needs, then you can go through," the security agent said and waved his hands toward an open space next to the security line.

Stunned, Fred said forcefully, "No, my assistant has the meds and he's already at the gate, we don't have a lot of time."

The inspector picked up the metal detector and cleared his throat. Alex slumped deeper in his seat and made a soft, plaintive groan.

"Please," Fred said to the security agent.

The security agent rolled his eyes then waved the metal detector around Alex as Susan presented the boarding passes and passports. He fumbled with the three boarding passes and passports, made a mark on them, then handed them back to Susan. He then quickly scanned Susan and Fred, then let them through.

Fred leaned toward Susan and quietly said, "Quickly, take Alex to the gate to get his medication, Dr. Frank is waiting."

Susan nodded, then wheeled Alex down the hall while

Fred tried to stay calm as the luggage passed through the x-ray machine. Once they came out the other side, he picked them up, balanced his on top of Alex's and wheeled them down the hall to catch up with Susan and Alex waiting for him twenty feet down the hallway. Fred had Susan watch their luggage while he wheeled Alex into a men's room and ditched the wheelchair in a toilet stall, then joined Susan and made their way to the gate, where they waited to board the plane. When boarding started, Fred, Alex and Susan casually walked up to the gate, presented the boarding passes. Fred held his breath as first Alex's and then his were scanned and the light turned green, letting them pass. Susan breezed through, they boarded the plane and went to their seats. Susan and Alex sat while Fred stuffed their carry-ons in the overhead compartments.

Alex sat near the window, Susan in the middle and Fred in the aisle seat. Susan held Fred's hand, then reached over and took hold of Alex's hand. As they waited for takeoff, Fred closed his eyes and concentrated on his breathing. Everything would be fine, or so he told himself. He kept his eyes closed while the flight attendants explained what to do in case of an emergency, then the plane began to taxi into position.

MOSCOW SUITE

MOSCOW, MAY 21

NINE HOURS LATER, Fred woke up as the plane began its descent to the Moscow Sheremetyevo airport early the next morning. Susan yawned. Alex woke and yawned as well. The plane brightened up as window shades were raised. Fred leaned over Susan and looked out the window as they flew through a layer of clouds, then the landscape became clear. It looked dreary. He leaned back in his seat, thinking that the craziness was about to begin again.

The plane touched down and some of the passengers clapped. Alex unbuckled his seat belt and stood up, bending to fit the contours of the ceiling.

Over the intercom, the attendant said, "Please return to your seats."

After they came to a stop at the terminal, with a strong Russian accent, the attendant on the address system amusingly said, "Get out."

They departed and emerged from the enclosed ramp into Sheremetyevo airport. Fred thought it looked like any other major airport, but the dazzling signs in Cyrillic reminded him that they were very far from home. As he walked, he was thankful that most signs were in English as well as Russian. Then he noticed that the signs for *entrance* and *exit* were only in Russian and curiously, they were nearly the same: выход, входа. He paid particular attention to these signs in the unlikely event that he might be leading the way. Fred held his breath as they approached customs. He paused as Alex pointed them through the green pathway under the sign, *Nothing to declare*. Alex went to the right, along a different path for those with Russian passports.

Floating through customs was a breeze, then they came together in the grand concourse ready to face Moscow. Alex showed a decided change in self-assurance. He was in a familiar place and took charge, which made Fred feel confident.

"Taxis are this way," Alex said. "Don't get in one unless I say it's okay. Cheating is a custom here, so let me pick the taxi." He paused in front of an ATM machine, then said, "Wait, we need to get some rubles." The glittering Cyrillic instructions on the screen were mesmerizing and eventually a small pile of currency slipped out. "Here, you should have some money on your pocket," Alex said as he handed Fred and Susan some bills.

Outside, in the cool, misty fog, Fred zipped up his jacket and turned up the collar. The cold didn't seem to bother Alex as he stepped out to the curb and swiftly hailed a taxi. Alex sounded assertive as he spoke with the driver, then they got in the cab while Alex and driver put their luggage in the trunk and they were on their way to the hotel.

Fred looked out the window as they drove past endless generic gray buildings covered in fog. *So this is what the Soviet-era apartment houses look like,* Fred thought, finding the stark raw concrete construction depressing. He glanced over at Susan, who was taking in the endless shades of gray.

"Not quite as exciting as you would have hoped," Alex said.

As they drove closer to the center of Moscow, the mood changed. Traffic slowed and Fred rolled down his window to get a better look at the new surroundings. The streets were vibrant with well-dressed people and elegant shops. The broad avenues curling around magnificent monuments awed him. It felt much like any major European city, the major exception being the number of high-end BMWs jamming the traffic to a standstill.

As they drove through the city center, Fred was surprised to notice that in Moscow, pedestrians didn't jaywalk; they lined up at the cross-walks and stood still until the light changed. Everyone appeared healthy despite the fact that so many people smoked.

Alex had reserved a suite of rooms in a hotel away from the center of the city. When they arrived, Fred got out of the taxi and looked up in wonderment. The hotel was tall, ornate and full of color. "I guess things aren't all gray," he said.

"Come on, let's check in," Alex said. The walls of the lobby were white, heavily ornamented with plaster sculpted curlicues and flourishes. Columns gave the high ceiling an even loftier appearance.

Susan pointed to the white marble floor with black dots and said, "Look at that floor, it looks like ermine fur. We're walking on Russian heraldry, with a not-too-subtle trace of wealth."

A bellhop met them at the front desk. He grabbed the suitcases, but Fred waved him away as he held onto his own suitcase. They squeezed into the elevator and when the bellhop was unable to pull the brass gate closed, Fred picked up his suitcase, set it on top of Alex's and took a deep breath. Once on the second floor, they followed the bellhop down a long, poorly lit hallway and waited while the man fumbled with the key and opened the door. He presented the room with his arm outstretched and hand open.

Alex dropped a five-ruble note in the man's hand and closed the door behind them. The suite was sparsely furnished, but appeared clean and recently painted. They explored the rooms and looked at the view of Moscow alleys from the large window in the smaller bedroom. Fred switched lights on and off by pressing black enameled buttons on ornate switch plates. "This place is like a museum of living in the fifties. It's amazing that it all works."

Off the common room were two doors, each leading to a bedroom. Between the bedrooms was a common bathroom. Susan took the smaller bedroom while Fred and Alex took the other. Susan's room had the large window that opened onto a fire escape. Fred and Alex's had a small window whose frame had been painted shut.

"Let's keep both bathroom doors open when we're not using it," Susan said. "Housekeeping hasn't been too restrained here. It has the fragrance and atmosphere of a public convenience."

Fred nodded and wondered what was being covered by the smell of the cheap perfume.

As it was already late in the day, Fred said, "Let's use room service, and instead of lunch, get an early dinner and then go right to sleep. I didn't really sleep on the plane and it's already getting dark."

Alex pulled a menu from the desk against the far wall of the common room and said, "They have chicken, beef and fish? I suggest the chicken; I'd stay away from the fish."

Fred and Susan nodded, then Alex called room service, rattled in Russian, put down the phone and said, "They said a half hour. We'll be lucky to see food before midnight."

Dinner was not much better than hospital food, and given its heaviness, more difficult to digest. It was also slow in arriving, as Alex predicted, so that by the time they finished eating, an early bedtime was out of the question. Since the bedrooms were tight, Alex and Fred set their suitcases on a desk in the central common room. Susan pushed her suitcase into an armoire cramped in the corner of the common room.

Although it was quite chilly in Moscow, the rooms were warm and suffocatingly close. Susan paced across the common room, into her bedroom, then back to the common room. She opened the door, leaned into the hallway, looked left and right, then returned to the suite. She walked to her bedroom, then said, "It feels like a sauna in here."

To lighten the atmosphere, Fred yelled through the bathroom, "It's like a Sonja Henie," referring to a vintage Hollywood actress.

Fred shouted through the bathroom, "Susan, why don't you open your window a crack to let some fresh air in? Ours doesn't open."

"Good idea." Susan raised the window, allowing the chilled air to pour in. "Ahhh, this is better," she said. "I prefer to sleep in a cool room with a comforter pulled up to my nose."

Fred welcomed the chill flowing through the bathroom. Susan turned out the lights, then Fred called out, "This has been a grueling day and we have a lot to do tomorrow. Sleep tight."

Alex added, "And, as you say, don't let the *postyelnee klop*" (bedbugs bite).

Fred lied in bed, noting that it was so dark that a slim moon made barely any difference when he closed his eyes and then opened them. The only sound was Alex and Susan's heavy breathing. He soon fell asleep.

Hours later, the moon had set and the lack of any nightlights made the rooms turn pitch black. The cool night air continued to pour through the barely open window. Hoping to sleep soundly, Fred pulled the comforter up to his nose and snuggled tighter in the comforter, then fell into a light sleep.

Fred woke to the sound of a creak. He kept still and listened. There was another creak, this time from a different direction. It could be Susan, or so he hoped. He sat up in bed and listened for the subtlest of creaks. He cautiously reached across the bed and felt for Alex, who was still there. He listened for Susan, who was breathing loudly, not quite snoring, but clearly sleeping. Fred held his breath, then heard it again. Yes, there *was* movement. He couldn't decide whether to make a sound and wake up Alex and Susan or investigate on his own.

He listened, heard a faint sound, like a footstep coming from the common room. Fred closed his eyes, took a deep breath, then slowly placed one bare foot on the cold floor and walked to the door leading to the common room. He opened the door a crack and peeked into the darkness hoping his eyes would adjust to the darkness, then he smelled something. It was faint and familiar, like magnolia. Susan never used strong perfumes, if any at all, nor did Alex.

"I want you to leave," Fred loudly said, then quickly backed away lest he be in the path of a swinging blade. He stood silently waiting for his bold statement to do something.

Susan startled and groggily said, "What's happening?"

Alex awoke, too and said, "Fred?"

A chair was knocked over and rattled across the floor, then a lamp toppled as footsteps headed into Susan's bedroom. Fred charged after the prowler.

Susan turned on the bedside lamp and sat up in bed just as the intruder looked back, then dashed out the window.

"Sophie!" Susan screamed, then ran to the open window, but it was too late, the intruder was gone.

Susan shut the window and said, "What fresh hell is this?"

REVERIES

MOSCOW, FEBRUARY 22, 1893

PETER ILYICH TCHAIKOVSKY sat pensively at his desk thinking about his meeting with the committee and his death sentence. He idly flipped pages of sketches for his new symphony, ideas that had haunted him during his most difficult time. He stopped to look out of the window at a young boy slowly ambling by in the bitter cold, with his head drooped low, looking down at the ground as if he walked in a daydream. An intangible force lifted Tchaikovsky, transported his thoughts from the darkened studio to the street below and related to the spirit of the boy whose life had yet to unfold. He felt his head flag heavy as he wandered through memories. He thought how naively optimistic he was that the world would change.

Peter's image of the committee burned with the hateful words of the chairman. A phrase kept ringing in his head, muddled but refusing to fade. All of a sudden, it rang true:

There are more things in heaven and earth, Horatio,
Than are dreamt of in your philosophy.

It gave him strength and he thought about all the hypocrisy in his world; the Tsar's brother, openly gay, and a target, not of doom, but of harmless jest. Why him?

Peter felt the loneliness of abandoning certain friends long ago, fearing a budding affection—an affection that his world saw as an affliction. He pictured those friends walking beside him and then straying away, confused by his apparent indifference. Peter watched the boy in the street beneath his window as the boy stopped and looked up at the trees. A couple of squirrels chased freely. *How wonderful the world can be,* he thought. He was that boy not so long ago; a boy like that lived on within him, battered by hostile daily events.

A late winter wind howled against his window, drumming the pane with an incessant beat. It was the scaffolding to a melody in his ears, a new melody. A squall blew apart a pile of leaves that had been painstakingly piled along the street, anchored by a layer of new snow. All was becoming undone. Peter watched the boy walk toward the remaining pile, kicking his way through the leaves and bringing a mild chaos to things in his path. The fallen leaves had been returned to the starting point.

Peter turned back to the shadowy room, sat down at the piano and glanced across the strings, at his desk and the miniature carved chest that contained the infusion that would be the ultimate abuse in his chaotic life. Perhaps it would finally bring solace to a life of fear and mind-induced illnesses. He looked down at his empty score paper and smoothed it on the piano's easel. He put a Roman numeral two at the top and began to write a new movement. He started with the marking, a statement that would suggest what was in his heart. He wrote *imaginatively*, then crumpled the paper and started again. He wanted the thoughts in his head, his music, to be interpreted with grace, perhaps performed lively. The melodies and counterpoint resonating in his mind created a mood that inspired him to challenge the orthodoxy of the church and the fear that was beat into him and his friends.

Gracefully, that was how he would have it. The venom in the carved chest so closely perched on his desk was only another in the long chain of poisons that had been forced onto him over his lifetime. But for the moment, at least, he was no longer sinking.

Cellos would chant this phrase and then the flutes would sing it. The melodies that flowed onto paper were carefree and carried by the gust of newfound buoyancy. These were the forces that he lived for. They were distant from the dynamics that solely benefited the inbred corporation known as The Orthodox Church. He thought the church could be damned for labeling him as an evil threat. He couldn't imagine himself being a threat to anyone. Why would they consider him a threat? Was it because he would never propagate offspring to fill the church's coffers?

Peter turned to the hideous small chest harboring the bitterness of his culture and stared at the ecclesiastical carvings on the top. The fearsome monsters, the whimsical delusions of glory, the fantasy of salvation, all an illusion. And the cost of helplessly following his homosexual urges was encapsulated in that gnomish wooden chest that dominated his room. And would he want to be any different? If that boy down there desired as he did, what would his life be?

Absorbed in reverie, Peter went to the desk, stared at the blank paper and smoothed it over and over and finally wrote a letter to his nephew, Vladimir "Bob" Davidov.

> *My Dearest Bob,*
>
> *I initially thought that I was too weary to write another symphony and yet, at the same time, I was energized by the need to express my feelings about the past, the future and love. My head, swimming with thematic ideas, seemed to be controlled by my hands when I sat at the keyboard. I instinctively felt my way through the opening phrases and my hand fell into the B minor key. There is little disagreement among my fellow musicians that this key embodies the solitary feelings of melancholia. It is the leitmotif[12] of my life and there is no better framework in which to describe it.*
>
> *As a summary of my career in Russia and my life, this work is the most inspired as it is the sincerest of all my works. I love it as I have never loved any other musical offering. In a sense, this work is honestly autobiographical and the ending that is sketched shall express the inevitable dying light of Mother Russia in my soul. I have quoted the Orthodox requiem at the end*

---

12 A leitmotif is a recurrent theme in music, usually related to a person or situation.

of the first movement as segue into the inner peace of the finale.

[My new symphony has] a program, but a program that will remain an enigma to all. Let them guess for themselves.[13] [The sketches are] permeated with subjectiveness, so much that not once, but often, while composing it in my mind, I shed tears. You cannot imagine the joy it gives me to know my day is not yet done, and that I am still capable of work. Of course I may be mistaken, but it doesn't seem so.[14]

My love for you is stronger than ever. It is one of the few enabling factors in my renewed inspiration.

Pyotr Ilyich

As Peter continued to sketch the second movement, he refocused on happier times. He also envisioned a future that might have been. After a while, he stopped writing and moseyed back to the window. The boy was gone. The sun cast dark shades upon warm colors that only the golden hour can produce. He defiantly started planning a future and, for the moment, his feeling of optimism brought warmth into the music, overcoming the long shadows that darkened it. He turned and walked back to his desk. His mood was transformed into a rebellious frame of mind. Peter took a deep breath, spiraled around his desk with spirit, humming melody and lifting his shoulders to the rhythm. He swung into his chair with a new grace that had the ingredients of hope and choice.[15]

As Peter sat, pen in hand, melodic phrases soared through his mind, and the resignation of doom that had hung over him like a cloud started to lift. The space it left was replaced by the need for guidance. He could no longer put his composition down on paper. His mind was crowded and the music was crashing down on him with an intolerable chaos. He put down his pen, walked

---

13   After the first performance of *Pathetique*, Nikolai Rimsky-Korsakov inquired if the symphony had a program (narrative). Tchaikovsky assured him that there was one but would not reveal it to him or to anyone else.

14   This paragraph is excerpted from a letter to his nephew, Bob Davidov dated February 22, 1893. The rest of the letter is interpreted.

15   Tchaikovsky's brother, Modeste, said of this moment, "[It] was like an act of exorcism by which Peter Ilyich cast out all the black spirits that had possessed him for so long."

over to the window once again and stared at the neighborhood outside. A couple walked by hand in hand, looking contented and quite happy. His mood changed to anger, then to a stubborn fury. He swung around, and instead of returning to his piano, he went to the small writing table in the corner of the room. He started to write a letter that would change everything:

Dear Claude . . .

MAYHEM IN MOSCOW

MOSCOW, MAY 22

STILL STUNNED FROM the burglar a few minutes before, Fred stood in front of the window and looked into the night.

Susan threw a blanket over her shoulders, then walked from her bedroom and sat next to Fred.

"Gone?" Susan said softly. "Sophie took the music?"

Alex walked up to Fred and looked at the empty suitcase. "It's all we had for the ransom. Fuck." He kicked the sofa and roared, "Fuck!"

Fred nodded solemnly. "I know."

"What're we going to do now?" Alex said.

"I don't know," Fred said. "I just don't know."

Alex picked up his suitcase and flung it across the room, where it hit the wall, opened and spilled its contents. He went to the scattered pile of clothing with contempt and kicked the pile. Fred began to collect Alex's clothes from the floor and stack them on the sofa as Alex fell back on the sofa and wailed, "Shit. Who is this Sophie?" He looked at Susan. "Is she some fuckin' friend of yours?"

"Remember the Winking Wok and the woman who introduced herself like a long-lost relative that you had no interest in? That was Sophie. She's no friend."

"Alex, didn't you mention back then that she looked familiar?" Fred said.

"I'm not sure. It was more like she knew me." With his head hung low, Alex walked through the common room and back to his bedroom, kicking the desk, then the sofa on the way. He then calmly walked out and back to Fred and Susan.

"She knew we were in Moscow, in this hotel. Who else knows?" Fred said.

"This is such a mess," Alex said, his face in his hands. He pushed away from Fred, kicked the sofa and then went to the chair lying on its side, spun it across the room and in a rasping whisper said, "*Dérmo, Dérmo*[16] . . . *pizdéts!*"[17] He grasped a cushion from the sofa and flung it across the room.

"Calm down," Fred said softly as he grabbed Alex's shoulders and pulled him close. "We have to think."

Alex shrugged Fred off, then stomped into the bedroom.

Fred went into the bedroom and found Alex in a fetal position on the bed. "Alex, I'll never feel this disaster as you do, but I'm in pain, too. Of all the times, now's the time we have to hang close."

With a plaintive look on his face, Alex looked up and said, "I don't know how to cry anymore." He curled up tighter on the bed.

Fred sat down and slowly rubbed Alex's back. "Fuck, things are more complicated now. Will this never end?"

Susan came to the bedroom door, stood still a few minutes, then sat down on the edge of the bed next to Alex.

Alex looked up at Susan, then dropped his head in a state of total fatigue, closed his eyes and moaned.

Fred glanced around the bedroom and took a deep breath. The lingering fragrance of magnolia nagged of Sophie's presence.

"Anna is doomed," Alex said as he lifted his head and began to weep. "My dear Grandmother."

Fred hugged him tighter as they reclined on the bed.

---

16 Shit.

17 We're fucked (*pizdéts*) пизде́ц—a widely used exclamation referring to the termination of something.

Susan got up and circled the room. "Sophie fucked up everything. New York, Moscow. It makes no sense. We're screwed."

Alex shot up out of bed and said, "I'm not going to lie here like some roadkill in an alley. I'm going to find Sophie." Alex grabbed his jacket and marched out the door.

"Alex, wait. It's the middle of the night, you'll never find her now," Fred said.

"I know Moscow. She probably walked to the Metro. I'll find her," Alex said as he slammed the door.

Susan looked at Fred. "Fred, what—"

"This is insane. Get your coat, Sus. We've gotta find him. He's never going to find Sophie, we waited too long for that."

They ran to the elevator and waited a few seconds, then Fred pulled Susan toward the stairs and they ran to the street. "The Metro," he said. "Where the fuck is the Metro? It's dark as hell around here."

"Let's split and cover more ground," Susan said.

"No, I don't want to have to start looking for you, too. Stay together."

"Is that a Metro sign way down there?" Susan said. "He probably went that way."

They walked hurriedly down the street. Not wanting to attract attention, Susan cupped her hands and said, "Alex. Alex. Wait, the Metro's not running at this hour." She looked around the dark street. "Alex?"

"There's no one on the street. He's not hiding from us. Let's keep quiet."

They stopped and stood on the murky roadway, looking around for a few minutes until Fred said, "This is hopeless. We don't know where anything is; we're not going to find him. Let's head back to the room. He'll be back."

"Do you think we could possibly find Sophie?" Susan said.

"How could we? We don't know her last name or anything about her. We don't even know if her name is really Sophie. I have no idea how she found *us*. No, we have to think about how we go from here. Let's go back." Fred pulled Susan close and they walked back to the hotel.

Back in the hotel room, Fred and Susan sat on the sofa. Fred looked at his watch, then slumped and closed his eyes.

An hour later, he shook his head and looked at his watch. "My God, what is he doing out there?"

Susan placed her hand on his thigh and shook her head. Fred stood up, walked to the window, looked out, then sat down again.

The sound of a key in the door caught Fred's attention and he jumped up. Alex walked in, threw his jacket on a chair and sat down. Susan got up and walked up to Alex and said, "Where've you been? Alex, you scared us."

"I walked until I felt so alone that I wanted to cry. Everything is falling apart. It's hopeless."

"We need a new plan," Fred said as he hugged Alex tightly. "Let's stay close together. We've got to do that much. We'll figure it out."

"Let's sleep on it," Susan said, then loudly exhaled. "If we can sleep."

Fred crossed his arms and leaned back against the wall. Nobody was going to sleep tonight. How could they? Alex wiped his tears and slowly stood up, taking Fred's arm. He went to the bathroom, followed by Susan, then Fred. Susan walked around the suite turning off lights, then returned to her bedroom, lifted the window, slammed it shut and turned the lock tight. "This is literally locking the barn door. Good night. We'll figure this out, we always do," Susan said, then turned off the light.

In the darkness, Alex whispered faintly, "We always do."

THE CONSERVATORY

MOSCOW, MAY 22

IN THE MIDDLE of the night, Fred felt a poke in his side.

"Fred, are you awake?" Alex whispered.

"Yeah. Who can sleep?" Fred said.

Alex whispered softly, "I was thinking, there are two options open to us at this point. We could try to find Sophie and get the music back, if in fact she still has it, or we could try to find something that might work as a substitute. Both are long shots, but there are no other options."

"There might be other music with his handwriting, a letter or something. We could go through Tchaikovsky's papers and stuff and try to find something. If we keep working at it, Sophie might try to get to us again," Fred said.

"I don't think we're going to see Sophie again. How could we get the kind of stuff that those bastards want?"

"Hmmm," Fred said as he pulled his pillow higher. "We do know the name of the student. We could start looking for evidence leading to proof that Tchaikovsky had a lover named Ivan."

"And we could enroll in a course at Moscow University." Alex threw the comforter aside and jumped out of bed. "Dammit, what you're saying takes time. We don't have that kind of time." He walked across the room. "I'm still pissed. Y'think that those fucks put Anna up in Catherine-the-Great's Winter Palace giving her caviar on toast points while she rocks to a string quartet? They could have her sharing a cage with rats in some wet cellar."

"Alex, please."

"No, we've got to walk the streets until we find that Sophie bitch and strangle her until she gives back what we need." Alex sat down on the edge of the bed and rubbed his eyes. Alex started to get up, but stopped when Fred leaned over and held his arm.

"Alex, we can't go flailing about in the streets hoping everything'll be alright. We have to be clever about this. I know you feel the same way."

Alex walked to the dresser and picked through his small pile of shirts. "I'm sorry." He pulled a blue shirt from the middle of the pile and shook the wrinkles out. "We can do this. At this point, we probably know more about Tchaikovsky and Ivan than anyone ever knew before."

"That's a small comfort," Fred said. "All I know is that we need something credible to give those shithead kidnappers."

Alex said, "I know where we should start. The Moscow Conservatory of Music."

"You think they have the kind of stuff we want?"

"Well, it dates back before Tchaikovsky. It's the most prominent music conservatory in Russia."

"Great idea," Fred said. "We'll tell Susan in the morning. She'll be happy to hear that we have a plan."

From the other bedroom, through the open bathroom, Susan said, "Hello. You think I could sleep? I heard everything. It's a plan. Now, go to sleep."

Fred stepped out of the hotel into the bright morning sunshine and said, "It's colder than I expected," then zipped his jacket up to his neck. He put his sunglasses on and waited for Susan and Alex.

Alex took the lead and said, "Let's get some breakfast. There'll be a better choice if we go over to the main street. We might not be able to eat until later in the day." He charged ahead. Fred put his arm around Susan and they walked briskly to keep up with Alex. Alex turned and said, "The Metro to the conservatory is only a few blocks away. We'll head that way."

Alex led them to a bakery. Susan tried to peer in, but the small-paned windows were fogged with moisture. Alex stepped ahead and pulled the door open. Fred started to enter, paused, but then smiled as the fragrance of yeasty bread wafted out. As he walked in, a young woman smiled and pointed to an empty table and Fred escorted Susan followed by Alex.

"I would have never thought of coming into this place," Susan said. "This feels like Russia. If you could translate the menu, it'll be perfect." Susan lifted herself from her chair so she could see into the kitchen "Look at that, this is wonderful." She pointed to an array of shiny pots crowded on a small gas stove. "Alex, you're such a guide."

Alex looked at the food on other tables and said, "Let's get the blini. It looks like it's a specialty here."

"*Blini*?" Susan said, looking around.

"Yeah, pancakes with all kinds of stuff piled on," Alex said. "Open, it's a blini, closed, it's a blintz. If we were in Paris, we'd say crêpe. You had them at Anna's."

"Sounds perfect. Order the blini and coffee," Susan said.

"Same for me. Make sure there's plenty; I'm starved," Fred said.

They were quickly served a huge pile of pancakes and an assortment of preserves and creams for garnish. Fred watched Susan study the artwork on the walls as she dug into her blini. Over brunch, Alex said, "We'll take the Metro to the Moscow Conservatory of Music. We'll be there in half an hour."

Susan asked, "How do we know that there's a worthwhile Tchaikovsky presence there? Do we need a plan B?"

Alex said quickly, "You have the tour book. Look it up. I guarantee you'll agree with me."

Susan fumbled with her bag and pulled out her guidebook, turned some pages and said, "Here it is. When it was opened in 1886, Tchaikovsky was appointed as professor of music theory and composition, a move that made it very prominent. Exactly the place that we want to start."

Fred said, "Right, let's get going."

Alex leaned back, lifting the front legs of his chair off the floor and rocked. "Yeah, if anyone retained memorabilia of Tchaikovsky, this would be the place."

"How're we going to find where to look?" Susan asked. "From the pictures, it looks like a pretty big place."

Alex kept swaying his chair. "Yeah, it's an old mansion expanded into a sprawling compound."

"Yeah, but how do we get into the archives? We can't just parade around until we find it," Fred said.

Alex said, "The archives are not open to the public, but I'm confident that we could talk our way in. All we have to do is get into the main area and get a detailed map of the building layout. It's a tourist attraction, so there surely will be diagrams."

"Just wander in? Geez, I don't know," Fred said.

"Trust me," Alex said, "Okay?"

"This feels really risky," Fred said.

"Really, risky," Susan said. "Okay. But if we get stopped, everything is over. Getting tossed out is one thing, but I don't want to spend the night in a Russian jail."

Fred, Alex and Susan exited the bakery, walked energetically to Bolshaya Nikitskaya Street to the Moscow Metro. Alex got tickets at the attendant's window and put them in the turnstile as Susan, then Fred went in with Alex following. Alex led them to the escalator and down to the station. The station was opulent with spotless polished marble floors and walls framed in mosaics, lit by art nouveau fixtures fitting for a palace. A train soon rolled into the station and they hopped on. They got off the metro at the Arbatskaya Station and walked briskly in the chilly Moscow weather. The sky had become overcast. Alex said, "We should hurry. It looks like rain."

The turned around a corner and Fred pointed to a large complex of buildings and said, "Is that it?"

"Yeah, that's the place. Impressive, huh?" Alex proudly said.

Sunlight lit the building in an amber glow, accentuating the white pilaster columns on the ornate Greek-revival mansion.

Susan said, "This place is really imposing." She pointed to

the portico. "What does that say?"

They paused and Alex said, "Bolshoi Hall, big concert hall. I'd love for you to see it; it's beautiful. But it's not where we want to go."

Fred stood and gaped at the mass of intricate ornamentation and how it all seemed to fit. Windows framed in ionic columns were set within tall Corinthian columns and crowned with alternating arched and peaked caps. Crowded on either side were add-on buildings in a similar style. Behind the main entrance, a semi-circular bay bulged out and extended more than five stories with a conical copper roof. "Wow," he mumbled.

"Hard to image that this was once was a residence. It would take a lifetime to visit every corner," Susan said.

Fred admired the building as Alex walked ahead. "Six, maybe seven floors, but those tall windows must make it like eight stories. Well, I guess as a conservatory, it's, wow, pretty nice," he said. The rows of small eyebrow dormers poking out along the original roofline and the tender decoration to the imposing façade made the surrounding buildings of the complex appear uninspired.

Alex walked over to Fred and Susan and said, "Anna took me to free concerts here when I was a kid."

Fred put his hand on Alex's shoulder. "We'll all be going to a concert here, with Anna. You'll see."

"I played in the Moscow Youth Orchestra here once, string bass. Anna and I went to a special dinner afterward. She invited my friend, Boris, to come with us. This isn't easy for me," Alex said taking a deep breath.

Alex led them to a large bronze statue of Tchaikovsky on a granite pedestal in a small semicircular park-like site set back from the sidewalk. "Isn't this amazing?"

"Tchaikovsky looks like a god at Valhalla looming over us mere mortals," Susan said. "It sure is a strange pose, with his arms stretched out. Is he conducting sitting down or yawning?"

Fred looked up at the statue and said, "This was the man they subjected to a life of misery while they worshipped every stroke of his pen and every nuance of his baton." Fred turned away from the statue and began walking down the few steps to the sidewalk.

Susan followed, then paused and looked back at the statue. "It's chilling that a cult exists today that would destroy every person who might bring a speck of truth to their perverted view of history."

In a hushed voice, Fred said, "What they heaped on this poor man continues today and the crosshairs are now aimed directly at us and worst of all, at Anna."

Alex waved his hands and guided them along the sidewalk to a narrow driveway made of polished gray granite blocks that led to the entrance.

"Now, how are we going to get inside without getting arrested?" Fred asked.

"Not to put a jinx on the whole thing, but the address is number thirteen," Susan said. "I hope that doesn't suck the luck out of everything."

Alex waved his hand and said, "Let's go around the block and see what this place looks like all around. We want to make sure we get inside the right section." They walked along *Bolshaya Nikitskaya* Street and around to the narrow street behind it."

As they turned the corner, Susan said, "The conservatory looked so inviting from the front, but the building looks daunting from behind. This is never going to work."

As they walked, Fred said, "We can't just barge in and hope for the best."

Alex said, "See those workmen down the street? Let's be bold, like we're inspectors of something or other. They won't see that as unusual. Just keep your mouth shut and let me do the talking. The last thing they need to suspect is that we're tourists, or worse, terrorists."

As they walked closer, Alex put his arm out and stopped Susan. "And don't look all over like a sightseer, look straight ahead. Look bored."

Fred and Susan walked behind Alex as they approached the workmen at an open rear entrance door with yellow tape stretched across it. Fred recognized the word for *enter* preceded by the words for *do not*.

Alex turned to Fred and quietly said, "Ahhh, we go for the man with the clipboard. Hopefully, he had his vodka this morning."

Alex walked over to the man and talked to him, then Alex reached for his wallet and Fred hoped he wasn't going to bribe the guy. Alex slipped a card out, flashed it to the workman, then quickly put it back in his wallet. To Fred's amazement, the workman opened the yellow barrier tape and allowed passage.

Fred and Susan followed Alex into the dark hallway, and as soon as they were alone, Fred said, "What did you show them?"

Alex smiled and said, "My membership card for the regional merchant's association, the closet thing we have to a Better Business Bureau. We had it for the shop on Karandash Street. It looks official."

A male voice behind them called out, "*Stop.*"[18]

Fred and Susan froze as Alex spun around and said, "*Shto?*" (What?)

Alex sauntered up to the man and after a brief conversation with the workman, Alex returned to Fred and Susan.

"What was that?" Fred asked.

"Oh, he told us to be careful of holes in the floor—scared the shit out of me for a minute. But we're clear to go," Alex said.

"I think this hallway leads to the main lobby. At least all these posters make it seem so," Susan softly said.

As they entered the main lobby, they swiftly merged with a small group of people waiting under a sign that said *Performance Hall Tour* in English and Russian. Alex went over to a slight woman behind a counter in the center of the main lobby and picked up a map of the Conservatory building. He studied the map while Susan and Fred looked around at the impressive layout, trying as best they could not to look like tourists. They were both pleased that Alex was taking his time to figure out the next step so that they could absorb the ambience of this place. In spite of the stir of personnel, it maintained the feeling of a nineteenth century building.

Alex returned to them a few moments later and whispered, "Let's go, follow me." He waved his hand, making Fred and Susan stand up and dash behind him as he quickly walked to the end of the hallway and turned out of sight. Susan and Fred walked behind him, trying to look relaxed to avoid the appearance of anything unusual. They all ducked into a poorly lit side hall and

---

18   Curiously, "Stop" is the same in Russian as it is in English.

waited for their eyes to adjust to the dim light.

The smell of disinfectant was poorly concealed by a cheap balsam scent. A woman was singing scales that rang through the hallway.

Alex walked ahead, down the long hallway, looking around. He stopped occasionally and peeked into a rooms, then said, "We have to test out our method for seeking a sanctuary, should we need one." He ducked into an empty office, pulling in Fred and Susan. Inside the empty office, Alex studied the map. "There are two floors that aren't open to the public, I assume they're for storage. The upper floor is very small, so I assume it's the peak of the attic. This is where we should go, the attic. But getting there is not simple. There appears to be no single stairway that goes from here to there."

As they guardedly left the empty office and walked toward the far end of the hallway, Alex sauntered boldly with his chest out and shoulders back. He winked at Susan, who tried to look as official as possible.

After a couple of people passed, Fred whispered to Alex, "Students?"

"Seems that way." Alex said, dismissively.

At the far end of the hall, Alex walked to a door with a security window and peered into a stairwell. Alex pulled the door open, then looked back and Fred and grinned as he held it open for them to enter. As he closed the door, he made sure it clicked shut behind them.

They tiptoed up three flights of stairs until they reached the top landing and had no choice but to exit onto a deserted vestibule that opened onto an extensive exhibition hall. Large, arched windows rose up from the floor, reaching the ceiling. Fred looked at them in awe as he held his breath and glanced at Susan, whose mouth was open as she looked around the vast expanse. *This had to be a ballroom or a concert hall,* Fred thought. He exhaled, "Wow." At the far end of the room, sitting at a worn, wooden desk approximately six feet long and three feet wide, there was a scrawny young woman.

Alex lifted his head, threw his shoulders back and marched to the desk and said, "We're reporting to survey the Archives." He then quickly said something in Russian.

The woman nodded, then pointed to the right to a stairway at the far end of the room that went up to the next levels.

"*Vkhod yest*" (The entrance is), the woman said, swallowed, then pointed to an alcove at the far end of the room. She opened the desk drawer, rummaged a bit and took out a bulky keychain. The keys clanged as she moved them around on the ring, finally holding onto one and dangling the ring of keys from it. She handed it to Alex.

Alex snatched the ring from her hands and, under his breath, grunted *"Spasibo"* (Thanks).

The woman looked away.

Fred stepped back and commented quietly to Susan, "That wood stick on the key—like the type used at American gas station toilets."

Alex nodded and took the keychain. He paused, then spoke in Russian for a bit. It was incomprehensible, but Fred caught the word "Sophie."

The woman gestured *no* and lowered her head.

As they walked away, Susan, acting relieved that they had overcome this hurdle, turned back to the young woman and graciously said, *"Bolshoi spasibo"* (Much thanks).

They all froze for a moment when the woman replied in perfect English, "You are quite welcome."

Susan froze at the response. She took the serve and returned the greeting, starting a conversation. "What a lovely place this is. What is this magnificent space used for? How long have you been working here?"

The woman looked at Susan with lifted eyebrows and smiled mechanically. The smile then drained from her face as if it would never return. Fred hooked his arm under Susan's elbow and dragged her off.

Alex gave Susan a stinging stare and growled, "Shit. Now we have to do this as quickly as possible. Do me a favor and don't pretend that you can speak Russian. Now that woman knows more about us than you think."

"What was that bit that you said to that woman at the end?" Fred said, "I thought I heard the word *Sophie.*"

"Just a shot to see if she knew someone named Sophie. She didn't, not that it would have done any good. I just want to get my hands around that bitch's neck," Alex said. "Shhh, we have to focus," and he walked ahead of Fred and Susan across the expansive room.

A PLAN

MOSCOW, SEPTEMBER 17, 1893

PETER ILYICH TCHAIKOVSKY fervently continued to compose his letter to Claude Debussy in Paris, tossing one version after another into the trash. This was to be his lifeline and it couldn't be frayed. He remembered the summer of 1880 when Debussy was only eighteen and was in Moscow teaching piano at the home of his benefactor, Nadezhda von Meck. Young Debussy spent some time with Peter, then forty years old, during his stay in Moscow and Debussy's respect for the greatness of this man continued to grow. Nadezhda von Meck, an influential and often cruel critic of others, often spoke exaltedly about Tchaikovsky, further impressing young Claude. Over the years, Debussy's friendship with Tchaikovsky grew although they met on few occasions.

In his letter, Tchaikovsky told of the turn of events and the clandestine decision of the Tsar's council of advisors. He mentioned his love for Ivan and his new symphony, which was well under way. He asked for Debussy's advice, mentioning that he could not trust anyone within the sphere of influence of the Tsar. Peter made it clear to Debussy, living in the relatively free society of Paris, Debussy he was the only person who could save Peter and Ivan. As mail was routinely opened for surveillance purposes, especially if it appeared to be from someone of importance, Peter sealed the letter and disguised it with a phony return address for safety. He had no doubt that Debussy would recognize the decoy and respond to Peter's real address. He had to have faith in something at this point.

A couple of weeks later a letter returned from Paris. As soon as Peter saw the postmark, his pulse quickened and his fingers quivered to such a degree that he fumbled with the envelope like an awkward infant. It arrived unexpectedly fast and Peter hoped that it implied a wholeheartedly positive response. He examined the envelope to assure himself that it had not been opened and resealed. He carefully held it up the light and convinced himself that it had slipped through the censors and was in its original condition. With his heart racing, he finally tore it open. Debussy was indeed sympathetic to Peter's plight and offered to help. The letter was clear, dangerously clear.

Dear Peter Ilyich,

Your situation is despicable and I wish to do anything, everything that I can to help. You must flee Russia as soon as you can. The danger that exists in your country, other parts of Europe and Eastern Europe hardly exists here, if at all. Come to Paris. I have made arrangements for you to live here safely. I have rented an apartment in a lovely part of Paris. It is near the Place de République where you and I strolled when you were last here. The address of the apartment is 14 rue Bérenger, apartment #17. It is not large and not very fancy, but it will suit you quite well. I hope that you maintain your health, because it is high up and there is a climb of 67 steps from the courtyard. I was short of breath when I reached the door to the apartment and I consider myself to be in excellent health. The apartment is rented under the name Razi and Albert leShoopierre. You and Ivan will be out of harm's way there. I have enclosed the key to the apartment in this letter. Keep it safe. I am not sure that it can be duplicated. I trust that this is the key to your future.

There is a music school nearby that rents their piano practice rooms very cheaply, so you will have an instrument available to both you and Ivan. You have much to give the world of music. This time the coda will direct you to a happy and productive cadenza rather than a dreadful finale, and in wonderful Paris.

Much love and admiration,
Claude

P.S. I anxiously await your latest symphony.

Peter was overjoyed reading the letter. He was elated at the vision of a new future that exorcised for the moment, the pathos in his heart. He returned to his manuscripts with a passion and expressed these elated feelings in his work. However, the plan to escape to Paris was to be seen by no one except Ivan. He was now being shadowed every moment of the day. If his intentions became known, his life would be snuffed out quickly. He had to communicate this plan to Ivan in writing, in such a way that if it were lost, no other person could comprehend what it meant.

Peter unwrapped the bundled item enclosed in the letter. It was rolled in tissue paper so that it became a fat cylinder of soft paper. He held the end of the paper and let the bundle unfold. It unrolled quickly and a large, heavy key fell to the floor. Tchaikovsky picked it up and studied the curious shape. He spoke as if he were talking to Ivan, "The key cannot be duplicated. This is the key to our happiness together—Pyotr and Ivan together—that, as well, cannot be duplicated." He slowly lifted the key to his lips and planted a soft kiss on it. Then he picked up the strip of tissue paper and rolled the key as he found it.

Peter ran over to his music cabinet and snatched the first few pieces of music off the top of the pile. He took a copy of his published work for piano, *The Seasons*, and laid it down on his writing desk. It was not a difficult piece, far below the technical and musical abilities of his student and lover. It was a convenient folio and he had no patience to attend to unimportant details. Ivan was to be part of this plan. In fact, Ivan was the reason for this plan. He set to work to write his last love letter to Ivan, enclose the key and thus set the arrangement in motion.

Peter annotated the sheet music as a teacher would do to instruct his pupil. This would not look unusual. Nonetheless, the annotations were unlike any notation that a teacher would place on a pupil's music. This was poetry from Tchaikovsky's heart. He had to include the address, *14 rue Bérenger* and instructions in the annotations, but not in a way that was obvious to uninformed observers. He worked for hours on the music. *The Seasons* were eventually littered with writing that would segue the beginnings of a new life; Peter and Ivan in Paris, a new season.

Peter summoned a carriage and rushed to Ivan's apartment. He carried the music folio in a large envelope sealed with wax. As he arrived at Ivan's street, he asked the carriage driver to slow down to a crawl. He wanted to savor this last trip to his lover's quarters. The finality of this visit aroused emotions of sadness mixed with anticipation of a new beginning, a coda indeed. The conflicting emotions were hard for Peter to bear, but seeing Ivan for possibly the last time in St. Petersburg, gave him a rush. The plan was detailed and carefully encoded so that only Ivan would understand. This was a formula for a union between Peter and Ivan that would never end. It would sweetly and unhurriedly drift into a dream. That reverie now had a beginning.

Ivan was not at home. Peter presented the music package to his landlady and explained that it was music for Ivan to study carefully. The landlady appeared happy to receive the package. Peter smiled warmly as she fumbled her words and threw in a series of inarticulate compliments to the great maestro, then she giggled with the awkwardness of her informality.

Peter knew that Ivan would easily discover the covert message in the music, that he was instructed to go to Paris as soon as possible following the directions encoded in the pages. Ivan had sufficient funds to make the trip and set up a home in the tiny apartment on the top floor of this ancient building. *Ivan is strong—he will laugh at Claude Debussy's complaint that there were sixty-seven stairs to the apartment.* Peter smiled to himself at the vision of Ivan bounding up the long climb, two stairs at a time, as he saw him do on many occasions.

Arriving back home, Peter began to feel the impact of his career in Russia tumbling into a dark abyss. He loved St. Petersburg and Moscow and the villas that his patron, Nadezhda von Meck, offered him. Nonetheless, the love of his countrymen would be shadowed by the guarantee of blind hate if it were known who he truly was. He returned home to his studio, and with a fiery passion once again reviewed his new symphony that was to be first performed on October 28· and then, to be published and named Number Six, *The Pathetique*; the last under the name of Pyotr Ilyich Tchaikovsky. Rehearsal had begun and although the musicians did not appear to understand the music, Peter was confident in its significance. He looked over the opening phrases, which he marked *Adagio*. The melody that slipped into his head during the odious council meeting sung out from the paper as if it were an echo in a deep valley. This was the centerpiece of the symphony. It was more symbolic to Peter Ilyich than just a creation of a beautiful thing. It was the angel that gave him hope during his darkest hour while he wore a mask of indifference to his tormentors. This was Tchaikovsky's life, a façade of deception that masked his inner truth. He had planned to construct a glorious finale as a testimonial to his brilliant career, but this symphony was an autobiography. To express his view on the conclusion to his life in Russia, he marked the finalé *Adagio Lamentoso*.[19] This was the most descriptive expression of his soul.

Peter and Ivan had talked about a halcyon life and possible plans to achieve it. Ivan had agreed with Tchaikovsky to tell no one of any plan that they might devise. "When more than one person knows, it is no longer a secret," he had said to Ivan whenever they discussed the future. If no one knew, there would be no pursuit. It was clear how imminent the risk was to his life.

Danger was everywhere, in Moscow, in St. Petersburg, and on the railroads. The minions of the Orthodox Church and the Tsar stalked Tchaikovsky and knew he friends. He was an important part of Russian commerce and needed to be managed. There was little doubt to the spies that Ivan was more than a student and if it became known to the world, Tchaikovsky would have to be disposable.

Tchaikovsky agreed to the Council that suicide was an acceptable solution, a compromise if you will. The alternative was likely murder. There had to be no fear that a shadow clouded

---

19 Literally, slow and complaining.

their future. As he wrote down his autobiography in the music of his final symphony, he thought of his family and his lover. His first inclination was to dedicate the work to Ivan. The love that could not be printed would embrace the listeners and disclose it aloud. As he wrote, it nagged at him that it was his family that would ultimately suffer the most. He finally dedicated the symphony to his dear nephew, Vladimir Davidov.[20] To Peter, this was the son that he always wanted—the son he would not have because of the circumstance of a miserable marriage—and the son he could not have because of laws prohibiting adoption under his terms. Scholars would describe this symphony a hundred years later as a magnificent suicide note. Tchaikovsky had every intention of evading the act.

---

20 It is unclear about Tchaikovsky's relationship to Vladimir. From some of his letters, it appears that Tchaikovsky was unaware that Vladimir was gay. Others suggest that Tchaikovsky had a gay relationship with his nephew.

ANOTHER ARRIVAL IN MOSCOW

MOSCOW, MAY 22

MARGO DISEMBARKED FROM her plane and entered the Moscow airport. Unfazed by the swarms of people rushing around like cockroaches exposed to light, she scanned the crowd for her pickup. She hadn't been able to sleep on Aeroflot flight 316 from New York and the gaggle of chauffeurs, hotel drivers and tour guides waving placards was dizzying. Off to the side, there was a man in a black suit and bow tie impassively holding a sign with the name, Margo Demidova. With a limp, she pulled her suitcase up to the man, nodded at him and then followed him to the street.

The driver took her rolling suitcase and swung it into the trunk, then shoved it into a collection of rags and tools before slamming it closed. He drove through the outskirts of Moscow in a drizzly fog making anything that might have been attractive appear lackluster. The prefab Soviet-era buildings of raw concrete loomed large against the roadway, reminding her of detention centers. *What a dreary place. How could I have lived in this tedious crap?* Traffic was bound up in a snarl, but no horns blared. She gazed at a BMW crushed in a collision with a rusty Seaz.

Margo's driver looked at the ruins and grunted. Margo raised her eyebrows and thought, *Yes, vodka at breakfast, lunch, dinner and anytime in-between, the cause of everything Russian.* She shook her head. *Russia will never change.*

Forty minutes later, the cab rolled up to an apartment house on Tverskoy Boulevard. Margo got out of the car and the driver opened the trunk, grabbed her suitcase and flung it to the ground. She extended the handle and slowly walked through the front door, then looked back out to the street and watched the driver depart. Margo walked to the elevator and pressed the up button. She dragged her suitcase onto the elevator, annoyed at how it no longer rolled smoothly, pulled the polished brass metal gate shut, and then banged the button for the fourth floor. As she watched the numbers above the door slowly count up, she wondered why she wasn't pulsing with adrenaline. Her head felt like a corkscrew was twisting into her brain.

The elevator jerked to a stop and Margo peeled open the metal gate and stepped onto the fourth floor. She grabbed the extended handle of the suitcase and lumbered down the long dark hall to Room 414.

The last time she'd been in this hotel was more than a year ago and she was happy they'd laid new carpet and put up new wallpaper, even if the dark red floral interpretation unsuccessfully tried to warm the chillingly silent passage. At room414 she heard muffled voices inside as they discussed cigars. She stiffened and knocked on the door.

"Leonid," Margo said.

"Dzyevooshka Demidova" (Miss Demidova).

The valet closed the door and secured two large bolt locks.

"Your room is ready. You refresh yourself, meeting in ten minutes. Come back to here, I take you to meeting room. They are waiting for you."

From the cloud of cigarette and cigar smoke in the foyer, she assumed that several of the usual contacts were somewhere in the apartment.

She followed Leonid to her room at the end of the long, narrow hallway. Since her last visit, several apartments had been joined into an array of big rooms. She gaped at the array of antiques in every niche and rich burgundy carpets that nearly covered the dark wood floor. Images of Russian saints were on every wall, their eyes eerily tracking her position as she walked. She stopped in front of a painting of Saint Cyril with the Cyrillic alphabet that he developed engraved on the huge frame. He stared out at her with sad eyes, a look made even more despondent by his lowered head. She took a deep breath and, staring at Saint Cyril's gloomy eyes, let out a sigh. She looked at the religious theme paintings and other Orthodox icons with gold-leafed images of various saints and wondered if they actually believed in mystic presence. As she walked past shadowy, heavily furnished rooms, she looked in amazement. In every room, the windows had heavy curtains that were drawn closed, making the rooms feel airless and confined. It had the overall impression of being a landmark museum that had been shut down and locked up for the night.

"Your room," Leonid said and opened the door to a small room, sparsely furnished. "Be in the gallery in ten minutes."

"Thank you, Leonid."

Margo felt ragged. She had just arrived on a grueling overnight flight from New York without sleep. The time change pounded her like a hangover. She looked at her watch. 3:45 PM here in Moscow and 12:45 AM in Manhattan. *Fuck, this job is a pain in the ass*, she thought. She walked to the window, looked out at the street below and wondered whom she would be meeting with and what they would ask of her. She had worked with this client before and delivered quickly and without complaints. Because this project required finding a package of music, it was a bit more complicated. *What if he starts griping about the music still not destroyed? Is this going to be a blame game?*

Margo emerged from her bedroom a short while later and wandered down the hallway, not remembering where the gallery was. Everything was different now. She returned to the hallway where she'd entered the apartment and stood alone in the ghostly quiet foyer. Leonid soon came to Margo and led her through a maze of turns entering the gallery at the far end of the sprawling suite.

There were a number of club chairs in the room. Four solemn-looking men sat in a cluster around the center, all smoking cigarettes with the exception of a heavyset man smoking a cigar. Margo recognized some of them and confidently sat down to complete the circle. She took a handkerchief from her pocket and grudgingly resisted the desire to put it to her nose. Margo glared at the men smoking as she waved her hand in front of herself. She'd been in America too long and had gotten used to the lack of smokers everywhere. She needed to concentrate on the men addressing her and not her surroundings.

The men sat silently for what seemed to be an eternity, three of them occasionally glancing at the heavyset man, making Margo feel something she rarely felt: discomfort. She had dealt with the stocky man before, referred to as Vlad, but was never formally introduced. Vlad signaled to a well-dressed man across from him and grunted his name, Dmitry. He nodded, poured a glass of vodka and placed it on the table next to Margo. She leaned back in her chair and casually surveyed the walls made of rich, precious wood carved with columns and thick shelves; an obscene display of wealth.

A tall, thin man dressed in black with a heavy white beard that covered most of his face, stood up and cleared his throat. The other three men looked up to him, waiting for him to speak. Margo had not met him before and from his stately manner, assumed that he was a Russian Orthodox priest.

"Thank you for coming to see us today. It is our pleasure to meet you. You are key to our mission."

Margo nodded.

He crossed himself with a sweeping motion, raised his chin and puffed a cloud of smoke that swirled and rose to a large amber glass chandelier hung in the center of the room. The man slowly stepped to the wall and leaned on a bookshelf. The shelf was lined with leather bound books, stamped in gold lettering, making this man seem like a gilt-framed icon. This room could be used for an exaggeratingly lavish movie set.

The burly man, Vlad, smoking a cigar stood, walked slowly around the periphery of the room. As her eyes followed this man, and took in more of the decorations, she felt a combination of admiration and contempt. The man fetched a box from the shelf and brought it to Margo. He held it for a moment, then walked to her in the matter-of-fact manner of a fellow soldier. She looked at the box and recognized the emblem, the letter *G* snaking around smaller letters, *Glock*.

THE ARCHIVES

MOSCOW, MAY 22

FRED LOOKED AROUND the magnificent sprawling space on the fifth floor of the Moscow Conservatory of Music, admiring the ornate pilasters against the arched windows. It was empty, but three stains on the parquet floor showed where a grand piano once sat. He focused on the nondescript door at the far end, then glanced back at the woman behind the desk, trying to avoid eye contact as she stared ahead like a figure in a wax museum. It was satisfying to have passed so many barriers to get this far, yet there was nothing to use for Anna's ransom. He gritted his teeth at the thought of Sophie. Now something might be within reach if luck held out in their hunt.

Alex glanced at his map of the floor plan, then said, "There it is, the door to the Conservatory's Archives." He led Fred and Susan across the expansive room to the far end of the room.

Susan walked slowly, gaping at the carved moldings while Alex, focused on the door to the archives, continued to walk briskly.

"Susan, come on. Don't act like a tourist," Fred whispered. "It's a miracle that we've made it this far."

They walked quickly toward the unremarkable door. Susan

turned and glanced back at the woman behind the desk. "She's watching us."

"Susan, you're acting suspicious. Don't," Fred said.

They crossed the room, passed through the plain doorway and turned into a small stairwell landing. A hefty iron gate secured the passage to the archives. "This is it, the mother lode of Tchaikovsky memorabilia and correspondence," Alex said quietly, standing at the gate to the attic.

"Well, here's hoping that we can get papers here about Tchaikovsky's romance with Ivan to trade for Anna," Susan said.

"Is there an alternative?" Alex whispered.

Fred stood before the large iron gate that sealed the entrance to the next higher level in the Conservatory and peered through. Shadowy boxes were piled as far as he could see. Alex inserted the key, which made a loud jangling sound as it turned. When the latch released, it reverberated like a kettledrum making Fred flinch. Alex pulled the gate open slowly, squinting as the hinges squealed.

"After that, silence doesn't seem necessary," Fred said.

"No, we have to rummage as quietly as possible," Alex said as he pulled the key out of the lock. Before them was a different type of stairwell made of open mesh stairs and a railing made of black pipe.

Susan coughed loudly and then coughed again into her handkerchief as they started to climb the stairs. "Cleaning crew on break . . . for a century," she said, brushing spider webs from her face. As she looked up the stairs, Susan turned to Fred and said, "What a mess."

"Shhh. The woman at the desk might still be able to hear us," Alex said.

Fred surveyed the stairs that were littered with boxes. "Does anyone know what's here? That's a hell of a lot of stuff; where to begin?"

Susan said, "This is a gold mine, maybe."

Alex quickly put his finger to his lips and softly shushed them. Fred slowly walked up, stopping at each step wondering if anyone knew what was stashed here. It looked like boxes were hauled to the first open spot and dropped.

Susan dug her hand in one of the boxes, lifted some pins and buttons, then let them drop like sand on a beach. She grabbed a handful of leaflets from a nearby box. "Old concert programs, loads of them," she said.

Again, Alex turned with his finger on his lips.

Fred walked up several stairs and stopped in front of a large trunk perched on the step. He bent down, jerked the blackened brass clasp and opened the trunk; the smell of vanilla and dust rose up and assaulted him like a ghost. He backed away, then reached down and thumbed through the papers inside. He looked at documents dated as far back as the 1920s. Placing them back in the box, he sighed and looked up at the stairs and the weathered boxes rising up before him. This was like the stairs to his grandmother's attic. *How many people have tried to catalog this stuff and simply gave up?* The job had to have been daunting. He walked up further and rummaged again, finding yet older documents.

Fred reached the top of the stairs, looked back at Alex and Susan rummaging through boxes and stepped through the double-wide door and into the open attic. He paused to survey the large space with wide unfinished wood plank floors and ceiling. The shape of the building made the space appear very long, seemingly narrow because of the unusual proportions, but it was at least thirty feet wide. He walked by piles of old furniture stacked against one long wall. On the long south wall, there was a row of small dormers with curved peaks. Windows in each dormer lit the space with diagonal stripes of sunlight. For an instant, Fred felt the presence of old Russia and workers that hauled the boxes up to this level. Just inside the door was a large pile of boxes, apparently deposited by the uphill flowing river of artifacts, and neatly packed for further consideration.

Fred looked around trying to orient himself. He said, "I think I know where we are. These are the eyebrow dormers that we saw from the street. I saw a second row of dormers above this; there must be another level above us."

He explored further as Alex and Susan probed in a different direction. Not far from the stairway they had just ascended, Fred found another stairway going up to the next level. He led them rapidly up the stairs and they entered a much narrower space conforming to the sloping roofline.

Fred pointed to the row of similar dormers against the long south wall on his right. "Just as I thought." He could now see the rafters supporting the roof. He walked around and saw above both the dimly lit east and west ends of the floor were a pair of catwalks across the narrow width of the attic space. Fred ran his hand along the curved handrail of the very narrow metal circular staircase that led up to the west walkway. He looked up, but the arrangement of the dormer windows cast deep shadows onto the catwalks, making it difficult to see what was up there. Each step left a small swirling cloud of dust. Fred tried unsuccessfully to stifle a cough. After poking through a few decaying cartons, he took out a handkerchief and snorted into it. The space had that awful musty odor of an attic that's been sealed for years with smells like old wood and stored paper.

Alex started to rummage around the boxes lined up against the south wall, then stopped and stood by the window. Fred walked down to the far end and looked back at the long narrow space; so much stuff piled in small mazes. He poked around some old furniture and wooden crates. Against the north wall, he stopped at a credenza and thought about what sort of person might have used it. Fred pulled open a drawer and thumbed through a pile of faded photographs. Photography was relatively new when Tchaikovsky was with Ivan; there might be some pictures. The images were of mostly of large groups who sternly stared at the camera like they were facing a firing squad. *No, too recent,* he thought. He pulled the rest of the drawers open, then moved on.

He walked up to the window to see what Alex was looking at and was in awe. The tower of the Anglican Church rose up on the Russian skyline, its squared construction gave the appearance that it was intended for another place.

"It's the only Anglican church in Russia," Alex said.

"It looks out of place."

Alex nodded. "It's a relic in more ways than one. That church was started in the mid-1500s when Tsar Ivan the Terrible allowed English merchants permission to worship."

"Neat," Fred said, and continued to pace, occasionally glancing at Susan, who seemed mesmerized by the views from the dormer windows. He continued to wander the floor, looking at Alex rummaging aimlessly, flapping a box cover here and rifling through a pile of papers there. *Focus, be systematic,* Fred thought. *How in the world are we going to fish out of this huge mess the compelling evidence that would be in exchange for Anna's ransom?* Time was running out and they had to find something about Tchaikovsky's Ivan now that the music was gone. He was nervous and wanted Susan to realize the urgency that he felt, not overwhelmed by her surroundings.

Fred walked to Susan, then she turned and said. "I can still plainly see Sophie scooting out of my bedroom window onto the fire escape with a package in her hand. Because of that friggin' woman, I'm stuck in this musty attic looking for—well, I'm not sure what."

Fred whispered forcefully, "It's getting late and we haven't begun to sort things out yet. We really have to dig into this stuff."

Susan, lowered her head, walked slowly away, then gazed up at the catwalk. She wandered over to the circular stairs and studied them for a bit. Then she took one stair at a time as if she were in a processional. Meanwhile, Alex and Fred started to rummage through boxes as fast as they could manage. Susan continued to climb the staircase until she got to the landing and stepped out onto the open steel catwalk.

"Dammit, these piles of boxes stacked against the wall make it awfully narrow." Susan said. She poked though a box, turned around, looked over the edge and quietly screamed, "Yow!"

Fred looked up and said, "Geez, Susan, stay away from the edge. Be careful, you could've fallen."

She sat down on a box and said, "I'm coming down. There's no railing and looking down through the open grid on the floor— sorry, I can't help it; makes me dizzy and unstable."

On her way back to the stairs, Susan opened boxes and quickly stood up, exclaiming, "These are letters. There are loads of photos here too with dates around 1880. This might be what we wanted. Shit, everything's in Russian. Alex, come up here. I'll change places with you. There isn't room up here for the two of us. Besides, with no handrail, I wouldn't want you near me. One bump and I would make a graceful swan dive into the nineteenth century. And I'm not sure that floor would stop me."

Susan twirled down the stairs with a satisfied and somewhat smug look on her face. She appeared pleased with herself that she made an important discovery. Fred hoped that this was the case.

Alex rushed over, hustled up to the top of the catwalk and exchanged places with Susan. He began at the box that Susan left open and started moving papers, folders and photos. Light slipping in through the dormer windows crept across the room and nagged at Fred that valuable time was passing.

After a long period of rummaging, Alex said, "These are letters to Anton Rubinstein. Interesting. Here is a box of letters from the Tsar. My God, this is amazing." He continued to open box after box. All of a sudden, Alex stopped. "I have something. This box is all full of memorabilia and letters of Tchaikovsky. God, there are a dozen boxes of the stuff. I'll pick some stuff out. And bring it down."

Fred looked up and was pleased that Alex started to make piles of papers and photographs that might be helpful. Alex emptied a few folders that contained old newspaper clippings and set them aside to help sort out his discoveries as they emerged. As he worked, Alex muttered names that he read from the documents. "Aaah, here is a newspaper page with ramblings of a gossip columnist about who was seen at a concert that Tchaikovsky was conducting. We have to save this and review the names later."

Fred dug through box after box, but they yielded nothing of interest. Looking over at Susan, now working feverishly, Fred assumed she found nothing useful as well. He looked up at the catwalk. Alex was sitting on a wooden crate, bent over a box, stacking papers into several piles.

"Wow," Alex said. A bit later he said, "Yeah."

Fred was encouraged by what he heard. Nevertheless, he had an uneasy feeling that more knew their presence than the woman at the desk. Fred opened a carton of photographs on glass, each wrapped in a sheet of soft paper. Someone had written in white ink on the bottom of each image, probably the name of the subject. He slid the carton into a beam of sunlight and opened each one, looking for an image of Tchaikovsky or his name in Russian. As the beam of sunlight slowly drifted across the room,

Fred kept feeling that time was not a reliable companion to the search. Fred stopped and listened; a creak in the floor made him jump. A beam of sunlight progressed onto a glass surface making a sudden flash of light. The place bristled with danger.

THE HUNT

MOSCOW, MAY 22

IN THE AIRLESS salon, Vlad showed the box labeled *Glock* to Margo and grunted softly. Reaching for it, she had the box rammed into her hands. She opened the box and looked at the gun set alongside the cobalt blue silencer. She looked at the man who handed it to her and thought about her assignment to get the music from Susan's apartment. It had been easy disposing of Harry and moving in with Steve so she could have easy access to Susan's dwelling. But the rest of the effort had embarrassingly failed, and now she was in Moscow in a smoke-filled apartment with some of the most powerful men in Russia. After this, there would be no more opportunities to bring this operation to a satisfactory conclusion. If she failed, she would be just one more mercenary who had quietly disappeared.

Margo watched as Vlad flicked his cigar into an ashtray, took a deep breath and pointed a finger. The priest stroked his white beard and nodded in return. Vlad made a few shallow coughs, then said, "Margo, we have been tracking this foolish music and other stuff. Homosexual proof, indeed." He tightened his lips and sneered, then shook his shoulders as if he was warding off an evil spirit and regained his composure. He nodded to the others sitting in the circle and finally gave a deep nod to the Orthodox priest standing to the side, and said, "Father Konstantin."

Margo leaned forward.

Leonid entered the room with a tray of glasses and a bottle of vodka. He cleared old glasses and placed a full glass next to each person. Margo glanced at her glass, then looked back at the priest who was speaking.

Father Konstantin took his glass of vodka, stood, downed it in a single gulp, belched loudly, then looked up at the ceiling and said, "These rumors surface periodically about every important person. It would be a disgrace if this kind of material ever surfaced in this case, no matter how fictitious it might be. It would empower those who want to undermine our church, our Fatherland." He paused and grunted. "We must root out such individuals and either stop them or end them, whichever is most expedient." He stopped to suck out any vodka from his glass that might have escaped his first gulp, then returned to his seat.

Vlad walked to the other side of the table "Margo, do whatever you have to do to get this music and stop these people and the damage they're headed for." He sucked on his cigar, then wiped some drool from his mouth and spoke with a gravelly voice. "No more dancing around the problem. Do it now!" He shuddered in a pompous display of disgust, then stared at Margo and mumbled, "The Fatherland."

Margo lifted her chin and took a deep breath. She did not care if what they believed was true or not. She was a mercenary and her work was her work. She sat in this room of another century trying to keep her breath as shallow as possible to avoid the thick cigar smoke. Margo stiffened and moved to the edge of her seat. Back in New York City, it had been only the music that had to be destroyed; now it was the people.

The priest stood and stroked his long white beard as he spoke. "I do not understand why this group of Americans continues to research material to try to discover, whatever. We have been watching them ever since they arrived in Moscow. I am told that they have just arrived at the Music Conservatory Archives. What foolishness."

Margo nodded. She looked at the glass of vodka next to her and began to reach for it, but snapped her hand back to her lap.

Coffee would be a better choice.

"Margo, I agree that they must be stopped any way possible. I have seen this kind of problem before," Father Konstantin added. He paused for a few seconds, shook his head and chanted, "They must be stopped. Homosexuality . . . no." He shook his head.

One of the other men picked up his glass of vodka, drained it in one gulp, leaned back in his chair and turned to the priest. In a mocking tone, he said, "Father Konstantin, your main interest is keeping your Orthodox flock from seeing a prominent gay luminary. You wouldn't be able to speak so strongly about such evils once your flock discovers the rampant population of your gay colleagues."

Father Konstantin cleared his throat. "The priesthood may have some errant—"

"Who cares about errant fools!" Vlad said with a loud voice.

With a bold voice, Father Konstantin chanted, "God watches—"

"Yeah, really," one of the other men said.

Margo rolled her eyes. She did not expect this infighting and mockery. But it did not change her job. Her position was to look attentive and to finish the project as soon as possible.

Turning to the other men, and conspicuously avoiding the priest, Vlad sucked on his cigar, wiped his mouth and said, "This is all more serious than that." He waved his hands, sprinkling cigar ash over the other men. "The hell with the Orthodox Church. This is our history that we are talking about here. The world will use Tchaikovsky as a homosexual martyr. This will not promote Russian interests. Not at all." He shook his head so violently that his jowls wobbled, muddling his closing words.

Father Konstantin sat down on a wooden bench against the wall, away from the others. Margo looked from one man to the other. This was not a sect of colleagues, but a group of Mafioso with cultish self-interest.

Leonid led Margo back to her room, where she assembled the things she needed and then headed out. She got her directions from the cabal of nationalists and followed the lead that the Americans had been tracked to the Archives. Information transmitted by phone from an attendant on the fourth floor gave their exact location.

As Margo walked from the guest bedroom, down the long hallway to exit the apartment, she overheard the men talking and stopped to listen. From the darkened passage, she could see the group. The stubby and restless man, Vlad, said, "It was wise to hold back the information about the old lady. Margo need not know where she is being held. Too much information can easily screw up the mission. If Margo fails again to conclude this episode, we can use the old woman as an expendable resource."

The others in the room grumbled in agreement.

"Leftovers are hard to deal with. They will hand over the music and whatever else they have for that old lady and that will be the end of the whole group of them," another one mumbled.

"Yes, no leftovers," another man said.

Margo was thankful that the end of the job was near. Failure this time was not an option and she took a deep breath, coughed to reveal her presence and left the apartment.

Margo headed directly to the conservatory, knowing that Alex, Fred and Susan were now cornered and on her turf. Tired and somewhat punchy from the long trip and the time change, Margo headed to confront the targets. She was irritable and no longer interested in clandestine movement. She called the cleanup crew to be ready to remove the bodies following the assassination. She wanted this job finished as quickly as possible. As she walked up the street to the Conservatory, she passed a shop with the unlikely name of Coffemania. It was just what she needed, another strong dose of caffeine to heighten her senses— or at least to keep her awake.

Twenty minutes later, Margo entered the Conservatory and marched past the guards and over to the stairs. She was instantly recognizable. The guards looked at her and then looked down at the ground. The doorway to the stairs was locked. It was past four o'clock and security was preparing the building for evening activities. She looked at a poster of an evening student concert, which explained the swarms of patrons wandering everywhere.

Margo stood at the door for a few minutes and, seeing a janitor wheeling a cart along the floor, signaled him to approach her. He dutifully pulled his cart and broom over to Margo and in a vacant manner he stopped and said, "What?"

She threw her shoulders back and flashed an impressive looking Spetsnaz badge[21] with its ominous looking bat and firmly said, "Unlock the door." The janitor stood, looking puzzled, silently considering the request. Margo was well aware that unlocking doors for strangers was strictly forbidden. He flashed his eyes back and forth as if he was checking for observers. The janitor stood still, nervously grimaced, then tightened his posture.

Margo clenched her teeth and said, "Unlock it." Her eyes opened wide and her nostrils flared. "Now!"

The janitor stood rigid and silent.

Margo's nose broadened as she took a deep breath, then her eyes widened and her lips tightened. Enraged, she put one hand in her pocket and felt for her pistol. The janitor lifted his hand and reached for his pocket. Keys jingled in his pocket as he put his quivering hand in and while slowly shaking his head took out a ring, fumbled for the correct key, unlocked the door and walked away. After he quickly walked several yards, Margo noticed him take a cell phone from another pocket. As he looked down at the cell phone, Margo grabbed his head from behind, pushed it down and gave it a quick twist. His neck snapped and the janitor fell to the ground.

Margo pulled his body and the cart into the stairwell and let the door swing locked behind her. She arranged his body to appear as though he had fallen on the stairs. Margo peeked back through the small window and saw two young musicians saunter down the hall seemingly oblivious to the evil a few feet away. She was trembling with rage and in no mood for diversions.

---

21 The Spetsnaz metal badge "VALOUR AND SKILL" is given to Russian Spetsnaz troopers. It is an acronym for Special Purpose Forces. There are many versions of this type of badge and replicas are easily purchased.

LOVE IN PRINT

MOSCOW, 1893

IVAN RETURNED HOME to his apartment in Moscow in a mad rush to pick up his portfolio and run to rehearsal. He was late and he was already thinking of a litany of excuses for the headmaster. He was not experienced with excuses and practiced looking sincere while floating a tale of disaster. Ivan mumbled the gratuitous excuses to himself in a pleading tone, knowing it would not work and rushed even more. His landlady greeted him as she often did. He had no time for the small talk that she often entertained. This time she was holding a neatly wrapped package with the return address shown only as ПИЧ.[22] Ivan recognized the initials with a rush of joy as he bounded up the stairs to his apartment. He pressed it to his chest with the prescient thrill of opening it, but there was no time now. He flung open the door to his apartment, hurried to the ornate armoire, rummaged amongst the clothing stacked on the bottom and slid out the leather covered box in which he kept the treasured letters of Peter.

The package was slightly larger than the box so he did not try to squeeze it in. Hurriedly, Ivan closed the box and put it away. He pressed the large envelope from his lover to his lips, knowing that he would be filled with cheerful anticipation until

---

22 Peter Ilyich Tchaikovsky's initials in Cyrillic.

he got home later in the day and saw the contents. In spite of his adrenaline surge, he slowly placed it neatly on his desk and carefully arranged it as if it was a beautiful and precious ornament. He placed a cloth over it as if to give it comfort and a touch of security. Ivan floated down the stairs two at a time, emotionally hovering in air for seconds. His soaring stride carried him into the sky and he took flight for a period that only the jubilant mind can create. He and Peter Ilyich had discussed what would be conveyed in the package, and he could not wait to study the details and dream of their future together.

Ivan's landlady was busy outside, polishing the brass ornaments at the end of the cast-iron railings. As he soared past her, Ivan grabbed her shoulders and spun her around in a flirtatious dance. She sputtered a giggle as she absorbed some of the contagious joy that overflowed from him. She could have no clue as to the reason, but smiled at the moment anyway.

"So shameful," the landlady said, complaining about the undignified spontaneity with a grin and unconvincing reprimand.

As he skipped down the street, Ivan spun around and waved to the landlady who stopped what she was doing and beamed a broad smile.

As it was far too dangerous to write anything in a letter, Ivan was unaware of any specific plans at this point. He was aware that the Council of Honor was uneasy about Peter's reputation and watching his every move. It was reasonable to assume that his letters were being intercepted as well. Ivan was also very cautious. He thought about living in the same structured society, although he was a nearly invisible fragment in Peter's world. He remembered clearly what Peter had discussed and what a life might be like without the extreme supremacy of a fundamentalist church. He recalled their talks about the likelihood that the Tsar's staff was probably sprinkled with homosexual courtiers and was empathetic to gay people. Ivan recollected the discussions of political expediency and why these servants of their master zealously went along with the Orthodox Church. It was clear to him that the Church had influence derived from a flock kept tight with fear and from patrons that were powerful and generous with the goal of securing their agenda.

But today was bright and filled with hope. As Ivan soared through the air, the melodies of Peter Ilyich's symphonies accompanied his dance of optimism. At his rehearsal that day, his playing was ebullient and expressive and brought generous comments about his musicianship. No one could suspect that there was a reason that his contemplative performance at the previous session had changed to elation this time.

DEADLY
CONFRONTATION

MOSCOW, MAY 22

WITH A DETERMINED pace, Margo climbed the stairs of the Conservatory with her hand firm on her gun. She stopped for a moment and felt for the silencer in her waist pack, then slipped it out and assembled the cobalt blue silencer on her Glock pistol, making the deadly weapon ponderous. The contract that had become her life was finally coming to a head. This had been a long journey, unlike the ordinary quick jobs. Margo felt a sense of relief that this snarled odyssey would soon end. *It should have ended in New York. Now the target has been broadened from the music to its possessors. Those three bothersome people must be swiftly eliminated.*

Margo limped up the stairs, tapping a syncopated rhythm. In the musty stairwell, she kept her hand around the cool gun switching hands back and forth. Three shots are all it would take to finish here and move on. Kill and call for cleanup. She knew that if she failed here, she would be the hunted. She tightened her grip on the cold gun. Her hand felt clammy; she switched hands. Today, the mission was to be quick, decisive and move on. Margo's conviction for an expedient conclusion turned her limping steps into a swagger as she combed her finger over the trigger guard. She strode up the stairs and swung around the landings.

Margo shoved open the double doors and walked up to the woman who was busy wiping down the desk. "Where is the trouble?" Margo said.

The woman at the desk jumped to her feet, pointed to the door at the far end of the room, then pointed to a key at the edge of the desk and in a dry voice, said, "In case gate closed."

Margo snatched the key from the desk, coldly said, "*Kharasho,*"[23] and holding the attic gate key in her fist, walked directly toward the door. Beyond the door, she found the heavy iron gate left open and cautiously walked through.

The long travel, time zone change, and copious amounts of caffeine made Margo more edgy than usual. She was a package of dynamite with a stunted fuse. She tightened her finger on the trigger guard, ready to detonate at the appropriate moment.

Margo tiptoed up the stairs, pausing on the first landing to stop and listen. Nothing. She took off her shoes, adjusted her grip to hold the gun with two hands and slowly made her way up the stairs, prepared for any sound. Her targets were upstairs and she needed the element of surprise.

A melody from a French horn boomed up from below, then repeated, stopped, then repeated again. Margo ground her teeth, listened when the horn playing stopped, then continued up the stairs. The horn continued, allowing Margo to be stealthy with little difficulty. She was now able to use the horn as a shield, allowing her to move quickly and secretly when it blared.

At the first attic level, Margo looked through the doors and saw nothing. She closed her eyes, crouched slightly and heard voices from above. She reached in her pocket, took out a map of the floor plan and verified that there was but one single entry to the top level; no way out. She climbed the stairs trying to move as few uninvolved muscles as possible with the stealth of a leopard focused on her target. The French horn player continued. She advanced to the double doors of the upper level attic and listened. She could see Fred through the space between the double doors that were slightly ajar. Margo stiffened her grip on the trigger guard and tightened the muscles in her arms.

23 хорошо, Good.

"Let's get this pile organized," Susan said.

Margo bent down and looked through the crack between the doors. Fred was moving some boxes with Susan. She rolled her eyes and wondered what they might have found. She watched Fred rummage through a box while Susan sifted papers through another carton.

"Might be a lot of good stuff here," Susan said.

Margo listened, hoping to hear something to report back, and waited. Although she was eager to rush in and kill them, she had to stick to the plan.

Susan mumbled to Fred below the catwalk, "Do you think that anything we find here will be as important as the music?"

The music? Margo moved her finger to the trigger.

"Poor Anna. We're going to get more ammunition for this situation if it takes us until the moment we have to meet at Anna's shop," Susan said.

The talk about Anna made no sense, but she was not in the mood for sense. Margo took a deep breath and replaced her finger back on the trigger guard. Margo stepped to the side to see through the window on the door. She watched Fred move boxes on one side of the room while Susan studied Russian characters on the boxes.

Susan kept looking at notes. "These letters (Иван) mean *Ivan* and this lettering (Пётр Ильич Чайковский) is *Peter Ilyich Tchaikovsky*," she said. She rummaged through some more papers and said, "Ivan and Peter, Ivan and Peter." Susan then said, "I'm optimistic. Optimism is our fuel."

Margo clenched her teeth and snarled. *It's time.* She kicked the doors and marched into the attic space.

When the door flew open, Alex looked through the grate of the catwalk to find Margo standing below him. He closed his hand around the photographs he just found and stood firm.

"Oh my God!" Susan screamed.

Fred stood still, his eyes wide, his mouth open.

This was horrific. Margo pointed the gun at Fred.

Alex froze. He put his hand up to his mouth and pressed tightly against his lips. A chill flashed from his toes to his neck as Margo stood facing Fred and Susan. *What new Hell has fallen on us?* Fred turned toward Margo and stiffened.

Alex trembled as Susan muttered, "Margo, you—" Susan's jaw dropped. "You—" She stepped back.

Fred did not blink for at least half a minute, stepped back and raised his hand in front of his face. Margo stood with her gun pointed at Fred.

Alex mouthed, "No, no, Fred!" as Margo moved her finger to the trigger and walked farther into the room. She turned facing the door so that Alex could now see her face. He began to shudder. "Please, no. Fred," he mouthed.

Silence.

Alex prayed that Margo would not look up.

"What do you want?" Fred said.

Margo kept the gun pointed at Fred. "You have the music. You have Anna. We have nothing."

Fred said. "What do you want from us?"

Margo stood fast with both hands holding the gun pointed at Fred. Alex looked down at Fred staring at the gun that moved slowly back and forth like a cobra about to strike.

Alex watched Susan move slowly away. He put his hand over his mouth and stopped breathing.

Margo turned toward Susan. Susan stiffened, squinted tightly and mouthed, *No.* She started to look up toward Alex.

From the catwalk, Alex glared at Susan and mouthed, *Don't look up, don't look up, don't.* He moved his hands back and forth. *Do not look up!* Susan looked down and Alex breathed a sigh.

Alex leaned to move back but his legs froze by the edge of the catwalk.

"Where is the music?" Margo snarled. Then, turning to Fred, she said, "And where is Alex hiding?" She took a few steps toward Fred. "Well?" she roared.

Alex tried not to move as the photographs dropped from his hand.

Margo said, "You don't have a choice. Give me the music."

Fred raised his hand as if that would stop the impending bullet. "If we had it, I would give it to you. We have nothing. It was stolen." He leaned back. "We can give you what we found here. That's all we have."

Margo raised her gun and pointed it at Fred's head. "Last chance."

Fred turned his head away.

Alex wanted Susan to make a distraction, but she didn't move or say anything. Susan was frozen, breathing heavily with her mouth opening and closing but uttering not a single word. Margo turned toward Susan aiming at her chest.

Alex looked down at Margo standing under the catwalk. He slowly moved over to a huge wooden box full of manuscripts that was positioned near the edge, aware that the slightest creak would be his death.

Alex heard his heartbeat thumping like kettledrums and his breathing like a windstorm. He moved as slowly and noiselessly as possible. He concentrated on sounds from below and coordinated his movement.

"Margo, don't," Fred said.

Alex nudged the crate an inch.

"No more chances," Margo said.

The crate made a squeal moving on the steel grating. Alex backed off, froze and shut his eyes tight. He tried not to tremble, but that wasn't working.

Susan glanced up and coughed loudly, which resonated from the far side of the room.

Thank you, Susan, he thought as he breathed deeply.

Alex put his hands onto the crate again and nudged it a bit closer toward the edge. It made no sounds as it moved ever so slightly.

Alex prodded the crate nearer to the edge, viewed down at his target, and finally gave it a shove. He stood back as it teetered at the edge for a moment and watched it tip, almost balanced. Then like the slowness of cold honey, it tilted and with a snarling growl slid the rest of the way off the catwalk.

Margo spun around and stared up. She glared at the box as it came straight toward her eyes. Alex inhaled loudly as it seemed to hover in mid-air, giving Margo enough time to raise her gun. She looked up and fired three shots toward Alex.

Fred wailed, "No."

Alex clenched his fists and raised his hands to his chest. The crate plummeted toward Margo's head, hitting it with a thud. Margo lay directly beneath him on the raw wooden deck, her wide-open eyes staring at him and blood trickling from her mouth.

The explosive rumble recoiled from the far end of the long room with a roar. The room then became bathed in freakish silence. Fred screamed, "Alex."

"I'm okay," Alex said in a trembling voice. "It's all right."

Fred put his hand on Margo's neck, then stood up and said, "Done."

Alex grabbed several folders of manuscripts and with tears rolling down his face he breathlessly said, "The blood will be dripping down through the floor to the room below in a few minutes. Let's get the fuck out of here."

Fred turned and said, "Susan, you okay?"

Susan stood, staring at Margo's lifeless body. Fred grabbed her hand, met Alex as he scurried down the catwalk stairs, pushed through the double doors and bolted down the stairs.

They retraced their path down the main staircase to the first floor. As they approached the exit, they stepped around the janitor, lying dead on the floor in the stairwell. Fred quickly led Susan and Alex from the stairwell to the lobby, pausing to hear the door click locked. They pushed through a horde of people in the lobby outside the concert hall. Alex stretched his arms slowing the pace and they walked out the front door and onto the street.

"Geez," Susan said, then took a slow, audibly deep breath. "I thought it was all over." She draped her arm on Alex's shoulder.

"My God," Fred said, putting his arm on Alex's shoulder and then remembering where he was, dropped his arm to his side.

They kept walking briskly.

"I hate to say it," Susan said, wiping her forehead. "When I looked at the gun pointed at me, I thought—" She began to cry. "—we're gone and Anna's next."

Fred looked up at the gray sky, then turned to Alex and said, "It's getting dark. Where are we going?"

For that time of day, it was darker than expected. A fine mist filled the air.

"I think it's starting to drizzle," Susan said as she walked faster getting ahead of the others. A strong gust marked a change in the weather. "Damn, it's raining," she said, hunching as they walked into the breeze.

Fred said, "Alex, those old papers are getting wet. You better stuff the folders under your shirt."

Fred led them into a side street, a narrow road not much bigger than an alleyway. It felt comfortable to slow down even with the steady shower. Fred pulled his collar up to protect himself from the rain, then helped Susan adjust her jacket collar.

Susan raised her head and wiped the rain from her face. "We have to get a new hotel. We can't go back to where we've been seen before."

"The police might be looking for us. I don't know," Alex said. "Could that mess look like an accident?"

"She has a gun in her hand. Who knows what they'll think," Susan said.

"We just don't want to make any contact with police at all. They'll question us for days and fuck up any chance of getting to Anna," Alex said.

"I remember a hotel a few blocks down this street that we passed on the way here," Fred said. Let's scope it out and see if we can stay there. We'll get our bags later."

They entered the hotel lobby and stood dripping on the marble floor. Fred looked around for a clerk. Alex walked up to the front desk, a window surrounded by ornate pilaster columns and a worn marble surface. He tapped the bell on the counter and waited.

"There's no one here," Susan said.

Fred wandered around the lobby looking for someone. He admired the space, decorated with high columns and plaster ornamentation and although the plaster was chipped and the paint peeling, it still gave a feeling of elegance, albeit decaying elegance.

A woman with a red and yellow floral kerchief on her head lumbered from behind a marble pillar with a mop in her hands. She mumbled something under her breath and started mopping the floor.

Alex asked, "Where is the hotel manager?"

The housekeeper reluctantly put down her mop, walked behind the counter, removed the kerchief, shook her hair and briskly said, "*Shto?*"

Susan whispered to Fred, "Is she the only one working here?"

"Multipurpose," Fred said. "This isn't a Hilton."

Alex asked, "Is there a room for the night?"

The woman looked at the three of them and said, "Only single rooms. You take three rooms. Yes?"

Susan walked over to Fred, poked him and nodded toward the door. A slender woman with a kerchief over her lowered head, obscuring her face, stepped in from the street and stood motionless. It was her lifelessness that mesmerized Fred.

Alex took the three keys and led Fred and Susan to the staircase. Fred looked back at the motionless woman, then walked up to this room. Arriving at the three adjacent rooms, Fred said, "I don't like the idea that we're separated tonight."

As they went into their rooms, Susan said, "Sleep tight. Well, as best you can."

"Good night," Fred said, and they closed their doors onto an empty hallway.

Fred found a wrinkled magazine on the dresser from 2001 extolling the virtues of Moscow and threw it on his bed, then tucked himself in and sat up mindlessly turning pages. A short while later, he heard the wail of police car sirens in the distance. Clearly there was more than one patrol car. The sound came closer. Fred slid down, turned off the light and pulled the covers up to his neck and listened carefully.

He heard a light tapping, went to the door and listened.

"Fred, it's me."

Fred opened the door a crack, letting Alex slip in. "They must've found Margo," Alex whispered. "Keep the lights off. I think we're okay for now. I didn't use our real names when I signed in here."

The doorbell to the hotel clanged several times, then stopped. There was a scratching at Fred's door. "It's Susan," Alex said, then quietly let her in. They stood by the door listening. The hotel was quiet and the police car sirens wailed, clearly receding.

Susan whispered, "What's a Russian jail like?"

"Y'don't want to know," Alex said. "We need to stay together, Susan. You should stay in this room tonight."

Fred went back to bed with Alex squeezed beside him and

Susan in the single bed alongside. He lay there listening to sirens in the distance, then replayed the sound of bullets firing at Alex. He expected the night to be sleepless.

Fred awoke as the first light of daybreak streaked through the window. He sat up in bed listening for any activity in the hotel. Fred tried to return to sleep but could not shake the stress of the day before. He propped up his pillow and thought about the new people in his life and the dreadful situation that had developed with the music. Fred adjusted his pillow, looked up at the ceiling and had a vision of Anna softly smiling the first time that he and Susan wandered into her shop in Brooklyn. He thought about Alex, who was so politely curious about meeting new people and now was tormented about Anna. He couldn't imagine the suffering that Alex was going through. He tried to picture his late mother in Anna's predicament. It was incomprehensible. It all seemed to be salvaged from a far more distant memory a long time ago; friends he had loved and lost. He slid down and put his face in his pillow.

A short time later, Susan leaned over Fred's bed and whispered, "Let's get going, guys. I'm all ready."

"Alex," Fred said.

"I'm up. I don't think I slept at all."

"Let's go downstairs and get some breakfast. It's included in the rate," Susan said. "And here, this note was slipped under your door. I didn't read it. I think the manager wants to date you, Fred."

Fred snatched the note from Susan.

Alex, Fred and Susan,

You are being followed and observed everywhere you go and are unlikely to shake that off. Some that follow you are intent to cause harm. You need a friend in Moscow or you will be in mortal danger. You have one already. You would be wise to trust no one but me—I am that friend. My goal is to find Anna and safely free her.

Tonight at 9 PM, come to the south side of the Large Polyanka Bridge on the canal. I will be waiting there with my boat tied up against the stone sea wall. You will recognize our boat by the white flag. Be there promptly at 9, neither earlier nor later. And most of all, do not attract attention.

Remember, you are being observed—everywhere. When you come to the canal this evening, walk directly to the mooring. If there are other people walking around, use them as your shield. If you are early and do not see us, keep moving—walk around the block once and come back. But do not be late. We can only wait for so long. We do not want to arouse any suspicion. Once we get the boat launched, no one will be able to follow undetected. If they do, it will be damn obvious.

Bring nothing. My brother will get your bags from your hotel. No one must think you are checking out.

"This is bizarre. Is this note for real?" Susan said.

"Do we dare get on a boat on the Moskva River at night? This is crazy," Alex said. "And it was even mentioned in the note, tracking a boat in the dark is nearly impossible. This'll be the riskiest move yet." He paced across the room. "But what else've we got? I have a feeling that we're going to do it."

In the hallway, outside the breakfast room, Fred saw a painting of a peasant woman and couldn't help but think about Anna and wonder how they were going to get her back. He glanced at Alex, then gently placed his hand on the small of his back. Alex looked at the same painting. Alex was being so brave. He could only imagine what Alex was really feeling.

Entering the breakfast room, Susan stopped, looked up at the vaulted ceiling and said, "Wow, can you imagine this place in its heyday?"

Fred walked over to the wall painted with folk art and said, "Look at the detail. This was painted by a really talented artist." Fred studied the detail in the crown molding and pictured the room in its finest moment, a tribute to the Imperial architecture period. He stepped to the center of the room, looked up at the paint peeling from the ceiling and said, "This place could be classy again—just a paint job."

"I know," Susan said, then pointing at a flickering sconce, "And that kills any ambience it might have had."

Susan walked ahead to an empty table and stood waiting for Fred and Alex. Fred glanced at the only other person in the room, a woman sitting at the far table, dressed in black with a dark purple scarf over her head. The woman was reading a book with her head lowered, apparently oblivious to any movement around her. Susan pulled out her chair, making a screeching sound and sat down. Fred rolled his eyes, then he and Alex gently pulled out their chairs. A few minutes after they sat down, coffee was served along with a large basket of rolls and brown bread.

Breakfast was served and the three ate in silence, each thinking about the eerie beauty of their surroundings and the danger they avoided. Finally, Susan smacked her hands on the table, palms down.

"Okay, let's summarize: we don't know who left the note, we don't know if this is a setup, and most of all, there's no name. Why would anyone who claims to be our friend not want to leave their name? We're going to be shanghaied, I can feel it."

Alex looked at Susan for a minute and said, "The note started out with our first names. We didn't use those names when we checked in. This isn't some random nutcase."

Fred thought a minute, then said, "All good points. And, what if that note got into the wrong hands? I would hesitate to put my name on it. That much makes sense a little."

"But why on the river?" Alex said. "Yesterday, you stared down the barrel of a gun and today we're talking about jumping on a stranger's boat in the Moskva. I don't know."

"Look, if we sit here talking, wanting and wishing, Anna will not come waltzing through the door," Fred said. "We have to do something, anything. And here, a plan has been dropped into our laps."

"Okay, I'm in," Alex said as he nodded. "Let's plot our path and hope tomorrow they don't find our bodies bobbing in the Moskva."

Susan searched for a map of the city in her bag and spread it out onto the table. "Don't write on the map. We don't want to have anything revealing that can be stolen," Susan said.

Alex turned the pen and poked a dimple on the map. Susan quickly folded the map, becoming even more unsettled trying to use the original fold lines on the map to get it back to the way it was. They sat silently while the state of affairs sunk in. Music began playing in the hallway of the hotel.

Fred said, "How apropos, Tchaikovsky, his *Serenade for Strings*, chopped in the middle as if it had been guillotined."

Alex got up from the table. "We're either going to find Anna or we're going to be shanghaied. Now let's check out and get out."

THE BOAT

MOSCOW, MAY 23

LIGHT WAS FADING as Fred walked with Susan and Alex along the waterfront on the large island in the Moskva River, stepping over creaking wood planks covering the damaged stone pathway. Shops lined the opposite side of the canal, just across the Luzhkov footbridge. Fred watched the people milling about on the other side of the canal, clearly standing out as they perilously did. He looked at his watch. Seven-thirty. Perhaps they had arrived too early, he wasn't sure.

Fred thought for a minute and pointed across the river. He wanted to go where there were people roaming around to be part of a crowd. They began crossing the Luzhkov footbridge. Susan stopped and scanned the crowd.

At the middle of the bridge, Fred too, stopped and looked back at the cluster of gold onion-shaped domes dazzling brilliant in the setting sun and exclaimed, "That's magnificent."

"C'mon, keep moving," Alex said, then spun around and said. "Pretty grand, huh? Those are all inside the Kremlin walls." He walked ahead at a faster pace, looked back and said, "C'mon, we'll find something to eat on this side of the canal." A short walk down a neatly bricked pedestrian footpath, Alex pointed to the Klassica restaurant, guided them in and selected a table near a piano.

"I'm glad the service is slow—we have lots of time to kill," Fred said as he looked around the sparsely filled room.

Susan said, "And I'm kinda enjoying the music coming from outside." She leaned to look out the open door. "It's somewhere around here. It must be a rehearsal—I've heard the same section a few times."

"Yeah, we're not far from a music conservatory. There's a wonderful folk orchestra there, an orchestra of balalaikas. That must be what we're hearing," Alex said.

After dinner, the sky turned to dusk. Fred squirmed restlessly in his seat and watched the crowd outside move more quickly, reacting to the nippy air.

With her hands clasped like a child, Susan sat on one side of the tiny table in the restaurant looking at Alex and Fred. "What are we supposed to do for the next hour?"

Fred looked at a clock on the wall and said, "Fifty-five minutes."

Alex said, "We can't go back to the hotel and get our bags. That would be a signal that we're on the move."

Susan said, "The note clearly said that our bags will be fetched, if you can believe it."

Fred said, "Just stay here and have another dessert. We shouldn't have left so early." Fred shifted his position, first crossing his left leg and then his right. He arranged the empty glasses on the table, fiddled with the silverware, then rearranged them again. He glanced at the clock on the wall. The minute hand hardly moved since the last time he looked.

"We should go back to get some warm clothes," Susan said. "I've only got this light windbreaker. I'll freeze on a boat at night."

Alex said. "This is not a cruise," and shook his head. After a moment, he said, "But I agree, we should have some warmer clothing with us."

Fred left a generous tip on the table and hurried to join Susan and Alex who were already walking briskly toward the hotel. As he caught up, he said, "It gets cold really fast here when the sun sets."

They located a nearby Metro on their map and rode to their hotel, then walked swiftly into the hotel, got some warm clothing and headed back out to the street. Without knowing exactly where to wander, they retraced their steps to the Metro to get to their meeting spot even though they were warned not to arrive early or linger there. Fred thought it seemed prudent to scope out the spot while there was still at least some light.

They took the Metro to the Cathedral of Christ the Savior station and as they emerged to the street level, Susan stopped and looked up at the huge floodlit golden onion dome. "That's bigger than enormous; truly amazing."

"Wow," Fred said as they backed away from the site toward the river, "That's quite a sight."

They walked to the nearby Patriarshiy Bridge and crossed the Moskva River, then walked across the narrow end of the island and the rest of the bridge to the south shore of the canal. They found their way to a path along the stone sea wall that went along the shore and walked northwest toward the meeting spot under the Large Polyanka Bridge.

As they walked in the dim light, Alex pointed to a tiny chapel set back from the path and said, "Let's go inside that church to sit out the remaining time."

As they stepped inside, Fred imagined a movie setting perfumed with damp incense. The air felt like it had been imprisoned for a century. Stained glass windows and flickering candles colored the dim light.

"This is like stepping back a century and a half," Fred said. He looked around and puffed out, "Whew. How can people breathe in here?"

Susan covered her mouth and coughed. "Heavenly, but toxic."

They sat down in the last row of pews and looked around at the gilded icons in the flickering light. As they sat silently, Fred thought, *This was the atmosphere that Tchaikovsky breathed. This is the level of light that he worked in. The man could have been sitting in these very seats gathering his thoughts that he embodied in his final symphony, his musical statement of life.*

As they looked at the gilded icons of saints hanging on the walls, sparkling with the light from dozens of candles, Fred had a ghostly sense of the root of Tchaikovsky's persecution, a century and a half after he was gone from his public that worshipped his achievements. He leaned over and whispered to Susan, "Religious orthodoxy still haunts."

Susan whispered, "Nothing has changed." She coughed lightly. "Fumes, toxic with hypocrisy—thick with it."

A young man wearing a black robe emerged from behind a partition in the front of the church and walked across the front of the sanctuary, moved some objects, then departed toward the rear. Fred became uneasy and said, "It's time to go." They quietly left the church onto the court surrounded by drooping trees and out to the street. Twilight was nearly gone and a slight mist covered everything with a glossy wetness.

"I'm glad we went back for coats," as she tightened her coat and buttoned it up to her neck.

When they approached the bridge over the canal, Alex said, "Over there's where boats usually tie up, there, against that mossy stone sea wall."

They stopped at the head of the bridge, "Remember, the note warned us about arriving early. We should cross to the other side so we can see them better. Otherwise, we'll be pacing back and forth attracting attention." Alex led them to the pedestrian path on the bridge, crossed to the other side and walked with a metered pace along the edge of the canal.

"This does give us a better view of the moorings," Fred said. Susan grabbed Fred's arm and snuggled as they meandered along the dank waterfront.

Ahead of them, a group of tourists had just spewed from a tour bus and were being herded by a tour guide. "Here, let's attach ourselves to the back of that tour group—we'll blend with the cluster," Fred said. "This'll allow more time to study the waterfront and find the boat." The group walked along the canal, stopping to admire the colorfully lit fountains in the canal.

"There it is, on the other side," Alex said. "See the white flag; it's them. I pray that this is not a trap." They walked with the group. "We have to cross the canal again to get to the boat," he said. Alex paused, looked around and said, "Over there, we'll have to break from the tourist group."

"Alex, shouldn't we take that small bridge that we crossed earlier rather than the one that the map shows us to cross?" Fred asked.

"Yeah, that's better," Alex said, and led away from the tour group toward the closest bridge. Starting to cross the small bridge, Fred became aware of two hulking men that stood in the middle of the walkway looking over the edge at the dark water below. As they got to the middle of the bridge, Fred started to get nervous seeing the men stand up and move to the center of the roadway. He thought it would not be possible to pass them without some sort of confrontation. Alex put his hands against Susan and Fred to signal that they should slow down.

In a hushed voice, Alex said, "Look casual."

Fred looked away, pretending he was interested in the fountains in the middle of the canal. As he turned back, he inadvertently looked straight at one of the men. The light from a lamppost made the stranger's eyes glow amber, drawing Fred's glance into a brief stare. Fred spun back.

Alex reached out and poked Fred to keep walking. To Fred, everyone looked like an agent of some nefarious and murderous gang out to seize them, but these men looked particularly onerous. He whispered, "Come, let's back off and get away from here."

Fred walked up to Susan and linked arms. He slowed his pace in an attempt to appear more casual.

"Maybe I should have brought extra underwear," Susan said.

Fred grinned and willed himself not to look back. He could be wrong about being followed, but didn't want to chance it. They merged with the tour group and were swallowed by the babbling herd once again. They were invisible for the time being. Fred peered back at the bridge through the shield of a cluster of tourists and could no longer see the men watching them. Fred said, "I still have the feeling that we're under surveillance."

Alex waved his hand and said, "The boat is waiting for us. Now, we've got to get there promptly. They'll leave without us and then what? Let's move it."

They stood on the long, narrow island with the Moskva River to the North and the canal to the South. Fred felt that someone had been stalking them all along. Moving unobserved was going to be difficult. As they passed a vendor at the edge of the canal with a cooking stand, roasting something with a seductive fragrance, Fred turned his head. Susan said, "Smells like roasted potatoes. Wow, I can almost taste 'em. We should bring a snack for the boat."

"Susan, c'mon," Fred said, "This is no time to think about being hungry. This vendor could have a cell phone and a video camera pointed at us for all we know. Let's stay on course and not get diverted."

Rather than go directly to the bridge over the canal, Alex led them in the opposite direction, ducking into doorways and looking around.

They huddled tightly in the dark entranceway of a large building, Fred and Alex in front, Susan behind and surveyed the surroundings. Fred stepped out cautiously and looked back and forth. "It looks like we've lost those two men for now."

"We're good," Alex said, leaning out.

"Well, let's get out of here. I'm getting squashed back here," Susan said.

They hurried back to Bolotnaya Boulevard and walked west to the Bolshaya-Polyanka Bridge, weaving around parked cars and busses. "What is that throbbing sound?" Susan said.

"This is the clubbing district, a tough place," Alex said. "You're hearing the music, well, the part that escaped. Just keep moving."

Fred looked up at a clock mounted on a lamppost on the bridge and said, "It's time—it's now, we should be there."

On the south side of the canal, they quickly walked east on Kadeshevskaya Street to the spot where they last saw the boat with the white flag. It was dark now, except for streetlights twinkling in the mist and fountains in the center of the canal spraying above colored lights.

"There it is, the white flag," Susan said, waving her arms.

"Cool it!" Alex quietly said, and rushed ahead.

There was one person on the deck facing away from them, wearing a dark coat and a dark wool cap. A raised collar obscured the face. A young man was on the dock with the boat. Fred assumed that this was the brother mentioned in the note.

As they approached the boat, the person on the deck turned around and raised her hand. As she turned around to greet the passengers, her fair skin framed by a dark coat made her face look like it was disembodied, floating in the air.

The three froze as if they had glanced at the hideous Medusa and had turned to stone. Like a clap of thunder, Susan belted out, "Sophie? What the fuck?"

Sophie smiled and waved. "Hi, yeah, I'm the friend, your friend. Come aboard."

Fred repeated Susan's sentiment, "What the fuck?"

THE RIVER

MOSCOW, MAY 23

LOOKING DOWN AT the deck of the boat and staring at Sophie with wonder, Fred still felt the fear of being shanghaied. Alex stepped onto the rusting ladder that was bolted to the embankment and carefully stepped down. Once on the deck, Alex looked up at Fred and Susan, then nodded to come aboard.

Fred walked around the deck noting the odd-looking repairs and mismatched vinyl cushions. He ran his finger over patches of duct tape holding fittings on the boat from falling, hoping that the boat ran better than it looked. Fred looked up at the nearby bridge occasionally, distracted by the rumble from a passing car. The row of fountains in the middle of the canal sprayed a fine mist when the breeze came toward the boat, making discomfort from the cool night air unavoidable, but Fred raised his collar to try to block it. He looked up at Susan and nodded. Susan looked straight down when she approached the ladder and hesitated. Sophie's brother went over to Susan and steadied her shoulders as she stepped onto the ladder. He kept his hands on her shoulders as far as he could reach while she climbed down to the deck. Sophie's brother then slid down the ladder and jumped onto the deck. He hurriedly went to the controls and started the engine, then let loose the ropes and gunned the engine. The boat jerked forward and the mossy granite block sea wall at the docking site quickly shrank in the distance.

Sophie directed the travelers to their seats at the rear of the boat as she said, "I'm the one that left the note. I'm on your side. I'm the friend you badly need and I'm truly sorry for any confusion that you may have. Let me explain."

Fred moved to the edge of his seat and said, "*Confusion?* Confusion is miles away from how we feel. The restaurant, the hotel, what is it with you? Who are you?"

In a composed and affable tone, Sophie said, "First, let me begin with—yes, I have the music. It's in a safe place. If it had fallen into the wrong hands—and it most assuredly would have—it would have made you and Anna far less secure than now. And, let me convince you, you are far from secure. Katyusha, Anna's longtime friend from Moscow, sent me. I am Katyusha's niece. I live in New York now and see Katyusha from time to time. We're still close with our family here in Russia. Katyusha is so troubled about Anna's abduction that she is practically out of her mind. She repeats and repeats that she knew that something like this would happen when Anna kept the music."

"But she didn't keep the music," Alex said.

"True," Sophie said. "When Anna gave the music to Fred and Susan we expected things to ease up. But then you got entangled. That made Katyusha and Anna decide that I should get involved and keep an eye on things. So here I am."

Fred sat back in his seat. Susan let her hand rest lightly on his and, still dazed, he listened to Sophie. "Anna and Katyusha gave me a brief history of the music without very many details. Now that the situation has progressed to this dreadful point, I had no choice but to come over here to be part of the solution."

"Dreadful point, yeah," Fred said.

Sophie looked Fred in the eye and said, "The axe isn't far from your heads."

"How did you find us?" Fred said.

"It was easy. You stayed in one of the most obvious tourist hotels in the city. I'm staying in a small village a ways out of Moscow with my family. It's safe there."

"Sophie, where's your family?" Alex asked. "What's the name of their town?"

"My grandparents have a farm on the river to the north of Moscow. My parents live there now. My brothers and their families run the farm. Two have families and one, the youngest," she said, then pointed to her brother, "he hasn't found the right woman, yet. We have other relatives in the village. We look after one another."

"What town?" Alex said, "I know some towns north of Moscow."

"The village used to be called Volkamir, but it has been absorbed into a larger village and that name is hardly used anymore. Other villages have also lost their names."

"Why? Isn't this a bit unusual?" Susan asked.

Sophie smiled. "It is probably because a large part of these villages were Jewish. After the Jews were driven out, all references to the village's existence were erased. These were called *shtetles*, not even a small village. The show, *Fiddler on the Roof*, took place in a shtetle. It was exactly like that. That's where we live."

"What goes on there? Is this *actually* a farm?" Fred asked.

"It's a beet farm," Sophie said as she turned to look over her shoulder. "They grow beets to sell. They also grow vegetables and raise some farm animals for our own use."

"Sophie, how can you support multiple families on a beet farm? How much land do you have?" Alex asked. "I think it's time for you to tell us what the real story is."

"Yeah, there's more. We live on this, the Moskva River. There's a huge commerce on the river that is, how can I say, not what you read about. My family started a half century ago when there were political prisoners being brought from Hungary. These people were bribing their way out of prison and fleeing the best way that they could. My family aided these escaping prisoners and helped them get as far away from the prisons as possible. We had a safe house and a transportation service. That business continues to this day, although we mostly transport materials rather than people."

"So you're smugglers," Susan said.

Sophie tilted her head and slowly broadened her smile. "If you want to put that it that way," she looked Susan in the eye and said, "so be it."

Fred now knew the ransom was intact, given the assumption

that Sophie had it. But apparently that was not all, Fred thought. It had been confirmed that he, Alex and Susan were a festering lesion to a perverse cult. Margo had said so in no uncertain terms. If things had gone differently in the conservatory, they might be there lying on the floor rather than Margo.

"It's important that we are getting you out of Moscow right now. You were doing no good there and you might cause harm to yourselves and to Anna as well. The whole family has talked about this. My brothers are well aware of this situation and they are trying to get some information as to where Anna is being kept. I want you to meet them. I'm sure that you'll like them. They speak some English and would love to practice it with you. My youngest brother, here, at the helm," She turned to the helm and smiled. "You'll get to know him and, I'm sure, love him as I do."

"I assume that we're going to your farm now," Fred said. "Where are our bags and stuff?"

"Yes, We're taking you to our farm. My brother got your bags from the hotel and they're stored below. The trip should take a few hours, but since we're traveling by boat, no one will follow us. It'll be safe." Sophie got up, looked around, then moved over to Susan and sat. "Trust us," as she laid her hand on Susan's.

Fred looked into the blackness of the wooded shoreline with the uneasy feeling that they might be far from safety. They were now depending on someone they barely knew. But at least for now, ambiguity was fading. Sophie made it clear to them that there was a well-known cult of zealots bent on protecting Tchaikovsky's reputation from being fouled. He was red in their minds and they would not allow anyone to produce evidence that he might be lavender.

Fred hugged his chest with tightly folded arms as it became cold and clammy on the river. He felt some relief that they appeared to be familiar with the waterway and were more interested in new obstructions than in the curving boundaries of the banks and masonry walls.

Sophie looked ahead; her dark coat and dark hat gave the illusion that she had disappeared. But when she turned, her face, once again, floated like an incorporeal ghostly creature. Fred put his arm around Alex and pulled him tight to share his warmth, snuggling like two kittens in a basket. Susan had already positioned herself next to the number one seat, near the captain. He saw the man at the wheel take her lead and move his sitting position slightly in her direction. Fred smiled seeing Susan lean toward the captain and then rest her head on his shoulder. The moment seemed to be perfect for Susan and Fred was quite happy for her. He became relaxed since they appeared to be safe and protected from the shadowing of strangers for now. They nestled tightly as the cold moisture from the river rose in an attempt to swallow those that were unguarded.

The city lights of Moscow retreated in the distance as the boat left the city limits and the sky became black. The boat's lights were turned off as they glided along the eerie water, the only light being the half moon and the distant glow from the city lights. Alex's eyelids were drooping, then he nested into Fred's arms and fell asleep. As best as he could see the surroundings, Fred was watchful of something that they might hit, but he too was spent. In his drowsy stupor, Fred heard Susan take the opportunity to get to know the captain better and chat with enthusiasm about river boating.

"Tell me about life on the boat," Susan asked.

"Ah, yes," the captain said. "The boat has good life on Moskva."

"How long have you driven a boat?" Susan asked.

"The boat is eight meters," the captain said.

"That is so interesting," Susan said.

Fred had dozed off and then was startled by a boat horn groaning in the distance. He briskly sat up, pulled Alex closer, and stared into the darkness. Hours passed, and the night became cold and apprehensive. The captain opened a locker on the deck behind him and pulled out a couple of blankets. He tossed one over to Fred and Alex and the other he put over his shoulders, draping it over Susan's as well. For the moment, Susan seemed distracted from her worries and snuggled deeper. Fred scanned the banks of the river for anything discernable, but everything was now shadowy. They passed villages and waterfront warehouses with dimly lit windows and junkyards along the river. This now was farmland interspersed with forest. Occasionally, a small cottage illuminated the banks of the river from its windows. Sophie hardly moved from her post, occasionally looking back at the crew. Fred felt the burden of the late hour and knew that everyone was chilled, fatigued and hungry.

Suddenly, a loud clunk from the bow of the boat rang through the still air. Susan jumped up to look around, but the river was black. Nothing could be seen. The captain gave a slight chuckle and carefully said, "No problem. Small log in water—No, was probably empty vodka bottle. Many empty vodka bottles in water. No problem." He reached over to the controls and slowed the engine, then stretched down into the locker and pulled up an old metal thermos bottle and a few aluminum cups.

Fred was content that Susan took the part of hostess as she took the stuff from the captain, sat, and prepared to serve. The engines ramped up to full speed once again and Susan opened the thermos and the aroma of coffee escaped. She poured one cup and set the rest down. She walked it up to the front of the boat and handed the cup to Sophie. Sophie smiled for the first time, a warm and compassionate smile. Susan held back a smile, still reacting to their meeting in the hotel room. But a smile slowly emerged. Susan went back and poured two more cups. She sipped the hot black coffee and squeezed her eyes shut and grimaced, reacting to the extremely strong brew.

The captain laughed and said, "I think now is time I introduce. My name, Stanislaw, but friends call me Stas. We like strong coffee. No problem."

Alex whispered to Fred, "American films; that's how we learn English." Alex chuckled and then said, "Stas picked up the last phrase from an American film and thinks that it's a cool closing to every American chat."

"Now I hear Hollywood dialogue in every sentence," Fred said. As much as Fred tried, he could not resist trying to identify the movie as Stas spoke the lines.

"Where are we?" Alex asked.

"And, how much longer?" Fred added.

"We in our village. Will be only few minutes. No problem," Stas said.

Stas slowed the engine down and coasted past a few old wooden docks. He then maneuvered into a slip partially shielded by a low hanging tree. Sophie hopped off the boat, then Stas threw her a line. Stas jumped off and secured the boat. He then went over and reached onto the boat for Susan. Fred extended his arm to help Susan as she tried her best to climb off the boat gracefully, but it was dark and she stepped on a rope across the gunwale. She made a small sound as her foot rolled on the rope and she waved her arms to regain her balance. Stas grabbed her and lifted her to the dock. Fred thought, *This is better than Susan could have planned.* A slight coo gave her delight away.

Sophie led them all through a small meadow to a cluster of modest homes. The shadowy light made the houses appear to be huddled together for security from the surrounding rubble of haphazard farming. Away from the river, the mist was low to the grass and, as Fred looked up, the moon seemed to be straining in a futile attempt to break through the clouds. Dogs barked in one house, which ignited another dog to bark in another house and then back again. It seemed very far from Moscow to Fred. And in many ways, it was.

Fred tried to figure out the setting as they were led to a wood farmhouse. In the shadowy moonlight it appeared unpainted. He lowered his head as he passed through the short doorway and then through to a vestibule to a small parlor. He recognized the incense of ages from the heavy drapes on all of the windows and across the entryway that they passed through. It was clear to Fred that the long curtains were thick enough so that the house could become invisible in the night by pulling the drapes. Alex introduced Fred and Susan to members of the household who greeted them with baffling Russian phrases.

"This is Sophie's brother, Volodya. He's the oldest."

Volodya nodded to Susan, then took Fred's hand. Fred wanted to smile, but he shook quickly hoping Volodya's grip would loosen.

As Fred stood at the doorway to the kitchen, the aromas, the sounds and the plethora of religious decorations brought to him, for the first time, the culture of old Eastern Europe. It was an intoxicating experience.

They all sat down at a large wooden table and an old man brought out a stack of mismatched dinner plates. The old man sat down at the table and smiled with a nod to everyone in turn. A small, very thin old woman emerged from the kitchen a few moments later. Fred looked up at the cloth on her head and the shawl over her shoulders and felt that she was the personification of a Russian *babba* (grandmother). She carried a tray of assorted appetizers and set it down in the middle of the table. Fred gently smiled at the babba as she slowly studied each of the guests and then stopped her stare at Alex.

The old woman cautiously looked Alex over from head to toe and then, like a burst of fireworks, gave him a broad smile. She opened her arms and rushed toward Alex. Alex stood to meet her arms and they hugged as the old woman said, "Sasha,[24] my little babushka." And then as she spoke with a thin, shrill voice, Alex glanced over to Fred and translated, "We'll find Anna. Don't you worry. We'll make our revenge." Her hug was so tight and long that Alex had to gently peel her off as if escaping from an amorous octopus.

It was a warm but hardly carefree reunion with an air of solemnity hanging heavy over the party. In the raucous chatter, Fred heard the frequent *Och Gospodi, moi dorogoya Anna* (Oh, God, my dear Anna) and eventually felt the despair woven into the otherwise incomprehensible chatter.

Alex explained to Fred and Susan, "Babba is Katyusha's older sister and an old friend of Anna." Hearing *Babba*, the old woman turned and with both hands threw a kiss to Alex, then pushed her way to Alex. She pressed Alex for descriptions of her sister, Katyusha's house and her neighborhood. Alex explained to Fred and Susan, "Babba is a fan of all things American and admires me for being there, perhaps on my way to becoming a citizen."

Alex tried to shorten the travelogue and get down to business, but quieting the group was ineffective. Although the conversation was all in Russian and there were never less than

---

24   As Alex is a nickname in English, Sasha is an endearing nickname for Alexander in Russia. A common construct is to use the ending of a name and add 'sha.' For Alexander, the ending is 'sander' but instead of Sandersha, it becomes Sasha.

three people speaking at once, Fred tried to gain understanding through Alex's scant translations. One man stood up and with his teeth clenched, yelled "*Chert pravoslavnuyu tserkov*" (Damn the Orthodox church) and then spit on the floor. Alex turned to Fred and said, "Everyone is blaming the Orthodox Church." Alex shrugged when several in the group swung their hands in a cross.

The conversation around the table turned quieter, but with no less grit. Alex turned to Fred and said, "Everyone is repeating the phrase *povesit' ublyudkov*, hang the bastards. This'll go on for a while." Alex sat at the table, listening. "No one knows what to do to find Anna. The best idea is to ask everyone in Moscow if they saw her. But we don't even know if she's in Moscow." Alex shook his head slowly as the banter continued. Fred understood nothing except the concern, anger and hate.

It was very late and Fred's eyelids started wilting. He occasionally turned to Susan who was trying to stay alert, but obviously understanding nothing and able to contribute nothing, she nodded off once or twice herself. Alex was given instructions and he went to a bedroom in an adjoining cabin. The old man led Fred to a second bedroom in the cabin where a bed was made up. Fred was pleased to see his two suitcases stand in the entryway of the cabin. It looked comfortable enough. Fred undressed, stretched out and fell asleep immediately.

Stas took Susan's hand and led her up to a bedroom above the kitchen. Susan took comfort seeing her suitcases were already there. As she looked around the room she saw that the room was tiny but tastefully furnished. With an innocently sweet smile, Susan said to Stas, "Thank you so much for everything. I can't thank you enough. Your family is charming. I love them already." Stas stood by the door of her bedroom trying to parse the words into Russian. In the dim light she saw his handsome appearance magnified. Susan wondered if it was the warmth of the house that motivated Stas to unbutton his shirt. His slender, muscular body transformed Susan's glances into a compelling stare. She could not look away. She could see that Stas sensed her attention and he walked closer and finally sat down on the bed next to her.

Susan wondered if Sophie would wait all night for Stas to return from her bedroom.

THE STRATEGY

THE COTTAGE ON the banks of the Moskva River was oddly quiet when Fred joined the family in the dining room. A dozen people were sitting or milling around and the room was quiet but conspicuously uneasy.

Sophie's older brother, Volodya, sat with his elbow on the table, his chin on his fist, looking across the table, rarely blinking, his foot tapping rapidly. People walked past each other with at most a subtle nod. The mood had a dreamlike quality, but actions were erratic as if an earthquake was rumbling. Alex, sitting at the table, looked up and welcomed Fred with a slight smile.

Sophie's grandfather walked toward Fred and gave a razor sharp *"zdraasti"* (hi) emphasizing the rolling *R*. The old man looked past him, gave a strident growl and continued ambling around the long table. In a sudden rage, he threw his hands in the air and shouted *"Pizdets"* (fucked-up situation), and walked to his plump easy chair and fell back into the pillows grunting softly. Fred smiled at Sophie, then walked over to Babba, extended his hand and said, *"zdraasti"* (hi). She looked over to the old man, took a deep breath, then said, *"Ebanashka"* (crazy person), picked the salt and pepper shakers off the table, moved them to a shelf, then set them down at the other end of the table.

At the middle of the long table, the package of music sat like an untouchable museum artifact. Fred moved back to the wall and watched the people move about. A man he hadn't met before walked toward him and extended his hand. "Next farm, we live," he said grabbing Fred's hand energetically. "Americans we welcome." He pointed to two other men, who briskly walked around the table and shook his hand. "My brothers, also next farm," he said. They then stood against the wall with Fred watching the family.

Alex was cutting and flattening large brown paper bags spread out on the table. He seemed out of place, occupied and focused in the midst of the edgy crowd. "Hey, Fred. Have a seat," Alex said pulling a chair away from the table. "Here, use this tape when I get the music wrapped."

"Let me do that," Fred said. "You're making a mess of it."

Handing the package of music to Fred, Alex said, "They'll rip it apart anyway and probably burn it."

Fred carefully folded the brown paper around the music and Alex taped it tightly. Babba sat down across the table from Fred and watched him work. She studied his work as he patted the wrapped package. Fred politely smiled when she mumbled something in Russian, scrunched her face so tight that her eyes got nearly lost in the wrinkles. She leaned across the table and took the package from him, then re-wrapped it. Alex whispered to Fred, "She wants everything to look as perfect to the kidnappers as possible."

"Yeah, we wouldn't want those shitheads to think that we're inelegant and dishonest," Fred said.

The room was filled with chatter and, even yelling. Susan entered and said, "What's going on? What happened?"

"It's not as bad as it sounds," Alex said. "It'll get worse." The shouting became shriller. Alex said, "I don't think they've aired their emotions before today."

Sophie's oldest brother, Volodya, hammered his coffee cup on the table and shouted, "We should mangle these men."

Babba stood up and in a piercing voice, screamed, "Behave."

Fred said, "Alex, when do dishes get thrown?"

Alex said, "This'll be over in a minute. It always does. I can tell you who'll be left standing. Watch."

The cacophony grew louder, then suddenly stopped as Stas stood up, folded his arms and stared across the room. He stretched out his long, thick arms as he looked over the people at the table while he rambled off in Russian.

"He wants everybody to be quiet," Alex said to Fred.

Stas said, "There is going to be no fooling around. Everybody understand?" And then repeated a few words in English. "No fooling. Alex. Your friends, you must lay low so not spook whatever thugs meet us at Anna's old shop. Understand?"

Susan walked to the table and leaned between Alex and Fred. Stas calmly said, "Anger and revenge—I expect that, but it's Anna we want to rescue—that's all." He looked at Sophie's grandfather, then his brothers and with an abrupt changed in tone, he said forcefully, "Do not display your temper. I forbid it."

Some of the family took chairs at the table and turned to Stas. He waited until the shuffling quieted and slowly said, "The plan is that Alex will go into the shop and deliver the package alone." He paused while Alex translated to Fred and Susan. "Fred and Susan will be visible across the street to demonstrate that others are involved, like a backup. They will be a distance away." Stas glared at Susan, then pointed a thick and calloused finger at her. "You be there for one reason, to keep Alex safe. You do nothing, you say nothing."

Susan's eyes grew wide, then she quickly nodded.

There was a moment of silence, then Stas said, "Do not be threatening in any way; do not make an already dangerous situation worse. The goons will surely notice you." He looked around the table. "Get it? Or should I play it again, Stas?" Fred refrained from rolling his eyes.

Any plan that put Alex in a perilous position was unacceptable to Fred. He looked at Alex, then he rubbed his cold and clammy hands together. He wanted to reach over to Alex, but held fast in his seat.

"Let me make it clear," Stas said, "The main goal is to identify the car that will bring the messengers back to the location where Anna is held. That car, we then follow. This is strategy."

Stas went to the short passageway between the kitchen and the dining room and grabbed an old wall-mounted phone that looked as if it preceded Lenin. Stas took a small directory from its shelf and reached for his cell phone, dialed, spoke fast and ended with *d'skorovo* (see you soon). He dialed again, repeating the same pattern, said *d'skorovo* and hung up. The fourth time he dialed, Fred tried to catch some phrases, but Stas talked fast with few breaks.

Susan turned to Alex and Fred and said, "What's going on?"

"Stas is asking some of the neighbors to join us. They're going to bring their trucks and cars to various locations surrounding Karandash Street."

"This is going to be a circus," Susan said. "They can't all show up. This crowd can't keep tempers down."

"This is strategy," Stas said. "No problem." Susan nodded somewhat and huddled back to Alex and Fred.

"It's okay," Alex said. "They'll all be out of sight and communicating on their cell phones. They're practicing the conference call right now. They'll all be able to speak and locate the enemy's car no matter which direction the departing car will go. Stas says that they could not escape detection and can then be tracked as they leave."

"Have they checked cell phone reception on Karandash Street? So much depends on that," Susan said.

Fred turned to Susan. "Good point. This strategy's balanced on a knife-edge that could end, well, not so good. Fortunately, Stas is well organized. He is amazing."

"In all, there will be seven cars," Alex said "At least one of our cars will be in a position to see the pickup men's departing car. Fred, you can use your cell phone too in the event that the thugs exit from the front of the store. I'm glad that we got you a Russian mobile phone, not that I care about phone charges at this point." Alex leaned across the table and said something in Russian to Babba, then turned to Susan and said, "And by the way, yes, cell reception is good in our old neighborhood. To quote Stas, 'No problem.'"

The room became quiet. Stas sauntered over to Susan and Fred, leaned in and said to Susan. "I didn't want you feeling you are left outside. Not to worry."

Susan smiled. "Thank you."

"Sophie agrees with me; plan is foolproof," Stas said.

"Foolproof," Fred said quietly.

"We have lookout at rear of store also. I went there. No way anyone could leave from shop without—we see them, we follow them. Everyone agrees."

"I heard Stas say 'twenty-three hundred hours.' That's eleven o'clock p.m.; it'll be pitch black. How the hell will we see anything?" Fred said.

"That whole neighborhood is lit by a few bare-bulb streetlights. That's enough to see. I'm nervous," Alex said. "If we give away the music and lose these bag men, we'll lose everything. Anna. Everything."

"*Dyerma*" (shit), Volodya said loudly. He turned to Susan, swept his hand down, said a few words in Russian, then said in English, "Cat or mouse; which are we?"

Susan leaned forward and said. "When the kidnappers approach—"

"They have cheese; we are mouse," Volodya said.

Sophie's grandfather stood and shouted, *"Da."*

Babba shrilly said, *"Shto?"*

Susan said, "But—"

Volodya leaned back in his chair and said, *"Nyet,"* followed by a few more words in Russian.

Alex leaned to Susan and said, "Sorry for that, Susan. Your voice doesn't carry much weight in this crowd."

It was after five o'clock and Babba, waved her hands and spoke quickly. Alex said, "It's dinnertime and she wants everything off the table."

Fred backed away from the table as Babba pushed her way to the package of music and placed it on a shelf of the sideboard and patted it down. She started to set up for dinner, while Sophie's mother wiped the table and placed cloth place mats in front of each chair. Babba counted the people milling around the dining room, pointing to each in turn and as she marched around, she slipped dishes from the stack in her arm onto a cloth place setting. She then turned each plate so the pattern was oriented correctly and counted off, *"Ahdeen, dvah, tree, chetyhree . . . "*

Wow, she spins plates like a Las Vegas dealer, Fred thought.

Sophie lined up chairs with the place settings and everyone sat down at the table. Alex translated as best he could as the conversation turned to fine-tuning the plan. It wasn't easy as in the tradition of the family, once again there were clearly more people talking than there were listening.

Volodya said, "Alex, how about carrying my pistol in your pocket in case it gets rough?"

Stas waved his hands and said, "No, no, no way. You cannot have a duel in the street—not Alex."

At the same time, over Stas's voice, one of the men at the far end of the table, said, "Alex, you should have your cell phone recording voice. Who knows what they will say?"

The group became silent.

The women came out from the kitchen and placed several bowls on the table, first, sliced beets in a horseradish sauce, a small bowl of mustard, then a large bowl of steaming sauerkraut.

Fred leaned over to Susan and whispered, "Does this ever end?" The first course was paraded out next, a large tray of kielbasa sausage and a great loaf of pumpernickel bread. It was placed in front of Sophie's father, Nikolai at the head of the long table. He smiled and nodded.

Alex adjusted his cloth napkin on his lap and said, "There are several kinds of kielbasa, smoked and so-called 'fresh.'" With a gentle smile he said, "Have some restraint, this is the first course; there's a lot more to come."

The fragrances of assorted meats and sauerkraut filled the room with a mouth-watering aroma. Sophie's father picked up a carving knife and fork and was about to start cutting, when he stopped, put down the utensils and lifted his glass. *"K'Anna. Ee zdaróvye. My lyubim tebya, Anna"* (To her health. We love you, Anna). All raised their glasses and said, *"K'Anna."* He then, ceremoniously cut the sausage into bite-sized chunks and slid a pile onto his own plate. The platter was slowly moved down the middle of the table and as if this was an archery competition, a gaggle of forks were plunged into the large stack to snag pieces of meat. The women slipped into their seats and sat quietly while their spouses filled their plates.

Sophie, sitting across the table from Fred and Susan, leaned forward and said, "This is usually what a trip home is all about."

She slid some meat and sauerkraut onto her plate. "I wish Anna was here with us." She brushed tears from cheek. People near her turned her way and several nodded and grunted.

Fifteen minutes later, Sophie's mother went to the kitchen and returned with a large bowl of roasted potato wedges, then a platter of sliced meat and a proud smile on her face. A while later, she brought out a tureen and said to Fred and Susan, "Poor man's soup."

Alex leaned over to Fred, "Poor man's soup is a culinary trash can, anything left over in the kitchen is thrown into the pot."

A large bowl of green salad was placed on the table and passed around. When eating had slowed down to a series of burps and belches, a tray of cookies and a pot of strong coffee were placed on the table.

"No vodka?" Fred said.

Alex laughed. "We don't always have vodka," he said. "Well, we do, but this evening is too important to dull our senses with alcohol."

After dinner, the women collected plates and the men leaned back and sipped coffee.

The tone of the conversation became more civilized and the men leaned back in their chairs and chatted. Fred leaned to Alex and said, "What is the discussion? What am I missing?"

"Oh, it's nothing," Alex said, and nodding toward the last man to speak, "He said, what if we kidnap the kidnappers? We can persuade them to tell us about Anna."

Alex nodded to his left and said, "That man said, what if we have the date wrong? Did you double-check, Stas?" Alex soon gave up translating. He turned to Fred and said, "Everyone has to say something."

"What if the bastards turn north? What then?" Sophie's grandfather said.

Another yelled out, "What if they flee the wrong way down a one-way street—can we follow without worrying about being detained by the police and perhaps get arrested?"

Stas stood up and addressed the throng, "We think of every possible turn, consider every car. Plan will not fail." He then turned to Susan, smiled and said, "No problem."

Sophie came from the kitchen and said, "We should go over the plan and see if there are any snags."

Stas nodded and said, "We have seven cars. They will see only one, the one with Alex and his friends. I'll be in that car too, but I'll stay low."

Volodya said, "I'll be in a car with Papa. He knows every crack in the sidewalk. We should be at the end of Karandash Street where it's dark."

Stas nodded and said, "Remember, all we have to do is watch and listen, not to start a battle in the street. It would do Anna no good."

Fred turned to Alex and said, "I hear *shto eslee* repeated over and over. What is that?"

"It means *what if* and everyone is answering with something clever about how failure will not happen because of good planning. I'm afraid that some are getting a bit too sure of success. Before the night is out, they believe that they'll know where Anna is being kept. I pray that they're correct. Oh God, I pray."

"So we have a two-part plan; tonight we learn *where*, and then we have to start all over to decide *how* to rescue," Fred said. "I guess first things first. It makes sense to secretly find out where Anna is." He leaned toward Alex. "What if they get rid of Anna after they get the music, before we can do anything?"

Alex shook his head.

RENDEZVOUS

MOSCOW, MAY 24

FRED SAT ON a bench outside the cottage as he checked his watch and waited for the plan to get started. At nine-thirty, twilight was fading as cars creaked and clunked, arriving at the cottage on the pothole filled road. Three cars parked next to Stas's car and a small truck parked behind Volodya's. Two more old cars arrived a few minutes later. A rusty truck stirred up dust as it sped toward the cottage, then parked at the end of the line. After the cars lined up on the scraggly lawn in front of the cottage, Alex hurried everyone involved in the ransom delivery out of the cottage and toward their assigned cars.

"Come on, we have ninety minutes to set up our positions around Karandash Street to watch and wait."

Fred checked his watch again, then got up from the bench and joined Alex.

Stas walked along the row of parked cars, then leaned against one and said to a man sitting in the passenger seat of an old sedan, "Papa, you are in car number one. Remember now, when you identify yourself, say 'Car one.' This is way is done; it works." He went along the row of cars ushering people in and giving directions. He handed a card to each driver showing their destination in the neighborhood surrounding Karandash Street.

"This is a narrow alley, you will have to back in," he told one driver.

Stas walked to a small sedan in front of the cottage door, opened all four doors and moved some things around that were piled on the seats. He waved to Alex and said, "Alex, Fred, you are with me. Come."

Alex and Fred climbed into the back seat and shoved a pile of rags and small boxes on the floor. Stas waved to Susan and held the front passenger door until she looked comfortable in her seat, then gently closed it. He walked around the car, sat in the driver's seat, turned and said, "We are car number six." Alex held the ransom package tightly. He scratched the wrapping with his fingernails, then tapped on the package with a staccato rhythm.

Sophie's mother, Tanya, emerged from the cottage, paused, looked around, went to Stas's car and handed a small bag to Fred and then Alex. Fred opened his and found a plastic bag of raisins and a package of cookies. She hurriedly went from car to car passing out the paper bags as if the drivers were going to summer camp. She returned to the doorway and stood as everyone who was assigned to a car settled in their seats.

"Try to stay cool. Look relaxed even if you have to fake it so you don't give the appearance of weakness," Fred said to Alex. He tried to give him a hug, but Alex was stiff and shrugged it off. Alex rolled down the window and leaned his elbow on the sill watching the others enter their cars. This was not the gay Alex that Fred knew in New York.

Alex grabbed the snack pack, flung it to the floor of the car and through clenched teeth, said, "This is not a picnic," then slumped in his seat.

Fred pressed against the door, giving Alex as much room as possible. He watched Stas go from car to car giving final instructions.

Alex sat in his seat tapping on the package. He said to Fred, "I'm angry—it'll be hard not to spit in their faces and strangle the men I'm going to meet. How am I supposed to appear calm and unconcerned when I'm so desperately concerned?"

"You'll do okay," Fred said.

"I'm gonna be face to face with someone who knows where Anna is."

"You've gotta stick with the plan."

"I want to know how Anna is, how she's doing."

"I know," Fred said and put his hand on Alex's lap.

"How can I look at someone who knows the answers to these questions and say nothing?" In the dim light, Alex's face looked flushed and he trembled as he spoke.

Fred took Alex's hand and said as softly as was audible, "It'll all be okay."

"Yeah."

Fred rubbed Alex's hand, then rubbed the back of his head, and combed his fingers through his hair. Alex lowered his head and put his hand on Fred's kneecap. He softly massaged Fred's knee, occasionally squeezing his kneecap. Alex took deep audible breaths, then slumped in his seat. He sighed, leaned to Fred and gave him a brief, gentle kiss on the lips, then leaned back in his seat. It killed Fred to see Alex so vulnerable and sad.

Stas stuck his hand out of the window, waved to the others, started his car, roared the engine, then took out his cell phone. "Car one, okay? Car two, okay?" He spoke to the other six drivers, then drove away from the cottage onto the bumpy road. Stas pulled over, allowing three cars to pull ahead of him, then he got back on the road. He put his arm out the window and waved to the three cars that followed.

Alex raised his head and said softly, "Fred, I'm afraid."

"That's natural. It'll keep you sharp."

"I guess."

Stas turned onto the main road and sped up. Susan turned to Stas and then turned to the window. "Very pretty countryside," she said, then turned back toward Stas. "That church; how old do you think it is?" Fred leaned forward and put his hand on Susan's shoulder. She slumped in her seat and nodded. A few minutes later, she sat up, looked out her side window and said, "That's a beautiful bell tower. Is that also Russian Orthodox?"

Stas good-naturedly said, "*teesha teesha*—oh, in English, shush."

Fred patted Susan on the shoulder. She turned to Stas and quietly said, "Sorry," then sank low in her seat.

Twilight turned to darkness and Stas turned on his headlights. In the rearview mirror, Fred saw the cars behind him do the same, reminding him of a funeral procession. One of the three cars in front turned off to the left and beeped his horn twice. Stas beeped twice in return and waved. They drove for another ten minutes. Then, passing a gas station, the second car in front slowed down, signaled a right turn and left the group. It was after ten o'clock when Alex spoke up. "Where are we, Stas? It's impossible to figure out anything in the back seat here."

Stas said, "We are very close. We are near old section. Karandash Street is only few blocks away. I keep going slow; we don't want to draw attention." There was one car of the procession still in front. It signaled a right turn, beeped twice and left the group.

Stas stopped on a dark street near an intersection and waved as the three cars behind drove around Stas, turned, two to the left and one to the right ending the procession. Stas waved as each passed him.

Several minutes later, Susan said, "Ahhh, Karandash Street. I can read it."

Alex leaned forward, staring out the side window and said, "Karandash Street. There it is, Number 46. Nothing has changed. It still looks empty."

Alex reached for Fred's hand. Fred squeezed Alex's hand tightly. "Fred, I'm nervous."

"Me too," and he put his arm around Alex's shoulders. In the cramped rear seat, they both stretched their arms across and hugged.

Stas continued to creep slowly along Karandash Street.

"It's deserted." Fred said.

Alex said, "That's the way it always is at this time. We're more than thirty minutes early. Stas, you should drive a few blocks away to wait out the time."

The car continued to move slowly. Stas turned off the headlights, revealing the blackness of the street. One dim lamppost in the distance cast long shadows. Stas drove around the corner to a narrow lane, then made a U-turn to face Karandash Street and turned off the engine.

Susan slid down further in her seat until her head was barely above the seat back. Alex looked out the window, then turned to Fred. "This is it. After all this time, this is it."

Fred looked out his window and down a dimly lit alley. He put his hand on Alex's and felt his hand tight around the package of music. "It'll be over soon. Then we can find Anna."

Alex tightened his grip and Fred heard the wrapping crinkle. He heard Stas breathe deeply and rapidly.

TARGET

MOSCOW, MAY 24

IN THE EERIE quiet of the dark lane, Alex got out of the car, holding the package of music, and started walking around the corner to Karandash Street. Alex looked at his watch: five minutes before eleven. All the storefront windows on Karandash were dark—no need to attract attention on the murky streets of Moscow at this hour of the night. Going toward number 46, Alex looked back at Stas's car, now barely visible a half block away. Stas waved as he started the car and moved it out of sight to the planned waiting spot. The car designated as *three* was on the street behind Anna's old store. There they should be able to see the contact men enter and exit from the rear and slip out through the alley that connected all the stores in the back. This was the obvious way for them to arrive and withdraw. The plan felt sound.

Alex paused and turned to watch Fred walk from Stas's car on the opposite side of the street and stop in a recessed doorway about fifty feet away. Alex looked at Fred, now barely visible in the shadows, took a deep breath and sighed. Alex walked a bit farther and looked back at Fred again, pleased that Fred was well hidden in the darkness, not too far from him.

In spite of the group of friends and family in the shadows nearby, Alex felt dreadfully alone. He breathed deeply and slowly, tightening his grip on the package of music to stop his hand from shaking and kept walking. Alex glanced back at where Fred stood, and although he couldn't see him in the dark doorway, he felt the comfort of his nearness. He moved on down the street, moving his fingers along the edge of the package and assessing the doorways and alleys. It was hard to fathom that after so many weeks of preparation, the next few minutes would save Anna's life.

Alex arrived at the storefront just before eleven o'clock. He tried to see in the front window of the shop, but it was dark inside. It was better not to see how his home had changed. He rubbed his fingers on the bundle again to confirm the reality of the situation. Alex looked back at the lamppost across the street several houses away. It cast a dim glow on the house, making the place murky, barren of color. He paced back and forth for a bit and then sat on the old wooden bench in the entranceway of the store.

From a nearby apartment, the aroma of roasted potatoes wafted past Alex, reminding him of Anna working in the kitchen, stirring a pot and softly singing. He ran his hand along the floral carvings on the bench, something he used to do in years past. *Anna, where is she now?*

After about fifteen minutes, the doorway of the store across the street opened slowly and two men walked out, then sauntered across the street as if they owned the neighborhood. The two men slowly walked toward Alex. He studied them carefully as they swaggered with their hands in their coat pockets. His sweaty fingers curled tightly around the package, Anna's ticket to freedom and safety. The two men approached, stopped and one of the men, the taller one, dug his hands deeper into his pockets. They stood in front of Alex and stared at him, making him wonder if they might grab the package and shoot him. Alex was reluctant to just give it to two anonymous men confronting him in the street. He shifted his position a bit to the left to see their faces better, but it was dark and the light behind them persisted, making them sinister silhouettes.

"Are you here to pick up the package?" Alex said boldly.

The men stood still.

"When will I see Anna? Is she all right?"

The men said nothing.

Alex swallowed, then said, "Well, is she alright?"

The man on the left reached out for the package. The short stocky man on the right said, in a soft and gravelly voice, "Anna is fine. She has her own room in the basement. The church feeds her well. She'll be all right."

Alex recognized the voice, then squinted to see the man's face. "Boris?"

After a pause, the man said, "Yes, old friend."

"What the hell are you doing here?"

"I have to work, you know. This is what I do," Boris said, as he crossed himself with a sweeping wide motion. "Saint-Vladimir-have-mercy."

Boris said quietly, "Alex, you are next. Get out of Moscow." Boris backed away slightly with his head lowered, then hesitated and extended his hand toward Alex. Alex raised his hand to meet Boris's. The setting of his old neighborhood had taken a sorrowfully bewildering turn.

The other mobster stepped forward, grabbed the package from Alex, then backed away from Boris. He drew a tire iron from underneath his coat and made a wide sweep at Boris. It landed a forceful blow against Boris's skull making Boris grunt and fall to the ground. The other man swung the iron piece high and slammed it again at Boris, then ran back toward the house from which they emerged.

Alex rushed over to Boris as the attacker disappeared in the darkness. The skin looked swollen and red where the tire iron had hit his head and blood seeped from a gash on his temple. Alex kneeled and straightened out Boris from the awkward position in which he landed as he folded. He felt that Boris' arm was broken. Alex peeled off Boris' coat, rolled it up, and tucked it under Boris' head.

Alex gently wailed, "Boris, we are still friends. This is our street, forever."

With a distant stare, Boris spat blood and said, "Mother is . . . fine." He coughed and moaned softly. "She's fine. She has a bread for you." He gasped a most ghastly sound on the final syllable of the nonsense phrase. Tears rolled down Alex's cheeks. Boris looked barely conscious and was bleeding from his mouth and ear. His eyes rolled back and his head fell to the side. Alex looked away as Boris exhaled his last breath. He put his hand on

Boris's neck and felt no pulse. He felt dizzy and disoriented with the only sound, his own heartbeat. He owed it to Boris to make him comfortable as he dragged Boris's body to the sidewalk and sat him against the wall of the building. He looked at the body searching for a way to help. Alex took Boris's coat and rolled it behind his neck to make a bolster, then placed his arms at his side. He turned to where he last saw Fred, then looked down at Boris.

Alex stood above the lifeless body on the dark street reluctant to walk away. A part of Alex had been snuffed out with Boris, the sweetness of the memories of them together now obscured by sadness. He looked to where he last saw Fred, then began to walk faster, sobbing more with each step. "Fred," he softly wailed as he saw him.

Fred walked quickly to meet Alex in the middle of Karandash Street. Alex approached with his hands clasped at his chest, his head bowed.

"Alex, what happened?" Fred said.

Alex was breathless. "The package is gone. A single man has it—now, that is. There were two men. One was an old neighborhood friend, Boris. He is dead," Alex said, choked up.

"Where did the man go? Where, Alex? Where is Anna?"

"He probably left through the back of the store that leads to Eesteeratel Street," Alex said and then fell into Fred's arms and wept.

When they arrived back at the car, Stas and Susan were standing outside. "*Shto? Shto?*" Stas said.

"It's done," Alex said, wiping tears from his face.

"Where did they go?" Stas said.

Alex shrugged. "Don't know. Maybe Eesteeratel Street."

Stas quickly spoke on his phone to the other drivers. "It is all done. They are gone," he said.

"No, I do not know the direction."

"No, I have no description of the car. All cars, you go and check out all around." Stas looked compassionately at Fred and Alex, "We will wait to hear."

Stas picked up the phone and said, "Car three, where are you? What do you mean, you followed a blue sedan until it went to a gas station and two old women got out? Car four, what do you have? Nothing?"

"None of the cars got anything." Stas said, shaking his head. "Shit, shit, shit."

Alex sat in the back of the car moaning. He whimpered, "Boris. They killed Boris. We went to school together. They have the package."

Susan said, "Alex dear, who is Boris?"

"Boris was one of the men who came to pick up the music. He was an old friend. We talked and then the other man hit him with a tire iron. Boris was murdered; I don't understand why. He's dead in front of Anna's shop."

"I am going back to the shop," Stas said as he put the car in gear and started rolling toward the shop. He stopped the car in front of the shop and Alex bounded out.

Alex stood motionless in front of the shop, looked back at Fred and howled, "Boris is gone."

Alex said, "He was dead. He was here. He's gone. He was right there . . . right there."

Fred got out of the car and pointed. "What is that rolled up against the wall?"

Alex quickly said, "His coat." He ran to the building and picked it up, hugged it tightly as if Boris was still inside of it. He stood with his eyes closed.

Fred put his arm around Alex and brought him back to the car. Stas walked around the car, opening, then shutting each door, then he got in and started the car. Fred pulled Alex close.

"I have his coat. See, here hold it for me." Alex reached to the front and put it on Susan's lap. "At least I know Anna is well and has her own room. I hope the church is treating her with some dignity."

Fred glared at Stas, who turned to the back seat and looked at Fred with his mouth open and eyes that were so wide they looked like ping-pong balls glowing in the darkness.

Fred said, "Alex, what do you know?—"

"Alex, tell—" Stas said.

"Nothing," Alex said. "Boris is gone." He rested his head on Fred's shoulder and wept. Fred held onto Alex and Susan turned and placed her hand on his thigh as they drove back to the farm in darkness.

Stas's car was the first to return to the cottage. They went to the dining room where the rest of the family was waiting and sat at the dining room table. Car doors slammed outside as the other six cars returned and, they too, went to the dining room. Alex gave a brief, but somewhat confused account of what had happened. Stas spoke with his head hanging low, "I am discouraged we did not follow the pickup men."

Alex mumbled, "A pickup man and a corpse."

"We know nothing about where Anna is being held," Stas said "Or I should say, we know next to nothing."

"Alex, tell us everything you know. Every detail," Fred said, then held Alex's hand. "Everything, every part."

Alex said, "Boris was a childhood friend. As soon as he said something, I recognized the husky voice and connected it to the shape of the silhouette. Boris's family was Georgian. They're all stocky, no neck. You can always spot a Georgian."

"Okay, okay, go on," Fred said.

"He said that Anna was fine." Alex took a deep breath. "He said she is fine for now and that the Saint Vladimir church people are feeding her well and she has her own room." Alex whimpered, snorted, then said, "We'll never find her."

Sophie was the first to blurt out, "Alex, do you understood the importance of what you've just said?"

Alex looked at Sophie's mother and softly said, "Can I have something to drink?"

"Yes," she said and ran to the kitchen. She returned quickly with water and a tray of cookies.

"Alex, tell us more about this Boris."

Nearly two dozen unblinking eyes stared at Alex who sat quietly sipping his drink.

"Poor Boris. He was always in trouble at school. He always cut class. He hung out with the wrong people. Everyone knew that he was headed for problems. And now all I have to remember him by is lying in the road and his coat." Alex looked down at the coat rolled up on his lap.

All eyes lowered to look at the coat. Everyone leaned forward, then Sophie ripped it from his lap. "Pockets, we have to see what's in his pockets," Sophie rattled as she fumbled with the coat.

Alex said, "So sad," as Sophie straightened out the coat to find pockets.

"Who is Vladimir? I never heard of him. Is he a saint? God, we have so many damn saints," Sophie said. Sophie stopped for a minute, looked at Alex, and then continued searching through the coat for something, pulling out pockets and shaking them.

Sophie's father asked, "Alex, why do you mention Saint Vladimir?"

"Boris mentioned Saint Vladimir in our short conversation. I never heard that name before."

"Is there a Saint Vladimir church?" Sophie's father asked. "Does anyone know a church named Saint Vladimir?"

There was no response.

Sophie fiddled with Boris' coat and pulled out from an inside pocket a folded newspaper clipping. She unfolded it and smoothed it on the table. The crowd huddled together and leaned in her direction waiting anxiously as Sophie read it aloud. "Luncheon at the rectory . . . hmm hmm hmm hmm . . . my God, this is so yellow. This is for an event at the Orthodox Church of Our Father Saint Vladimir. So Boris was at the church. It mentions the village of Pravdinsky. Where the hell is Pravdinsky?"

Sophie's father got up from the dining room table and said, "I get map," He returned quickly and unfolded it on the table. It was very large and everyone poured over it looking for the stated town.

One of the neighbors piped in. "Did you say *Bronnitsy?* I have a cousin in Bronnitsy. You wouldn't like him,"

Fred tried to get closer to the map, but it was in Russian so he stepped back, allowing someone else to get a good look at the map.

Sophie studied the newspaper clipping, then said, "Wait, there is a faint scribble in the margin the of paper. I think that it says—'bring towels down to Anna.' My God, Boris was taking care of Anna. And the word *down*—she's downstairs. We could hardly have learned more if Boris was here himself. Anna is in the basement of that church, wherever the hell that is."

There was a rush to examine the large map. "Here it is. It is near the intersection of the M8 and the A107 roads. Pravdinsky. It is in middle of, how you say, no place," Stas said. "Alex, you have done what seven cars did not do. I am proud of you." He reached out to Alex and gave a tight hug, lifting him off the floor, spun around and with a firm pat on the back set him back down.

Sophie's father let out a roaring, "Yow, yow, hooray! We're on the road to get Anna." He stood up and said, "Wonderful, Alex. Wonderful."

Alex said, "Boris in a church? The only reason that poor Boris would be at a church in such a remote place is if he worked there with his gangster comrades. We have our destination. Now we're ready for the rescue." He grinned slightly then opened his mouth and smiled.

Stas got up, lifted Alex from his chair, and gave him a tight hug. Alex looked puzzled at first, but let loose a beaming smile and softly said, "Anna."

Sophie's father brought out the vodka. He lined up glasses on the table and as he poured, he embellished the mood joyfully bellowing a soft, "Haa, heh, heh . . . whoo hoo hoo."

Alex turned to Fred who walked over to Alex and rather than hug, touched his hands and closed them in a furtive embrace. Alex put his arms around Fred and returned the warm touch. The hug lasted forever and tears of relief dripped down Alex's and Fred cheeks until they merged.

SUICIDE NOTE

A COTTAGE BETWEEN MOSCOW AND
ST. PETERSBURG, 1893

PETER ILYICH TCHAIKOVSKY sat pensively at his desk torn between the doom of the present and dreams of the future. He glanced at the wooden box containing the lethal dose on the small table next to him with a presence that cloaked the room with an infernal darkness. He studied the brass clasp that secured the box thinking that one flip, one gulp and the enigmatic conflicts of his life would end. Peter feared that he would have a prurient curiosity to peek inside, but to the contrary, he was revolted at the thought of opening it, even if it was just to look. Nevertheless, the box dominated his vision as images of his friends and patrons floated in and out of his consciousness. His mind was at the same time blank and teeming with memories.

He recalled outdoor concerts in the park on the banks of the Moskva River where lovers picnicked on blankets, openly displaying their affections enriched by his romantic music. But then, staring at the box, he thought of his own closely guarded amorous moments and he felt scorned by the tomblike coffer that would deliver the ultimate punishment—*For what?* He reached and shoved the box away.

On the far side of Peter's studio, in a heavily carved frame, a large gilded portrait of the Virgin Mary stared across the room with an elusive smile. Now, that incorporeal expression and all that it stood for mocked Tchaikovsky. He felt cornered. He thought, *Either I must yield to its silent hypocrisy or stand up to it. Or, Pyotr Ilyich Tchaikovsky might vanish, leave forever, perhaps to be reborn elsewhere. The youth of Ivan buoys the health of this fifty-three-year-old man. Rebirth in Paris or death in Moscow; the curtain will fall on this act and rise to a new and better one.*

He glanced once again at the box. It seemed to have edged closer and become larger since his last glimpse. Now, it sat there taunting him. Inside was the potion that would supposedly save the lifeblood of the Fatherland he had enriched. Rather than be mugged in some shadowy alley, he had magnanimously been given the chance to end it with a perverted dignity. That box, it stubbornly pulled at him to end it all, his struggle to become Russia's most revered and celebrated musician—a punishing end. Everything he had worked for, his dedications, his collaboration with patrons, hovered at its finale. It was time to express his feelings to the world. It was time to complete a suicide note in a language that he could speak from his heart, for every one of these people to see and understand. It would be his memoir, voiced from his innermost feelings. It would be his sixth and final symphony.

Tchaikovsky thumbed through pages of sketches of a new grand work that he had created in the previous months. He sluggishly pushed the folder aside, less interested in grandiose histrionics than in heartfelt communication. These sketches reflected the majesty and grandeur of his countryside and his friendships. He felt his career crumbling because he was condemned a criminal—a criminal who, he felt, did nothing to hurt another soul in any way. Peter thought, *This is the law of my country, the law of the Church; damn the law, damn the church.*

Peter sketched ideas as they appeared to him, as images in a dream sometimes do, to express his long-smothered thoughts and speak to those he would be leaving behind. He expressed recent memories in a melancholy theme that he visualized as the end of one journey and the start of another. It was the termination of one day and a new morning simultaneously. This was to be a memoir of a career he loved and devoted his life to develop. As he wrote, he heard the orchestra lament the circumstances that touched him, compelling the final message that was to be written under the name of Peter Ilyich Tchaikovsky. This farewell to the world would be the most expressive suicide note ever written.

Yet there was a plan to emerge into a different world with a new identity, a new persona, and a vision of hope. The identity of Peter Ilyich Tchaikovsky was to die, there was no escaping that, but it was not to be the end.

The somber mood churned with visions of a future with Ivan, the harmonies that came to Peter were sumptuous creating blissful images of long-ago moments with his family and especially his nephew whom he loved and admired in many ways. He reflected on the strolls through the countryside, his oasis of bounty in a landscape of personal want. These happy times flowed from his pen and onto the page, emerging in the second movement.

As Peter put his pen down on a blank sheet of paper and titled it *III, Allegro molto vivace* (very lively and fast), he felt defiant in his misery and began a playful, uplifting melody filled with humor. He glanced at the box and grinned; he had soared to a new place that was bold and optimistic. His pulse quickened as he wrote quickly, trying to keep up with the allegro tempo.

The first movement had been with Peter for some time. It was filled with the sweeping melodies that haunted him in the shadowy chamber of the court of honor as that dreadful sentence was pronounced. This was the sweet song that appeared in his gravest hour of condemnation amidst the heavy fumes of smoldering candles and the suffocating vapors of the gas lamps. He felt that it was appropriate to begin his story with the breath of fresh air that came to his aid at his worst hour. This was his love. No matter how dark his thoughts became, his final note to his friends should embark on a communication of tenderness. As his pen scratched harmonic poetry onto the paper, it had no name, just a saving compassion.

But it was the final movement, in an unorthodox introspective and sullen manner that would orchestrate a transition to a new life, a richer one. As he wrote with the visions of Russia past, he felt the budding future of Paris embracing him. *This is my life,* he thought, *and this is what I want my audience to remember when they think of Ivan and me.*

Peter walked over to the credenza and picked up a snow globe of Red Square with Saint Basil Cathedral in the center. He shook it gently, walked to the window and watched the snow crystals glisten in the last light of day as they fell on the miniature cathedral. When the crystals settled on the scene, he walked back to the credenza and gently set the snow globe down, knowing that he would never again be in that scene.

RESCUE

A RUSSIAN VILLAGE, MAY 25

FRED LINKED ARMS with Susan and the two of them joined Alex, the family and some close neighbors to assemble in the dining room of the family cottage and gather around the large table to review the situation. Alex selected a seat at the table and Fred sat down alongside him. Susan stood with the women of the family. Fred winked and Susan smiled as she posed with the group of Russian womenfolk. Fred leaned back in his chair as Sophie's father, Nikolai, commanded attention and bellowed, "The situation is now all too clear. There never was any intention to trade Anna for the package. Those bastards." Alex squirmed. Under the table, Fred put his hand on Alex's lap in a sign of restraint knowing that much more thundering was expected to follow. Sophie's father roared, "Anna's life for Tchaikovsky's honor, he got sick and died. What more is there?"

Fred whispered to Alex, "I think you should explain to the group."

Alex stood, waited for the group to settle down and said, "You need to know this. We did research in the Archives in Moscow and learned a lot. There was overwhelming material evidence that we gathered from the archives that Tchaikovsky not only had a lover, a life partner, but there was a possibility that he may not have been in the sealed coffin that was ceremoniously honored in St. Petersburg."

Sophie's father waved his hand dismissively and said, "He died of cholera. Every schoolchild knows that. Case closed. End of discussion." He slammed his hand on the table. "Rumors, hah."

Alex took a deep breath and said, "There was documentation from witnesses, servants and friends who provided substantive evidence that Tchaikovsky's death was suspicious."

"Everything to you is suspicious," Sophie's father said.

Alex looked at the old man and said, "These lunatics that have Anna believe that any evidence that sheds light on what they call the misrepresentation of Tchaikovsky's death has to be destroyed at any cost, if history is to be as simple as what's accepted in the Russian children's history books."

Sophie's father mumbled, "Yeah, yeah."

Alex raised his hand and said, "No, there is more going on here. Anna knows what is in that music. Her danger is more immediate than we have conceded."

Fred leaned back to Sophie and said, "We've got to get Anna out of that church as soon as possible. They're not going to keep her around much longer."

Sophie patted Fred on the shoulder and nodded.

"When we find the church, we won't know anything about the layout except that there are assembly rooms in the basement," Sophie said so that all could hear. "This is where the captors most likely congregate and perhaps where they live. I believe—"

"It will be impossible to storm the basement rooms," Stas said. "First, we don't know the floor plan. We would not know where to enter and where to escape. Second, we don't know where Anna's room is."

Fred sat with his arms folded, thinking that they'd come so far, yet there seemed to be no clear way to proceed. Without more information, they were helpless.

The table shook, startling Fred and he turned to Sophie's father slamming the palm of his hand on the table saying loudly, "We will make a false fire alarm and then wait for everyone to exit and then we could rush in."

A chorus of *Nyet* in rude disapproval rattled around the table.

Volodya waved his arms and forcefully said, "Papa, *nyet*."

The scene looked dismal to Fred as no worthwhile ideas surfaced from the group. An image of Anna in a barren dungeon tormented him.

Alex turned to Fred and said, "All the ideas that're being brought forth are ruthless and extremely risky. They're all being dismissed quickly. We've got nothing, *nothing*."

Fred looked around the room as it eventually went silent and all heads hung low.

"Now what?" Alex said.

The hush in the room underscored the hopeless lack of direction. Fred squirmed in his seat, then stood up to get everyone's attention. "A situation that I once experienced might be successfully applied now."

Heads turned to Fred.

"I once worked in a facility that had a lot of very expensive high-voltage electronics. It was imperative that if fire broke out that it be extinguished immediately. The facility was fitted with tanks of compressed carbon dioxide with quick-opening valves. In the case of a fire signal generated, the valves automatically burst open and the facility was quickly flooded with the gas."

Fred paused while his discourse was translated into Russian. Stas waved his hands at the group turned to Fred and said, "Go on."

Fred looked at the staring eyes and coughed to clear his throat. "It sounds simple and harmless, but there are circumstances that make this scene very menacing. "

Stas held his hand up to pause Fred while he translated.

Stas's father shook his head, Stas emphasized, "Papa, carbon dioxide, *uglekislyy gaz*."

One of the neighbors waved his hand and said, "We get it, carbon dioxide is okay, we call CO_2."

There was loud chatter around the room, then all quieted and turned to Fred.

"Carbon dioxide is odorless, colorless and tasteless," Fred explained. "Your senses require it to be undetectable because we breathe out that gas all the time. That property makes it invisible to us. It is also heavier than air, so it drops to the ground, just where a person might regrettably go if they sensed that something was wrong. But here is the most important factor—it is deadly." Fred paused. "*Deadly*," he said with emphasis. "It suffocates quickly—very quickly, much faster than pinching closed a victim's mouth and nose. Let me explain why."

Fred paused for a babble of translations and explanations, then continued. "The human body is geared to react to an excess of carbon dioxide in the blood. The body responds by breathing faster and deeper. If the person is immersed in carbon dioxide gas, the body takes in more of the gas in the process of trying to expel it. It's a runaway disaster."

There was some rumbling from those around the table. "But it gets worse," Fred said. "You cannot hold your breath and escape. Carbon dioxide, CO_2, is absorbed through the skin. The gas soaks in through your skin and forces a reflex to gulp air in, but it is no longer plain air, it is now more CO_2. Deadly. Deadly *and quick*."

Fred could tell he was getting through because he heard a few utter *boje moi* (oh my god). He paused for a few seconds while the room became silent. "I was in a training exercise a long time ago where the gas tanks were let open and the facility was filled with the gas. The purpose was to demonstrate, and warn us that if a buddy was trapped inside, you could not jump in to pull him out without dying yourself. In the training, we stuck our arms through a crack in the door. I felt the unstoppable impulse to suck in a deep breath. If I were inside, I would have died. Just one more thing—carbon dioxide, being so dangerous, was replaced in modern installations with a harmless gas that also puts out a fire. So carbon dioxide is not used any more, the way I described, I believe. It is far too dangerous. But it is still used in refrigeration—think of dry ice. That is frozen CO_2." Fred sat down and leaned back in his chair.

The group was silent.

Alex said, "If it's so deadly, then how can we do away with the enemy bastards without killing Anna?"

Fred expected this question and nodded. "In America we call them a Scott Air Pack. It's a small tank of air that you strap to your shoulders and then breathe the fresh air through a mask. It's similar to a scuba diving tank, but much lighter. All fire stations have several of these portable air tanks so that firemen can go into burning buildings without breathing the smoke. By the way, if you are exposed to the carbon dioxide in an outside, open space, there's no danger because it quickly dissipates."

Sophie's jaw dropped. "We can do this immediately. We know that they are in a basement suite of rooms. All the rooms will probably have small windows to the outside. We can flood the basement apartments with the gas. They will all die quickly. And for Anna—"

Stas said, "Papa, you worked in the fire department. You have many friends there. We will get one of those 'Scottish air packs' and fit it with two masks, one for you and one for Anna. No problem."

His papa, Nikolai, raised his arms and cried out, "I can't just march into the place with a tank of air and not look like trouble. They will kill me."

Stas grinned and continued. "You will put a priest's robe on to cover it and go down to the basement to be with Anna. You would look just like an Orthodox Priest. They will call you Father instead of papa."

Baba, who was sitting quietly against the wall, piped in with a rusty voice, "Nikolai, stop shaking your head; it will fall off, and I have heard enough *nyet*s from you. No need to get irritable, you will be a priest." She then leaned back and squealed, "Father Nikolai—Hah!"

Nikolai stood and said, "I want to save Anna, but I will not be called an Orthodox Priest. That church is a circus and they are the clowns. I will be an actor, a jester for an hour, but not a priest."

Stas stood up and finalized the outburst with his usual "No problem."

Papa Nikolai, said, "How could you possibly know how much carbon dioxide to bring? What do we know about the size of the church building?" He crossed his arms, sat down, then said, "We know nothing."

Sophie seemed to expect this question and quickly answered, "These rural churches are all built alike and this one is probably no different. It's probably located in an area where there very few people live. It can't have a floor plan much bigger than this house."

Fred looked over at Susan standing by the doorway, her head hung and looking disturbed. "Susie, what's wrong?"

Susan lifted her head and looked around the room. "This is horrible. We're going to kill people. We don't even know how many. We're rushing into something without thinking it through."

"These people are murderers," Fred said. "They kill for reasons that are medieval. They hide from the truth and kill anyone that seeks it. If we don't squash them, they will certainly come for us. And they have Anna right now. They're going to kill Anna and they could kill us all."

Susan lowered her head and said, "Well, of course, you're right."

"What are the alternatives?" Fred asked. "Meet with them and try to talk them out of the perverted religious beliefs that have been instilled into them since childhood? We could expose the church for the self-preserving institution that it is, but that would take a century. We must do something now or there will be tragedy. That the Church seems to be a willing partner with these zealots is troublesome. They want to deny the existence of gay people and do it retroactively."

Sophie stood and said, "Alex and Fred, we will need you with us. Susan, you stay here. It won't be safe for you to come with us."

Susan got up and defiantly said. "I didn't come all this way so I could sit around and watch the beets grow. You'll need me. I've seen Russian women in church here. I'll be in the church, deep in prayer, watching for anything unusual. I'll either warn you or divert attention. I'm good at that and we'll need that. You work the downstairs; I'll attend to the upstairs. Simple as that."

Sophie smiled warmly and Susan nodded. Susan said, "I know where the usual location of the vestments would be. I'll enter the church and go to the rack of robes. You follow and I'll bring the liturgically proper vestment out. Every church is the same. At least this will be one good thing that I can bring from my Catholic upbringing."

Nikolai waved his hand. "No, that will be unnecessary. I will call Father Krinsky and borrow one of his robes. I will say that Mamma wants to make another one to donate to the church and she needs one to copy. He will be delighted. They are all greedy for donations. That old fart will help in a flash. They bask in luxury—one more priceless robe to strut around in—he will help. I will bring a liter of expensive vodka for insurance." Nicolai let out a hoarse chuckle that changed the mood of the crowd as if his laugh was contagious.

Stas put on his coat and said, "The factory that sells dry ice—I believed they manufacture it there. We go." Stas and Volodya left the cottage and hopped in the old truck. The transmission made grinding noises, the engine coughed, the tires squealed and they drove off in a curl of dust.

Sophie said to Fred and Susan, "Stas is always very resourceful and there's no doubt that this will take only a short time. They'll be back at the house in less than an hour."

Sophie outlined the finalized plan. "We'll drive to the church and eliminate the members of the cult without harming Anna with the CO_2 gas. Nikolai, papa, you will quietly parade into the church with the air pack on your back, under your robe. It will make you look hunchbacked, but that would make you look all the more pious."

"I will bring a *kadeelah*[25] and march around the church," Nikolai said, nodding. "That will give me time until I find the stairway to the basement."

Sophie said, "Yes. Then, you go downstairs, find Anna and make sure she recognizes you so she doesn't get panicky. Hopefully, Anna will cooperate calmly with you after that."

Susan stood up and said, "I'll take a seat in the pews and move near the stairs to the basement when I finally discover where it is. I'll appear to be deep in prayer so that I can't be disturbed."

Fred whispered to Alex, "This is the theatrical part. She's good. Even though she doesn't speak the language, she could generate a distraction. Susan's talented that way."

"Hopefully, she won't ham it up too much," Alex said.

"Stas, Volodya and their friends will carefully move the tanks of carbon dioxide outside the cellar windows and prepare to discharge them," Sophie said. "I'm sure that they will bring enough cylinders to fill a very large space so quantity will be of no concern. I'll check on that. If anything, I would guess that they'd be over equipped."

Fred looked at his watch. It was still morning and their plan

25 A pot of burning incense on a swinging harness of chains.

was to depart before noon. He paced, put his fingernails against his teeth, then paced again. Although the ensuing discussions he overheard were in Russian, Sophie and her two brothers spoke with conviction and without the emotion that the family earlier exhibited. Fred was fired up, confident and believed that the team was capable of saving Anna. It was going to happen soon.

DISCOVERY AND DEPARTURE

MOSCOW, EARLY SEPTEMBER 1893

IVAN SAT ALONE in his quarters holding the package that Peter had sent, then carefully unwrapped it to find a large piece of music accompanied by a small cloth bundle. He grinned at the choice of music, the piano version of Tchaikovsky's suite *The Seasons*, a facile piece, far below his abilities. He was not particularly ruffled by the simplistic instruction written boldly across the opening passage, *Mind the key*. It was not such unusual notation for a teacher to write. It was not uncommon for a student to mistake the key in which a piece of music is written. But at the level of Ivan's accomplishments, it was a surprisingly shallow instruction.

In a flash, Ivan understood what lay before him and a sense of the irrevocability of what had been set out rushed over him. They had talked about a plan many times before and Ivan understood that Peter would make all the arrangements. Ivan thought about the warnings of Peter, that they were being watched and everything spoken or written could be intercepted. But delivering music, now that was so normal as to be scanned by hostile eyes quickly and ignored. Now he had the plan locked in cryptic phrases to sidetrack unwelcome eyes. He needed the key.

While his other teachers annotated with few words, these annotations were phrases of emotion and passion, but still instructional. He read the comments feeling the warmth that his lover intended. And then Ivan noticed a note: *Examine the tempo on page 51.* He turned to that page and moved his finger past the jotted notes until he realized that this was the part of the suite titled *November.* "How appropriate," he mumbled. They talked about going to Paris in November. "Here is my guide." At the top of the page in this particular published edition, was a short poem, as there was for each of the twelve sections. This poem had bold pen strokes alongside of it to draw attention. Ivan slowly read the text by poet Nickolay Nekrasov, remembering that he and Peter Ilyich often talked about the bothersome distance between Moscow and Paris and the separation from his family. He read it over and over again:

> *Do not look at the road with sadness,*
> *and do not hasten to follow the troika,*[26]
> *and smother the dreary anxiety*
> *in your heart quickly and for the good.*

Ivan stared down the page knowing that the poem had been written long ago, but the meaning was as heartfelt now as it was to the author. Further down the page, Ivan noted how curious the annotations in Peter's hand were worded. There were the words *love* and *encouragement,* phrases with the words *hope* and *future.* Yet they were arrowed to spots in the music to make it look like a pedagogical spray of instructions from a dedicated music teacher. Uneasiness crept upon Ivan: there was too much poetry and not enough details. He needed to know *when* and *where.*

He studied the notations down to the bottom of the November song. At the bottom, Peter had written a peculiar phrase, *Apply the rhythm of two as is done in the July song.* He quickly flipped pages back to the July movement. The subtitle of the July movement suggested to Ivan what he needed to satisfy understanding the *when* part of the message as well as *what.* July was subtitled, *The Reapers Song.* A reference to their discussions

---

26 A sled drawn by three horses.

that the only way Peter could leave the Fatherland was to have died. Death was the *what* that would start the journey. And, the date encrypted for this planned charade was the strange reference to the two-rhythm. It was marked as four beats to a measure, but it was not unusual for a musician to interpret this as two stronger beats.

Ivan looked across the room and said, "Why stress *two*?" as if Tchaikovsky was in the room with him. He stared at the comment, running his hand through his hair and then pressing his finger back on the page. Suddenly, it came to him; Ivan realized that the November Song comment conveyed the date. 'It would be on November 2. Peter would begin his journey to Paris on that day.

Ivan now understood the day that Peter would leave Russia to meet him. To *where*, precisely? He knew that Peter had made all the arrangements for them to meet in Paris. Ivan had already made preparations for travel, but he needed an address as a destination. Step by step, Ivan connected clues that referenced pages in the music. These clues referenced other pages and from numbers repeated or references to bogus musicians, he understood the place to go was to be rue Bérenger, number 14 on the third floor. Ivan suspected what was in the cloth bundle and unwrapped it to find the key, assumedly to an apartment. He ran his fingers over its smooth, unusual shape and felt the promise of a new life with Peter.

Weeks later, Ivan stood in the center of his small apartment surveying all of his belongings. Each of his souvenirs represented a landmark in his life. He went to the window and looked down the street and across the rooftops of his Moscow neighborhood. In a short time, these would be visions of a past that would not, could not, be revisited. Ivan had studied the music that Peter Ilyich left for him once again and was confident of the message imbedded in the annotations. He had memorized the address in Paris and no longer needed Peter's writings. His baggage was light and books of music would have been an unnecessary burden.

Ivan waited for his brother and his family to arrive to make final goodbyes before he left for Paris. When they asked why, he planned to tell them that his voyage was to study more seriously in a European city, but he assumed that they likely knew his reasons. They probably knew of his love interests but it was never spoken of. His brother had mentioned that Europe would be a safer place for Ivan and Paris had a reputation for being the best choice. Ivan knew they could not talk about it for fear that a suspicious neighbor or an official might analyze their choice of destination. There were few secrets in Russian neighborhoods, and those concerning personal safety were vital to defend.

It was early afternoon and he heard the commotion at the front door and the rapid footsteps of the landlady rushing out to the front porch to greet his family. They had brought their young daughter, Ranya, and Ivan cherished her enthusiasm when she visited. Ivan and she had been close since the girl was very young. In fact, Ivan always felt that part of his soul was expressed in the young girl. Now she was ten years old and they had grown even closer. They trusted each other as close friends do in spite of her youth. Ivan could hear the clamoring light steps of a young person springing up the stairs. There was also a soft girlish cooing as if a dove was approaching his apartment door. Ivan could feel the rush of affection as the footfalls came closer and the girl finally burst through the door.

"Ranya," Ivan said, "Where are Mommy and Daddy?"

"I wanted to see you first, before they came up the stairs."

Ivan lifted the little girl up and swung her around as they hugged and she made sounds that children love to make and to hear. Ranya gave a little giggle of joy, but it was not the silly laugh of a ten-year-old. It was a mature expression of happiness. Ivan was well aware that she knew that she would not see him again for a very long time and this feeling of elation had a somber undercurrent to it. A minute later, his brother and sister-in-law reached the apartment and entered the room to join them.

"Ivan, you look well."

"As do you," Ivan said.

"How is the music?"

"My studies go well."

Ivan finalized the initial greetings with the usual hugs and near-miss kisses. He offered his guests a place to sit, even though, with the exception of the single chair, these places were on the edge of his bed. After everyone got settled, the real visit began.

"I am leaving everything in this apartment for you," Ivan said. "Nothing here is terribly important. Take what you want—the landlady will do what she wishes with the rest . . . Ranya, this precious box is for you—please take care of it." Ivan picked up the wooden box covered in leather containing all his correspondence with Peter.

"For me?" Ranya said in a soft voice as she stood and clasped her hands tight to her chest.

Ivan was about to present it to Ranya, but paused. "Wait a moment," he said as he took the package of music with the encoded message and stuffed it into the box. It did not fit easily so he pressed it and forced the box closed.

"Ranya, this package is the most important thing in the box. Keep it all together. And finally, promise me that you will not open the box until you have a Ranya of your own."

Ranya nodded acknowledging the solemn promise. She took the box and hugged it. "Now it is our box—together."

Ivan took a key from his desk and locked the box. He took a thin red ribbon from a sachet of debris on his desk and threaded it through the hole on the key. Then, he planted an exaggerated kiss on the key and regally placed it around Ranya's neck.

"Ranya, you are now the guardian of the box. Keep the box close to you and we will always be together."

Ranya blushed at the little ceremony and beamed with happiness and sorrow. She revealed to Ivan a closeness she had not displayed before and he knew that she would unfailingly honor his request. Ivan had the uncomfortable feeling that many years would pass before they would repeat the hugs.

The family visited in Ivan's cramped quarters for a while longer. Ivan treasured the small talk and remembrances of times that they spent together as a family. The landlady brought up a pot of tea and several glasses. She set down a plate of nutmeg-lemon sugar cookies in front of the girl. Ranya nibbled the cookies, occasionally touching the key on the red ribbon around her neck and smiling at Ivan. Ranya's eyes followed Ivan carefully, imitating his nuances. At this moment they had never been closer. He watched Ranya look at the leather box on the bed and he knew she would, one day, treasure its contents. He felt that this would preserve their togetherness for the long period until they might be reunited.

Everyone exchanged hugs, but rather than the polite greetings and air-kisses of their arrival, the departure hugs were different. These were the hugs that must last a lifetime. Ivan's eyes moistened when his brother gave him a goodbye embrace. When he sensed that his strapping brother sniffed back some tears, he too wept, trying to hide his emotions from the others. Ivan lifted Ranya and held her tightly. He felt her small hands pull the back of his head closer. Ranya and Ivan shared tender smiles. Ivan bit his lips so that he could hold back tears. Paris was far away and he could not predict when they would see each other. No doubt he would never hug Ranya the child again.

The family carriage was waiting in front of the house. As his family settled in for their journey home, Ivan stood on the front steps gently waving his hand. Ranya had the leather box on her lap. He saw her fondle the heavy weight of the object and held it by the corners, being as affectionate to it as possible.

The family left with Ranya holding up the box, struggling to demonstrate she would treat it as their pact avowed. She once again touched the ribbon around her neck and slowly let her finger slip down to feel the key. Ivan knew she felt a part of her beloved Uncle Ivan with her as she receded in the distance.

Upstairs, the apartment was terribly lonely as Ivan stood studying the objects that would be artifacts in a diminishing memory. He thumbed through the music that he first brought to the daunting Professor Tchaikovsky's studio for his first performance, when he shivered with anxiety that he might be chosen as a student of the great Maestro. There was no need for it now, as it had served its purpose and led him to a love that he trusted would last forever. He reached for the key to an apartment in Paris and squeezed it tightly warming the cold brass in his perspiring hand. It was a tender moment that was steeped in the sadness of goodbyes.

Ivan sat on the windowsill and watched his family's coach recede in the distance, as newly arrived winter winds bowed the trees without apology.

SAINT VLADIMIR

PRAVDINSKY, MAY 25

IT WAS LATE in the afternoon when Stas turned a bend in the dusty road and the Church of Saint Vladimir became visible in the distance. The sun lit up the golden onion dome and a large filigreed cross on top, making it dazzle against the dark forested hills behind. As they drove closer, Fred said, "There are three cars in the parking lot. Every other church like it that we've passed was deserted." He put his hand on Alex's and said, "Alex, it's happening. Won't be long 'til we see Anna." Stas slowed the truck down to a crawl. Approaching the church grounds, Fred leaned forward and said, "Stas, we should park in the overflow lot, way on the side. It looks like the right spot for a service truck." The tanks of carbon dioxide and coils of plastic tubing rattled in the truck bed as they drove over the rutted entrance, then parked on the weedy area to the side of the church. Stas parked and they sat quietly in the truck leaving the engine running. Alex squeezed Fred's hand until it hurt.

The church wasn't very big but seemed unfittingly large for its neighboring countryside of scattered cottages. It sat on a knoll backed by steep hills and faced a wide plain of farms peppered with small fenced in areas that were probably kitchen gardens. Fred got out of the truck and walked back down to the road, then paced the road examining the building and its surroundings, then walked back to the truck. He looked out from the knoll, took a deep breath of the cool air and surveyed the farmland from the road to the distant ridge of mountains.

Susan got out of the truck, ambled up to Fred and said, "What a godforsaken place. You think there might have been an expectation that this church would draw development, maybe the center of a community? Where do they get the money for such extravagance?" She pointed to an elaborate gilded cross atop the impressive gold onion dome.

"Still, it looks like it draws a crowd," Fred said pointing to ruts in the large grassy parking area. "And they have extra room in back. We could browse the cemetery over there and see how old this place is."

Susan looked up at the onion dome and said, "Nice as it is, it's actually not so unusual compared to hundreds of Orthodox churches scattered around the countryside. We should go back to the truck and wait. We look suspicious milling around."

As they walked back, passing the parish house, looking at a small sign next to the front door, Susan said, "Well, the priest lives well. I don't know what the rest says, but I got *Father Konstantin.*"

Stas turned off the ignition and the car made a cough, then a loud boom. Fred said, "Where did you get this truck? We were supposed to be invisible." The hacking truck was not reassuring. "I hope that the crew knows how to handle these tanks and tubing."

"We needed a small pickup truck, so I borrowed this from a plumber friend, Vladimir Kugen. I wanted a truck that was undistinguished, but Kugen thought otherwise."

Fred walked around the truck with *Kugen's Plumbing* written in simple Cyrillic lettering on both sides.

"Kugen had no idea what use his truck would be put to or where it would be taken, but he was satisfied with the case of vodka I put in his garage in return for the favor," Stas said. "Vodka is our national currency." Stas sputtered a laugh. "Yes indeed, our currency."

Alex jumped out of the truck and said, "In spite of the fact that he knew nothing about the maneuver, Kugen slapped that magnetic sign on the rear of the truck just to be sure that the trip had maximum benefit to him. Undistinguished, my ass. I'm ripping it off."

"No," Stas quickly said. "It makes us look common. Leave it."

Susan walked to the truck and said. "I guess everyone here will know the virtues of Kugen's for plumbing and refrigeration services."

"I'll move the truck to the side of the grass-covered area away from the church entrance," Stas said, opening the door to the truck. "That will make it seem that it really is a service vehicle on a business trip. Then we will wait until everyone is here before we do anything. Yes indeed."

A short while later, all the cars had arrived at the church and assembled in a tight formation in the rear grassy area near the cemetery. Everyone sat in their cars and waited, trying to look as innocuous as possible. Stas went to each car and said, "In case you are noticed, look casual." Fred was not sure why they were waiting, but it seemed better to sit for a while and contemplate the upcoming episode rather than be seen by someone and have to come up with an explanation of who they were. The plan was all set and rehearsed, but waiting for the right moment felt like he was standing at the edge of a deep chasm ready to leap.

"Well, everyone is ready," Stas said.

Susan reached into her pocket and pulled out a white lace cloth, then placed it over her hair and tied it around her chin. Without saying a word, she opened the door to the truck and walked slowly to the entrance of the church with her head bowed.

Susan opened the door to the church, bowed her head deeper, paused, then reverently crossed herself in a tight pattern three times before walking in. It was curtain time and Fred was terribly uneasy. Fred glanced at the three parked cars, then walked briskly to catch up to Susan in case the occupants might be waiting inside. From inside the doorway, Fred scanned the church. It was very simple inside, unlike other provincial churches that he had toured. Susan hobbled down the center aisle, hunched over, making her body look twenty years older, immersed in the role of abject devotion.

Fred backed out of the church, went back to the truck and exclaimed, "It's happening." He sat with Alex and Stas and silently stared at the front door.

Moments later, two large limousines unexpectedly rolled up to the front of the church and parked on the grass next to the stone path leading up to the front door. Stas dropped down behind the steering wheel and Fred quickly slumped down in his seat, grabbing Alex's shoulder pulling him down, out of sight. Alex raised his head high enough to peek and said, "Shhh. There are four well-dressed men getting out of the cars."

"What do they look like?" Fred said softly.

"They're dressed in dark suits and they act as if they are attending a funeral. Two of the men, the heavier of the two, are walking away from the entrance deeply absorbed in a conversation. They're coming this way," Alex said.

"Get down. Make yourself invisible," Stas grumbled.

Alex and Stas strained to hear the voices of the men conversing in Russian.

"I understand we have all the material evidence that exists for now. Now let's get rid of the rest of this mess and exercise our duty to guard the name of the Fatherland," one man said. "And the respect and holiness of the church," added another. "Those perverts, they're not going to hijack our national icons to advance their degenerate agenda."

"Let's clean up the mess and end this," the first man said.

The other man said, "The rest of the mess? Shit, that's that old woman. We'll clean that up now."

"Oh my God," Alex groaned. He grabbed Fred's hand and gripped it tightly. "They're going to kill Anna now."

Fred couldn't help but peek out the truck window. He saw the other man lower his head and nod in agreement. The two men looked up at the cross atop the dome, raised their right hands, lowered them, then swept across right to left waving a broad cross in the air acting like that this gesture would sanctify and legitimize their position. One of the men followed the other two into the building while the last stopped to urinate against the stone foundation. Fred slipped back down to the floor of the truck.

Alex turned to Fred and said. "Let's get this show on the road. Time is not on our side."

Stas rolled down the window of the truck, put his fingers to his lips and whistled three short bursts. The prearranged signal had been given and the cars unloaded their crews. Fred and Alex got out of the truck and watched the crew work.

Sophie got of her car, closed the door quietly, and waved to Fred. Then they ran around the church together, surveying the cellar windows and returning quickly to her car. Sophie said to her father, "Papa, put on the air pack, it's curtain time." She adjusted the straps and the two masks while he gestured mockingly with every twist of his body. Sophie took his vestment from the back seat of the car, threw the robe over his head and draped it on his shoulders. She placed the hat on his head and adjusted an ecclesiastical ribbon around his neck.

Nikolai squirmed in his vestment, adjusted his hat and grumbled, "I am in a clown costume. Where is my big red nose?" He was visibly nervous. But he threw his shoulders back, puffed out his chest and said. "Well, I suppose I play a leading role in this drama," he said. "For Anna."

Nikolai lit his incense pot and marched into the church, swinging it slowly from side to side. He mumbled some faux prayers with minimal articulation as he walked. Fred thought, *In a sense, he is praying*. Fred and Alex slipped into the church and took a seat in a dark pew near the left wall. Nikolai marched through the front door and down the center aisle of the church. It was dark with scant light filtering through the stained glass windows. Nikolai acknowledged Susan pray-acting in a pew far to the right side of the church, occasionally peeking from her shawl. As Nikolai passed her, she leaned her head toward the door to the basement, as was planned. Nikolai stepped back and Susan nodded to signal that he was at the stairway that he sought.

Fred watched him open the door ceremoniously and pause at the top of the stairs. He swung the incense pot wider, intensifying the musty odor of the church. He stayed at that spot.

Alex grabbed Fred's arm and whispered faintly, "He stopped. He's freezing. This is not going well. Shit."

Fred slid out from the pew, hunched over and tiptoed along the rear wall in the blackness to the other side of the church and over to Nikolai. Fred grabbed his wrist and pressed him forward. He gently pushed Nikolai in front of him down the steps, then stayed several steps behind and tried to blend into the dark stairwell.

At the bottom of the stairs there was another door. It was dark except for the light that escaped through the crack at the bottom of the door onto the stairwell. Fred went back to Nikolai, patted him on the shoulder, then urged him down the stairs and again stood back in the shadowy passage. Nikolai took a deep breath then raised his shoulders and acted as a priest on a mission as he opened the door slowly and entered the large assembly room. Fred pressed against the wall of the stairwell to stay concealed.

The four men who had driven up were at the center of the room. One man had a fat cigar in his mouth belching smoke that battled with the incense and clouded the air with a nauseating stench. Along the wall were three more men wearing holsters across their chests. Nikolai ceremoniously marched up to the assassins and boldly said, "I am here to give the old lady her final communion. Lead me to her," he insisted.

Fred leaned forward to see through the open door. "Where is she?" Nikolai said. At first, the men in the room looked confused, but one of them rose and signaled the others to let the priest in. The four in the center of the room traced a cross on their chests, then the other gunmen did the same. It was oddly comforting to see such reverence from these noxious-looking men. Fred shifted his position so that he could see further into the room but stayed pressed against the wall of the dusky space.

Fred saw Nikolai approach Anna, who was sitting in an old torn soft chair with her head in the palm of her hand, elbow on the armrest. She was awake, but heavy-eyed and lethargic. She looked so different from the Anna that he first met in the antique shop in Brooklyn. The strong woman that Anna always was, who seemed in control of her world, appeared pale and fragile now.

Anna looked up slowly as if the room had been entered many times before, but this time there was something different. The priest wore an expression of dread and glanced irregularly at the men in the larger assembly room outside Anna's small room.

The assassins, appearing bored, watched, and waited for Nikolai to leave. One leaned back in his chair and put his feet on a table.

Nikolai set down the incense pot, raised his hands and began to talk softly. Anna, glassy eyed and bent over, listened to Nikolai speak until he said Alex's nickname, *Sasha*. Anna lifted her head high, then smiled broadly. She straightened her bearing and leaned to Nikolai. Fred looked at the guards slumped in their chairs. Apparently they were not listening.

One of the gunmen got up and walked around the room, sometimes peering into Anna's space, sometimes to the open door to the stairs. Fred pressed against the wall and closed his eyes, hoping that would prevent the armed guard seeing that there was someone there. Fred mouthed, *Anna, do what he says. Let's get this over with.*

Fred heard Nikolai talk unhurriedly to Anna as Anna nodded slowly. Everything was going well. Then Nikolai looked toward the stairs, looked back at Anna and used the phrase containing the word *Fyodor*, the Russian word for Fred.

Anna looked toward the stairs and bowed indistinctly.

Racing through Fred mind was, *Nikolai, don't explain to Anna that everyone sitting outside the room will be dead in a few moments. Stick to the script; sleep, remember to tell her 'sleep.'* In a long string of Russian, Fred picked out the words *spotch* [sleep] and *gaz* [gas], then Nikolai showed Anna the masks. Yes, things were going well, but lethal risk was dangerously close.

Fred tightened his fingers into a tight fist, curled his toes and stiffened the muscles in his legs. Standing so still, Fred's foot started to cramp and he changed his position ever so slightly. The stair creaked. It was a slight sound, but it seemed like a roar. One of the gunmen stood quickly, knocking his chair over. A second gunman jumped up. Fred closed his eyes thinking that the gunshot would be quick, that his end would be painless and Anna would be freed. He gritted his teeth and waited for the bullet. He heard the floor creak as the gangster walked slowly toward him and the odor of vodka and foul breath strengthen. He closed his eyes tighter and stiffened his jaws. The gunman walked away.

Nikolai stood up and wriggled two masks from under his vestment, then pulled out some long black tubing. He put one mask to his face and breathed deeply, then offered the other to Anna. Nikolai breathed from the within the mask, then gestured to Anna to do the same.

Father Konstantin, resident priest, sensed motion outside and looked out of the window. He noticed that two limousines had driven up and thought, *My benefactors have arrived.* He hustled to spruce up quickly and welcome them to his church. He quickly moved in front of a mirror on the dresser, combed his beard and arranged his collar. He rummaged in the top drawer of his dresser for a mint, stored there for just such a moment, and popped it into his mouth. Father Konstantin went before a full-length mirror in the hallway, checked that his clerical uniform was perfect, rubbed his shoes on the back of each trouser leg, stepped out of his front door and walked the few steps to the church.

Father Konstantin walked in a stately, measured manner, even though he didn't want these benefactors to wait. He needed to continue to be part of their mission, as distasteful as it sometimes felt. It seemed like yesterday that he sat with these men in a luxurious apartment in Moscow briefing with that woman, what was her name, Margo, to destroy all evidence. He had to continue as servant of both the Mother Church and the Fatherland. These benefactors, no matter how unsavory they were to our Lord, were there financial lifeblood. He had no choice but to follow their lead. Homosexuality? The Church condemned that and he had to do what he could to preserve the sanctity of his Church. Besides, without these benefactors, his church would be a crumbling shack in a faraway village. He did what he had to do.

Father Konstantin entered the church expecting to see it empty, as it always was this time of day. Glancing at the far right pew, he thought that it was lovely to see a woman deep in prayer. He felt that he should comfort her, and he walked over to Susan and spoke gently to her in Russian. Father Konstantin noticed the door to the basement was open and thought, as soon as he did his duty to this poor soul, he would visit his patrons downstairs.

In the stairwell, Fred heard a stream of Russian coming from above. *That must be the resident priest, Father Konstantin. Fuck. Father Konstantin will be coming down the stairs any second, killing the whole plan, along with me and the rest of us. Susan, sweetheart, do something, and do it fast.* He had to communicate with Nikolai about Father Konstantin approaching but there was nothing he could do. He depended on Susan's ingenuity and he needed it now.

Suddenly, from the open door at the stop of the stairs, Fred heard Susan groan. He feared that she was ill. *Surely she knows that the toilet is down here.* There was a continuing of Susan's groaning and a shuffling of feet at the top of the stairs followed by Susan clopping loudly down the steps.

Susan raucously thundered down the stairs. Fred cautiously crept up the stairs to meet her, lest she give his position away. When Susan passed Fred, she held his hand for a fraction of a second, gave a short grasp on his hand and a slight shake, then moved past him. She entered the assembly room where the menacing gangsters stood, then exaggerated her groans. Susan kept moving from spot to spot, looking for Nikolai.

Fred took advantage of the brief distraction, moved back to his position at the bottom of the stairs and watched Susan make a successful reprise of her performance for an emergency run to the toilet. One of the guards mumbled a few words, including *tualet* and Susan was directed to a small lavatory out of sight. Susan slammed the door, sounding like a cardboard box slapping shut.

Fred peered into Anna's room and from Nikolai's steady droning to Anna, he appeared oblivious to Susan's alarm. The church was much smaller than anticipated and the basement rooms more confined than foreseen. Fred, not far away from Anna's room, wanted to tell Nikolai that Father Konstantin was approaching, but he had to leave it to poor Susan, tucked in a tiny lavatory room now with the door closed. The only thing that Susan could know for sure is that a door hardly more substantial than cardboard was the only thing that separated her from a volatile situation. Only she could tell Nikolai that Father Konstantin's appearance would be imminent. Fred could do nothing.

From the lavatory, Susan made a loud retching noises accompanied by extensive moans. The assassins cringed with disgust and mumbled something in Russian.

Nikolai gave the short shrieking whistle to start the action.

The call alerted the guards who drew their guns. Suddenly, the hissing sounds of the CO_2 gas began entering the basement. Surely Susan could hear the hiss through the paper-thin door to the toilet and would have a minute or so to escape. The guards drew their pistols and walked nervously around the space. If she bolted out into the assembly room, she might have only seconds. Surely, Susan knew that running for the stairs would spark the thugs, reveal Fred's position and bring certain death to them both. She couldn't walk, she couldn't run, she couldn't stay put. Adrenaline swirled through Fred's veins and he tried to muster enough composure to think through this nightmarish situation. The hissing sound came from everywhere and Fred could hear movement from inside the lavatory door. The quantity of CO_2 planned was for a space more than twice as large.

The effects of the CO_2 started immediately. Fred felt his knees weaken and his hands start to shake. He worried that Susan would be trapped and die in the toilet.

No one but Fred knew where she was. If anything happened to him, both would die. He heard the lavatory door open, then slam shut. Susan walked into the center of the assembly room with her head bowed, the shawl tight around her head and continued the drama. She stood in full view, blotting her lips, then bowing to the guards and faced the stairway.

Believing that the plan was back in the groove, Fred ran away from the ensuing gas and halfway up the stairs to the church main floor. Through the open door to the stairs below, Fred could see Susan walk, acting calmly toward the door that led to the steps. Anna and Nikolai should be exiting next with masks on.

Feeling numbness from the CO_2 in his fingers, Fred ran up the remaining stairs as quietly as possible and staying against the dusky walls, slithered past Father Konstantin and slipped out the front door.

Susan approached the stairs and proceeded to climb up to the main floor of the church. She felt a slight tingling in her nose and a slight effervescence on her tongue. From the sensations on her nose and tongue, she knew that she was being covered in a blanket of carbon dioxide. If she held her breath and kept her lips closed as tightly as possible, she should be able to get out of there, or so she believed. Her heart was pounding like a kettledrum and her knees were shaking. In spite of her terror, she couldn't dash. The drama had to continue, lest she tip off the guards. She believed she was going to die in a church—not what she had planned.

One step at a time, Susan repeated. She tried to assure herself if she held her breath, she could make it up the stairs—*do it, Susan*, she thought. One step at time—she clutched the iron pipe railing—she believed it would hold her up—she leaned and put her other hand down on the stair for balance. *One step at a time. I can do it*, she kept repeating to herself. She knew that the gas was rising—*I can keep above the tide. I can hold my breath*, was her mantra and she repeated it with a steady rhythm. You're doing well, Susan, she kept echoing. Suddenly, Susan felt a reflexive wheeze that could not be restrained, and she knew this was a signal that there was a dangerous excess of carbon dioxide in her blood beginning its lethal effect.

In a dazed fog, Susan heard the guards gasping and whooping below her; they were succumbing. She had to keep dragging her quivering body upward. The effort was crushing; *should have lost more weight*, she thought. Her chest was paining to breathe deeply, and as she sensed that, her chest pulled to draw in a breath, her lungs reflexively sucked a deep gust of the venomous gas and Susan got dizzy and stumbled. As she fell she made a loud whooping shriek that reverberated on the stairway and echoed in the church above. Susan lay sprawled out, barely conscious on the stairway. Each shallow breath brought her closer to death.

Anna linked her elbow with Nikolai's and they emerged from their door into the assembly room. The four assassins sat slumped in their chairs, either unconscious or dead. "Those two laying on the floor are already asleep," Nikolai said as he crushed a smoldering cigar that had fallen on the wood floor.

Anna stared at the well-dressed men and said, "Like crumpled pieces of wastepaper." Anna gasped. "Nikolai, that guard, he's holding his gun—he is pointing toward me—straight at me. I knew this would happen."

The gunman held the gun at arm's length with two hands and slowly waved the firearm in the air settling its aim at Anna. Anna froze in her tracks, pulling back Nikolai, waiting for a painful end. The gunman held his lips in a tight "o" and made repeated, uncontrolled gasping sounds while he swayed his pistol in random directions. Anna stood still and watched him as his eyes each focused on a different place on the ceiling, then he fell straight down as if he were a marionette with its strings suddenly severed.

Anna and Nikolai walked briskly to the stairway. As her eyes swept the place where she had been held captive, Anna spotted a securely wrapped package on the table in the center of the room. "Wait," she said, "The music." She grabbed the package as they passed. Anna paused for a moment, stretching the air tube connected to Nikolai's tank. Nikolai grunted and tugged gently to keep her moving. Anna made a loud humming series of grunts in return and pulled toward a shelf in the back of the assembly room. "My ball of ribbons—from my old sheet in Moscow," Anna said.

"Oh, that crumpled mess. Let it be, Anna," Nikolai said, pulling at Anna to go.

"No, that package," she said, unable to be budged as she became transfixed with the object. "That's the package robbed from my shop on Karandash Street in Moscow months ago." Anna waved her hands at her partner tethered to her by a stretched breathing tube. She pulled Nikolai to the end of the room, grabbed the package and the frayed ribbons. Nikolai kicked to fully open the door at the bottom of the stairs and the two of them pushed through to the dim stairway.

As they opened the door and started to climb up, Anna let out a muffled scream. "Susan. It's Susan. Is she sleeping, too?"

"No, this is terrible," Nikolai said, "Hurry." They rushed to the top and fully opened the door to the church sanctuary. They emerged face-to-face with Father Konstantin who stood at the door ready to open it to see what the shriek was that he had heard seconds before.

As Anna and Nikolai brushed past Father Konstantin, they took off the masks and Anna said, "Father, go, please bring Susan up to the top of the stairs. She needs fresh air." Anna and Nikolai continued to hurry out of the church toward the cool outside air. "What is that tingling I feel all over my skin?" Anna asked.

"I feel it too, Anna. Let's get the hell out of this church," Nicolai exclaimed.

Father Konstantin watched what he assumed was a fellow priest with Anna rush down the main aisle to the outside door. He turned to the dark staircase, and then swung to the sudden bright light from the open church door. Father Konstantin paused for a moment with his knuckles up to his chin, then ran halfway down the stairs and stumbled. He fell just above Susan, face down with his head below his feet. His ankle painfully sprained, lying crumpled on the narrow stairs, he could not muster the strength to right himself. The sea of gas continued to rise.

Anna and Nikolai flung open the doors to the church. "Hooray, we've done it," Fred shouted.

Alex rushed to the front steps of the church and grabbed Anna in a tight hug.

Nikolai immediately looked behind her to see if Susan and the priest had emerged safely. They had not. He screamed "Susan" to Fred and Stas and pointed to the door. Stas ran inside the church first. Fred lumbered behind, still woozy and ill from the gas he had inhaled.

Fred yelled from behind, "The door on the right side." They both rushed to it. Seeing Susan and the priest lying on the stairs, Stas jumped down several steps, grabbed Susan by the shoulders and started pulling her up over the priest. Father Konstantin grabbed Stas's ankle in a death grip.

Fred, unable to get close enough to help, shouted, "The priest; he knows he's dying." In a fury, Stas kicked the priest's arm free with his other foot and dragged Susan over the desperate cleric and up the stairs. The priest moaned, pleading for help. Stas emerged from the stairwell and passed Fred who was still struggling to breathe.

"The priest," Fred said.

Stas said angrily, "This priest knows what is going on. He is part of it all and should be left to die in the rising gas." Stas exited, put Susan on a bench and began giving vigorous resuscitation.

When Fred failed to emerge after Stas, Alex entered the building and began calling, "Fred, Fred, where are you? What's happening?"

Alex ran over to Fred by the doorway to the basement stairs. Fred said with fretful speed, "The priest. I don't know what to do. I feel the same revenge toward this priest. He's the host of this kidnapping."

Father Konstantin moaned and repeated over and over with a sinking voice, *"Pomogite mne"* (Help me). Haunted by the wailing. Fred moved one step down the stairs. He saw Father Konstantin try to turn himself facing up the stairs and crawl up a single stair. But overcome with pain and difficulty breathing, he slipped back down to where he had started. Fred made his decision. He climbed down the stairs and grabbed father Konstantin's arms. The gas had reached the priest and he was already starting to breathe in gulps. Fred could see that he had turned his head above somewhat and he was not yet in danger of suffocating. In a few more minutes, though, he would succumb.

Alex shouted into the stairwell with anger. "He's the enemy. He's done everything in his power to torture us. Let him be. Let his God decide what to do with him."

Fred thought otherwise. Seeing the man powerless and near death, he saw a helpless victim. There was no time to think further much less debate. Fred dragged Father Konstantin up the stairs and laid him on a bench.

Fred turned to Alex and the two of them grabbed each other, hugged tightly, bounced a bit and celebrated their victory. Alex placed his lips on Fred's neck and kissed as Fred whispered in his ear, "My precious Alex." They held the tight hug in the muted light of the sanctuary for a prolonged time. Neither of them wanted to abandon this comforting moment.

Father Konstantin gasped and coughed, awakened in a stupor, still lying on the bench, as Fred and Alex stood above him in a tight embrace. Fred gave Alex a prolonged kiss on the mouth. "It's over," Fred said. "It's all over," he howled as they hugged.

Father Konstantin looked up with blurry eyes and witnessed this affection in his holy sanctuary. They were silhouetted against the stained glass window that rose high in the apse of the church. Tranquil but still confused, he saw this as a pair of angels looking over him. "Thank you, God," he mumbled. In a state of drugged euphoria, he saw two male angels kissing. "My angels," he chanted. He lay on the bench in a quiet delirium, not to disturb the message he imagined being sent from God.

Alex, Fred and the other rescuers said nothing to the priest. Stas gathered the team, loaded them in the truck he borrowed and quickly headed down the road to safety.

A few minutes later, Father Konstantin regained full consciousness, still fuzzy about what had just occurred and what he witnessed when near death.

Later that day he grabbed a cane and hobbled to the basement of the church to survey the damage. He went to the phone and said, "We will be needing seven generic grave markers and a front-loader operator to dig graves in the field behind the church." He paused in the church and looked up to the stained glass window in the apse where he had seen his angels, then bowed his head.

The priest returned to the rectory, sat down in his favorite soft chair and relived his apparition of the pair of angels that he witnessed in the sanctuary. He got up, went to a phonograph and carefully searched the shelf of recordings to pick just the right one. "Ahhh, Tchaikovsky, our national icon, Symphony Number One, 'Winter Daydreams,'" he said to the empty room, then slid the record out of its sleeve and placed it on the turntable. Father Konstantin returned to his chair, closed his eyes, and pictured the silhouettes of the two gay angels against the stained glass window. He felt a bit closer to Tchaikovsky.

It was time to go home. Fred watched Anna walk around clutching her packages, looking up to the blue sky tinged with gold, and a gentle smile on her face. Alex pressed by her side, tears rolling down his cheeks, looking at her face as she walked. Everyone else was busy collecting the paraphernalia around the rear of the church that was used for the event, but Fred walked over to Anna and Alex and escorted them back to the truck. He hugged Anna, stood back to see her smile, then hugged her again. She scooted to the middle and Fred sat down beside her. Alex got into the other side of the truck sitting beside Anna. Stas sat down at the wheel and Susan entered the car and sat next to him.

They sat silently. All the empty tanks were loaded onto the truck, then Stas said, "Kugen's Plumbing, here we come. We return the truck and cylinders, and then home for big celebration. Yes, indeed. No problem."

THE PLAN CONTINUES

MOSCOW, NOVEMBER 6, 1893

PETER'S BROTHER, MODESTE, stood by the coffin in the parlor in his flat in St. Petersburg acting grief stricken. It was little more than a week after Tchaikovsky conducted the premier performance of his Sixth Symphony and Modeste appeared to be strongly affected by the tragedy of the great maestro's death, while others in the house wept with little sense of control. The rumor was spread that there had been an oversight and the servants had forgotten to boil the water in spite of a general alarm of cholera. However, when tales of suicide were overheard, Modeste displayed no objections to the story. Tchaikovsky had shared with Modeste his prescribed duty to The Fatherland and how the Tsar's counselors demanded he honor his country. The flask at Tchaikovsky's bedside was indeed empty. As the roomful of mourners came and went, Modeste played the misfortune well, sobbing and beating on the casket as others had done before him and continued to do. Modeste was well aware of his brother's predicament and, being gay himself, was supportive in every possible way.

Modeste edged the maid into a corner and said, "Please stop boasting that you had kissed the body. It discredits the solemnity since everyone knows that the coffin was quickly soldered shut with a lead seal as it is always done to the remains of cholera victims." Then Modeste looked at the coffin with a large log wrapped in a blanket stuffed inside on its way to blissful eternity. The scene was well done with visitors praying and moaning, some kissing the casket. Modeste joined in and, with passion, chanted the melodies of the mysterious sounding Orthodox liturgy.

In the incense-filled room, Modeste reminisced how, in the months before, he and Peter had discussed what to name the final symphony that Peter Ilyich worked so hard to complete. Peter, having discussed the entire situation with Modeste, selected Tragic; Modeste suggested *Pathétique* and Peter agreed that this was indeed an expression of the pathos that haunted him. As he chanted the liturgy, Modeste pictured his brother energetically conducting the premier on Saturday eve, October 28, 1893, in St. Petersburg. He remembered discussing travel to Moscow with Peter for a second performance, but that had never happened. He thought how he selfishly tried to discourage the move to Paris even though he knew it was Peter's only means to a happy life. He had to agree with the critics when they published their puzzled review. Rather than a dynamic finale to an incredible lifetime of great work, the Pathetique Symphony ends in a dreamlike state, drifting to a vague place undefined in previous musical repertoire. *My brother and a dream—an end to suffering.*

As the family hovered around the casket in the overheated, emotionally still room in the darkened home, a small, anxious group was reported standing outside the door. The rattling of the doorknocker stopped the chanting several times. Modeste was relieved when the knocking stopped, but then it started again. He signaled the maid, "See who is there." He held up his hand and said, "But allow no one to enter."

The household maid went to the door and opened it just far enough to peer through a crack. "*Shto?*" she coarsely said, an unusual and somewhat brusque greeting at the Tchaikovsky home, especially at this time.

"We are from the Church of Saint Turov and have brought our priest to offer blessing to Maestro Tchaikovsky at this most sacred time," a stout woman said with a loud, crass and demanding voice.

"I am sorry," the maid said in a fragile voice and began to close the door.

The stout woman was pushed aside and an Orthodox priest stepped forward and spoke in a forceful, somewhat chanting voice, "I have the sacred sacrament ribbon to place on the head of the deceased. We must come in, it is our duty to our Lord."

Modeste came to the door, stood outside in the cold and closed the door loudly behind him. "It is not possible to see nor touch the Maestro's body," Modeste said angrily. "Please leave us in peace."

"We act on behalf of the Lord," the priest forcefully said.

Trying to be calm, Modeste said, "The coffin has been sealed because of the cholera. It is the law and it cannot be opened. You must leave."

"This has happened before. I have attended several cholera deaths and have opened the coffin and resealed it," the priest said. "Our mechanic, Alexander, is equipped to do that immediately. We will only be several minutes. Our scriptures require this." He reached for one of the group and tugged him forward gracelessly by the lapel of his coat. "We will not leave; God before law."

Modeste pictured the wooden contents of the coffin and became increasingly uneasy. "I am sorry, the family cannot be disturbed. All services have been performed and you must now leave," and grabbed the doorknob to go back inside. As he opened the door to go back in, the group pushed their way in with him and followed the scent of the burning candles to the parlor where the coffin lay. The maid ran circles around the obstinate group with no success at turning them away. "Call the police," Modeste demanded.

Alexander, the technician brought by the priest, studied the metal that sealed the coffin and pulled some tools from his coat. The priest began to chant the traditional Orthodox service for the dead. Alexander continued to pry at the coffin while the priest laid out a headband with a sacred prayer written on it. Modeste, picturing the log wrapped inside, started to rant. "You must leave, you must leave now."

Modeste called the butler to expel the intruders. The butler appeared with a double-barreled shotgun and pointed it at the group. "Leave or I will shoot. I will count to three—I don't care how much blood splatters on the walls. He began counting, "*odin ...dva...tri...*"

"Insults to God are not easily forgiven," the priest said to Modeste and he and his entourage backed out.

Modeste turned away and said to the butler, "Clear this room out quickly."

The maid stood by the open door as the group withdrew from the house. She slammed it shut and pulled the deadbolt lock to secure it. She crossed herself with a wide, sweeping cross, then repeated it over and over again. She joined the mourning group back in the parlor. Modeste went to the butler and silently nodded his head in approval and thanks. The plan was back in motion.

Modeste played the act of reverence for his brother in St. Petersburg as the casket was buried in the Alexander Nevsky Monastery. He was amazed that sixty thousand people showed up for the service in the Kazan Cathedral, with eight thousand of them jammed inside. Later, he read the Moscow newspapers how the news of Peter Ilyich Tchaikovsky's death from cholera was announced to a stunned public. As he read the reports, Modeste thought, he hoped that the controversy would subside. Cholera was seen to be a disease of the lower classes, not something to which a person of Tchaikovsky's stature would succumb, and certainly not as quickly as stated. The newspaper journalists were no doubt suspicious.

Peter Ilyich had quietly slipped out of St. Petersburg leaving the faceless weight in the coffin behind. He set out for Paris on the eighth of November, six days later than he wrote in the coded music. He arrived after an arduous journey early in December hoping throughout the trip that Ivan would not worry about him being late. He had shaved his beard and kept his coat collar high around his face to prevent being recognized during the journey. While all the passengers in the coach slept, Peter sat on the edge of his seat, energetic with anticipation.

Paris was dusted with snow when he arrived at the Place de République. As the carriage progressed down rue Bérenger, a childlike sense of freedom for his passion that had been denied to him awakened. The world was once again a place in which he could happily live. He twisted his head and balanced at the edge of his seat, studying the imposing doorways as the coachman announced number 14 and stopped the carriage. Peter pushed through the massive door to the inner courtyard and stood silent for a moment feeling the joy of arriving at a new home. Clearly remembering the directions from Claude Debussy, he went to a small door just to the left. There were sixty-seven steps to the top apartment, and Peter floated up with increasing energy as he approached the top. As he was about to knock, Ivan opened the door and grabbed Peter. The two stood in the open door swaying in a tight hug. Peter leaned over and kissed Ivan's neck. He did not move, breathing the fragrance of Ivan with his heart pounding from the climb combined with an aching craving for love.

The haunting strains of the *Pathetique Symphony* were in his head. But the melodies joined other sounds in his mind and became a mosaic that erupted into a joyful cacophony. Peter swirled Ivan around the apartment, then flung open the windows letting the December air flood the space. But the winter air could not quench the flames of their passion. "Look at Paris," Ivan said, "This is where life begins for us," and they went to the open window and leaned out to see the lights of Paris.

Peter held Ivan close in the biting breeze and said, "I've waited for this so long. I want to run down the stairs and dash up once more to feel the thrill of our first kiss in Paris. The plan is complete and the haunt of hate is a lifetime and a world away."

A few days later, Peter and Ivan joyfully lunched with Claude Debussy and his girlfriend, Gabrielle. They sipped wine and they laughed as Debussy toasted, "Here's to a new life, new identities and new pen names."

Peter stood up and with watery eyes said, "And here's to our new friends, Claude and Gabrielle—from us, Pierre and Jean."

Debussy raised his glass and, pointing to Tchaikovsky, said, "Pierre," then turned to Ivan and said, "Jean, long life."

Peter wanted to express his joy to this loving group, but he was so choked with emotion that he only smiled and nodded, then clinked his glass with Ivan's.

ON THE FARM AGAIN

RUSSIAN COUNTRYSIDE, MAY 25

DURING THE RIDE home from the church, Fred felt the gentleness of Anna's hand and, as no words could express the warmth of the moment, they watched the countryside, occasionally glancing at each other. Anna leaned over and gave Alex a light kiss on the cheek, then she turned to Fred and gave him a subdued smile. Fred returned the smile and tilted his head slightly and bit his lips lest he tear up. He squeezed her hand and Anna responded by clasping his. She then cupped Fred's face in her hands and lightly kissed his cheek. Fred sat back, staring out the car window as he took a deep breath and saw beauty in each passing junkyard and ramshackle cottage.

Rolling through farmland, they watched the long shadows stretched along the countryside. Susan said, "Fred, I remember you saying that this is the golden hour, and here we have golden color only a setting sun can paint. Isn't it beautiful?"

Fred looked down and saw Alex take Anna's hand and squeeze it with great affection. He took Anna's other hand and held it gently. Anna lifted her hands and drew them together, joining the hands of Fred and Alex. She wrapped her palms around the joined hands and Fred knew that she felt the love whose name she knew. Anna turned to Alex and softly, said, "My Sashka," as tears trickled down Alex's face. Fred held his tears back for a moment, then surrendered to his emotions and wept. Anna sat with her hands cupped around theirs with a contented smile on her face. All three rested their hands on the packages of music that lay on Anna's lap.

Susan looked out the window at the farmhouses and vegetable gardens as Stas drove them home. Her head tilted more and more, then sleep overtook her. Fred's wonderful mood was lifted further when Stas put his arm around Susan as she drifted. Susan deserved this.

Fred leaned forward and rested his hand on Susan's shoulder. Susan tilted her head back. *It's wonderful that Susan had found Stas,* he thought. *She did the coy act so well; surely Stas noticed her.* Fred gave Susan a little push toward Stas and she inched a bit closer to him. Then Stas put his arm over Susan's shoulder and gently tugged Susan toward him.

Fred turned to Anna and said, "How did they treat you while you were locked in the church basement?"

"Oh, I suppose it could have been worse. If it weren't for Boris, I would have starved. Dear Boris, the chances he took for me. I guess you say that he saved my life." She looked at Alex and said, "Alex, you have to find a way to thank sweet Boris, for his kindness."

Alex looked at Fred, then lowered his head. "Yes, Anna. I owe Boris." He rubbed his eye with the sleeve of his shirt.

The sun was dipping below the tree line when the truck pulled up to the family home. Anna slipped out of the truck, still clutching the packages of music. She walked with care along the stone path, a bit wobbly from the long period of confinement. Alex took her arm and held her close. Fred opened the door and Alex and Anna, arm in arm, stepped through the door to the cottage and were greeted with cheers. Anna's face lit up as she squeezed Alex close to her, then turned to Fred and kissed him on the cheek. Fred blushed, then gave Alex a wink.

Anna walked amongst the cheering group, saying a tearful *spaceba* (thanks) over and over, giving out hugs to everyone and then doing it again. Anna had come full circle, back to her homeland, her grandson, her family.

"We have you to thank for this," Alex said, putting his arm around Fred's waist.

Fred pulled Alex close and kissed the top of his head. "It was a group effort."

Anna, still blushing from all the reveling, said, "You treat me like a folk hero. I've done nothing except survive. I guess that was an achievement considering the circumstances."

Sophie's mother said, "I guess it is my generation of Russians—expect the worst, and everything is better. However, in my heart I knew we would all be together again and in keeping with tradition, I have a feast prepared."

Sophie clapped her hands and said, "We're Russians; we always worry that the nastiest will happen. It's our nature, but screw that. The best has happened. Papa, bring out your squeezebox. *Egrai v'moosikee* (Play music)!"

While everyone hugged, Sophie's grandmother joyously danced around the table with Anna while Sophie's mother briskly slid dinner plates off the stack that she balanced against her chest. She paused for a moment with her finger to her lips and with a toothy smile, said to Sophie, "Go to the breakfront and bring out the linen napkins. This is an occasion."

Sophie's father winked at Fred, raised his eyebrows, put his lips in a tight "o," went to the closet, and brought out two bottles of Shlivovitz and said, "The best plum brandy that one can buy." He popped the cork and yelled, "For everyone."

One by one, members if the family gathered in the dining room, took a seat, lifted their glasses and made a short speech. Alex began to translate, then said, "You can read the expressions on everyone's face and understand without getting a word of Russian. Just wait, one slug of this brandy will sweep away any remaining worry in anyone's mind, if there is any."

At the dinner table, Sophie got up and said, "A toast to all of us. This is a landmark celebration that will be repeated for generations. We were all amazing. We've never worked so well together."

Susan walked to Fred and said, "Tomorrow, we should go to the American Embassy and tell them the whole story. That's the only way we can get back home without a hassle."

Fred smiled at Susan and gave her a tight hug. "Susan, how could we have done this without you?"

After the dishes were cleared, the family and friends returned to the living room. Most brought their glasses as the Shlivovitz was still being poured to keep them full. One by one, the family wilted into a quiet repose. Every perspective of the recent events had been discussed several times until everyone was exhausted. Susan sat next to Anna, put her hand on Anna's and quietly and as cautiously and politely as possible, asked, "Anna, I've wanted to ask for a long time now. What happened to Alex's parents?"

Anna sat motionless for an extended time, then turned slowly toward Susan and Fred and said softly, "Alex was a baby. He never knew his parents. My daughter had a tragic time at childbirth and died shortly after Alex was born." Anna gave Susan a nervous smile. "Alex's father fell into deep depression and was unable to take care of a baby. He traveled a lot with the National Symphony. We don't know where he is now. Oh, he visited occasionally for the first year, but then he disappeared and that was the end of that. It was clear at the very beginning that he wanted out completely. We, my husband and I, raised Alex as if he were our son. I should say that he is my son. When Alex was a boy, he talked about finding his father, but we grew to be his parents." Anna paused and looked around the room for a bit and then added, "I should say I am his parent. My husband died several years ago." Susan took Anna's hand and rubbed it gently.

"At the church, you called Alex *Sashka*, other times, *Sasha*. What is that nickname?" Fred said.

Anna smiled and said, "Sasha is the common nickname for Alexander. If we want to express a bit more love, we add a *ka* at the end. Like the word for water—in Russian it is *voda*. But if it's special, we call it vod*ka* and we have a weakness for our special water. You have to love our language."

Stas put his arm around Susan's shoulder and Fred heard him say softly to Susan, "Stay in Russia for a while. We get to know each other better. I have extra room in cottage next door. Yes, indeed." Fred caught Susan's glance and winked. Fred took a deep breath, got a bit teary-eyed and backed away to not interfere. He saw Susan try not to blush, but she was not completely successful.

"I have a better plan," Susan said, "Come to New York. I have a spare bedroom in the best apartment, in the best house, on the best street in surely the best city in America."

Stas raised his eyebrows and smiled. He reached for Susan who gave a welcome embrace and ran her fingers down Stas's back. Fred got up, walked over to Alex, put his arms around him and whispered, "Can love be contagious?"

PARIS, CHRISTMAS EVE

PARIS, DECEMBER 24, 1893

"I HAVE A surprise. I have tickets to the ballet this evening. But there is more to the surprise," Ivan said breathlessly as he stood at the open door to their apartment. "And, by the way, I found that it takes less than thirty seconds to climb the sixty-seven stairs, but I swear that there are more than that, perhaps sixty-nine—hard to count when I take two at a time." The apartment in Paris turned out to be a happy sanctuary for Ivan and Peter. Of course, they never used those names in public and they tried to use Jean and Pierre in private, but often failed. They laughed at these mistakes in the apartment, but scowled at one another in public when there was a slip of the tongue. Although they both spoke fluent French, there was no mistaking their Slavic accents. When someone inquired about those accents they claimed that they were from Bohemia. That seemed good enough.

The ballet was scheduled to have an intermission between seven o'clock and nine-thirty to allow patrons to leave for dinner and return for the second half. Ivan had made reservations for dinner at a new restaurant that was notoriously difficult to secure on short notice. Plans were for a special Christmas Eve.

"I have the possibility of a commission to write a new ballet under my new name," Peter said. "We don't need the money, but the challenge to create something new has me excited. I have so many ideas. And I want to write a piano concerto expressly for you."

"We're lucky to have a true friend in our new city," Ivan said.

"Claude Debussy is indeed a true friend. He has investigated new contacts and potential commissions, far beyond anything that you could do for yourself," Peter said. "Claude is very much sought after in Paris and has more business than he can handle anyway. Paris is ravenous for new concert material and new ballets," Peter said. It was a golden age of musical culture, *La Belle Époque*. They had been in Paris for only a couple of weeks and a new life was well under way.

Peter straightened his bow tie as the carriage pulled into the courtyard. He was uncomfortable going out in public with Ivan, but this was one of the times it was a delight. He glanced over at Ivan, who grinned and winked.

"We can't avoid the unavoidable," Ivan said. "We have to mix with society."

On the way to the theater, Peter asked, "What is the program for the evening. Is it something I know?" Ivan chuckled. "Is it something by the new modernists?"

Ivan replied with a gentle laugh each time Peter asked the same question. Peter leaned out of the carriage and said, "Driver, a bit slower please," and turned to Ivan and said, "We want to avoid being early and having to mingle with the crowd."

The ballet was a very social affair and the patrons wanted to be seen as well as to see who was there. It was not unusual to strike up a conversation with a new face. Ivan and Peter were not comfortable in these situations and tried to avoid them as much as possible. They would arrive just in time to be seated.

Peter could hardly hold back a grin as they approached the theater. It was a special night out with his love on Christmas Eve, the first Christmas of many that they would spend together. Peter watched the restaurants setting up their outdoor tables with small portable ovens of charcoal to warm the area against a chilling breeze. He wondered which of these Ivan had selected for dinner. The coach soon arrived at the theater and lined up behind a long line of other coaches waiting to deliver their customers. Peter and Ivan were let out of the carriage and Peter gave a generous tip to the driver. They walked directly up the stairs to the main entrance without acknowledging any other people and stood in the central lobby. It was a warm and brilliant environment that Peter loved so much, and he had a wonderful feeling that he belonged.

As they approached the doors to the theater, an usher looked at their tickets and a second usher took them to their seats. The orchestra members were already in their seats and the usual random symphonic fragments wafted from the orchestra pit, from musicians warming up and showing off. Peter did not have to look at his program to learn the surprise that Ivan had prepared for the evening. A flute played a short line from the ballet. He reflexively glanced at the program and read on the cover, in bold letters, *Peter Ilyich Tchaikovsky, The Nutcracker*. A thrill raced through his body, touching his toes and raising the hair on his neck as he appreciated the loving thoughtfulness of his partner. As they were amongst the last to be seated, the lights dimmed soon after they took their places. The conductor walked smartly to the orchestra podium and bowed to the audience. He raised his baton and Peter squeezed Ivan's hand as he heard the playful overture of his work. In his head, the ambiance of the Paris ballet merged with the theater in St. Petersburg and he heard the music in his mind more from his memories than his ears.

Toward the end of the first act, the chorus of children stood up from their seats surrounding the audience and performed their chorale. The effect of encircling the audience with singing children was designed to lift the spectators and bring them into the dream world of the performers. No longer spectators, but drawn into flight, to a wonderland of toys, the audience turned their heads, marveling at the spectacle. But this time was different. In their midst was the composer, drawn into the wonderland of dreams alongside of them. It was an extremely happy time for Peter. Wanting to share the joy, he put his hand on Ivan's, violating a rule that they had agreed to before leaving Russia. Ivan turned his hand over and squeezed Peter's. *Rules can be abandoned for important moments,* Peter thought.

After the lights came up for the intermission, people hurriedly strolled out to find their waiting carriages to take them to dinner. They were given a generous interval for supper before the start of the second act. The restaurant that Ivan had arranged was a short walk from the theater and as they walked through the dimly lit lanes to find it, street musicians and carolers buoyed the festive, uplifting mood. Nevertheless, both preferred to have the melodies of the ballet floating through their minds. Ivan loudly hummed the song of the children's chorus—the chorus seemed to surround them and fill the street. It was an enchanting stroll.

The restaurant was perfect. Ivan and Peter ate and drank wine, reviewing the first act of the ballet. "What did you think of the poor children who danced to the wrong side of the stage to meet their mother?" Ivan said as he laughed.

"Oh, it wasn't awkward until their mother waved outstretched arms to their backs," Peter said and started to chuckle. "These things happen; no one really cares."

"And how about the woman two rows in front of us who coughed in time with the music? She had a talent, didn't you think?" Ivan said.

Toward the end of the dinner, Peter suggested, "Let's buy a bottle of wine and take it back to the apartment. We know how the ballet will end. The only way the evening could be better is to share the wine back in the apartment and toast the holiday season in Paris. I'll sing Act Two on the way home." They paid the waiter and complimented the dinner.

It was nearly nine o'clock and even though it was December, they did not mind the chill in the air. Peter put his arm over Ivan's shoulder, sharing warmth, giving Ivan a secure and wonderful feeling. Sometimes an empty carriage slowed down to tempt them to ride the coach. But their walking was comfortable and unhurried. It was not long before they approached the Place de République. They walked along the avenue until they got to their street, rue Bérenger, and turned the corner. The traffic circling the open square was congested with carriages, some with agitated horses. Drivers yelled at other carriages blocking the way. It was unruly and difficult to negotiate, but it was Paris and the mood was upbeat and exciting.

They turned onto their street and walked side by side down

the narrow sidewalk. In spite of the fact that rue Bérenger was just off the raucous Place, it was a different world, quiet and dark. The tight walkway made it difficult to avoid the occasional step down onto the cobblestone street. Peter walked on the outside in his usual manner, protective of Ivan. The street was usually deserted at this time, but tonight, on Christmas Eve, there were others on the street. It was difficult to be sure how many people there were or who they were since the only illumination was a gaslight at the head of the street toward Place de République and a small number of windows with oil lamps and candles. Peter attributed the presence of others to the holiday evening and thought nothing of it. The dinner wine did its part to soothe anxieties.

As they approached number 14, a man dashed from behind, passing between them, forcing Peter and Ivan apart. As he went by, he thrust his shoulder into Peter and ran ahead. Peter swayed for a moment. He stumbled and with one foot on the sidewalk and one foot on the cobblestone street, he leaned toward the street trying to regain his balance. He reached out to grab Ivan and Ivan grabbed as well, but both missed. On the previously still street a loud noise made Ivan spin around. "Peter, watch out—a carriage," Ivan shouted.

The carriage came roaring down the street, booming on the cobblestone with thunderous noise while Peter flailed. Ivan again yelled, "Peter, Pierre, Peter, the carriage." Ivan reached to grab Peter, but he didn't catch him.

Even though the street was plenty wide for the carriage, it rolled toward Peter and the horses brushed him as it roared by. The impact twisted Peter toward the carriage and straight to its wheels. Peter became entangled in the furiously spinning machinery and was thrust into the air, then smashed to the ground. The bottle of wine that Peter was holding crashed on the sidewalk near Ivan. The carriage raced down the street and turned the corner at the end. Suddenly, the street was deadly quiet. "Peter . . . help . . . someone help us, *aidez-nous*, please," Ivan cried and dropped down next to Peter. "Peter . . . say something . . . ", Ivan yelled continuously for any response from Peter, but none came. He cried *"aidez,"* again and again, but the street remained ghostly quiet. The dark street that felt populated minutes before was empty and silent.

Ivan, blinded by tears, dragged Peter to the sidewalk and propped him against the wall. He wiped Peter's face to clean off the splashed wine.

Ivan lifted Peter from the street and carried him to the doorway. Entering the stairwell, in the flickering gaslight, Ivan saw that what he wiped from Peter's face was not red wine. He moaned as he saw blood trickle from his mouth and nose. Ivan strengthened his grip and began the climb up to the apartment. All senses ceased. Ivan trudged to the top holding the dead weight of Peter in his arms. He heard the children's chorus from the ballet in his head and imagined them to be angels. Once in the apartment, Ivan, began sobbing uncontrollably and collapsed onto the bed with Peter.

As if that moment was marked to be observed by all of Paris, bells rang out from the church nearby, then by steeples in the distance. It was midnight. Christmas had begun. But the sound of the bells made no impact on Ivan. He held Peter's still body tightly and sobbed until his endurance drained. He slumped down to the floor and lied there.

In another part of Paris, hundreds of music lovers were captured by the uplifting emotion of a masterwork. The broad, descending notes of an exultant ending to *The Nutcracker* expressed the finality of a fantastical journey. The audience poured out of the theater, lifted to a happy place, humming melodies created by a musical genius. The poetic and romantic justice that transformed the *Nutcracker* to a loving prince inspired the children. This was a blissful evening created by Peter Ilyich Tchaikovsky. But at 14 rue Bérenger, that same man was dead, crumpled like a discarded document that spoke the wrong message at the wrong time.

MEMORIES OF RUSSIA

ANNA SAT IN her favorite chair staring at the empty wall, transported to a distant place and time. Her memory was of springtime on narrow Karandash Street in a small neighborhood in Moscow. The large flowerpot in front of her shop had been recently planted with red geraniums seemed almost within reach and promised a luxurious display of color. She imagined opening the door to the shop, peering inside, then remembered the trinkets arranged in the shop window. She recalled the comfort of her home since childhood. *Ahhh, the fragrance of blossoming lilacs in the backyard,* she thought, *I can almost get a whiff of it now.* She remembered the night that everything changed. It seemed so long ago, and yet the biting scars that remained made it feel like yesterday.

She pictured the two packages wrapped in ribbons torn from an old bedsheet stacked neatly on the table. Once again, she was haunted by the chill of that night last December in her shop in Moscow when a package had been robbed from her shop and believed lost forever. *Oh, that bundle of music,* she thought, *the music manuscripts autographed by one of the most important celebrities of his time in a most caring and heartfelt manner, and in our family for so long.* She had read it on many occasions and had examined the graceful French script, *À Ivan et à Peter, Félicitations de votre nouvelle vie ensemble, Votre ami, Claude Debussy, Paris December 14, 1893.* "To Ivan and Peter, Congratulations on your new life together, Your friend . . . " But it was not as significant as the other package, which divulged the key to the plans Tchaikovsky made to flee the mores of Russia and restart his life with his love, Ivan.

Anna took a pen and a piece of paper and started a letter to *The New York Times.*

> *Dear Editor,*
>
> *For a long time, I have resisted sending you the package that I now remit. It has been in my family for nearly a century and a half and contains evidence that the world would be better off knowing. I trust that you will—*

Anna stopped. How could she relate the awful events that this package had triggered in a letter to a newspaper? She wanted to recount how involving Fred with the music was a dangerous gamble, but it brought such love into Alex's life that it was worth it in the end. Her friend, Katyusha, had lectured her about donating the music; perhaps she should have listened to her. *Her suggestion was good that we involve her niece, Sophie, such a nice girl, so energetic and resourceful.*

Anna continued her letter.

> *Our journey began with the old Russian family name Tochinovich. I still find it amazing that someone came into my shop in Brooklyn with that same family name—and so deeply interested in music. You see, it is a rare family name, the same as Tchaikovsky's lover, Ivan, the same Tochinovich as my great grandfather.*

As Anna thought about the series of recent events, a smile formed on her lips and she felt that her heritage had been a faithful companion. And then, she thought, *no, I will make a copy of the music and send that to the* New York Times. *It belongs to my family—it's time to make my mark.*

Anna got up from her chair and went to the linen chest in her bedroom. She rummaged beneath the blankets as mothballs clinked to the bottom of the chest and pulled out a leather covered wooden chest. Anna gently peeled the tape from the box, freeing an envelope, yellow with age. She shook the envelope and a key with a thin red ribbon tied through the hole in the key fell into her hand. Anna held the key in her hands and felt the love and romance that had survived nearly a century and a half. She reread the inscriptions on the envelope for the thousandth time.

> *To my beloved daughter. August 14, 1920. From your mother, Ranya.*

And on the line below that in a much simpler handwriting,

> *To my beautiful daughter, Anna, from Mother. January 23, 1940.*

Anna fetched a fountain pen from her nightstand and scratched it on a piece of scrap paper to test its writing and with her best penmanship, she wrote a third line.

> *To my grandson Alex and to my other grandson, Fred, I will always love you. Baba Anna, June 18, 2013.*

She looked at the blank space below that line imagining a sanguine future.

Anna returned to the linen chest and carefully placed the box on top of two neatly stacked packages, each with *The Music* written on top. She sighed as she folded an old woolen blanket over the packages and closed the chest.

Anna went back to the kitchen to finish her letter.

> *Considering the pain that some have caused to eliminate the evidence about Tchaikovsky, I have destroyed all other copies of this music. Please tell the world about the suffering that has gone on merely to share love.*

Anna returned to the linen chest and opened it to make sure that the music packages would be snug for a long time to come. She sat down on the chest, pulled back the curtains and looked out the window. The big maple tree outside the window filled the air with a soothing perfume. It was springtime. All was serene.

ACKNOWLEDGMENTS

IT'S ONE THING to conceive a story, quite another to produce a novel. Without the remarkable guidance of the editor, Ken Harrison, this book would have remained marred with coarse edges. He was my personal trainer, guiding the development of the narrative with wry, welcome comments.